"If I decide I don't [ ] **because he was big a** [ ] **made her lose all sense of self-preservation.**

A slow, slow curve of his lips that had her toes curling into the sheets. "Oh, you like my kiss, Liliana. I felt your tongue stroke against mine."

"Micah!"

He tilted his head to the side, the black retreating to reveal winter-green that glowed in the dark. "Am I not supposed to say that, either?"

"Yes."

"I'm the Lord of the Black Castle. I can say whatever I want."

She didn't know whether to scream or laugh. "You're not the least bit civilized, are you?"

He gave her the strangest look, as if she'd asked a silly question. But to her surprise, he answered it. "I live at the gateway to the Abyss."

"Yes, I suppose the civilized graces aren't exactly useful here." If she wasn't careful, he'd turn her as wild. To be quite honest, she wasn't sure she minded.

NALINI SINGH

New York Times and *USA TODAY* bestselling author Nalini Singh loves writing paranormal romances. Currently working on two ongoing series, she also has a passion for travel and has been to places as far afield as Tahiti, Japan, Ireland and Scotland. She makes her home in beautiful New Zealand. To find out more about Nalini's books, please visit her website, www.nalinisingh.com.

NALINI SINGH

LORD OF THE ABYSS

&

DESERT WARRIOR

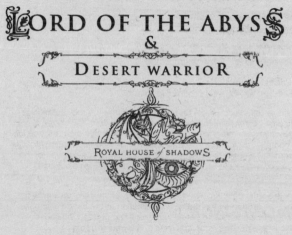

ROYAL HOUSE of SHADOWS

™ **Harlequin**®

TORONTO NEW YORK LONDON
AMSTERDAM PARIS SYDNEY HAMBURG
STOCKHOLM ATHENS TOKYO MILAN MADRID
PRAGUE WARSAW BUDAPEST AUCKLAND

Recycling programs for this product may not exist in your area.

ISBN-13: 978-0-373-83775-5

LORD OF THE ABYSS
Copyright © 2011 by Harlequin Books S.A.

The publisher acknowledges the copyright holder of the individual works as follows:

LORD OF THE ABYSS
Copyright © 2011 by Nalini Singh

DESERT WARRIOR
Copyright © 2003 by Nalini Singh

This edition published by arrangement with Harlequin Books S.A.

For questions and comments about the quality of this book please contact us at Customer_eCare@Harlequin.ca.

® and TM are trademarks of the publisher. Trademarks indicated with ® are registered in the United States Patent and Trademark Office, the Canadian Trade Marks Office and in other countries.

www.Harlequin.com

Printed in U.S.A.

CONTENTS

Dear Reader,

I've always loved dark, dangerous heroes, and Micah is very much that. The lord of a terrible place called the Abyss, he's known only death and violence, seen only fear on the faces of the men and women who cross his path. It's why he's so fascinated with Liliana, this strange intruder in his domain who looks him in the eye. Liliana, in turn, has come prepared to face a monster…only to find herself tempted by the dark lord's sinful kiss.

I adored spending time with Micah and Liliana, and the world of the Royal House of Shadows. Working with fellow authors Gena Showalter, Jessica Andersen and Jill Monroe to create that unique world was a fun process—one that included the exchange of many, many emails to ensure the story line was seamless from book to book.

I truly hope you'll enjoy stepping into this magical, dangerous and seductive world.

With the warmest regards,

Nalini Singh

To my fellow adventurers into Elden

PROLOGUE

WHEN I PICKED UP THE PEN and ink that are the tools of the Royal Chronicler, I took an oath to record only the truth. Now my old bones ache with the knowledge that the truth I must put down is one I wish I could erase. But it cannot be. I know no one will read these archives now, but still the history must be written. The past must be known. And so I must begin.

For many years the Blood Sorcerer cast covetous eyes on the kingdom of Elden, a proud, ancient land overflowing with riches and power, its long-lived people watched over by the good king Aelfric and his wise queen, Alvina. Though strong as rulers, they were not brutal, and Elden's people flourished under their guiding hand.

So did their children.

Nicolai, the oldest and some say the one with the darkest heart.

Dayn, second-born and with eyes that saw everything.

Breena, gentle of spirit and much loved by mother, father and brothers all.

And Micah, the youngest, his heart that of an innocent. Born long after his siblings, he was but a babe of five when the blackest shadows engulfed Elden, on the dawn following a night of celebration to acknowledge that milestone. But the singing and dancing had long grown quiet, the castle yet dark with sleep, when the

Blood Sorcerer appeared at the gates—accompanied by monsters such as were unseen in all the kingdoms.

Perhaps they had once been spiders, but now they were horrific creatures with razor-sharp blades on their furred legs and a taste for human flesh, their eyes roiling red. They were accompanied by men turned into hulking beasts with fists akin to steel mallets, and tiny scurrying insects that dug into the soil and turned it to poison.

Hands drenched with the life force of those he had murdered, the Blood Sorcerer's power was an immense thing, bloated and malignant. It seemed nothing could defeat him, but the king and queen would not surrender their people to such darkness, though the Blood Sorcerer taunted them with promises of a quick death.

King Aelfric's strength was a profound force and he wounded the sorcerer with a terrible blow, but fed by the putrid evil of his malevolent power, the enemy would not die. Again and again the Blood Sorcerer attacked, until the king started to bleed from his very eyes.

The queen, weak herself from battling the creatures the sorcerer had brought with him, saw the king begin to fall under the onslaught of evil, and knew the battle was lost. Using the last of their strength, for their spirits were one, she sacrificed her life to do a great magic, one that has never since been repeated and may never be known.

There is a lineage of blood that ties mother to child, a lineage that can never be broken. And it is this lineage the queen used to cast her children away from Elden, to safety, so they could one day return and reclaim their stolen birthright.

It was a mother's last loving gift, yet the Blood Sorcerer boasts even now that Queen Alvina failed, that he twisted her magic at the end so that instead of finding

safe harbor, the heirs of Elden fell into death. There is no one left alive to contradict him.
—From the Royal Chronicles of Elden, on the third day of the Reign of the Blood Sorcerer

CHAPTER ONE

HE WAS THE MOST BEAUTIFUL monster she had ever seen.

It was the first thought Liliana had as she lay weak and drained across the black marble of the floor, her face reflected in its polished surface. As she watched, the one they called the Lord of the Black Castle rose from his ebony throne at the head of the room and walked down the ten steps with a lazy grace that spoke of power, strength...and death.

Trying desperately to close her hand into a fist, she attempted to push herself up onto her knees, unwilling to meet him at such a disadvantage. But her body was debilitated beyond bearing by the blood she had spilled to make the crossing, her wrists spotted with it, though her magic had sealed the wounds. Her father would've sacrificed another without a thought to the life he took, would call her a fool for using her own blood.

"Weak." He had spit the judgment at her more than once. "I took a beautiful witch to wife and got a hatchet-faced mewling brat in return."

Sensing the vibration of the monster's boots getting ever closer, she took a deep breath, able to feel it rattle in her throat. It wasn't meant to be like this. The spell should have deposited her in the forests outside his domain, not in the midst of his great hall, where he stood as the lone, lethal shield against the vicious beings beyond. She could feel eyes on her, hundreds of them. And yet no one made a sound.

The boots were almost to her now.

Cruelty was no stranger to her, not after having grown up with the Blood Sorcerer for a father. But this man, this "monster," was meant to be completely without heart, without soul. His castle held within it the gateway to the Abyss, the place where the servants of evil were banished after death to suffer eternal torment at the hands of the basilisks and the serpents, and he was the guardian of that terrible place. It was said that even the most inhuman of the dead quivered when confronted by his visage.

But that was a lie, she thought as he crouched down beside her, his boots heavy in her line of sight.

He was not ugly at all.

Strong hands gripped her by the shoulders, pulled her roughly to her knees.

And she found herself staring into the face of a monster.

Sun-kissed hair, eyes of winter-green and skin that held the golden brush of summer even in this black place devoid of warmth, he could have stood in as the model for the mythical Prince Charming spoken of in childhood storybooks. Except Prince Charming did not wear armor of impenetrable black, and his eyes were not full of nightmares.

"Who is this?" A quiet, quiet question.

It made the hair on the back of her neck rise. She tried to force her tongue to work, but her body refused to cooperate even that much, still stunned from the leap she'd made from her father's stolen kingdom to this place that stood as the dark ward between the living and the most depraved of the dead.

"An intruder." He stroked her hair off her face, the act almost tender…if one ignored the fact that he wore gauntlets over his forearms that extended to his hands in spiderwebs of black. A spray of razors rode over his knuckles, while his fingers were tipped with bladed claws the same shade as his armor. "No one has dared enter the Black Castle without invitation in…" A flicker in the green. "Ever."

He didn't remember, she realized, looking into that face that was only of the Guardian. There was no echo of the boy he must've once been. *None.* Which could only mean one thing—according to legend, it was Queen Alvina who had cast the final desperate spell that had thrown her children from Elden, but Liliana's father had ever gloated that he'd thwarted the queen's magic with his own.

What only Liliana knew, because he'd once betrayed it in a rage, was that the Blood Sorcerer believed he had failed. Perhaps he had with the three oldest children, but not with the youngest…with Micah. Her father's blood enchantment had held strong as the child grew into a man, into the dread Lord of the Black Castle.

Oh, he would be pleased. So, so pleased. For those he bespelled rarely, if ever, broke through the veil and found themselves again. Liliana's mother had not—she haunted the hallways of his castle to this day, a slender woman with skin of the dark, lush honey-brown that spoke of Elden's southern climes, and eyes of uptilted gold.

Irina believed herself the chatelaine of a great keep, childless and with her only duty being to see to the needs of the master—even if those needs meant nights filled with screams and bruises ringed around her neck more often than not. Her gaze glanced off her daughter even when Liliana stood directly in her path and pleaded for her mother to remember her, to know her.

By contrast, the winter-green eyes on her face right then saw her when she wished they would not. She had meant to slip unnoticed into his household, learn all she could about him before attempting to speak the truth of his past. She'd been ready to cope with a lack of memory, for he had been only five when Elden fell. But if he was caught in the malicious tentacles of her father's sorcery, then her task had become a thousand times harder. The Blood Sorcerer's work had a way of mutating over time, so there was no knowing what other effects it might've had.

"What do I do with you?" the Lord of the Black Castle and the Guardian of the Abyss asked in a tone that held a faint, dangerous amusement. "Since I have never had an intruder, your presence leaves me at a loss."

Playing with her, she thought; he was playing with her as a cat might with a mouse it fully intended to eat—but wanted to torment first.

Anger gave her the will to stare back, her defiance born of a lifetime of fighting her father's attempts to break her. Perhaps it was futile, but she could no more help it than a cornered animal could stop itself from striking out.

He blinked. "Interesting." Steel-tipped nails grazed her cheek before he moved both hands to her shoulders again and pulled, bringing her to her feet as he rose.

She wobbled, would have pitched forward if he hadn't held her up. As it was, one of her hands slammed up against the cold black of his armor. It felt like rock. Her father's sorcery she thought, had grown upon itself, turned his mental prison into a physical truth. To counteract the spell, she'd first have to remove his armor.

Of course, before she could attempt any such thing, she had to survive.

"The dungeon," the monster said at last. "Bard!"

A heavy tread, one that made the ground tremble. A second later, Liliana found herself being picked up in huge tree-trunk arms as the monster watched. "Take her to the dungeon," he said. "I'll deal with her after I hunt those destined for the Abyss tonight."

The command echoed ominously in Liliana's mind as she was carried from the hall in a hold that was unbreakable. In contrast to the strange whispering hush that pervaded this castle of harshest stone, she could feel a big, steady heartbeat against her cheek, the speed of it so slow as to be nothing human. Unable to turn her head, she couldn't see who—what—it was that carried her with such ease until they passed through a hall of black mirrors.

His face appeared as if it had been formed of clay left in a child's hands. It was all knots and bulges, misshapen and without any true form. He did have ears, but the large protrusions stuck up far too high on the sides of his head. And his nose…she couldn't truly see it, but perhaps it was the small button hidden between his distorted cheeks and below the overhanging jut of his brow.

Ugly, she thought, he was truly ugly.

That made her feel better. At least one being in this place might have some sympathy with her. "Please," she managed to whisper through a throat cracked and raw.

One of those ears seemed to twitch, but he didn't halt his steady, relentless pace toward the dungeons. She tried again, got the same response. He wouldn't stop, she realized, no matter what. For the monster would punish him. All too aware of the cage created by that kind of fear, she went silent, conserving her energy.

It was as well, for this Bard's long, slow strides soon brought them to a dark corridor formed of crumbling walls, the only light coming from a single flickering torch. Then she glimpsed the stairs. The descent into the menacing maw of the Black Castle was narrow and tight enough that Bard's head scraped the top more than once, his shoulders barely fitting. She felt her feet brush the stone, too, but Bard just held her in a more restrictive way, ensuring she took no injury.

She didn't make the mistake of thinking it was because of any care on his part. No, he simply didn't want to be responsible for explaining why the prisoner had been harmed in a way that had not been mandated by the Lord of the Black Castle.

The stairs seemed to spiral down interminably, until she wondered if she was being taken into the very bowels of the Abyss itself. But the dungeons they finally came to were harshly real, the passageway lit by a torch that gave just enough illumination for her to see that each cell was a black square broken up by a small window set with bars. She strained her ears but heard only silence. Either there were no other prisoners...or they were long dead.

Opening the door to the nearest cell, Bard stepped inside and placed her in the corner, atop a bed of straw. His eyes met hers, and she sucked in a breath. Large and dark and full of sorrow, they were the eyes of a scholar or a physician, shimmering with compassion. But he shook his head when she parted her lips.

There would be no mercy from him, not here.

As he turned to step out, he grunted and rattled something in the other corner. Then the door slammed shut, leaving her in a darkness so complete, it was stygian. But no—a scrap of light flickered in from the flames of the torch outside, enough to allow her to navigate the cell.

Gathering her strength, she crawled to where Bard had rattled what sounded like a metal bucket. Her hands touched it after what seemed like hours, and she felt her way carefully up its side until she could dip her fingers within.

Water.

Her throat suddenly felt as if it was lined with broken glass. Sheer need gave her the strength to pull herself up onto her knees and cup her hands, drink her fill. The water was cool and crisp and sweet, the droplets trailing down her wrists. It was beyond tempting to gorge, but she stopped herself after a bare few mouthfuls, aware her empty stomach would revolt if she overindulged.

Her eyes more accustomed to the shadows now, she glimpsed something else beside the pail. A steel container. Opening it, she found a small loaf of bread. Hunger a clawing beast in her stomach after days without food, she ripped off a piece and chewed. The bread wasn't moldy or stale but simply lumpy and hard—as if the baker had been given instructions to make it as unpalatable as possible.

A skittering to her left, the sound of tiny paws on stone.

She turned her head, found her eyes meeting two shiny ones that gleamed in the dark. The sight may have incited fear in another woman, but Liliana had long made pets of such creatures in her father's home. Still, she examined her roommate carefully. It was a small, quivering thing, its bones showing through its skin. Hardly a threat. Tearing off a piece of bread, she held it out. "Come, little friend."

The mouse froze.

She continued to hold the bread, almost able to see the way the tiny creature was torn between lunging for the food and protecting itself. Hunger won and it darted to grab the bread from her grasp. An instant later and it was gone. It would return, she thought, when its belly forced it to.

Closing the container with half the loaf still inside, she placed it beside the water and made her way to the straw. For a dungeon, she thought drowsily as her body began to shut down, this place was not so terrible. The monster clearly needed to take lessons from her father in how to make it a filthy pit full of screams and endless despair.

THE DREAM ALWAYS BEGAN THE same way.

"No, Bitty, no." She was small, maybe five, and on her knees, shaking a finger at the long-haired white rabbit who was her best friend. "You have to fetch."

Since Bitty was a rabbit more enamored with eating and sunning himself, he didn't so much as twitch when she threw the ball. Sighing, she got up and fetched it herself, but she wasn't really sad. Bitty was a good pet. He let her stroke his long silky ears as much as she wanted, and sometimes he made enough of an effort to move to follow her around the room.

"Come on, slugapuss," she said, pulling him into her lap. "Oomph, you're heavy. No more lettuce for you."

Under her hands, his heart beat in a fast rhythm, his body warm and snuggly. She struggled to her feet under the burden. "Let's go in the garden. If you're really good, I'll steal some strawberries for you."

That was when the door opened.

And the dream changed.

The man in the doorway with his black hair brushed back from a severe widow's peak, chill slate-gray eyes and cadaverous frame, was her father. For a frozen moment, she thought he'd heard what she'd been planning for the strawberries, but then he smiled and her fear lessened a fraction. Just a fraction. Because even at five years of age, she knew nothing good ever came of her father seeking her out. "Father?"

He strolled into the room, his eyes on Bitty. "You've looked after him well."

She nodded. "I take care of him really good." Bitty was the only kind thing her father had ever done for her.

"I can see that." He smiled again, but those eyes, they were wrong in a way that made her stomach hurt. "Come with me, Liliana. No," he said when she would have bent to place Bitty on the floor, "bring your pet. I have a use for him."

The words scared her, but she was only five. Cuddling Bitty close to her chest, she toddled along after her father, and then up…and up…and up.

"How thoughtless of me," he said when they were halfway. "It must be difficult for you, all these stairs. Let me take the creature."

Certain she felt the rabbit flinch, Liliana tightened her hold on Bitty. "No, I'm okay," she said, trying not to huff.

Eyes of dirty ice stared at her for a long moment before her father turned, continued to climb the twisting, winding staircase to the tower room. The magic room. Where she was never, ever supposed to go.

However, today he opened the door and said, "It's time you learned about your heritage."

There was nowhere else to go, nowhere he wouldn't find her. So she walked into that room full of strange scents and books. It wasn't as gloomy as she'd expected, and there was no blood. Relief had her smiling in tremulous hope. Everyone always said her father was a blood sorcerer, but there was no blood here, so they had to be wrong.

Looking up, she met his gaze as he loomed over to take Bitty from her protesting arms. Her smile died, fear a metallic taste on her tongue.

"Such a healthy creature," he murmured, carrying the rabbit over to something that looked like a stone birdbath set in the middle of the circular room. Switching his hold, he suspended Bitty by his silky ears.

"No!" Liliana said, able to hear Bitty squeaking in distress. "That hurts him."

"It won't be for long." And then her father pulled a long, sharp knife from his cloak.

Bitty's blood turned the silver of the blade a dark, dark crimson before it flowed down to fill the shallow bowl of the horrible thing that wasn't a birdbath.

"Come here, Liliana."

Shaking her head, sobbing, she backed away.

"Come here," he said again in that same calm voice.

Her feet began to move forward in spite of her terror, in spite of her will, until she was close enough for her father to pick her up by the ruff of her neck and push her face close to the fading warmth of Bitty's blood, her blinding fear reflected in red. "See," he said. "See who you are."

CHAPTER TWO

LILIANA JERKED AWAKE ON A soundless scream, her mouth stuffed with cotton wool and her head full of the cold finality of death. It took her long moments to realize that the door to her cell stood open; Bard watched her with those large eyes of liquid black.

"Hello," she said, voice strained with the echoes of nightmare.

He waved her forward.

She got to her feet, ready to fight dizziness, but her body held her up. Relieved, she stepped out, following Bard's ponderous steps through the dimly lit passageway until he stopped at another narrow door. When he did nothing else, she pushed through and felt her cheeks color. "I'll be but a moment."

Taking care of her private business, she used the mirror of black glass to tidy herself up as much as possible—there wasn't anything she could do about her beak of a nose, or the eyes of dirty ice so wrong against her mother's honey-dark skin, or the strawlike consistency of her matted black hair, much less the slashing gape of her mouth, but she was able to sleek that hair back off her face at least and tuck it behind her ears, wash off the blood that still streaked her wrists.

"Well," she said to herself, "you're here now. You must do what you came to do." Though she had no idea how.

She'd grown up hearing the people her father had enslaved whispering of the four royal children, the true heirs to the jewel that was once Elden. The hope in their furtive voices had nurtured her own, fostering dreams of a future in which fear, sharp and acrid, wasn't her constant companion.

Then, a month ago, driven by a steadily strengthening belief that something was very, very *wrong,* she'd stolen away into the putrid stench and clawing branches of the Dead Forest to call a vision as her father could not, his blood too tainted—and seen the tomorrow that was to come.

The heirs of Elden would return.

All of them…but one.

The Guardian of the Abyss would not be there on that fateful day. Without him, the four-sided key of power would remain incomplete. His brothers and sister, their mates, would fight with the fiercest hearts to defeat her father, but they would fail, and Elden would fall forever to the Blood Sorcerer's evil. Horrifying as that was, it wasn't the worst truth.

Elden had begun to die a slow death the instant the king and the queen—the blood of Elden—had taken their final breaths. That death would be complete when the clock struck midnight on the twentieth anniversary of her father's invasion. Not so terrible a thing if it would strip the Blood Sorcerer of power, but Elden's people were touched by magic, too. Without it, they would simply fall where they stood, never to rise again.

Her father had spent years seeking to find a solution to what he termed a "disease." Which is why he would not murder the returned heirs. No, she'd seen the horror in her vision—he'd have them enchained and cut into with extreme care day after day, night after night, their blood dripping to the earth in a continuous flow to fool it into believing the blood of Elden had returned. They were a race that lived for centuries, would not easily die. And so her father would continue on in his heinous—

Thump!

Jumping at the booming sound, she realized her guard was whacking on the door to hurry her up. "I'm coming," she said, and turned away from the mirror.

Bard began to shuffle off in front of her as soon as she stepped out. It was difficult to keep up with him, for even shuffling, he was a far larger creature than her, each of his feet five times as big as her own. "Master Bard," she called as she all but ran behind him after reaching the top of the stairs.

He didn't stop, but she saw one of those large ears twitch.

"I do not wish to die," she said to his back. "What must I do to survive?"

Bard shook his head in a slight negative.

There was no way to survive?

Or he didn't know how she might?

Surely, she thought, not giving in to panic, surely her father's evil hadn't completely destroyed the soul of the boy who had been Prince Micah. She didn't know much about the youngest child of King Aelfric and Queen Alvina, but she'd heard enough whispers to realize that he had been a beloved prince, the small heart of the royal family, and of Elden.

"For who could not love a babe with such a light in his eyes?"

Words her old nursery maid, Mathilde, had said as she told Liliana a night-tale. It had taken Liliana years to realize that Mathilde's night-tales had been the true stories of Elden. And then she'd understood why Mathilde had disappeared from the nursery one cold spring night, never to be seen alive again.

Months later, her father had taken her for a walk, pointed out the gleaming white of bone in the slithering dark of the Dead Forest, a faint smile on his face.

Pain bloomed in her heart at the memory of the only person who had ever held her when she cried, but she crushed it with a ruthless hand. Mathilde was long dead, but the youngest prince of Elden still lived and, no matter the cost, Liliana would return him to Elden before the final, deadly midnight bell.

THE LORD OF THE BLACK CASTLE found himself waiting for his prisoner. It had taken longer than he'd anticipated to capture those spirits destined for the Abyss who had somehow managed to halt their journey at the badlands that surrounded the doorway to their ultimate destination. Usually, time had little meaning for him, but this past night he'd known the hours were passing, that the intruder who had dared look him in the eye slept in his dungeon.

He wasn't used to such thoughts and they made him curious.

So he waited on the black stone of the floor beneath his throne, aware of the day servants from the village going about their business in jittering quiet. It had been so as long as he could remember. They feared him, even as they served him. That was the way it should and would always be, for the Guardian of the Abyss must be a monster.

The thunder of Bard's footsteps vibrated through the stone just as he was getting impatient, and then came the deep groan of the massive doors at the end of the great hall being opened. The Lord of the Black Castle looked up as Bard walked in. His prisoner was nowhere to be seen—until Bard moved aside to expose the odd creature at his back.

She was…mismatched, he thought. Though her skin was a smooth golden brown that reminded him of honey from the redblossom tree, her eyes were tiny dots a peculiar sort of nowhere color and her mouth much too big, her hooked nose overwhelming every other feature. Her hair stuck out in a stiff mass akin to the straw in the stables, and she limped when she walked, as if one leg was shorter than the other.

Truly, she was not a prepossessing thing at all. And yet he remained curious.

Because she looked him in the eye.

No one had been unafraid enough to do that for… He could not remember the last time.

"So, you survived the night," he said.

She brushed off a piece of straw from the coarse material of her sacklike brown dress. "The accommodation was lovely, thank you."

He blinked at the unexpected response, conscious of the servants freezing where they stood. He didn't know what they expected him to do. Just as he had no awareness of his actions when the curse came upon him. He just knew that after it passed, parts of the castle lay wrecked, and the servants scuttled away from him like so many insects afraid to be crushed. "I shall have to speak to Bard about that," he murmured.

"Oh, don't blame him for my comfort," the odd creature said with an airy wave of a bony hand. "You see, I am quite used to a stone floor, so straw is the height of luxury."

"Who are you?" Whoever she was, she could not harm him. No one could harm him. No one could even touch him through the black armor that had crept up over his body until it encased him from neck to ankle. He'd felt the tendrils spearing through his hair of late, knew the armor would soon cover his face, too. All for the best. It would make it more difficult for evil to touch him when he went hunting its disciples.

"Liliana," his prisoner said, those tiny eyes of no particular color meeting his own with bold confidence. "I am Liliana. Who are you?"

He angled his head, wondering if she had all her faculties. For surely she wouldn't dare to speak to him thus otherwise. "I am the Guardian of the Abyss and the Lord of the Black Castle," he said because it amused him.

"Do you not have a name?" A quiet whisper.

It made him go still inside. "The lord does not need a name." But he had had one once, he thought, a long time ago. So long ago that it made waves of darkness roll through his head to even think of it, the monstrous curse within itching to take form.

He snapped a hand at Bard. "Take her back!"

LILIANA COULD HAVE KICKED herself as she was dragged away by a massive hand, her heels scraping along the stone floor. She'd attempted too much, too soon, and the twisted evil of her father's sorcery had struck back like the most vicious of snakes. "Wait!" she cried out to the retreating back coated in unyielding black armor. "Wait!"

When her jailor stopped to open the door, she glanced around wildly, trying to find something with which to save herself. There were no weapons on the wall nearby, but even if there had been, she was no warrior. The servants were too afraid to help. Maybe she could throw the bread, she thought with a dark glance at the hunk that sat on a platter on the huge slab of a dining table to her left—it certainly looked hard enough.

Oh.

"I can cook!" she yelled as Bard started to drag her through the doorway. "I'll cook you the most delicious meal you've ever had in your life if you—"

The door began to close on her words.

"Bard."

The big ugly lug stopped at his master's voice.

"Take her to the kitchen," came the order. "If she lies, throw her in the cauldron."

Relief had her feeling faint, but she managed to wobble around to walk beside Bard when he released his hold and turned to lead her down a different corridor. "He was jesting about the cauldron, wasn't he? You cannot have a cauldron big enough for a person?"

Bard halted, sighed, looked at her with those wide, liquid eyes. When he spoke, the sound came from the depths of some deep cave, so heavy and thunderous that her eardrums echoed. "We," he said, "have knives."

Liliana couldn't tell if he, like his master, was making a jest at her expense, so she shut her mouth and said nothing as they wound their way through black hallways free of all ornamentation, down a single wide step and through a heavy wooden door into a warm, sweet-smelling room at one end.

A startled pixielike creature looked up from where she stood by the large freestanding bench in the center. "Bard!" the woman said, her voice as high and sweet as her face was tiny and wrinkled in the most unexpected way—at the corners of her lips and along the bridge of her nose. The rest of her skin, the color of the earth after rain, was taut and smooth, the crinkled tips of her ears poking out through dark hair she'd pulled back into a thick braid.

A brownie, Liliana thought in wonder. She wasn't a pixie at all, but a brownie, a creature her father had hunted to extinction in Elden, for their blood made his magic so very strong.

Bard pushed Liliana into the room with one big paw. "New cook." He was gone the next instant.

The brownie's face fell.

Feeling terrible, Liliana walked over to stand on the other side of the bench. "I'm sorry." She hadn't even thought when she'd spoken. "I was trying to save myself from being sent back to the dungeon when I said I'd cook."

The other woman blinked at her. "Oh, no, oh, no. I'm an awful cook, I am." Picking up a biscuit from a tray on the bench, she dropped it to the floor. It bounced. "I do not know why the lord has not had me beheaded. Perhaps, oh, yes, perhaps he enjoys that my food matches this place."

Startled by her friendliness, Liliana said, "But you looked so disappointed just then."

The woman's ears turned pink at the tips. "Oh, no, that was nothing. Nothing at all. I'm Jissa."

"Liliana."

Reaching out, Jissa pinched Liliana's wrinkled and blood-encrusted dress. "I am not a good cook, but I keep this place clean. You are *not* clean."

"No." Embarrassed, Liliana scratched at her hair. "A bath would be much appreciated."

"You'll have to be quick, quick indeed, if you are to cook a meal," Jissa warned, shaking a rolling pin at her. "The lord will not wait past the early dinner bell before consigning you to the dungeon again." The brownie was moving as she spoke, waving at Liliana to follow with quick, birdlike motions. "Noon meal he will not eat today. Not in the castle, he isn't."

Running after her, Liliana found herself led to a small bathroom where Jissa was already working the pump to fill the tub. "I'll do—"

The brownie shook her head. "Take off your clothes and get in, in right now." Impatient words. "I'm sorry but it must be cold, so cold, for we have no time to heat the water."

Glad for the chance to be clean after spending days in her father's dungeon for the infraction of refusing to slit a man's throat, and then last night here, she gave up any attempt at modesty and stripped away her clothing to step into the frigid bath. Shivering, she picked up the bar of rough soap on the ledge, and dipping her head under the pump, wet her hair.

As she lathered it, Jissa said, "You are not very well put together, you aren't."

From others, it may have been an unkind statement. From Jissa, it sounded like simple fact, so Liliana nodded. "No." Her breasts were so small as to be non-existent, while her ribs stuck out from beneath her skin. Her behind, by comparison, was rather large, and one of her legs was shorter than the other.

"You will fit in very well here, yes, you will," Jissa said with a sudden smile that gave her a quixotic charm. "For *he* is the only creature of beauty, and even he turns into a monster."

Laughing, Liliana ducked her head under the water and washed off the suds before repeating the soaping process. Jissa stopped pumping to give her the chance to lather up her entire body, leaning against the pump as she recovered from the exertion.

"Where do you come from, Jissa?" Liliana asked, running the soap down her arms with a bliss even the cold couldn't diminish. "You are surely not a denizen of the Abyss." There was no evil in the brownie—on that Liliana would stake her life.

Jissa's face grew sad. "A mountain forest far from here, so far," she whispered. "The Blood Sorcerer came to our village and stole our magic. Stole and stole. I survived, but he said he couldn't stand the sight of me, so he enspelled me beyond the kingdoms, beyond the realm. This is where the spell stopped."

Liliana's stomach curdled. She knew Jissa would hate her if she learned of the murderous blood that ran in her veins, but Liliana needed her friendship. So she bit her tongue and stuck her head and body under the pump as Jissa began to work it again.

I'm sorry, she whispered deep inside. *I'm sorry my blood is responsible for the spilling of your own.*

CHAPTER THREE

Bath finished, she got out and rubbed herself down with a rough little towel while Jissa disappeared—to return with a black tunic that hit Liliana midthigh, black leggings and soft black boots. "I think these were meant for footmen," she said, holding out the garments, "when there were men of foot. There have never been any in the years I have lived here. Never, ever."

"Thank you, they look very comfortable." The leggings fit well enough but the tunic was baggy, so she was grateful for the thin rope Jissa found for her to use as a belt. "Do you have a comb I could— Thank you." Brushing it through the knotted mat of her hair, she pulled the whole mass severely off her face and tied it using a smaller piece of rope. She didn't look in the mirror. She had no wish to see the face "that would frighten even a ghoul into returning to its den."

"Can you truly cook?" Jissa asked as they made their way back to the kitchen.

"Yes. I spent many hours in the kitchens of the castle where I grew up." In spite of his cadaverous frame, the Blood Sorcerer liked to eat, and so he didn't brutalize the cook. As a result, the man had been the only one of the castle's servants unafraid to offer a little kindness to the child who clung to the shadows so as not to attract her father's attention.

"What raw ingredients do you have?" she asked Jissa,

shaking off the memories. That child was long gone, her innocence shattered into innumerable shards. The woman she'd become would let nothing stop her—not even the monster who was the lord of this place.

"Oh, many things." Moving to the bench where she'd been working, the brownie waved a hand and the mostly empty surface was suddenly overflowing with plump red and orange peppers, carrots, cabbages, ripe fruits of every description, a basket full of dark green leaves that would taste nutty when cooked, and more.

Liliana picked up a pepper with a wondering hand. "Where does this come from?"

"The village," Jissa said in a matter-of-fact tone that was already familiar.

"There is a village in this realm?" She'd always assumed the Abyss was a baleful place devoid of all life—but that didn't explain the servants she'd seen.

"Of course." Jissa gave her a look that suggested Liliana was being very dim. "We are the doorway to the Abyss. The doorway only."

"Yes, I see." The Black Castle was still part of the living world. "Is the village close?"

A shake of her head that sent Jissa's braid swinging. "You must pass through the gates of the Black Castle, and then you must walk through the forest to the settlement. Dark, whispery forest. Whisper, whisper. But not bad." An intent look, as if she wanted to make certain Liliana understood.

She continued at Liliana's nod. "I walk quick and fast with Bard when we need supplies, and buy from the merchants using the lord's gold. This and that and this, too." A sudden dipping of her head that hid her expression, but her words were pragmatic enough. "Bard carries everything back for me. Always he carries."

"*He* has gold?" The furnishings Liliana had seen were functional, but aside from a few grim tapestries, there was nothing of beauty, nothing to speak of wealth. All was black and hard and cold.

"It is the Law of the Abyss, first law, always law." Jissa began to stack the vegetables to the side to clear part of the bench. "Do you not know?" She answered her own question without waiting for a response. "Evil gold and evil treasure comes to the Black Castle with the condemned." A baring of those sharp, pointed teeth. "Only if an innocent, an innocent, you see, would be harmed by the taking, only then it does not."

Liliana thought of her father's coffers, knew this law was yet another reason he sought to live forever, though they, too, were part of a race that lived centuries. He had taken her into his vault after bleeding poor Bitty to nothingness. Gold in innumerable piles, jewels twinkling from necklaces still stained with their last wearer's life-blood, rings on skeletal fingers, it had been a glimmering nightmare.

"This," her father had said, his arms spread wide, "this is what you could have if you aren't weak." Picking up a necklace of tear-shaped diamonds splattered with flecks of brown, he'd placed it around her neck. "Feel it, feel the blood."

She had felt it. And it had made her choke on her own vomit. Her father had backhanded her so hard for her "weakness" she'd ended up resting on a mountain of gold coins. When he'd wrenched off the necklace, he'd made her bleed. She carried the scar on her neck to this day—it was a constant reminder of the vow she'd made as a defenseless child. Never would she be like him, no matter what he did to her.

And he had done things he didn't do even to his enemies.

"Dungeon you'll go to if you don't cook."

Snapping back to the present, Liliana nodded and chose an assortment of fruit vibrant with color and fragrance. "Will you chop these, Jissa?"

The brownie picked up a knife as Liliana hunted out the flour, butter and milk, and began to roll out a pastry on one corner of the massive bench. "The village," she said as they worked, "do you live there?" It would make sense if Jissa did—the Black Castle was a gloomy place full of watchful ghosts and shimmering darkness.

"I cannot." Jissa's sadness lingered in the air, settled on Liliana's skin, permeated her very bones. "I tried when I first came, and I…died, was all dead, after two days. The lord brought me back here and I lived again."

Liliana's heart caught, for she understood now. No matter her memories, Jissa hadn't survived the massacre in her village. The Blood Sorcerer had a spell he called Slumber. Such an innocuous name for such an evil thing. He used it on those magical creatures who were pure of blood and yet rare. Rather than murdering them when he might already be swollen with power, he broke their necks but whispered a spell at the moment of death that kept them breathing and slumbering.

Liliana had been locked in a room with her father's victims once, but it hadn't horrified her as he'd intended. She'd been grateful, her magic telling her the beings no longer possessed their souls. They had escaped. But not Jissa. Whatever her father had done to her, it had trapped her in this borderland between life and death. "I'm sorry."

"Why?" Confusion. "You aren't the Blood Sorcerer. No, you're not."

Knives in Liliana's chest, the lies of omission choking her up.

Jissa spoke again. "There are meats in the cold box. I can—"

"*No.* No meat on the table." Her own blood would be the only blood she would ever spill. Her father had delighted in forcing her to watch as he took his time torturing and mutilating creature after magical creature. It was when she was six that he'd begun to whisper spells that forced her to do the same vile acts even as she screamed and screamed and screamed.

Four more years it had taken until she'd grown strong enough to block his spells with her own. That was when he'd started to hurt the servants who dared to speak with her, to offer her any small kindness—all except the cook. So she had learned to remain silent.

"Oh." Jissa's brow furrowed, her sharp little teeth biting into her lower lip. "Meat, he always eats the meat," she whispered. "Even I, bad cook I, can't make it taste that terrible."

"Never fear, Jissa," Liliana said, kneading the dough with determined hands, her mind on eyes of wintergreen, so very beautiful, so very deadly. "He'll never notice the lack."

THE DINNER BELL RANG LOUD and sonorous. Seated alone at the head of a massive table of polished wood so dark it was near black, the Guardian of the Abyss raised his cup and took a sip of red wine. "Where is my meal, Bard?" he asked, though he wasn't looking forward to the food that didn't deserve the name.

If Jissa weren't already dead, he was sure he would have executed her long ago for attempting to starve him. Of course today it was his new prisoner who would face his wrath. He wondered if she would look him in the eye when he sentenced her to another night in the dungeon.

"I will see, my lord." The big man turned to open the door…to reveal the prisoner, Liliana, and Jissa standing there with huge trays in their arms.

"Thank you," Liliana said with a smile that was much too wide. "We couldn't open the door." And then she was walking into the great hall with that halting stride of hers, her face brutally exposed given that she'd pulled her hair back.

Again, he found himself fascinated by his strange prisoner.

Placing her tray on the table and waiting for Jissa to do the same, she whipped off the covers from the dishes and moved to serve him. "This," she said, placing a small round tart on his plate, "is not my best work, but you didn't give me much time, my lord. Jissa tells me the dinner bell rings early today."

He picked up the tidbit, wondering if all her food came in so small a portion. And if her words were meant to warn him that she'd lied about her ability to cook. If she had, he would have to send her back to the dungeon. Lines furrowed his forehead. He was intrigued enough by her that he wanted her around, but he couldn't spare her—he was the Guardian of the Abyss. Mercy was a weakness he'd never had. Though perhaps he would ask Bard to give her a blanket.

"Well, my lord? Will you not eat it or are you afraid I will poison you?" A question as tart as the miniscule bite he held in hand.

He considered punishing her for her impertinence, decided she was likely feebleminded and didn't know any better. "The Guardian of the Abyss cannot die."

She tucked a stiff strand of hair behind her ear. "But only while you are within this castle."

Amused by her, he decided to answer. "No. While I am in this realm."

"I see." Something whispered in the depths of her eyes, and he wondered if she was a very clever spy, come to assassinate him.

But who would dare raise a blade against the Lord of the Black Castle? And why would they send this creature so weak and small and strange? Ridiculous. With that, he ate the tart.

An explosion of flavors—sweet and fresh and spicy and— "What else have you made?" Swallowing the tiny tidbit, he waited with impatience as she served him two more of the same.

Then came the soup so clear and with round little green things in it that she told him were pieces of "spring onion." He blinked, having the sudden, nagging feeling that he hated onion. But that was an inexplicable thought—he ate what Jissa made, but then Jissa's food had no taste. "This is meant to feed me?"

"Try it, my lord."

He didn't bother with the spoon. Picking up the bowl, he drank.

And drank.

And drank.

There was a large square of something made of many layers in front of him when he finished the soup and set the bowl to the side. This time, he didn't question, simply picked up the fork and took a bite.

Cheese and a thin pastry and peppers and cabbage, tomatoes and other things, spices he couldn't name but that burst to life on his tongue with flickering heat. He cleared his plate with swift relish. "What is next?"

She spooned rice, soft and fluffy, onto his plate, before covering it with some kind of a stew, except that it was full of chunks of different vegetables that turned it into a storm of color. "Where is the meat?"

Putting down the bowl, his peculiar little prisoner folded her arms. "I won't cook it. If you wish for meat, you may ask Jissa to do so."

He was the Lord of the Black Castle and of the Abyss. He wasn't used to being defied. But he was also not used to eating food that made him eager to see the next course. So he tried this vegetable stew over rice. It was a thick, flavorsome concoction that lay warm and satisfying in his belly. Finishing the food, he pushed away the plate. "You will cook for me."

A slight nod—as if she had a choice in the matter. "I didn't have time to prepare a proper dessert, my lord, but I hope this will do."

She put slices of fruit in front of him, plump and fresh, alongside a small pot of something sweet and rich, with a scent that made his nostrils flare. "What is this?"

A faint smile. "Try it, my lord."

He hadn't been the recipient of any kind of a smile for so long that something creaked and crashed open inside of him as he looked into her face. "No, you will tell me," he said in a harsh tone, suddenly no longer amused.

She didn't flinch. "Honey with a bit of vanilla and some spices. It is sometimes called nectar."

More, please!

Shaking his head, he rid himself of that odd child-like voice. He didn't know such a child, and the smallest of the realms never came through the doorway to the Abyss. They didn't have time to grow into the evil that would mean banishment to this place of torment and repentance.

More, Mama!

"Take it away," he said, shoving back his chair with such force it clattered to the floor. "And do not bring me such a thing again."

His prisoner said nothing as she—with Jissa's help—began to gather up the remains of the meal. Stalking to the other end of the great hall, he used the power of this place to raise himself to the wall above the throne and picked out a giant sickle, black as his armor. The edge gleamed white-hot the instant it touched his hand.

He glimpsed Liliana watching him as he came back down to earth and turned to walk out into the cold dark of the soul hunt.

LILIANA'S EYES LINGERED ON the doorway through which the dark lord had disappeared, the echo of his chair hitting the floor still ringing in her ears. Something in him remembered the delicacy favored by the children of Elden, something in him *knew*.

"Liliana." Jissa's hand on her arm. "Go, go, we must go. Not nice to see souls being dragged into the Abyss. Always, they try to escape. Beg and bargain and plead."

"Where is the doorway?"

"Feet, below our feet. Down, down in the castle."

Liliana looked at the black marble of the floor and wondered what she would find if she were to crack it open. Likely nothing but rock. For it was said only the most blackened of souls and the Guardian of the Abyss himself could view that terrible wasteland full of screams and horror. And it was this place that the youngest Elden royal faced night after night. It was this place that had shaped him.

"We'll eat now." Jissa's bright voice broke into her

murky thoughts. "You and me and Bard, we'll eat your delicious food."

"The other servants?" Liliana asked when they reached the kitchens after cleaning up the table in the great hall.

"Returned to the village they have." Round, shining eyes filled with unquenchable sorrow. "Gone home."

Liliana's hatred for her father grew impossibly deeper. "Sit," she said, "eat. I'll be back after I deliver this—" picking up a tart "—to another friend."

When Bard began to rise, Liliana said, "Where will I go, Master Jailor? And what would I dare steal?" With that, she pushed through the door and made her way down to the dungeons. The door to her cell was closed, but not locked.

Walking inside, she placed the tart near the food container. "Little friend," she whispered, "this is for you."

Silence. Then a slight sound, a small body quivering in hope.

Rising, Liliana backed out and closed the door. She was about to return to the warmth of the kitchen when she found herself curious about the other cells. She'd heard nothing but silence the previous night, but she'd been weak and exhausted at the time.

Picking the torch up off the wall, its flames flickering eerie shadows over the crumbling stone, she walked deeper into the cold. The first cell beyond her own was empty, as was the next. But the third, the third was very much occupied.

"Sissssster," came the sibilant whisper as she stood with the flame held close to the small barred square in the door, "help meeeee."

CHAPTER FOUR

SQUINTING, SHE TRIED TO SEE within. But there was only blackness. An impossible blackness, so dense as to repel the light from the torch. Liliana hesitated. She wasn't stupid. The Black Castle held the gateway through which only the most vicious of the dead and the Guardian himself could pass—her sojourn here aside, its dungeons were unlikely to be populated by beings who meant her no harm.

Holding the torch in front of her like a shield, she backed away.

A slithering, as if some large creature was nearing the door. "Sissssster, it issssss a missssstake. I've done nothing wrong."

"Then," she said, continuing to keep her distance, "you would not have been drawn to the Abyss." It was said the Abyss was the one constant throughout the realms, its magic elemental, immutable—if your soul was rotted and foul, you'd be unable to escape it once your mortal flesh released its grip on life.

"Are you sssssssssssoooo certain?"

"Yes," she said, suddenly conscious that she was almost at the cell door once again.

She couldn't remember moving.

And she couldn't shift her eyes from the square "window" of the cage.

"Come clossssser, sissssster."

Swallowing, she squeezed her fingers into the palm of her free hand in an attempt to cut half-moons into her flesh, release her blood. But it was taking too long and she knew that once she was close enough, the sinister creature beyond would reach out—

"Stop."

The single, cold word was said in a deep voice that whispered with its own darkness.

An enraged hiss from beyond the door, before the Lord of the Black Castle raised a gauntleted hand and a mirror of black glass grew to cover the bars of the window. Only then did he turn to look at her, and his eyes, his eyes…

She stumbled back in spite of herself at the blackness within, all traces of green erased. Watching her with lethal focus, he stepped closer, until he could grip her jaw, hold her in place with those fingers tipped with claws of cold steel. "Are you so eager to spend another night in the dungeon?" As gentle as the first question he'd asked her in this realm.

She tried to shake her head, but his hold was firm, his grip unbreakable. "I am too curious, my lord," she managed to grit out. "It is my besetting sin."

For some reason, that made him soften his hold. "What would you see here?"

"I wanted to know if you had any more prisoners."

Black tendrils spread out from his irises and back again, eerie—and a sign of the sorcery that held him captive. If she didn't find a way to reverse it, he would soon be utterly encased in impenetrable black.

"Why," she said when he didn't reply, "is that creature here and not in the Abyss?"

"Opening the doorway is difficult work," he said, rubbing his thumb almost absently over her chin, the sharp point brushing against her lip in a caress that could turn deadly in a fragment of a moment. "It's less trouble to collect several of the condemned and deliver them together."

"Aren't you afraid of what they'll do to your servants?" It was hard to speak with him touching her, his body so big, so close.

"My servants are intelligent enough to know not to wander the dungeons once night has fallen."

She colored, wondering why he stared at her so; she knew she was ugly, but did he have to watch her with such focus? As if she was an insect? "I won't make the same mistake again."

Releasing her, he said, "But will you be curious again?"

Perhaps it would've been better to lie, but Liliana found her mouth parting, the words spilling out. "Yes, this castle is fascinating." As was its lord. Who would he have been if her father had not seized the throne of Elden? A prince golden and true? Sophisticated and elegant and learned?

She couldn't imagine him thus, this man with the ice of death in his gaze, his voice, his touch. "Did you complete your hunt?" He hadn't been gone long…or she'd been caught in the creature's snare for longer than she'd realized.

"Yes, for now," he said, his eyes still that eerie midnight shade. "Come. I will show you my castle."

Startled at the offer, she began to head after him.

"Beware, sissssssster," came the sibilant whisper from beyond the mirrored glass. "No maid is safe with the Lord of the Black Castle."

She felt more than saw anger sweep across the face of the lethal male at her side, but she snorted. "Clearly, you do not have good vision," she said to whatever lay beyond the locked door. "Or you'd know that I'm not a maid any man would want to ravish."

Turning to look at the Guardian of the Abyss, she found him staring at her again. Once more, she felt like a bug, an insect. But she straightened her shoulders and said, "Your castle, my lord?"

A long pause that made an icy bead of sweat trickle down her spine before he led her back up the winding stairs and into the dark heart of his domain. Stopping in the hall of black mirrors when she hesitated, he said, "Do you want to see?"

Everywhere she looked, she saw reflections. Him, so tall and sun-golden and piercingly beautiful—and her, so short and badly formed. "What?" she asked, looking away from her own image.

"The Abyss." He swept out a hand without waiting for a response and the mirrors filled with images of churning horror. At first there was only a wash of black and green flame, an impression of things burning. But then she began to see the faces. Contorted faces drowning in pain. Clawing hands asking for help before they dug out their own eyes in an effort to escape. Limbs floating in the black, twitching as if sensation remained.

And the screams. Silent. Endless. Forever.

Clapping her hands over her ears, she shook her head. "Stop it!"

"Do you feel pity for them?" He touched his finger to the image of a face flayed and torn, its eyes red orbs bulging with terror as a basilisk feasted on its body. "He sold his children to…a sorcerer. The…sorcerer tortured and murdered them because that is how he gains his power. The man knew."

No matter that she stood in the midst of such violent

anguish, she caught his hesitation. "Blood Sorcerer," it seemed, was something he couldn't say. But if he remembered her father, even if only in the most hidden depths of his psyche, then there was a chance he'd remember his family, remember what he had to do before it was too late.

"Please," she whispered, feeling as if her ears were bleeding from those silent screams that reverberated relentlessly in her head.

"This one," he said, pointing to another face so burned the flesh was melting, but with eyes of perfect alertness, "trapped those creatures he considered lesser—brownies like Jissa, the wise gazelles of the plains, cave trolls so small and shy—and butchered them for his own amusement. And this one, she poisoned an entire wood so that the creatures tied to the earth would curl up and die and she would have their land."

Unable to take the pressure of the screams any longer, her gut twisting from the horrors he was painting onto the walls of a mind that already held too much, Liliana ran forward to press her face to his back, her hands fisted against the hard carapace of his armor. "Stop, or I won't cook for you again."

A moment's pause.

The images disappeared.

Peace.

"You will cook for me." An order—but there was a thread of what she might've almost called disappointment in the tone of his voice.

Blinking, she wondered if he had been trying to show her something that was important to him, something he'd thought she would *like* to see. Surely not, for he was the Lord of the Black Castle, and yet…he was alone. A monster who stood as the last defense against the other monsters. "They say," she whispered, "that once there was no Abyss, that the world was innocent and its people, young and old, untainted."

He shifted away to face her, his eyebrows heavy over eyes become that beautiful winter-green. "You tell night-tales."

"Perhaps." In truth, regardless of what she wanted to believe, she'd seen too much not to understand that there would always be those whose souls were malevolent. "I do know many night-tales."

He cocked his head. "How many?"

"Many," she said, seeing in his intrigued expression a way to reach the boy who lived within the lethal Guardian, who had to live within. If she was wrong, if that boy was long dead, crushed beneath the weight of years and the soul-chilling armor of her father's twisted spell, then they were all lost. Her father would rule and Elden would become another Abyss.

HAVING BEEN "PERMITTED" time enough for a meal, she found herself in the great hall, perhaps half an hour later, able to feel hundreds of eyes on her—as she had the day she'd landed frail and disoriented on the marble floor. But when she raised her head in stiff pride, ready to stare down the audience, she saw only emptiness. "Who is watching?"

The Lord of the Black Castle turned from where he'd put one booted foot on the steps that led to the throne colored the same eponymous shade, as hard and lacking in ornamentation as the man himself. "The residents," he said, as if that were self-evident.

"The residents?" she pushed, fighting the urge to hug her arms around herself. "From the Abyss?" Legend said that despite the pitiless task that was his nightly duty, the

Guardian was always pure of heart. In this ancient legend she'd placed her faith, but if he allowed the putrid souls destined for the Abyss to linger above...

"Of course not." A grim stare that raised every tiny hair on her body. "There are other souls who are drawn to the Black Castle."

"Why?"

"They come and they do not leave." An answer that told her she was trying his patience with her questions. "The Black Castle welcomes them."

Liliana felt a glimmer of understanding, wondered if she might have more allies than she believed.

"You will tell the tale now." It was an order as he took his seat on the throne.

Hairs still standing up in alarm, she nonetheless put her hands on her hips and said, "It would be easier if I didn't have to shout, my lord!" He sat high and remote, an arrogant emperor.

He gestured her forward. "You may sit at my feet."

Dropping them from her hips, Liliana fisted her hands by her sides, her entire body rigid. Sit at his feet? Like an animal? *No.* If her father hadn't broken her after a lifetime, then the Guardian of the Abyss surely would not! But when she would've opened her mouth, given voice to her fury, she felt ghostly fingers on her lips, *almost* heard a whisper in her ear.

The shock of it cut through her conditioned response, tempered her rage, made her think.

Looking up into the face of the dark lord who'd commanded her, she saw impatience, saw, too, a quicksilver anticipation. "Is it an honor, my lord?" she asked, realization shimmering a golden rain through her veins. "To sit below your throne?"

"You ask strange questions, Liliana." It was the first

time he'd said her name, and it felt akin to a spell on its own, wrapping her in tendrils of black that gleamed with bright green highlights. "This throne is only for the Guardian. Any imposter who dares sit here will die a terrible death."

And so it *was* a great honor for her to be allowed so close.

Keeping that in mind, she swallowed her pride and climbed the steps to the throne—but instead of taking a seat at his feet, for that she couldn't do, not for anyone, she perched herself several feet away, so she could turn and face him. "Once upon a time," she began, her blood thunder in her veins—because it could all end now, with a single misstep—"there was a land called Elden."

Whispers rolling around the room, ghostly murmurs gaining in volume.

"Quiet!" The lord cut the air with a slicing hand.

Silence reigned.

"Continue."

Curiosity about the ghostly residents danced nimble and quick through her veins, but she kept it in check. First, she must discover if the Abyss had saved the last heir—or if it had consumed him. "This land, this Elden, it was a place of grace and wonder. Its people grew old at so slow a pace that some called them immortal, but they were not true immortals, for they could die, but only after hundreds of years of life, of learning.

"Because of their great love of this last, they were renowned for their knowledge and artistry, their libraries the finest in all the kingdoms." She carried on when her audience didn't interrupt, the ghosts as motionless as the green-eyed man on the throne of black. "Elden was also a land overflowing with magical energy, its people's bodies touched with it." That energy had given Elden its strength—and made it a target. "All of Elden's grace and prosperity flowed from the king and queen. King Aelfric, it is said—"

"No!" The Lord of the Black Castle rose, his hands clenched, his eyes black, the tendrils spiraling out to run across his face. "You will not say that name."

"It is only a name in a tale," she said, though the merciless cold of his gaze made her abdomen lurch with the realization that he could end her life with one swipe of that razor-gauntleted hand. "It is not real." Better to tell a small lie, if it would help her slip under the viscous cobweb of her father's spell. "Surely, you aren't a child to be scared of tales." It was a chance she took, that he wouldn't kill her for such insolence, but the stakes were too high for her to walk softly.

"You dare challenge me?" Quiet words. Deadly words. "I will—"

"If you send everyone to the dungeon, my lord," she said, brushing an imaginary speck of dirt off her tunic in an effort to hide the trembling in her hands, "it's a wonder you have any friends at all."

His eyes turned green between one blink and the next, the tendrils of armor disappearing from his face. "The Guardian of the Abyss has no friends."

She understood loneliness. Oh, yes, she understood how it could cut and bite and make you bleed. "I'm not surprised," she said, rather than offering him her friendship. That would most certainly get her thrown back down into the bowels of the castle—he was a man of power and pride, of arrogance earned through dark labor. "It's a dicey business," she said, taking her life into her hands for the second time in as many minutes, "talking with someone who locks up anyone who disagrees with him."

Anger turned his bones stark against his skin, but then the green gleamed. "Tell this tale, Liliana. I promise, whether it is good or bad, you won't have to spend the night in the dungeon."

Liliana didn't trust that gleam, her heart thudding against her ribs as her hands turned damp. "What are you planning to do to me?"

CHAPTER FIVE

HE SMILED. AND SHE CAUGHT her breath at the heartbreaking beauty of him. Now she understood, now she glimpsed the child he must've been, the one who had won a kingdom's heart. However, his words were not those of a child, but of an intelligent, dangerous man. "You must imagine what the Guardian of the Abyss might do to you."

It took every ounce of her will to find her voice again when all she wanted was to stare at him, this lost prince who had become a dark stranger. "King Aelfric—" she saw him clench his hands over the arms of the throne but he stayed silent "—was wise and powerful. It was written that his people would do anything for him, they loved him so much." She'd spent many an hour in the archives, a place her father never went, though he kept a chronicler on hand to record his "greatness."

"Kings are not loved." A rough interruption from the Guardian of the Abyss. "They rule. They cannot play games of nicety."

Liliana rubbed a fisted hand over her heart. "Some kings rule, and some kings reign," she whispered. "Some are loved and some are not. Aelfric was loved, for he was just and treated his people with a fair hand."

"Fairness alone does not engender love."

She looked into that gaze turned inscrutable, wondered if he was asking a question, or simply stating a

fact. "In Elden," she said, "it did." When he didn't interrupt again, she continued. "Its people, hungry for knowledge, did love to roam. Some even found a doorway to a
realm of no magic and came back with the most fantastical tales."

Ghostly whispers of disbelief, but it was the Lord of
the Black Castle who snorted. "A realm without magic?
It's like speaking of a realm without air."

"This is my tale," Liliana said with a prim sniff,
smoothing her hands down the wrinkled black of her
tunic. It was as shapeless as a potato sack, but better than
that ugly brown dress, he supposed.

"If you don't like it," she continued, putting that
large hooked nose of hers into the air, "you don't have
to listen."

No one said such things to him in such a tone, but
though part of her tale caused a primal fury within him,
it was an intriguing story, far better than anything he'd
heard these past several years. There was a storyteller in
the village, but the old man quaked and trembled so when
invited to the Black Castle that the Guardian of the Abyss
was afraid he would shake apart. And his teeth chattered
the entire time, a constant clattering accompaniment.

"Continue," he said to this curious storyteller of his,
this Liliana who had appeared from nowhere and was
stroked by a magic he knew he should recognize, a
magic that aroused a shadowy curl of anger...of hidden
memory.

He shook off the thought at once—he was the Guardian of the Abyss and had been so since the instant he
woke in the Black Castle. There were no other memories
within him. "Liliana." It was a growl when she didn't immediately obey.

Her head lifted. "In this land of no magic—" a stern

frown when the ghostly residents of the Black Castle twittered in amusement "—it is said that they do everything with mechanical creatures. They build monoliths with fearsome metal beasts and even have birds that fly through the air on steel wings."

Cold. Cold. Cold, the residents whispered, but the lord wondered what those towering structures might look like. However, when his lashes drifted down, what he saw instead was a castle tall and strong, with many-hued pennants flaring above the parapets while firedancers circled, the birds voices a shimmering chorus to the dawn. The windows were made of glass so fine they appeared created of air, the building growing out of the pure blue waters of a pristine lake.

The entire scene was drenched in a golden glow.

Impossible, he thought. No light such as that had ever touched the Black Castle, or the barren desert and bubbling pools of lava that were the badlands. Perhaps he'd read of that golden castle in another tale as a child.

But…he had never been a child.

"My lord."

Turning, he met Liliana's quizzical gaze. Such an in-between shade were her eyes. Neither blue nor gray. "Enough," he said, getting to his feet. "You may sleep in the kitchen tonight. Bard!"

Liliana was already rising. "You didn't like my tale?" she asked as Bard lumbered into the great hall from where he'd been standing watch outside.

He stared at her, at those strange eyes that seemed to penetrate the hard shine of the black armor and see things in him that should not, could not, exist. "You will make me breakfast when you wake." Then he turned and walked to the doorway that would lead him out into the night-dark world.

As Liliana followed Bard's hulking presence to the kitchen, she felt a ghostly finger tug at her hair. Then another. "Stop it," she muttered under her breath. When they persisted, she halted, knuckled fists against her hips, foot tapping on the black stone of the castle floor. "I have no intention of continuing the tale until the lord wishes it." She glared at the air. "If you pester me, I'll refuse to do even that."

Turning back around, she found Bard staring at her with those liquid eyes so wise and deep. "Don't pretend you can't hear them," she said, folding her arms.

Bard said nothing, simply carried on to the kitchen.

The ghosts, at least, whispered away, leaving her in peace.

"Thank you," she said when he pushed open the door that led to the cozy room.

He waited until she was inside before pulling it shut.

She heard a lock click into place. "So much for trust." A little surprised that she'd survived the Guardian of the Abyss, she looked around for something with which to create a pallet. The sacks of flour, perhaps, or maybe—

"Jissa, you sweetheart." A set of folded blankets, as well as a soft pillow, lay neatly in front of the stove that had been stoked so that it would burn all night, ensuring she'd feel no chill.

Unfolding the blankets with a smile, she realized one of them was heavy, stuffed with some kind of cotton. With that on the heated floor near the stove, it would be almost as comfortable as sleeping in a bed—something she hadn't done for months, having been banished to an empty stone room in punishment for not heeding her father. He hadn't locked her in, because he enjoyed tormenting her by making her watch her mother haunt the halls, Irina's face puffy and bruised from his fists.

A sharp hint of iron.

It took conscious effort to make herself unclench her fists, force her mind away from her hatred of the man whose blood ran in her veins. Face burning with pulsing rage, she got up to throw ice-cold water on her cheeks before hunting out some more food. No matter if her stomach churned with memory, she had to keep up her strength if she was to tangle with the dangerous, golden prince who ruled this place.

Taking out a thick piece of bread, she cut off a hunk of smoky cheese and rolled it up. The first bite was delicious, settling her stomach, the second even more so. Then she heard the skitter of tiny feet. Breaking off a bit of the cheese, she walked to the corner where she could see the gleam of small dark eyes, the skeletal push of bone against skin. "Here you go, my little friend."

She retreated after placing the cheese on the floor. Only when he'd eaten the food did she approach again and leave a second piece. It would not do to feed him too quickly when he had been starving so very long.

The same could be said for the Lord of the Black Castle.

She'd attempted too much too soon in speaking of Elden and his father at once, driven by the knowledge that time was running out at an inexorable pace. From his violent reaction to King Aelfric's name, it was obvious that the Blood Sorcerer's twisted spell was even more entrenched than she'd believed. Not even a crack marred the carapace that was the black armor that held him locked away from his past.

Worry turned her gut to lead, made the food lose all taste, but she forced herself to finish the sandwich, then a small apple. What strength she had came from her own blood, and she couldn't afford to allow that blood to grow thin and weak. If her father found her...

Bile, bitter and acidic, rose up in her throat.

"No," she whispered. *"No."* He wouldn't find her. She'd only discovered the location of the youngest prince because of her visions. Even then, it had taken her five attempts to get to a realm most knew only as the most terrifying of legends. The first two times that she'd failed hadn't been so bad— she'd been able to return home before her father noticed. The third time, she'd ended up with a fractured forearm after landing wrong, and the fourth...the Blood Sorcerer had been waiting for her.

Her skin tightened as if under the lash of a razor-whip.

"But I didn't break." A fierce reminder. That night, as her back was shredded, so much meat exposed to the air while she lay naked and chained to a massive stone table carved with channels that sent her blood trickling into collection pots, she'd managed to convince the Blood Sorcerer that her spells had been fueled by a wish to find a talisman that would cure her mother.

He'd believed her; he found it vastly amusing how much it hurt her that Irina never so much as acknowledged her presence.

"No matter what you do—" he'd paused to rub his finger over a seeping wound "—she belongs to me." A chuckle as he stepped away to flick the whip almost desultorily over her already ruined back.

Blood seeped out of her ravaged flesh, sliding down her ribs and into the channels. "She's my mother." A mother she loved.

Another laugh, deep and from the chest, as if he had never heard anything so ludicrous in his life. "Then I give you leave to discover this wonderful talisman. Do show it to me when you find it." A stroke of the whip over her shoulders. "I think my pets will enjoy their time with you."

Spiders—huge and mutated for use in another spell—fell from the ceiling to crawl all over her body, their furred legs rasping over her flesh, their mouths sucking on the raw meat of her back. Panicked, she tried to use her sorcery to escape, but her father was stronger and the restraints held.

The entire time they terrorized her, he sat where she could see him, a small smile on his face.

THE GUARDIAN OF THE ABYSS flew across the skies, his wings slicing through the night air in much the same way as that of the bat over to his right, his wings as leathery and as dark. He didn't know where his wings went when he landed—they simply appeared when he needed them and ceased to exist when he no longer wished them present.

A gift from the Abyss.

He thought of Liliana's tale of a realm without magic and snorted again. As if such a land could ever exist. An instant later, his mind pricked at him with the other part of her story, the part about *that* place, the name of which he couldn't even think about without a thunderous pain in his head, an anvil striking at his skull from within. He flew harder, faster, in an effort to escape the relentless pressure.

A whisper of oily evil.

Having located his prey, he moved toward it with furious swiftness. The man-shaped shadow was running over the ground in a vain effort to escape his fate, heading toward the borders of the realm. The majority of the condemned woke up from death to find themselves in the howling cold of the Abyss, but some were able to claw themselves to a stop in the badlands.

They had to be caught and sent through the doorway, for he would not take the chance that they might turn in the other direction, and seek to possess one of the villagers. However, sometimes, he allowed them to run—because waiting out here were creatures who could catch even shadows, crunching them up with sharp teeth before spitting out screaming, mangled tears of black.

It was a lesson no one had ever wanted to repeat.

Sweeping down on wings designed for deathly silence, he clamped his hands over the figure's arms. It thrashed, panicked that anyone could restrain it—for it was little more than smoke—but the lord of this place had always been able to hold those destined for the Abyss.

After all, that was the reason for his creation.

Crying, scared, a small child in a dark, dark place.

Guessing the alien images and emotions were the result of an attack by the creature in his grasp, he entrapped the shadow using thick black ropes infused with his blood, ensuring there'd be no more attempts at coercion. Then he flew through the cold, moonless and starless night, impatient to capture the others and return to the Black Castle. To get rid of his burden, nothing more.

But after he landed, the shadows locked up in the cages from which nothing could escape, he strode not to his room, but to the kitchen. The lock on the door was no impediment. Everything in the Black Castle obeyed its lord, flesh or ether or metal. Everything except the woman fast asleep on the floor near the hot belly of the stove.

Stepping closer, he stared down at her. She wasn't beautiful, this Liliana with the potent magic in her blood that he *knew* and yet could not name, this storyteller who told him outlandish tales as if she thought them true. Her nose was too big, her eyes too close together, her hair so much black straw.

But...

He watched her until she sighed and turned toward him, as if in welcome.

Crouching, he reached for her—and saw the gauntlet around his forearm, the spiderweb crawling across the back of his hand to turn into sharp claws above his nails, indestructible armor that kept him safe from evil, and shut him away from the world. He rose, his hand clenched into a fist, and left the room, closing the door behind him.

He stared at the lock for a long, long time.

If he left the door unlocked, she might decide to leave.

He snapped the lock shut.

It had nothing to do with Liliana. He just wanted to hear the rest of her ridiculous tale.

CHAPTER SIX

LILIANA WOKE TO THE SOUND of small feet moving around the kitchen. "Jissa?"

"Yes, it's me. I'm making sweet, sweet chocolate."

Liliana jerked into a sitting position at once. "Where did you get it?"

Jissa smiled, showing a row of pointed white teeth. "*He* brought some once. Nowhere, where, I don't know."

Astonished at the idea that the beautiful monster with eyes of winter-green enjoyed chocolate, Liliana rose to her feet, reaching back to twist her hair off her neck. "He must like it very much to have searched it out," she said, heading to the washing bowl in the corner.

"I made him some the first time he brought it, yes, I did. One sip he took and said it tasted not right. Not right." Jissa poured the liquid into two small cups. "Is right!"

Face washed and dried, Liliana came to take a sip of the rich, sweet liquid that made her toes curl. The only reason she knew and adored the taste was because the cook had had a weakness for it, and the kind man had shared his store of it with her on the days when her father had brutalized her to silence. Violence and chocolate were indelibly linked in her mind, but she refused to let that diminish her pleasure in the treat. "You're right. This is perfect." Licking a droplet off her lips, she remembered the cook reaching for something to sprinkle on top. "Unless…"

Jissa, having started to pull together the ingredients for a loaf of bread, wasn't paying attention. "Shall we make fruit porridge this morning, Liliana?"

"Perhaps we can put the fruit in the bread," Liliana muttered, putting down her chocolate to rummage through the cupboards. "It will taste lovely toasted."

"What do you search for?"

"Cinnamon."

A mournful shake of her head. "No, don't know. Don't know at all."

"I'm sure it must be here." If the youngest son of Elden had found chocolate and brought it home, then he may well have hunted out the spice that was so very common in his homeland that it was put in everything from casseroles to sweets…to a little boy's chocolate.

A squeak met her when she opened a lower cupboard.

"Mouse? A mouse!" Jissa turned with rolling pin held high, her face scrunched up into a scowl. "Nasty creatures! Show me, show Jissa."

Liliana closed the door. "It was only a squeaking hinge. Don't forget the sugar syrup or the bread won't taste as sweet."

"Oh, dear!" Distracted, Jissa dropped the rolling pin onto the table and ran to get the syrup.

Soon as she was far enough away, Liliana opened the door a crack, put her finger to her lips and whispered, "Have you seen the cinnamon?"

Small black eyes gleamed at her in the dark before her little friend darted out and along the edge of the cupboards to the very corner of the kitchen, where it slipped under a set of tall shelves just as Jissa returned. "Oh, you must help me, Liliana," the brownie wailed. "He won't, won't like what I make. I don't want you thrown back in the cold, so cold dungeon."

"I'll help, don't worry. Just give me a moment." Having reached the shelves under which the mouse had disappeared, she looked at the rows upon rows of identical dark brown jars, not a label in sight. "Well," she muttered, then glimpsed a flash of sleek gray run up along the side of the shelving. An instant later, one particular jar was nudged forward a bare millimeter.

Grabbing it, she twisted the lid open to find several long sticks of cinnamon. A bit old, but they had held their scent. "Thank you," she mouthed.

The mouse twitched its nose at her before disappearing behind the jars.

Turning, she walked over to put the jar next to the small tin of chocolate. Then she helped Jissa finish preparing the fruit bread, made a few crisp pastries covered with jam and churned some fresh butter.

"Oh, but there is no meat." Jissa twisted her hands. "He will growl and snarl and my bones will clatter, clatter against one another, they will."

Liliana had heard the Guardian of the Abyss growl, and while terrifying, it had also haunted her sleep in a startlingly different fashion—she'd dreamed of him making the same feral sound against a woman's…against *her* skin. And now that she'd allowed herself to recall it, she couldn't stop the sinful cascade of a lush fantasy that surely meant she was mad—for what kind of a woman would want the dark lord in her bed?

"Snarling and growling." Jissa continued to fuss. "Meat, he will demand. Meat!"

"We'll see," she said through a throat gone dry, and began to grind the cinnamon until it was a pile of dust that she scooped back into the jar. "Now, where's the milk?"

THE GUARDIAN OF THE ABYSS hadn't slept. He never slept. When the Black Castle went quiet for the night, he walked the halls in the company of ghosts. Sometimes, he went back out to hunt, for that was his reason for being, and sometimes, he went searching beyond the village and to the twilight lands, for those like Jissa and Bard.

He didn't know why he'd saved the brownie and the big lug. No one had ever asked him, but perhaps his strange storyteller would. If she did ask such an impertinent question, he'd tell her it was because he needed servants. A lie. He wondered if she would know, if she would challenge him. Hmm...

Striding into the great hall with that intriguing thought in mind, he halted.

The table was set with toast and pastry and fruit. But that wasn't what stopped him. It was the scent in the air, sweet and spicy at the same time. Aware of Liliana standing with suspicious meekness by the table, he crossed the black stone of the castle to take his seat, picking up the cup of steaming liquid at his elbow.

Rich and dark, he recognized it as chocolate. But that scent...

Drawing it in, he felt his mind spark, tumbling him headlong into memories that couldn't be his own, but that he found himself loath to repudiate.

A woman's laughter. Soft hands on his brow. Contentment.

"Drink." The whisper came from beside him. "Drink."

Looking up at his prisoner, who was most certainly a sorceress, someone he should not be listening to under any circumstances, he nonetheless lifted the cup to his lips. Sweet and wicked and wild, the taste seared his senses, took him to places he didn't know, showed him a kaleidoscope of faces he'd never seen in the Abyss.

The woman's face was the strongest. Eyes so bright and green, hair the color of sunlight, and a face of such beauty and grace it hurt him to look at her. But she was laughing, this being formed of purest magic, leaning forward to press her lips to his forehead.

Stubborn, so stubborn, my baby boy.

"What sorcery is this?" he asked, slamming down the empty cup and rising to glare at the woman who had likely poisoned him.

Liliana didn't flinch as she should. "No sorcery, my lord. It is merely a spice named cinnamon."

Cinnamon, he can't have enough.

Shaking his head to erase that haunting voice that made things in his chest tear and break, he stared at Liliana, spoke in the gentle tone that made the villagers tremble. "Where's my breakfast?" He ran the sharp tips of his gauntlet along her jaw. "I do not smell meat."

"Your breakfast is right here," she said, her face going white…but she didn't back down. "And it's quite delicious, as you'd know if you'd stop trying to terrify me." Reaching out, she touched him, her hand curving over the black armor of his upper arm. "Please sit."

He was so startled that anyone dared touch him, he obeyed without realizing what he was doing. When he would've snarled, she seduced him into silence by serving him bread studded with fruit and sprinkled with honey and sugar and…cinnamon.

This time, when the scent threatened to ensorcel him, he fought it.

Liliana laughed, the sound an invisible stroke that caressed him through the armor. "No one ever told me the Lord of the Black Castle was so stubborn." Her father, Liliana thought, hope a jagged pulse within her, had likely not realized the indomitable will within the child this dangerous man had once been. Far more of the prince might have survived his entrapment than anyone realized—though she'd have to be careful how far she pushed him. He might have allowed her instinctive touch, but he remained the Lord of the Black Castle, powerful and lethal.

"Speak to me with respect," he growled at her, but his lips were dusted with honey and sugar, his hair falling across his forehead. For an instant, he looked unbearably young, deliciously approachable, his mouth a treat for her to suck on.

Feeling her cheeks burn at the scandalous thought, her breasts taut points against the thin black material of the tunic, she went to pull away from the table.

A strong hand clamped down on her wrist, his palm hot and rough, the brush of the razored points extending from his gauntlet an unnamed threat. "Where is Bard?" It was a silken question.

"Outside the door," she said, realizing he was pulling her down.

She resisted.

He compelled.

Until her lips were on a level with his.

Her heart pounded hard enough to bruise against her ribs, but she couldn't take her eyes off those sugar-sweet lips. "My lord?" Her voice came out a croak.

His mouth curved, as if he could read her thoughts, and she held her breath, waiting to see what he would do. Right then, she had the sudden, shocking realization that she might permit him any liberty, no matter how darkly wicked, if he would only allow her to sup at those lips, to taste his mouth.

"You smell, Liliana." He released her wrist. "You must bathe."

Face so hot she knew she must be a dull, angry red beneath the brown of her skin, she stepped away from the table. "Bathing facilities are rather limited in the dungeon and the kitchen," she snapped, wanting to slam the candlestick in the center of the table on his beautiful head.

He glanced at her as he bit into a pastry, and she could've sworn there was laughter in his gaze, but of course, the Guardian of the Abyss didn't know how to laugh. "You remind me of a creature in the village," he told her as he gobbled up her pastries like some greedy, ill-mannered child. "The baker keeps it as a pet, though the kitten is forever spitting and clawing at everyone she meets."

Taunted, she was being taunted. "This spitting kitten is your cook," she said, unable to sit back and allow him to get away with it, though no sane woman would have argued with the Lord of the Black Castle. But then, as evidenced by her sinful fantasies, she was in no way sane. "I beg you don't forget that, or *I* might forget which is the salt and which the chili."

Ignoring her threat, he waved her forward. "Pour me more chocolate—" the order of an emperor to his concubine "—then you may go and bathe."

She *really* wanted to smash the teapot over his head, but she poured the luscious liquid into his cup, watched his eyes glaze over for an instant as his mind tried to drag him into the past. It was the truth she'd told. She hadn't ensorcelled either the cinnamon or the chocolate—but some sensual memories were strong enough to act as spells on their own. "Now, may I go?"

"My lord," he said, licking out his tongue to capture a drop of chocolate on his lip.

Her entire body hummed. "What?"

"You forgot to add 'my lord.'"

She grit her teeth and put down the teapot with extreme care. "May I go, *my lord?*"

He took a sip of his chocolate, paused for a second. "No."

"No?" Her vision was starting to blaze incandescent red.

"I haven't finished breakfasting yet."

Suddenly, she could see the spoiled princeling all too well—except that she was also certain there was a cackling imp riding on his shoulder at this moment. No, not a spoiled princeling at all. More akin to an adolescent boy pulling the pigtails of a girl to annoy her.

It should have been a ridiculous thought when faced with the black-armored Guardian, his hands tipped with bladed points, but this man had grown up in a cage of sorcery that had turned into a solid wall of armor. As she had never had a chance to be a child, he had never had a chance to be a boy, never had a chance to do mischief. The fact that he might be doing so now, with *her*—it created the beginnings of a terrible weakness inside of her, one she knew she should fight, but couldn't.

Several long minutes later, he finally finished his meal and stood. Picking up a piece of toasted fruit bread, he closed the small distance between them. "Try it. It's very good."

She took it with a bad-tempered scowl, attempting to hide the vulnerability within. "I know. I made it." Eating it though she wasn't that hungry, having snacked as she cooked, she narrowed her eyes when he continued to loom over her. "Now what?"

"My lord."

Oh, she just wanted to— "My lord."

"You don't mean it."

Smiling because it wasn't her imagination—he *was* teasing her—she finished off the bread, then dropped into a ludicrously ornate curtsy. "Oh, my lord," she simpered, fluttering her lashes. "What would you have of this poor wee maiden?"

A rusty sound, harsh and rough. Startled she looked up—and realized the Guardian of the Abyss was laughing. He was even more magnificent than she had believed.

"Why do you stare?" he asked suddenly, stopping midlaugh.

"I didn't know you could laugh."

A hush fell over the room, as if the ghosts themselves were holding their breaths.

Lines formed between his brows. "I don't remember laughing before."

"Did you like it?"

He considered the question. "It's a strange sensation." Not giving her any more of an answer, he said, "Come, I'll show you where you will bathe."

Will, not *may* or even *can.*

Gritting her teeth against the impulse to call down nasty curses on his golden head, she followed him as he walked to the back of the great hall. Once they were through the door and in a gloomy corridor that went on to a nothingness so deep it seemed impossible that light existed, he led her up a flight of stairs barely illuminated by a small window on the landing.

"Why must it be so dark in here?" she muttered. "A maid could fall and break her neck."

"This is the Black Castle."

"I realize this is the gateway to the Abyss, *my lord,* but surely you don't intend to harvest souls here on your staircase."

He turned and looked at her, then at the tiny window now at her back. "I can see in the dark."

She startled. "Can you truly?" But she knew it was no lie. How else would he hunt in the pitch-black of night?

He started up the stairs again without answering, his armor gleaming even in the muted light. Staring at it, she had another thought. "How do you bathe?"

"Mistress Liliana, you ask the most peculiar questions." Turning, he pinned her with a darkly intrigued look. "Do you wish to share a bath?"

"I meant the armor," she said, cheeks burning. "It doesn't come off—does it?" If it did, that meant her father had made a mistake. *Please.*

He paused, his hand on the railing. "It must, for I am clean." But he didn't sound too certain. "I don't remember bathing, but I know I do."

It was a puzzle, she thought, one she'd have to stick close to him to figure out. No hardship, that. And it wasn't because the Guardian of the Abyss was a monster most beautiful. She'd seen beauty in her father's castle— the Blood Sorcerer himself was an ugly man, but he surrounded himself with the most exquisite courtiers male and female. It had only taken a few overheard pieces of mockery, a sneer here and there, for her to learn that outward beauty was no measure of the person within.

But the Guardian—there was a strange charm to him, a wildness that was as innocent as she was not. He *truly* appeared to have no comprehension of the impact of his looks, trapped as he was in the Black Castle and regarded with fear by both his prey and the people of this realm, but he knew his own intelligence very well. And Liliana was discovering that a lethally fascinating mind was a temptation as sinful as those lips she wanted to lick.

"Surely you don't wish me to expire before we get to the bathing chamber," she said in an effort to derail the thoughts that had a sumptuous warmth uncurling low in her body. She couldn't afford to feel anything for him, for even though he would never look at her the same, that way lay distraction and failure. Her task was to awaken and return him to Elden so that his kingdom could breathe again, its people no longer crushed under the steel boot of the Blood Sorcerer's brutal reign.

"So weak, Mistress Liliana?" Stopping at the top of the staircase, he held out a hand, his green eyes intent. "Come."

CHAPTER SEVEN

HER HAND WAS HALFWAY TO his when she pulled it back, suddenly afraid that he'd sense her tainted blood. "I'm dirty, my lord. You said it yourself."

His hand curled into a fist even as his eyes darkened to black. Turning, he pushed open a door and she had the terrible feeling she'd wounded him. That could not be. For she was a hook-nosed, raw-boned, ungainly thing. What man would be offended that she didn't take his hand?

But he is ensorcelled, whispered another part of her mind. *He hasn't known friendship or love, or the touch of a woman's softness.*

Liliana was the last person to teach anyone those things, but even she'd had the friendship of the cook as a child. She was starting to fear that the Lord of the Black Castle had had no one. Biting her lip, she walked into the room to see him staring out the window, his back to her. "In there." He pointed to his right.

Peeking in, she saw a stone pool filled with cool, clear water, a bar of soap set on the edge beside a thick towel. When she sniffed the soap, she smelled the freshness of herbs, the scent sweet, the softness of the soap a luxury. Eager to begin, she dipped her finger into the water and winced…had an idea.

"The water is very cold," she said, stepping to the doorway. "I shall shrivel away to nothing."

He said nothing.

Taking a deep breath and hoping she wasn't about to humiliate herself, she crossed to him and very carefully placed her hand on his back, just below his shoulder blade, shocked at the warmth she sensed in the armor. It had been cold before, she was certain, but now it seemed to pulse with life, as if it was an extension of his skin. "Please, my lord. Will you not use your magic to heat it for me?"

She could've used her own, but that might give away her identity as a blood sorceress—and he was a Prince of Elden. He had incredible power within his own body, beyond anything that had been bequeathed him when he took on the mantle of the Guardian of the Abyss.

A slight shift of his head, as if he was considering her request, his hair shining golden in the light pouring in through the window. A sly look slid across his features. "You will tell me a tale while you are in your bath."

Her breath caught in her throat. "My lord, that is unacceptable."

Turning, he stared at her with eyes as curious as a cat's—and once more as green. "Why?"

"Well—" He confused her, this man with his intelligence and his darkness and his wild innocence. "I can't tell a tale naked!" she said at last.

He shrugged those shoulders covered by armor that had become living skin. "The water will protect you." With that, he walked into the bathing chamber.

By the time she managed to break out of her stunned shock and follow, steam was rising from the surface of the huge bath, the Lord of the Black Castle standing there with a small, pleased smile on his face.

She found her own lips curving. "I can't wait to bathe properly." Her entire body tingled in anticipation.

When the big, deadly man beside her didn't move, she folded her arms. "I will tell you a tale, but I won't disrobe in front of you."

A short, taut silence before his expression changed, the smile whispering away to be replaced by something hotter, not the least bit innocent. All of a sudden, he was no longer the dread lord, but simply a *man,* one who was looking at her in a way no man had ever before done.

It closed up her throat, caused butterflies to awaken in her stomach, made her blood run hot, then cold…but though her father often called her such, Liliana wasn't stupid. She knew she wasn't a woman men desired. However, the sorcerers who coveted her father's patronage had tried to make her believe they saw her that way, though they were revolted by her all the while.

She'd seen the shivers of disgust they couldn't hide, the smirks when they thought her back was turned. But those men hadn't hurt her. Her heart had already been so bruised by then that it felt little of their insults. Nothing they could do would ever compare to her father's cruelty.

"Perhaps you are my curse." Laughing as he made her stand in front of him, a young, fragile-hearted girl of twelve. "I lay with the most beautiful woman in the kingdoms and sired the ugliest creature ever born. Yes, perhaps you are the punishment for my sins."

Another day, another year.

"Come, daughter, you're not afraid to help your father?"

"Father, no, I—"

"Are you scared the magic will damage your face?"

"The acid—" Screaming, because he'd reached out and broken her nose with a single twist.

"There," he said with a nasty smile while she tried to staunch the blood using her apron. "It will heal back as

ugly as always, but now you don't have to worry about the threat of pain."

"Liliana."

A deep male voice, not her father's, not hurting and vicious and—

"Liliana." Impatience colored her name this time, breaking through the haze of memory.

Snapping up her head, she looked into winter-green eyes that said they'd very much like to see her naked. Heat seared her veins, but she dampened the simmering burn with cold practicality. This man wasn't like the others, didn't intend to humiliate her—but, given his life in the Black Castle, he was unlikely to have come into contact with many women. It was unsurprising that even the ugliest girl in all the kingdoms had managed to capture his attention.

"I said I won't disrobe in front of you." She kept her arms crossed, hiding the tight points of her nipples, mortified by her reaction.

His scowl covered his face as he mirrored her action. "I am the Lord of the Black Castle. You are my servant." A raised eyebrow. "Though you are also my prisoner."

"Does Bard bathe naked in front of you?"

"I don't wish Bard to bathe naked in front of me."

She glared, knowing if she gave in now, it was all over. To return him to Elden, she had to challenge him, awaken him. "No tale."

"You'll tell me a tale or you'll starve in the dungeons."

"Fine."

A growl. An actual *growl,* one that scraped over every inch of her skin. Then he turned on his heel and gave her his back. "Two minutes."

"You don't think I'll actually start disrob—"

"A quarter less than two minutes."

"It has been but a second!" Realizing he was going to cheat, she ripped off her clothing—including the underwear she'd laundered yesterday—with such furious speed that she heard something tear, and scrambled into the bath. Water sloshed over the side just as he turned.

His disappointment was open. "The steam hides you very well."

"Yes," she said, chest heaving as she tried to catch her breath. "It does."

"Next time, I won't make the water as hot." Walking over, he picked up her clothes. Then he proceeded to stare at them, paying particular attention to her underthings.

"What," she managed to get out through her mortification, "are you *doing?*"

"Looking." A scowl. "I don't like these." To her shock, he proceeded to tear the tunic and tights, her underthings, into small strips. "You may keep the boots."

"Stop!" She reached out over the edge of the bath, but he continued on in his methodical destruction even when her fingers brushed the black stone of his armor. All too soon, her clothes were reduced to a pile of rags that he pushed into a corner with his own boot.

Wanting to cry, she glared at him instead. "What am I supposed to wear?" She'd soaked her dress in an effort to remove the bloodstains, and it was still wet.

"Tell me a tale and I'll steal you a dress."

She didn't know whether he was serious—about either part of his statement—but she knew he had her exactly where he wanted her. That would teach her to fence with the Guardian of the Abyss. Blowing out a breath, she drew deeper into the bath and ducked her head under the water to clear her mind, wet her hair. When she rose back out, she made a startled, undignified sound.

He was crouching with his arms on the edge of the bath, so close that she could've leaned over and caressed his face with her lips— *Oh, dear.* Swallowing the insane urges that told her to react to him as a woman reacted to a man who looked at her as if she were some particularly delicious treat, she pushed herself through the water until her back hit the wall.

It still left them far too close, no matter that the bath was huge. "Where's the soap?"

He held up a hand, brought the square bar to his nose. "Smells pretty."

She was being taunted again. "Give it to me."

"No."

Frustrated beyond bearing, she splashed water at him, remembering too late that he was a man of power, of strength that could hurt. He drew back in startlement, but when the water hit him, there was no anger. Instead, he wiped the droplets off his face and…smiled.

Her mind simply stopped.

He was beyond anything she had ever imagined as a child when she'd dreamed of being saved by the lost heirs of Elden.

And he was inhaling her soap again, as if it was the best thing he had ever smelled. Would he do the same with her if she bathed with that soap? Biting her lower lip, she pressed them together in an effort to find control. Liquid with shocking desire or not, she didn't want the Guardian of the Abyss sniffing at her. He would only hate her all the more when he discovered whose blood ran in her veins.

That thought should've chilled her, but then he held out the soap…only to snatch it back when she went to reach for it. She froze. He held it out again…a little farther away. Though she knew his game, she kept playing—until she was back where she'd started, face-to-face with him at the very edge. "Give me my soap," she whispered, "and I'll tell you a tale of three princes and a princess." She deliberately left out the name of the kingdom of Elden. That struck too deep, and might make him refuse to hear what she had to say.

He hesitated. "Come closer."

"This is close enough." So close that she could see each separate golden lash that shaded eyes of such vibrant green she could lose herself in the clarity of them.

No.

The word was snapped out by the blood sorcery inside of her, a whiplash reminder that she didn't have the luxury of losing herself in his eyes, of forgetting that she was here to break him out of his prison of ensorcellment, take him home to Elden.

Afterward…

Her heart gave a bittersweet pulse, because she was unlikely to survive her father. Even if she did, she was the daughter of the Blood Sorcerer. If the kingdom of Elden didn't execute her, and perhaps they wouldn't, for she would've returned their lost prince to them, she would be exiled beyond the borderlands of the realm, to the dark empty places where only the stone eaters roamed.

"Liliana."

Blinking at the masculine demand, she reached out to grab the soap. He moved it out of reach so fast that she almost rose up after it, forgetting that she was very, very naked. "Do you want me to be clean or not?" she asked, dropping back down.

His expression turned thoughtful.

The skin on her shoulders tingling from the intensity

of his gaze, she folded her arms under the water. "Fine. No tale, then."

He leaned on the rim, satisfaction in the curve of those lips she wanted to taste so badly her toes curled. "You have no clothes." A silken reminder.

Her mouth fell open at the way he was telling her she was effectively trapped until he decided to let her go. "You— I—" Snapping her mouth shut, she turned her back on him, and began to rub at her skin with the water alone.

"Liliana."

Trying not to think about the fact that she'd just given her back to the man who scared even shadows, she made a face at a speck of dirt that seemed imprinted in her skin. It made her feel sick to think how filthy she was— *Oh.* That wasn't dirt. It was a burn scar, an old one, so old she forgot about it most of the time.

Come here, Liliana. The salamander only wants to say hello.

She'd screamed herself hoarse that day, and it had made him laugh so hard tears had rolled down his face.

"Liliana."

The way the Lord of the Black Castle said her name was as much an order as her father had made it—except that instead of causing her blood to freeze, the quiet demand of it made the most intimate parts of her flush with sinful heat.

"Liliana."

There was a dangerous impatience to him now. Part of her, the part that had grown up fearing a man's anger, said she should turn around right that second and give him what he wanted. But the other part—the annoyed, frustrated female part—made her keep her head turned to the wall in stubborn refusal. Perhaps it was that simple…and perhaps she did this so he would hurt her, destroying the seed of vulnerability growing within her, a softness that had her panicked.

"Here, you can have your soap."

Wary, she looked over her shoulder to see the soap on the rim and him in the doorway. She went to grab the bar, certain he'd use his magic to push it away before she reached it. However, he did nothing but stand motionless as she picked up the bar and brought it to her nose.

"Glorious." So rich and exquisite that she almost didn't notice he was leaving. "Where are you going?" There had been no hurt, no pain from him in spite of actions her father might have termed "insolent," and that deepened the softness, made her weaker when she couldn't afford to be if she was to kill her father.

"Leaving you to your bath." The words were stiff, the disappointment in his expression cut with anger.

It startled her, the wild clarity of his emotions. This man, she saw with dawning hope, didn't know how to hide his true face from the world, had never had cause to learn…and so she would never, ever have to wonder if he was about to strike out at her even when he looked at her with a smile. "I haven't told you the tale yet."

He hesitated. "You will tell it?"

"Of course. I always keep up my end of a bargain." Then, going with a feminine instinct that was rusty and unused—and though her stomach was clenched tight beneath the water in an attempt to quiet the butterflies—she began to rub the soap down the bare skin of her arm, unable to see a washcloth. "Of course, since you took such pleasure in tormenting me, I shall torment you, too."

There was a luminous spark in his eyes and then he was beside the bath again, his arms—solid, muscled, strong beneath the liquid caress of the armor—on the rim. "You were fighting with me, Liliana."

An odd thing to say, but not so odd when you considered that no one dared argue with him, this dark lord. "A little," she said. "But not seriously. It was almost a game."

He considered that, his expression thoughtful once more. "The children in the village play games."

Placing the soap on the rim beside his arm, she raised her hands to her hair. "What did you do when you were a child?"

"I don't remember being a child."

Fingers caught in the rat's nest on top of her head, she tugged and pulled as she tried to work out what the confluence of his mother's and her father's spells must have done to him for him to have forgotten his childhood so completely. Either the impact had wiped his memories—or perhaps he hadn't *had* a childhood. It was possible that he'd been held in a kind of limbo until he was old enough to care for himself.

"You'll pull it all out."

"What?"

"Your hair."

"Oh." She dropped her tired arms. "I'll cut it off after I get out of the bath. That's the only way to untangle it."

He made a low sound deep in his throat that had her thighs clenching. "I'll untangle it for you."

CHAPTER EIGHT

HIS STORYTELLER LAUGHED.

The Guardian of the Abyss had heard feminine laughter before. Sometimes, Jissa laughed. And he'd heard the women in the village laugh, too, when they didn't know he was near. But Liliana's laugh was different, full of something that made his own mouth want to curve, his chest muscles expand. He didn't give in. But he wanted to.

"Very well," the sorceress said to him, for he knew she was a sorceress. "But how will you work this magic?"

He ran his eyes over the slopes of her shoulders, so silky with water. "Turn your back and wait for me," he ordered, wondering what the water would taste like licked from her skin.

When she raised an eyebrow, then obeyed, he got to his feet. "Start thinking of your tale." Leaving her, he went quickly down to the kitchen using the secret passageways of the Black Castle that opened only for its lord, and found the cupboard where Jissa kept her "pretty-making things" as Bard called them when Bard could be brought upon to speak.

The Guardian wasn't interested in pretty-making, but he'd been curious about the light in Bard's eyes when he'd spoken of such things, so he'd explored. Everything in the cupboard had smelled very nice, and later, he'd caught one of the scents in Jissa's hair. *There.* Closing his hand around the bottle, he promised himself he would bring Jissa a bar of the special soap she liked when he next went flying over the village.

All the shopkeepers knew to leave a black box with some of their wares out for him in the night. No one dared steal from that which was the lord's, and the shopkeepers made sure of it—for he paid them very well. He wondered if Liliana would like to see his room of jewels and treasures as he retraced his steps to the bathroom. Part of him had expected her to be gone, but she was waiting patiently, her back against the rim.

"Liliana," he said from the doorway.

A soft smile over her shoulder that made his body tighten in painful ways, and yet it was a pain he craved. "I heard your footsteps," she said. "What have you got?"

"Nothing for you to see." If she knew of it, she might decide to do the task herself. "Turn your head to the wall."

Only the slightest of hesitations before she did as he commanded.

He knelt behind her, anticipation humming in his belly at the chance to touch this woman who spoke to him in ways no one else ever had, and who seemed to see something in him even he couldn't see.

"Once upon a time," she began as he poured Jissa's pretty-making lotion onto his palm, "there were three princelings and one princess. They were named Nicolai—"

A kick of his heart, his mind burning as his hands worked the lotion into Liliana's tangled locks, the sharp points of his armor having retracted themselves.

"—Dayn, Breena and—"

"—Micah," he found himself saying, his hands fisting in her hair. "The third prince must be called Micah. You will do this."

Liliana went motionless. "Yes." A whisper. "His name was Micah and he was the youngest prince of them all."

One of his hands brushed Liliana's nape as he un-clenched them, and she shivered. He didn't jerk back his hand, though it was obviously too cold for her. He liked the feel of her skin. It was different from his own, more delicate and smooth. "Where did they live?" he asked to distract her so he could continue to explore.

"In a kingdom," she said, her voice husky. "With their father and mother, the land's beloved king and queen. But this is not their tale. This is the tale of how the four sib-lings once summoned a unicorn prince, proud and dig-nified."

Wonder blazed through him, along with a tugging sense of knowledge. "There is a watch in the room where I would sleep," he said, sharing a secret with her because she was his prisoner and would tell no one, "if I needed sleep."

"A watch?"

Made of opals, emeralds and precious metals, it was his oldest treasure. "It has a unicorn on the face." A noble creature, as regal as any ruler.

Liliana sucked in a breath. "May I see it?"

"If I'm pleased with you," he said, because she was even softer now, her muscles no longer stiff. It made him wonder if he could coax her into lying naked for him as he stroked his hands along her skin, if she would go loose and limber all over, her thighs falling open to the caress of his fingers. His body grew hard, engorged.

"The watch is beautiful but broken," he said, schem-ing how he would make her naked even as he lulled her into softening even further. "The hands move so slow, I can never catch the motion, and they have ever tried to reach midnight." An extraordinary watch, that showed dawn, noon, evening and midnight, each quarter marked by a green gemstone.

"There aren't many minutes left, are there?" Liliana asked, turning to look at him over her shoulder, those eyes of no particular color suddenly piercing. "Before midnight?"

"No." With his finger, he traced a pattern on the skin of her nape, massaging his other hand through her hair as he did so. "Tell me this tale."

She shivered again. "My lord—"

"There is soap there," he murmured. "I'm just clearing it away." Not a lie. Of course, he'd put the soap there.

"One day," she began, and he was certain she arched a fraction into his touch, "when Micah was very young and his siblings full-grown, his brothers were teasing him as older brothers do, by saying that they could summon a unicorn and it was a pity he was so small and likely to be scared of such a magnificent being, or they'd show him.

"His sister, who was his champion, said for him to ignore his brothers, but Micah demanded they prove their boast, and so the four of them set off for the Stone Circle, a point of great power within the land."

"I bet they didn't expect Micah to hold them to their stories." The name flowed off his tongue so smooth and easy that he wanted to claim it.

"No." Liliana sighed. "Shall I duck my head under the water?"

He looked at the bubbles in her hair. "Yes, then I will untangle your hair further."

When she ducked under and rose back up, all slick and sweet smelling, he knew her hair was untangled, but he poured more lotion into his hands, stroked it through the rough, thick strands while imagining doing the same to the body hidden beneath the steamy water. Next time, he *would* make the water colder so he could see everything. "Tell me the rest."

"It was a long way to the Stone Circle, and Micah was but a babe—"

He scowled. "Micah wasn't a babe simply because he was the youngest."

"That's what Micah is said to have said," Liliana told him, "but finally Nicolai—who was rumored to be a sinful man in many ways, but who loved his siblings with the fierceness of the hunting lions that roam the plains—convinced Micah things would go faster if Nicolai carried him on his back, and so that is how they went."

A stirring in his mind, an image of a warrior with bronzed skin and silver-colored eyes streaked with gold. "Where did you hear this tale?"

"The cook told me," she answered, rubbing the soap over her arms. "He once worked for the king and queen."

He watched the soap slide over her skin, felt a dark stirring within him that tasted not of evil, but of a far hotter temptation. "Tell me more about Micah."

"Well, it's said that Micah might have been the smallest, but he had the biggest heart."

He wasn't sure he liked that. "Tales about boys do not involve hearts."

"Oh?" She made a startled sound. "I suppose not. But you see, Micah was loved. He was the youngest prince, and terribly spoiled."

"He couldn't have been so spoiled." It was an instinctive response. "He was a prince, after all. He had duties."

"Ah, but he was a babe then," she murmured. "He had two older brothers and a doting sister. So he was spoiled."

He tugged on her hair.

"Stop that," she said, slapping at his hand. "You must listen to the tale as I tell it."

Allowing her to catch him, he made a rumbling sound at the feel of her skin against his. "Turn around, Liliana." The mounds of her breasts were slight, but they would make the perfect mouthfuls.

Her hand dropped away and her voice, when it came, was a whisper. "No. It's not safe. You're not safe."

Since he wanted to bite the gentle curve of her neck, stroke his hands below the water to fondle and squeeze, he couldn't argue. "Continue." It was a growl.

"Micah," she said, a tremor racing over her skin, "he was spoiled and petted, but he wasn't cruel or mean like other boys might've been. He rescued so many injured animals that the queen gave him his own little block of land where they could roam."

Something in his chest grew tight and he found himself curving his hands over her shoulders, rubbing his thumbs along the skin of her back. "His mother was kind."

He felt a ridge under his thumbs but Liliana pulled away before he could explore it. "I think my hair is done."

He coaxed her back by promising to wash off the soap. "The queen?"

"The king called her his other half," she said after a taut pause. "Is that not strange?"

He considered it. He had always been alone, encased in stone. No one could join with him. Even were Liliana spread naked beneath him, her body flushed and damp, her thighs spread, his armor would lie between them. "Yes." He scooped up some water, watched it smooth over her skin.

"So," she continued, "the four heirs went to the Stone Circle, and they got their heads together and conferred about the best spell to use for the summoning. During the trek, it had become a shared challenge."

He massaged more lotion into her scalp, saw the goose bumps that rose up over her flesh. "You're cold. We will finish the bath."

"Yes," Liliana murmured. "I think that's a good idea." Dunking her head again, she squeezed the water out of her hair. "You must go."

He was the Lord of the Black Castle, could order her to stand wet and nude before him, but that would make her stiffen, and he wanted Liliana luscious and soft when he explored her. "I," he said, brushing her earlobe with his lips as he spoke, "enjoyed your bath, Liliana."

LILIANA LET THE SHIVER ROLL over her as the Guardian of the Abyss exited the room. Her reaction had nothing to do with the cold, and everything to do with the man who'd had his hands on her. Looking down to see her nipples beaded to shameless points, her meager breasts plump with heat, she bit back a moan.

A few more minutes and she might just have leaned back and allowed him to slide his hands down her front to explore her breasts the same way he'd been exploring her nape, her scalp, her shoulders. For the first time, she wanted rough male hands on her flesh, squeezing and petting and caressing. His fingers had been so strong, so assured. But not hurtful. In fact, she hadn't felt the spray of razors or the sharp black tips of his gauntlets at all. Pleasure, that was all she'd felt.

Forbidden pleasure.

He wasn't for her, might well slay her on the spot once he realized the truth of her lineage. Trying not to allow that to matter, to be the stoic Liliana she'd been since the day her father burned the final drop of childish innocence out of her, she stepped out of the bath and used the towel to dry her hair, wipe her body. Then she looked around.

To realize she had no clothes.

"I can't believe it," she muttered, wrapping the towel around herself and tucking it in tight before wrenching open the door. "If you think—"

The room was empty.

But that wasn't what had her tongue-tied.

It was the dress on the bed. The red, *red* dress.

Walking forward with disbelieving steps, she touched her fingers to the delicate, silky material, curling those fingers into her hands as sheer *want* washed over her. She'd never had a dress so saturated with color, so very pretty. Dull browns and grays, those were what suited her "nightmare of a face." Her father's words, but in this he was right.

"I'll give you three more minutes." The ultimatum came from the other side of the door.

Biting back a startled cry, she stared at the wooden surface. "I'm not the kind of woman who wears a red dress." Oh, but she wanted to.

"Do you not like it?"

"It's the most beautiful dress I've ever seen," she said, because to lie would be a desecration of his gift.

"Then you'll wear it. Or you will be naked." A pause. "Hmm…"

Every inch of her skin skittering with sensation at that considering murmur, she dropped the towel and pulled on one of the two identical pieces of flimsy underwear laid out beside the dress—there was no slip, nothing for her breasts, but then she didn't need it. Such luxury, she thought as the cloth whispered over her thighs to cup her behind.

"Oh." It was a shivering whisper as she realized the undergarment, cut high on her thighs and of a near-transparent material, exposed more than it covered.

"I'm coming in very soon."

"Wait!" Grabbing the dress after stuffing the extra pair of underwear in a drawer, she pulled it on over her head. Only to find that it laced up the back. Twisting to clench the sides closed, she stared at herself in the mirror. Her hair hung damp and sleek around her face, but it was still a shapeless mat, and her face hadn't changed. It remained that of a wicked witch right out of a nightmarish tale.

But the dress...oh, *the dress*.

It cupped her breasts, nipped in at the waist and flared out at the hips to give her a form that made her, for a bare moment, feel almost, if not pretty, then not ugly, either. Her lower lip quivered and she might have given in to tears had the door not pushed open behind her.

She swiveled to face him. "I need Jissa."

He stared at her, those green, green eyes lingering on her breasts. "Why?"

It suddenly felt as if her modest attributes were twice as large. "The back needs lacing."

"I will do it." Closing the door, he dared her to contradict him.

She couldn't think when he had his hands on her, her body reacting in ways that were simply not acceptable if she was to complete her mission and take him home. "It would be unseemly."

"We are in the Black Castle. The only rules that exist here are the ones I make."

"Just because you enjoy being a bully," she said, pointing at him with her free hand, "doesn't mean I intend to take it."

His eyes dipped to her chest, his expression intrigued, and she realized that by moving her arm to gesticulate at him, she'd caused the bodice of her dress—her gorgeous, precious *red* dress—to slip, revealing the upper curve of one breast. Face flaming, she pulled it back up and glared. "It's rude to stare."

He raised his eyes to her with such slowness that the heat in her cheeks spread throughout her body, a heavy, languorous warmth that was as terrifying as it was unfamiliar. When he began to stalk toward her, those winter-green eyes filled with dark, unknowable things, she backed up. He kept coming. She kept stumbling back.

Until the backs of her thighs hit the vanity.

He stopped so close she was scared to breathe for fear her breasts would press against the black armor that no longer seemed so very thick. "Turn around." A quiet order, his hands braced palms down on the vanity on either side of her hips.

CHAPTER NINE

REALIZING SHE'D WELL AND truly lost this battle, she turned. Tall as he was, she could glimpse his face above hers in the mirror, saw his gaze dip to her back. Her stomach clenched. Shutting her eyes in an effort to lessen the impact of his nearness, she continued to hold the back closed, and waited for the ties to pull tight.

Nothing happened.

Chest painful, she exhaled, sucked in another jerky breath. "My lord?"

"I've never before done this," he murmured, and she was almost certain he was talking about something other than lacing a dress even when he pulled at the strings. "Hmm."

She dared open her eyes at the change in his tone. When she looked into the mirror again, it was to see his face set in lines of concentration as he laced her up inch by slow inch.

"I can't breathe," she said when he pulled too tight.

Loosening the strings, he said, "What other colors do you not wear?"

She narrowed her eyes. "Brown, gray and black."

He laughed, and she was so seduced by the sound that she made no protest when he finished lacing her up and spun her around with his hands on her hips. Leaning close, his cheeks creased with pure masculine amusement, he said, "Liar."

Jumping at the whisper of his breath across her cheek-bone, she turned her head. "I must…" She didn't know what she had to do, was starting to panic at the closeness of him when her eye fell on the comb on the very end of the vanity. "I have to brush my hair or it'll become a rat's nest once more."

Reaching out, he picked up the comb before she could get to it. She thought she knew what was coming, but instead of ordering her to turn around again, he backed off, staring mock-thoughtfully at the comb. "What will you do for this?"

"What?" He was *blackmailing* her. "I'll tell you the rest of the tale."

He waved a hand. "You'll tell me the rest, anyway, the next time you want a bath."

Putting her hands on her hips, she fought the driving urge to pull him down, bite down on that taunting mouth. "What do you want?"

"Lushberry pie with real cream."

"Lushberry pie?" It was a well-known dessert in Elden.

"Yes." He folded his arms, comb still held hostage.

She knew without asking that he hadn't eaten lush-berry pie since the childhood he didn't remember—but he'd remembered the pie. Hope unfurled in her heart. However, she didn't give in at once to his demand. He'd get suspicious of that. "Where am I supposed to get lush-berries?" Even in Elden, the trees were dying like so much else.

"I'll get them." A grim look. "You'll make the pie."

"Give me the comb first."

"After the pie."

"It'll be no use to me when my hair's already dry and ratty."

A dark scowl. "Don't think to cheat me, Liliana."

Her abdomen grew tight at the sound of her name on his lips. "I'm not the one who refuses to follow the rules of civilized behavior." She held out her hand. "The comb."

Walking over until he was far too close again, he leaned in, sniffed the curve of her neck. "Pretty." Then he gave her the comb and walked out.

Knees crumpling, she stumbled to sit on the bed. *Oh, dear. Oh, dear.* The Guardian of the Abyss was not meant to be so very… "Yes. Just *very.*" Realizing she was babbling, she lifted her hand and began to run the comb through her hair. When she was done, it settled in sleek lines over her shoulders, and she knew it would be soft even when dry.

The feminine heart of her sighed in pleasure. Her hair had never been soft or silky like those of other women— her mother, the courtiers, the mistresses her father kept. Until she'd turned seven and learned to use her own sorcery to heat the water, her father had made her wash in an ice-cold bath, use the roughest soap.

Weak, so weak. It might give you a little more spirit.

What it had done was turn her blue and almost give up bathing. The only thing that had kept her going back was the knowledge that the punishment for defying the Blood Sorcerer would be worse than the chill that infiltrated her bones after every wash.

Putting the comb back on the vanity as the memories threatened to steal the warmth from her bones, she got up and brushed down the front of her lovely red dress. Then, checking to make sure no one was at the open door, she twirled in front of the mirror, the skirts flying out around her. "Thank you," she whispered to the dread Lord of the Black Castle.

LUSHBERRIES WERE SO CALLED because, when ripe, the fist-size dark purple berries were so lush with juice they all but burst open. It was a favorite trick of travelers to place them in a stream until they were chilled, and then to crush the berries into pulp, creating a thick, thirst-quenching drink.

"Sometimes on the farms," Liliana told Jissa as she created the pulp for use in the pie only twelve hours after the man who'd given her a red dress had told her he'd find the berries, "the cook said they add milk and sugar to it."

Jissa's eyes widened. "Delicious, sounds delicious."

That was when Liliana remembered that brownies were rumored to love sweets of every kind. "Shall we try?" she asked, mischief in her veins. "His Lordship will never miss it, he brought back so many berries." He'd likely denuded an entire tree, the greedy creature.

"Liliana," Jissa said in a censuring tone. "You must not say 'His Lordship' in that tone. If he hears, oh, no, oh, no."

"Don't worry, Jissa. He'll threaten to throw me in the dungeon and I'll bribe him with food." Laughing at the look on the brownie's face, she put aside some pulp in a jug. "Why don't you add the milk and sugar to your taste?"

Jissa bit her lip. "We shouldn't."

Liliana lowered her voice. "I won't tell."

Temptation won over Jissa's timid nature and soon the woman was standing beside Liliana stirring the mixture into a rich purple concoction while Liliana put aside the rest of the pulp and pulled across the thick pastry crust she'd already baked. It was her special recipe, so buttery and rich it melted in the mouth. Even the cook had praised her for her pie crust—especially because she only ever made it for him, not for her father. Never for her father. But she would make it for the Lord of the Black Castle.

"There!" Jissa's voice rose in excitement. "Try, try!"

Feeling like a child, Liliana brought a small glass to her lips, took a sip. Her eyes widened, met Jissa's across the top. Both of them tilted back their heads and gulped. They'd drunk half the jug when Jissa wiped off her milk moustache and said, "Bard would like this, I think. Yes, I think."

"So would His Lordship."

"Liliana."

Laughing, Liliana poured two more glasses. "Here, you go take it to them. If *he* asks where I am, tell him I'm slaving over his damn lushberry pie." It was dark outside, time for sleep, but he wanted his pie.

"So impertinent. Trouble, you are, trouble." Shaking her head, Jissa pushed through the door with the glasses.

A tiny chittering sound came right on cue. Liliana turned, put her finger to her lips. "Shh. You're not supposed to be in the kitchen."

Her little friend sat up on his hind legs and made the most arresting face—as if saying that he was a very clean creature, thank you very much. "Well, of course you are," she said in apology. "I've seen your fastidious ways." Liliana didn't find that as strange as she should have—the mouse had magic of its own. A tiny magic, but magic all the same.

"Lushberries are not something you'd like," she said, and, when his face fell, picked up the tiny but perfect pastry crust she'd baked the same time she'd done the large one. "Here, my friend. Now shoo before Jissa catches you."

Nose twitching with excitement, the mouse—its bones

no longer so sharp against its skin—dragged away its spoils as she washed her hands and returned to mix a rich sweet cheese with the pulp before pouring it into the pastry. That done, all she had to do was put it into the oven for but a quarter hour. She took the time to whip up the cream, since His Lordship had decreed he'd eat the pie the instant it left the oven.

When the door opened, the caress of lushberries lay heavy and mouth-watering in the air. "Jissa, I think the pie will be—" It registered then, the scent that had come in with the opening of the door.

Darkness and heat and something quintessentially *male*.

Keeping her eyes resolutely on the cream, she said, "You're in my domain now."

Instead of arguing as she'd expected, he walked to the oven, made as if to open it. "Stop!" she ordered. "If you open it now, you'll let out all the heat."

Growling low in his throat, he came over to stand beside her at the counter, staring at the cream. She knew what he wanted even before he tried to dip a finger into it. Scooting away the dish, she shot him a scowl. "If you don't behave, I'll put salt in your pie."

He shifted closer, went for the cream again.

Glaring, she jerked it away once more.

He stepped over.

She looked up, intending to tell him to stop it when she was caught by the laughter in his eyes. He was teasing her again. That knowledge turned her a little mad, mad enough to lift the whisk and touch it to the tip of his nose. "There."

He blinked, raised his finger to his nose and wiped off the cream. No jagged black tips, she thought in shock—his hands were bare of any trace of armor below the wrists. Then he licked the cream off his finger, and suddenly, the game wasn't a game anymore, her thoughts scattering like so many marbles across a floor.

Forcing her head back to the bowl, she began to whisk with all her strength. Maybe that was why she didn't notice him move, why she didn't realize he'd trapped her with his gauntleted arms on either side of hers until his hands came over hers, one on the edge of the bowl to hold it in place, the other closing around the hand that held the whisk.

She should've protested, should've pushed back, but she continued to whisk even as his body imprinted itself on her own. The sensation was indescribable. No man had ever touched her thus, had ever wanted to touch her thus.

Her heart grew heavy at the reminder that the Lord of the Black Castle had been trapped here his entire life. He didn't understand that there were women of stunning elegance and grace who would beg to come to his bed once he reclaimed his place as a prince of Elden. Beside them, she'd look the mountain troll her father had called her. Her pride shook under the blow, but she didn't pull away.

Because this man, with his way of looking at her as if she mattered, his way of touching her as if he'd like to do a whole lot more, captivated her. And she wasn't too proud to take the crumbs of his affection. Shame would strike later, she knew. But this moment when he was so hot and hard and strong around her, this moment was hers. To be kept like a jewel inside her heart, a treasure no one could steal from the ugly girl with the face of a wicked witch.

"You're very soft down here."

Jumping at the deep voice so close to her ear, it took

her a second to process the meaning of his words. Her hand squeezed the metal of the whisk. "You think me fat?"

"I didn't say that." He pressed a little deeper into her, his own body created of harsh edges and taut muscle. "You're all bony angles—except here."

Her skin blazed. No matter how much flesh other parts of her body might need, one part was quite happy to remain round and plump. "That's not something it's polite to mention."

"Isn't it?" Tantalizingly close to her ear again, his breath hot and wicked. "I order you to eat more. I like the softness." Lips brushing her earlobe.

She might just end up naked on the bench if he continued on in this fashion. "The pie!" she said, grabbing for the lifeline. "I must take it out of the oven or it'll burn."

He pulled back at once—but she was almost certain she felt the brush of his mouth against her neck before he released her. Already regretting the loss of his touch, she picked up a thick cloth, opened the oven and removed the pie. Taking it to the counter, she put it carefully on top of a flat stone she'd placed there for that purpose.

The Lord of the Black Castle was beside her an instant later. "Give it to me."

She wanted to turn, breathe in the scent at the curve of his neck. "It'll taste much better after it has cooled a fraction," she managed to say.

"You are not lying to me, Liliana?" That gentle, dangerous tone he used very much on purpose to get what he wanted; his hand—hot, rough—coming to curve around her nape.

Before she could respond, his head jerked up. "I must

go. The residents of the Abyss need a reminder of who rules them."

Liliana all but collapsed into a quivering puddle after he left. The man was potent. And she was playing a very dangerous game in allowing him to go as far as he'd done. If they went further, and then he discovered her identity...

"He won't hate me any less." It was a painful realization, but it freed her. "There is no happy outcome here for you, Liliana." So what did it matter if she stole a few moments of happiness on the road to Elden? If she allowed him to treat her as a desirable woman, though she knew she was no such thing? It made her a thief and a liar, but perhaps once she was dead or exiled, her father defeated, the Guardian of the Abyss would forgive her the deception.

Tears burned at the backs of her eyes and she might have given in to them had she not felt an ugly chill along her spine. The kind of chill that augured the proximity of dark blood sorcery. Stomach curdling with horror and rage, she pushed out of the kitchen and ran to the massive doorway of the Black Castle.

Bard appeared out of nowhere to stand in her way.

"Blood sorcery," she said, begging him to understand. "There is blood sorcery beyond." Terrible and vicious and fetid with evil.

The man blinked once. "You stay."

"No! You don't understand! This kind of blood sorcery—" tainted, putrid "—means someone is being sacrificed!"

A stolid expression. "You stay."

Liliana bit down on her tongue. Hard enough to spill blood. And then she whispered an incantation that had the giant slumping to the floor in a heap. "I'm sorry," she said as she bent to take a wicked curved knife from his belt. "You'll be awake again in no time." Pulling open one heavy door, she raced out into the black-as-black embrace of the night.

CHAPTER TEN

HER FEET, CLAD IN THIN embroidered slippers that had appeared in the kitchen a few hours ago, slammed down on sharp edges, rocks and branches as she ran through the agitated rustling of the Whispering Forest, almost slipped on the moss that covered the bridge that spanned the restless river, but she kept running, holding her skirt high above her ankles.

The lights of the village came into view. Twinkling and warm but for the haze of sulfurous magic. Fighting the urge to throw up, she ran pell-mell toward it, taking only enough care to ensure she didn't break her neck. For if she did, an innocent would die. Always, her father and his apprentices used innocents. Their blood was more vital, they said. Richer. Purer. But not tonight, she vowed, *not tonight!*

Stumbling into the periphery of the village, she had to halt so she could pinpoint the location of the evil. Slicing a small line on her palm, but not allowing the blood to touch the earth lest it give her away, she whispered for the magic to rise, to seek out its dark kin. Her power hesitated in distaste. *Innocents,* she urged, *innocent blood. Seek innocent blood.*

No hesitation now. Her power winding through the village in a crackle of deepest red, with her running in its wake. Around houses shuttered up for the night and courtyards abandoned, through the deserted main street and onto the clear surrounds of the village green.

Her power hissed at the filth it saw, went to wrap itself around the man's neck in a choking hold, but Liliana drew it back. *Wait. Wait. We'll have only once chance.* Dark blood sorcerers, distended with power stolen from those who couldn't defend themselves, were stronger than those like Liliana, who used only their personal reserves.

This one was a thin, handsome man, his face likely the reason he'd been able to persuade the young village maid at his feet to meet him in the thick black of night. She lay unconscious on the grass now, the sorcerer chanting incantations above her, a serrated blade in hand. That blade, Liliana knew, would go into the girl's abdomen. A slow, torturous death, her blood seeping out drop by drop while her murderer kept her silent even in her agony and grew drunk on the force of her life, her death.

Power blazed in the air as the sorcerer made a sigil above the girl and Liliana realized he was one of the old ones for all that his face appeared young. Old and powerful. It was foolish, part of her said, to give up her life for this one girl when she had come to save a kingdom. If Liliana died, the Lord of the Black Castle would not remember, would not return.

And Elden would fall into her father's clutches forever.

"No," she whispered, fighting that voice, that part of her the Blood Sorcerer had attempted to turn rancid with his own evil.

One life was worth everything. For how could Liliana hope to save a kingdom if she was willing to bow down to evil when it stood in front of her?

Stepping out of the shadows, she stalked toward the sorcerer on silent feet. But he sensed her, turned. "Liliana!" Shock. "Your father seeks you." Avarice glittered in his eyes. "Now I will be the one to take you home."

"What reward has he offered?"

"Lands, riches, power." He shuddered, in an ugly parody of pleasure. "The understanding with Ives is ended," he said, referring to the man her father had intended Liliana marry—with or without her consent. "The one who finds you takes you to wife and to his bed." Distaste he made no attempt to hide. "You are his daughter."

That link to power, she thought, would make it worth his while to wed such a hideous creature. Bard's knife hidden in the folds of her apron, she stepped closer. "Is that why you're here, in this village?"

"The others, they scattered to the edges of the kingdoms, but I knew you would do the unexpected. I've been keeping an eye on you—you're smarter than everyone believes."

It made her skin creep to think he'd been watching her. "You know what they say happens to those like you who trespass in the Abyss." Even her father feared it, wouldn't dare step foot in this realm.

A skittering behind his eyes. "We'll leave this place as soon as I replenish my power."

"Yes." With that, she struck out, going for his neck. She failed.

The tip of her knife skated off his cheekbone as she was thrown backward with brutal force. Retaliating with her own magic, she managed to make him stagger on his feet, but he didn't go down. Then, the skin of his cheek flapping grotesque and raw, he turned to the girl behind him. "First I will taste her. Then I will take care of you." He kissed the girl, digging his nails viciously into her breast. "Pity I won't have time to savor her."

Unable to breathe around the pain in her ribs, Liliana

nonetheless began to try to crawl toward him. The bastard thought her down, but she wasn't. Except it was too late. The sorcerer's incantations complete, he went to his knees, laid the edge of the blade on the girl's neck.

"No!"

He began to laugh…and then his head was turned in her direction, his eyes bulging as his neck was broken in a single hard snap by powerful hands made of midnight shadows.

HEAT ON HER FACE, A WARM damp cloth. Hurt around her rib cage, the comforting smell of spiced tea. Raising heavy lids, she looked into the face of the brownie who was becoming her closest friend. "Jissa." Her voice was hoarse, her throat dry.

"Oh, you're awake, awake at last." Tears, large and a haunting translucent blue, rolled slowly down Jissa's face even as she helped Liliana into a sitting position and held a glass to her lips. "I thought you were dead. All dead."

Pushing away the water after a few sips, Liliana touched her distressed friend's hand. "The girl?"

"Safe, safe." Jissa wiped away her tears, but they kept falling big and slow. "No memory, none at all."

"Good." Guilt heavy in her veins, she asked, "Bard?"

Jissa patted her hand. "He worries for you, hasn't left the door all this time. So much worry."

Liliana was quite sure that wasn't why Bard stood guard, but she didn't break Jissa's heart by saying so. "How long have I been asleep?" she asked, realizing she wore her rough brown dress again.

"Since the lord carried you home last night. Now it's morning, sun shining." Jissa's voice dropped. "Was angry, he was. So angry."

"I'm sorry."

Jissa shook her head, wiped away more beautiful tears. "Only quiet words to Jissa he said. But you—growls, there will be growls and snarls." The last was a whisper just before the door slammed open.

Giving a startled squeak, Jissa glanced from Liliana to the green-eyed male standing in the doorway. Liliana saw her friend hesitate, knew the brownie was fighting to stay and confront the Guardian of the Abyss with her, but she shook her head. "Go, Jissa."

Wide, wet eyes met her own. "Liliana…"

"Shh. I would love some lushberry juice later."

"Yes, yes. I'll make it for you. Sweet and rich and good."

The Lord of the Black Castle closed the door very carefully behind Jissa's form before coming to loom over the bed, gauntleted arms crossed over his chest. "You ran away."

That wasn't what she'd expected him to say. "Only to save the girl's life."

"You were not to leave the Black Castle."

She couldn't keep staring up at him, her neck tired. Looking down, she spread her hands on the sheet gathered at her waist. "You'll have to put me in the dungeon."

"You tore your dress."

"No!" Her beautiful red dress, the most beautiful dress she had ever owned. A fat droplet crashed on the back of her hand.

"Don't cry." A snapped order.

She sniffed, fought to hold back the tears. It had never been difficult before. She'd learned early on that her father fed on her fear, and so she'd given him nothing. But today, the tears kept falling.

"I'll get you another red dress."

She wiped the backs of her hands over her cheeks at the snarl. "You will?"

He glared down at her. "Yes. But you must not cry. I won't get you any dresses if you cry."

"I don't normally cry."

"You will never do it."

"Well, I'm afraid I may sometimes," she said apologetically. "Women need to cry."

Lines formed between his brows. "How many times in a year?"

"Maybe five or six," she said, thinking about it. "But really, it's usually a very small cry and not in front of anyone." Always she'd hidden her tears, curled up in some dark corner of the castle.

At that, his scowl grew even darker. "I will permit you to cry four times a year. And you will do it when I am here."

"Why?"

He didn't answer her whispered question. Instead, sitting down on the bed, he lifted his fingers to her jaw, a delicate touch that froze her in place. "You taste of blood sorcery." Something very shrewd in his eyes, a dark knowing.

Rocks in her throat, in her stomach. "Yes."

"You are a blood mage."

The panic that beat in her chest was a tight, fluttering thing. "I don't kill," she said, pleading with him to believe her. "I spill my own blood, as is my right." There was nothing inherently wrong with blood sorcery, only how it was practiced.

Thrusting out her hand, she showed him the cut on her palm. Then, when he remained silent, she held out her arms. "See." The thin scars bisected the brown of her skin—small, horizontal slices. "My blood. No one else's."

Dropping the hand on her jaw to her arm, he curved his fingers around it, rubbing his thumb over a scar. "Does it hurt?"

"Yes, but only a small hurt."

"My magic doesn't hurt."

Her breath stuck in her throat. This was the first time he'd referenced any personal magic, beyond that which came from his position as the Guardian. "That's because your power springs from a different place." It was the magic of the royal line of Elden, powerful and pure and infused in every cell of his body.

However, if her research, done in the Royal Archives, was correct, then the youngest Elden heir was also an earth mage. The instant his feet touched Elden, he'd be able to access the power of the land itself…if anything was left of it after her father's defilement.

"This place is on the edges of the realms," he said, instead of continuing with the topic that came so close to acknowledging his true heritage. "Not only do the evil ones fear it, there is little life here for blood sorcery— why did the sorcerer come here?"

Liliana had to swallow twice to speak past the knot choking her. "My father," she said, taking a precarious step along the tightrope of truth, "is a powerful man, and he wishes me to return home."

His expression turned black as night. "You don't wish to go?"

She shook her head and hoped with all her might that he wouldn't ask the next question. But of course he did. "Why?"

Because he is the Blood Sorcerer. Because he stole your kingdom, murdered your parents, forced your

*mother to scatter your brothers and sister through time
and space. Because he is evil.*

She could say none of that, but she could tell him another truth. "He wishes me to marry one of his men."
Ives's blood was as rancid as her father's. He watched her
with the eyes of a lizard, licked his lips when her father
whipped her raw and whispered the most obscene promises in her ear when he managed to corner her.

Though if the sorcerer she'd met the previous night
had been telling the truth, she was now a prize to be won
by any of her father's men. It mattered little. "He is not a
good man." None of them were.

"You will not marry." It was an order, cold and hard.
"You belong to the Lord of the Black Castle."

She blinked, stared. "You can't own people," she said,
her fear waning in the face of his arrogant pronounce-
ment.

A shrug, his hand tightening on her wrist. "Who will
naysay me?"

LILIANA WAS STILL FURIOUS as she walked to the village
two days later, dressed in a chocolate-brown dress she
was sure the lord had given her as punishment for "running away." Except this brown was lush, exquisite, quite
gorgeous—even if the man who'd given it to her was a
maddening beast.

The only good thing that had resulted from the attack,
and her subsequent confession, was that *His Lordship* no
longer considered it a threat that she'd try to escape, so
she'd been allowed to come with Jissa to do the shopping.
"Who does he think he is? Just ordering me about that
way. As if I didn't have a single thought of my own!"

Jissa, who'd been looking over her shoulder ever since
Liliana started ranting, shifted her empty basket to her

other arm and used her free hand to squeeze Liliana's hand. "You know who he is, Lilia—"

"He knows who we are, too!" Turning, she glared at the looming hulk of the castle before returning her gaze to the path that led into the Whispering Forest. "And we aren't his slaves!"

Jissa didn't say anything.

Liliana slowed her stride, anger transforming into a sickening lurch in her stomach. "Are we?" Had the youngest Elden royal been tainted by the evil that lived within the Abyss in the most subtle of ways?

Jissa shook her head. "Oh, no. Oh, no." Her distress was apparent on her fine features. "He was very, very sad when he brought me back to the castle after…after."

After you died again, Liliana thought, trembling as the lurching settled. "Will you be safe in the village?"

"Oh, yes. Just can't stay all day and night." Taking a deep breath, she began walking at a brisk pace through the Whispering Forest, touching her hand to the trees as if in greeting.

The tree branches shook, the leaves murmuring, *Jissa. Jissa. Friend. Jissa.*

"The lord," Jissa said, patting the trunk of a sapling, "told me he wished he could send me back to my people, but that my people were gone. All gone."

Liliana felt her heart twist. Her father had decimated the brownies, stolen their power too fast for those small, sturdy bodies to recover. "Do you believe him?"

"I do." A sad, sad sound. "He doesn't lie. Never, ever."

"No, he doesn't." Yet he was not naive. He was simply without corruption—arrogant and spoiled, but without corruption. "Why did you go quiet at my mention of slaves?"

"The lord said he didn't wish to make me a slave. I

could just stay, he said, do nothing." Jissa made a scowling face. "I told him, I will cook. That is fair."

"I can't imagine why you bothered," she muttered, trying to work up her old ill humor. "Bad-tempered creature that he is."

"Hush, Liliana." A chiding look. "He is alone, so alone."

Yes, but he was also a possessive beast. "Is the lord very rich?" she asked, to take Jissa's mind off her sorrow. "Will we be able to buy any ingredients we need?"

Jissa nodded. "He has treasures. I saw once, after I woke. Sparkly jewels. He gave me." Her eyes lit. "For me to keep, Liliana!"

Liliana's throat thickened. The Guardian of the Abyss had been trying, in his own way, to return Jissa's happiness, make her forget that she'd die after she left the protective magic of the Black Castle. "Will you show me your jewels?"

"Oh, yes, so pretty, pretty." Jissa chattered about her treasures until they hit the village. "We are about to turn into the market square, busy, busy." Even as the last word left the brownie's lips, they found themselves in a bustling marketplace filled with stalls holding green beans, carrots, pumpkins orange with health and so much more.

CHAPTER ELEVEN

"YE BE FROM THE BLACK CASTLE, then," said a red-cheeked man wearing a crisp blue apron over his clothing.

Liliana looked at Jissa to answer but the brownie had ducked her head. "Yes," she said to the man. "I'm Liliana and this is Jissa."

"I knows Jissa." He patted his large belly. "Wee thing doesn't say much, then, does she?"

Liliana touched a protective hand to her friend's shoulder. "She speaks when there's something to say."

A booming laugh. "Wish my missus would do the same." Picking up a small, ripe peach, he put it in Jissa's basket with a wink. "Enjoy now."

The friendly comments continued as they shopped.

"Are they not afraid of the Black Castle?" Liliana asked Jissa when they stopped to examine some hard green fruit that Jissa said made a good jelly. "After all, it is the gateway to the Abyss."

"At night, yes, oh, yes," Jissa confirmed. "Doors shut. Windows locked. But the lord protects the village, too. Very well, he protects."

"And he's not like them others," the stall owner said, having obviously overheard.

Liliana looked up at the raw-boned woman with the mass of twisting black curls and skin of ebony silk. "The others?"

"Heard stories, we have," the woman said, "of the

far-off realms. Past the plains and the bubbling lakes, beyond the mountains of ice, on the other side of the Great Divide."

"What do these stories say?"

The woman folded her arms, lowered her voice. "That there's them lords that come into a man's house and steal his daughters away. And if she be comely, his wife, too."

Liliana gave a small, quiet nod. Murdering, forcing carnal acts on those who could not defend themselves, abusing old and young with impunity, her father's men were monsters clothed in flesh. "Yes, I've heard the same."

"Well, then," the stall owner said, "the Guardian is plenty better than that even if we don't like as to be in the castle too much. Ghosts there, you know."

As Liliana followed Jissa to a stall filled with exotic spices, she couldn't help but wonder how the man who was the Guardian had managed to retain his honor, though he lived in the Black Castle, handled evil night after night.

A memory of ghosts, watching, listening...perhaps guiding?

"—big nose."

"Told you she isn't his mistress."

Jerked back to the present by the hissed comments of two passing women, Liliana felt her face begin to color. Though she wanted to run, she pretended she hadn't heard, and waited until the women were otherwise engaged before looking at them.

Tiny and dainty and doll-like, the golden-haired one was a princess dressed in the clothes of a prosperous shopkeeper's daughter. Her friend was taller, slender, more elegant. Lush black curls swept back from her face with shell combs, her eyes sparkled with the confidence of a woman who knew she was not only stunning, but sensually so.

"Liliana."

She turned to Jissa. "Are there many beautiful women in the village?"

Her friend's eyes filled with an unexpected fierceness, the rhythm of her singsong voice wiped away. "Don't listen to those spiteful wenches. You're the one he speaks to, not them."

Only because, Liliana thought, her heart heavy, their parents likely didn't allow them to consort with the Lord of the Black Castle. No, they'd only allow that when he was ready to make an offer. So she was his only choice, a big-nosed, ugly thing with a limp and no grace.

She'd always known that, been willing to swallow her pride to steal a few moments of happiness, but faced with the village women, women of beauty and sensual sophistication, women who had to have crossed his path, she realized he must know it, too.

Her heart broke with an audible crack.

Standing on top of the highest parapet of the Black Castle, its lord watched Liliana walking up from the village, laughing at something Jissa had said. He scowled. "Why does she laugh?"

Bard lumbered to his side, opened his mouth, sighed. It was as close as he ever came to a diatribe. The Guardian of the Abyss waited, knowing the other male had something to say, but Bard took his time; Bard always took his time, until most of the village thought him a big, dumb mute. It was to both their advantage to let that misapprehension continue.

"Women," he said, his voice a deep rumbling thing akin to the heart of a mountain, "laugh. Jissa laughs."

He'd never thought of Jissa as a woman. She was simply sweet Jissa, who jumped if he talked too loudly and smiled when Bard's back was turned. He tried not to scare Jissa, but she was so timid that, sometimes, it happened by accident. Bard always looked at him with accusation in those deep, dark eyes when it did.

But Liliana... Yes, she was a woman. His body heated within the black armor as he thought of how she'd felt against him in the kitchen, all soft curves and warmth. Exploring the luscious shape of her while she was naked had become not only an erotic desire but a raking hunger. Glancing down, he flexed his fingers and watched as the armor retreated from the backs of his knuckles, coming to a stop at his wrists.

"Armor." Bard's bass voice. "Moved."

"Yes." He couldn't touch Liliana with the armor on his hands—it might scratch her. And so it had retreated. "They've reached the castle gates."

Liliana stopped and looked up right then. He was too far way to read the expression in her eyes, but there was an odd stiltedness to her walk when she began to move again, her shoulders hunched in.

There was no more laughter.

He hadn't spoken to many women. The village ones squealed and giggled when he came near. It irritated him. When he got irritated, he scowled and scared them. He liked that—it made them keep their distance. And if they huddled as they walked, that was fine with him. But those women weren't Liliana. "Do you see?"

Bard said nothing, his eyes on Jissa.

LILIANA MANAGED TO AVOID the Lord of the Black Castle that night only because there were too many shadows in the dungeons and he had to open the gateway to the

Abyss. Ordered to lock herself in the upstairs room that had become her own, while Jissa and Bard did the same in another wing, Liliana didn't argue. Magical energy could be highly volatile. And when it came to the energy of the Abyss, its lord was the only person who could control it.

"Where did the old lord go?" she muttered, the house shuddering with waves of magic unlike any she'd ever before felt—heavy and brutal and cold—as the gateway was opened.

When the old lord is ready to retire, a new lord is chosen.

"Oh," she said, heart thundering where she sat on the bed. "Thank you."

The boy was strong, already sleeping below the Black Castle.

A ripple in the air on the right-hand side of the bed, a formless face that came and went. *You carry blood sorcery in your veins.*

All at once she knew this ghost understood exactly what—*who*—she was. "I mean him no harm," she said. "Please, you mustn't tell him. He's not ready."

Silence.

Ghostly fingers across her face, cold and skeletal. She sat still, let the spirit read her. And breathed a sigh of relief when the shimmer beside the bed began to fade.

He is ours. We will protect him.

A violent pulse of magic, one that made every hair on her body stand up in alarm…and then, silence. Peace. The gateway to the Abyss was closed once again. Letting out a sigh of relief, she got off the bed and unlocked the door. But when she looked out into the corridor, she saw only absolute darkness, all the lamps having been extinguished by the waves of battering power.

She could have easily relit them, but suddenly she was tired. Tired of being her father's daughter, tired of being ugly, tired of finding herself aching for a wonderful, powerful man who would never, could never, be hers. Turning from the door, she crawled into bed.

EVIL FOUND HER IN HER DREAMS, the Blood Sorcerer's spidery fingers clawing at her until she bled. "You think to escape me? You are my daughter, my possession!"

Shaking, she held up her hands, backed away. "No. You have no claim on me!"

His laugh made her bones tremble, her throat lock. "I *own* every part of you."

Her back hit a wall, and she looked around in panic, searching for a way out. There was nothing. She was trapped within a gleaming black box, her father's form a cadaverous shadow that melded with the darkness.

"Now you will tell me where you are." It was a sinister command, his nails knives that dug into her throat. "You'll tell me or you'll die."

That was when she realized this was no dream. It was a spell for which her father had spilled not only innocent blood, but his own. For blood would call to blood, and his ran in her veins. If she died in this nightmare prison, she wouldn't wake in the real world.

Calling her own magic, she tried to shove him away. But he was protected, had spilled enough blood to armor himself in it. Her power skated off the malice of him with a shrill shriek that sounded like a woman's scream. Choking as he tightened his hold, she clawed at his wrist. Her hands came away bloody, her nails snapped off.

Darkness began to squeeze the edges of her vision, his breath noxious on her face. "Where are you, dearest daughter?" Lips almost against her own, a terrible kiss. "Where do you hide?"

No. She couldn't die. She hadn't brought Micah home.

But her father was squeezing the life out of her, her heart a scrabbling rabbit in her chest. Lifting hands weak and trembling, she tried to pull him off once more, but her fingers slipped, slick with her own blood. *No!* She refused to give up, refused to surrender. Not to him, never to him. Even if—

A massive surge of power—clean, pure, *potent*—slammed through her veins.

Drawing it to the surface as her lungs released a final breath, she threw it at her father in a hail of razor-sharp daggers. His scream shattered the black box, sent her tumbling into the dreamscape, shards of obsidian falling around her, cutting and stabbing. Gasping, choking, she used the intoxicating power in her veins to break the final threads of his spell, falling back into reality with a jerk that had her bolting into a sitting position.

To look into the face of the Lord of the Black Castle.

His eyes burned with black, and when he shoved back her hair to bare her face to the lamp that flickered on the nightstand, she didn't resist. "You bleed." It was a harsh statement.

Leaving her to stride into the bathing chamber, he returned with a soft towel in hand. She raised her fingers to her throat, felt the welts, the stickiness of blood. Shocked and shaky, she didn't protest when he put the towel to her throat with his right hand, his left tightly fisted.

Her eyes locked on that fist.

Tugging at his fingers, she felt a dark wetness. "What did you do?" She stared at the massive gash across his palm. "What did you *do?*"

The hand holding the towel to her neck flexed, pressed again. "You do blood sorcery."

Shuddering, she understood. He'd seen her trapped in the nightmare, given her the surge of magic she'd needed to get herself out, his blood heady. Her own was paltry in comparison. Elden itself ran in his veins. "Thank you," she murmured, even as she took a second towel he'd dropped on the nightstand and pressed it to his cut. "You shouldn't waste your blood. It holds incredible power."

The Guardian of the Abyss gave her a look filled with such fury that she froze. "So I should've let you die, Liliana? Is that what you would will of me?"

She'd insulted him. "No," she said at once. "But you're far more important than me." *Far more.* "If you die, what will become of the Abyss?"

"There will be a new lord." Anger continued to glitter in the eyes become winter-green once more. "There will never be another Liliana."

Her heart kicked, stopped, and when it started again, it belonged to him, this Prince of Elden become Lord of the Black Castle. She couldn't stop the trembling of her lower lip, couldn't stop the tear that rolled down her cheek. For the second time, she was crying in front of him when she tried never, ever to betray such vulnerability.

The Guardian of the Abyss made a rough sound in the back of his throat, and then she was being scooped up and settled on his lap, against the cool chill of his armor. When he ordered her to continue keeping pressure on her wounds, she obeyed, even as she refused to let go of the hold she had around his palm.

"You're still bleeding," she managed to say through the tears. "I can taste the power." It was rich and dark and tempting. So tempting. The sorcery she could do with his blood… *No.* She threw aside his hand and the towel at her throat to huddle into herself, horrified. "Let me go. I'm evil." The Blood Sorcerer's daughter, after all.

Strong fingers against her face, his arm holding her tightly in place. "The blood you taste is freely given," he murmured in her ear. "It intoxicates."

She shuddered, because he was right. The exquisite beauty of it ran through her veins, curled around her senses, threatening to make her a slave. "Please."

"Have you smelled blood that is not freely given?"

She thought of her father's tower room, of her horror as she sat bound, unable to help his victims…and then later, when he'd stolen her will, forced her to assist. "Yes." A low, quiet word. "I was a child," she whispered, wondering if he would believe her. "I've never spilled innocent blood of my own free will."

"I know." Fingers in her hair, massaging her skull. "What did it taste like?"

"Putrid, vile, spoiled." She'd thrown up the first time, had had her face pushed into her own vomit as punishment. "Nothing like your blood."

"That was because it was stolen. Do you see, Liliana?"

Oh. "Then you must not give your blood to me freely," she admonished. "I'm apt to become drunk on it and murder you in your bed."

A rumble against her cheek, vibrations that… He was laughing. The Lord of the Black Castle was laughing, as if she'd said the most absurd thing. So when he lowered his head and kissed her, she was too startled to do anything but part her lips under the bold thrust of his tongue.

CHAPTER TWELVE

THE SHOCK OF SENSATION MADE her whimper.

He raised his head. "Do you not like that?"

It took time to find the wit to speak. "I've never tried it before." Ives had attempted to kiss her, his breath foul. She'd managed to avoid that indignity, though it had cost her a broken cheekbone.

"Neither have I," came the startling answer.

"There are women in the village who are not maidens." And who would surely have attempted to seduce him, this sensual, dangerous creature who held her in his lap.

"They stink of fear," was the unforgiving answer before he clamped strong fingers on her jaw. "Let's try it again."

The second time was just as big a shock, but she didn't want him to stop. So she dared touch her tongue to his. He groaned, his fingers tightening on her jaw. "Again." Licks against the roof of her mouth, his tongue stroking against hers with a sexual intensity that was utterly without restraint.

She was drowning in him, in the storm of erotic rain after a lifetime of drought. "Stop."

"Are you sure?" That hand on her jaw turning her toward his mouth.

"No." It felt good, his kiss, so good.

When he claimed her mouth again with that same

raw energy, she shuddered, bracing her hand against the black armor that kept them from being skin to skin. It was warm now, almost like skin—and it was one sensation too many.

Breaking the intimate contact, she buried her face against his neck. Even that threatened to overwhelm her, his skin hot, his scent different. *Male.* Pushing against the solid wall of his chest, she scrambled out of his lap, landing in an ungainly heap on the bed, her skirts rucked up over her knees.

His eyes lingered on the exposed length of her legs.

Face filling with heat, she struggled into a sitting position to push down the fabric. "You mustn't."

"Why not?" A big hand closing around her ankle, tugging her forward.

She tried to pull it back. He held on. "Micah, stop."

Time froze.

No, no, no, she thought. She couldn't have made such an elemental error after all her hard work. "I—"

"Micah," he murmured as if he was tasting the name. "Yes, you may call me that."

She let out a sigh of relief. It wasn't quite an acceptance of the identity he'd once had, but at least he hadn't rejected it out of hand. "Will you let go of my ankle?"

He moved his fingers on her skin, just enough to send a shiver up her body. "I want another kiss."

"You can't simply ask for a kiss."

"Why not?"

That stopped her. She had no answer to his question. All she knew of courtship—from what she'd seen of it among the courtiers—was that it was an intricate dance. Nobody ever said what they meant, everything being communicated through coy glances and delicate touches.

It had always seemed a horribly painful thing to her,

she who had none of the feminine graces and couldn't effect a coy smile on her best day. "I suppose," she said, "it's better to be direct."

"Good." The hand on her ankle tugged again.

She fisted her hands in the sheets to stop herself from crawling all over him. "Just because you ask doesn't mean I agree to it!"

Tendrils of black speared out from his eyes, beautiful and lethal. "If you didn't like it, tell me. I'll kiss you another way."

Heat uncurled low in her body, so sinful and wild that she had trouble stringing together her words. "I don't know if I want to be kissed!"

Scowling, he tightened his hold. "Why are you lying, Liliana?"

Oh, mercy. "Because you confuse me," she blurted out. "Kissing is… I need time to get used to the idea." *That you want me even though you know about beauty, even though there are other women out there you could take to your bed.*

He tugged at her ankle and, unbalanced, she fell onto her back. Gasping as he came over her, bracing his palms on either side of her head, she fought the urge to spread her thighs, cradle him with sumptuous intimacy. "I will," he said in that gentle voice that was so effective at chilling people's blood, "give you until tomorrow morn to get used to the idea."

It made her shiver, but not because her blood ran cold. "I want till the morn after." Before, she might have argued with him about the order, but now she'd learned that that wasn't the way to get what she wanted with Micah.

"No."

She made a mutinous face.

"Tomorrow eve." His tone said that was his final offer.

"If I decide I don't like kissing?" she asked, because he was big and overwhelming and made her lose all sense of self-preservation.

A slow, slow curve of his lips had her toes curling into the sheets. "Oh, you like my kiss, Liliana. I felt your tongue stroke against mine."

"Micah!"

He tilted his head to the side, the black retreating to reveal winter-green luminous in the dark. "Am I not supposed to say that, either?"

"Yes."

"I'm the Lord of the Black Castle. I can say whatever I want."

She didn't know whether to scream or laugh. "You're not the least bit civilized, are you?"

He gave her the strangest look, as if she'd asked a silly question. But to her surprise, he answered it. "I live at the gateway to the Abyss."

"Yes, I suppose the civilized graces aren't exactly useful here." If she wasn't careful, he'd turn her as wild. To be quite honest, she wasn't sure she minded.

THE GUARDIAN OF THE ABYSS slept that night. Dreamed. Of the firedancers and the castle with the pennants flying in the wind. A castle with windows full of golden light and sparkling music that floated across the night-dark lake to tickle his ears where he lay on his back in a small rowboat.

"Is it time, Nicki?" he asked the man with silver eyes streaked with gold who sat beside him.

Carefully stowing the paddle so they wouldn't be stranded in the middle of the lake, his brother shook his head and came down on his back beside Micah, stretching out his big, muscled body on the blanket they'd borrowed from the stables. It was kind of scratchy, but at least Mama wouldn't yell at Micah for spoiling her soft fleecy blanket like she had the last time.

"Is it time now?" He wiggled in excitement.

Nicolai said, "Not yet."

Micah liked lying there with Nicolai by his side. Nicolai was the strongest, with the most powerful magic. Breena was the nicest, and Dayn brought the best, most interesting things to show him. Micah, though he was the smallest of them all, was the "stubbornest," everyone said so. He liked being the stubbornest. Especially when it made Mama blow out her breath and then laugh. And laugh.

"Is it time *now?*"

Finally Nicolai said, "Yes. Look."

Micah sucked in a breath as the first star streaked across the sky. He didn't talk for the whole time the stars fell to earth, so entranced that he forgot to wish until Nicolai whispered for him to, "Hurry, or it'll be over."

Micah didn't want to miss even a minute of the sky magic, but he squeezed his eyes shut and made his wish. It was a strange wish had he thought about it, but he made it as the stars streaked across the sky, and forgot it by the time he scrambled out of the rowboat onto the rocks that led up to the castle.

But when the Guardian of the Abyss opened his eyes, he remembered.

"I wished that we'd all come home," he told Liliana the next day, while she tried to make something in the kitchen. "An odd wish, don't you think?"

Liliana gave him a startled look, her lips parting as if to say something, but then she pressed those lips back together. Lips he wanted to nibble at again. Prowling around the bench where she was rolling out the dough, he put his hands on her hips from behind. "Did you make up your mind about kissing yet?"

"Micah."

Pushing aside a tendril of her hair, he buried his nose in the curve of her neck. She smelled of the soap he'd given her, flour and something sweet. He decided he wanted to eat her up, so he took a bite.

She jumped. "Micah, did you just bite me?"

He thought about whether to answer her or not. She'd tasted good. He might want to take another bite later. Better if she didn't have warning. "You didn't tell me what you're making."

"Biscuits," she said, shooting him a suspicious look before returning her attention to the dough. "Normally I'd do it with dried lushberries, but since we haven't had a chance to dry them, Jissa found me a box of raisins."

REGARDLESS OF HER OUTWARD calm, Liliana wasn't sure she drew a single breath until Micah moved around the bench to pick up a small green fruit. That was when she noticed something incredible. "Your armor." It had vanished from his arms, all the way to his shoulders.

"Hmm."

His response startled her less than the fact that his skin was tanned, his muscles defined against skin stroked with warmest gold. "You don't always have the armor on." She'd assumed it was part of her father's twisted spell, but what if the armor had been created by the powerful magic of a small scared boy thrown into the void without anyone to catch him as he fell?

"When are the biscuits going to be ready?"

Looking down, she saw that she'd finished with the preparation. "Not long."

Micah walked over to pull open the oven door, the muscles in his arms gleaming in the heat. She felt her abdomen go tight, her mouth suddenly bone-dry.

"Liliana." A deep, coaxing voice. "It's not night yet, so I can't kiss you. But you can kiss me."

Blushing, she put the biscuits in the oven, watched him close it, wanting to lick and kiss her way down those arms. "Where are Jissa and Bard?" she asked, waving a hand to cool her face.

"Playing chess."

"Oh." She went to pour a cup of tea, but her hand was trembling so hard she sloshed it. Putting down the pot, she said, "Go away. I can't think with you here." And she needed to think. He was too deep in her heart now. She didn't want to take him back to Elden, to the evil that awaited there.

But she must.

If she didn't, Elden would fall forever.

And Micah would never forgive her.

She choked back a harsh laugh. He was never going to forgive her, no matter what. The touches, the kisses... they were stolen. Even knowing that, she couldn't stop herself. She would continue to be a thief for the fragment of time that remained.

It wasn't all selfish, she tried to convince herself when guilt reared its ugly head—he'd begun to shed his armor. Every instinct she had told her that that armor needed to be completely gone before he'd remember Elden. And once he remembered, he'd have to rebuild the armor for the biggest fight of his life. But time...time was trickling by so fast. She had only until the moon rose full again, the final midnight too close.

"Liliana."

Clenching her hands on the edge of the bench, she said, "The biscuits smell good."

"So do you."

She folded her arms, stalked across to look him in the face. "I'm not beautiful, Micah." It had to be said, because such sweet lies hurt. "You don't have to say things like that."

His lashes, thick and silky and long, swept down over those amazing eyes, lifted again. "Yes, you are."

That tone of his voice was already intimately familiar. "Just because you say so doesn't make it true!" She felt like stamping her foot like some bad-tempered child.

"I'm the Lord of the Black Castle," he reminded her once again with dark arrogance. "My word is law. Don't forget to think about our kisses. I'll lick up your taste again come sunset."

Liliana was still staring at the closed door minutes later when her smallest friend in this castle full of old magic and whispering ghosts skittered over her foot in sharp reminder. "The biscuits!" Grabbing a cloth, she opened the oven and pulled them out in the nick of time. "Well," she murmured, looking down at the twitching nose of the inquisitive creature who had come to look quite healthy, "I think, for that, you get a whole biscuit to yourself."

She swore he chortled in glee.

MICAH LEFT LILIANA A VIVID silver dress this time, the threads so fine they picked up every shimmer of light and multiplied it a hundred times over. She would look like a falling star, he thought, and he would kiss her.

His body heated within the confines of the black armor, and for the first time, the weight of it irritated him. Still, he couldn't take it off, not tonight. The air had grown heavy with a shadowy energy that told him the condemned roamed the badlands—they had to be collected before they did harm.

"I'll return two hours after moonrise," he told Bard as he left. "Tell Liliana to wait for me." As he stepped out into the velvet dark of the night, his wings unfurling to take him into the air, he thought of her kiss. The village women had attempted to lure him many a time, but underneath all their seductive looks lay a tremor of fear, a quivering hunger to dance with danger.

He had no desire to kiss a woman who would shiver because she was afraid. Liliana shivered, too, but not because she was afraid. His lips curved. It didn't matter that he hadn't kissed other women—he knew she shivered because she liked it. Especially when he licked his tongue against hers. He wanted to lick her in—

A rush of oily energy. The stench of putrefaction.

Fully armored once again, though he didn't recall a conscious thought making it so, he went after the soul. From the smell, it was a blood sorcerer. Not like Liliana. This one had spilled innocent blood and the taint clung to him.

The sorcerer, his body shrunken in death, his eyes endless pools of red, tried to drown him in a barrage of razor-sharp power. He ignored it. It was an old trick. The shards attempted to sink through the armor, and held such evil that one succeeded in causing a small burn in the black.

Using the cold power of the depths of the Abyss, he turned the shards back on their maker. The sorcerer screamed, high and shrill. Micah reached him to find a whimpering ball, shredded as if he'd been run through a great razored net, until the night was visible through the patches in his nonphysical self.

"The Abyss awaits you."

"No, no." The sorcerer's voice was less than a whisper, his magic dulled.

"How did you die?" For he was close to absolute death, his shadow self fading.

"I was sacrificed." Voice almost lost now. "He seeks his possession."

For another dark sorcerer to have sacrificed one of his own, he must've needed a vast amount of power. "Who?"

But the sorcerer was gone, faded into nothingness. Frustrated by the thought that he'd lost the chance to discover some important truth, he spent the rest of the midnight hours in a fury, collecting those destined for the Abyss without mercy.

Evil lingered everywhere. It was a thing to which he'd long become accustomed, for that was why he existed, to cleanse the lands. But tonight, the evil was darker, thicker, more insidious. Something in him keened, as if mourning a great loss, panic stuttering in his chest.

Time was running out.

He didn't know what that meant, didn't know what he had to do. But he could feel time trickling by at an ever-increasing pace. Each day that passed, each hour that passed, the darkness continued to spread, to dig its roots ever deeper.

Hurry, Micah.

Driven, he flew hard and fast, but found nothing except shadows, their evil tainting him, making him unclean.

CHAPTER THIRTEEN

LILIANA HAD BEEN WAITING for Micah long beyond the moonrise. When he did walk in, he went straight to the dungeons, his power rolling heavy and potent through the hallways. It seemed it took an eternity for him to return; she busied herself setting everything out on the table and lighting the candles.

Her hands trembled. "Stop it, Liliana. It's only going to be a kiss…maybe a little more."

Hard boot steps on stone. The slam of a door. The opening of the one to the great hall and more footsteps much closer now. Used to the way he crowded her, she turned from the table, bracing her back against it. But he wasn't behind her. He stood several feet away, his entire body encased in black, razor-sharp points arcing over his nails.

Her stomach fell. "What's wrong?" His face…she'd never seen it that way—so closed and distant and without emotion.

"The hunt was long. I need to bathe." Turning on his heel with those cold words, he left the great hall that she'd emptied of all inhabitants, including the ghostly ones, in anticipation of this night.

She didn't know what to do. For a minute, she just stood there, lost. Then her dress shimmered in the candlelight and she almost crumpled under the wave of humiliation. Pinching out the candles, she covered up the food, and made herself carry it all back to the kitchen, store it away. "Don't break," she ordered herself, though her chest ached, her heart terribly bruised.

It was better this way, she told herself as she left the kitchen to walk to her room. Now she'd be able to focus on her task without being distracted by the wild emotions that had held her hostage today. Already, the Lord of the Black Castle had reclaimed his name. Soon, he'd reclaim his title.

Then she'd take him home, to the castle of Elden, to the family that awaited him. Her father had to die, and so she would kill him, though the power needed would require a human sacrifice. Whatever fantasies of exile she'd allowed herself, she'd always known the brutal truth: it would be her own throat she'd slit for the death spell. But before she did that, she'd restore the blood rulers of Elden, bring the heart back to the land.

Perhaps then, the daughter of the Blood Sorcerer would go not into the Abyss, but to a peaceful forever good-night. She didn't expect to be sent to the Always, the place where the good went after death. She hoped only for an end to her existence. Or she had…before she met Micah. Before he kissed her, made her feel so very alive.

Pulling the silver dress over her head once she reached her room, she put it carefully in the closet. That dress wasn't made for someone like Liliana. It was better for her to wear the browns she'd always worn. Tucking her hair behind her ears, she went to pick up her coarse old dress, but then remembered it was in the laundry. She had only the beautiful chocolate-colored dress Micah had given her, and she couldn't bear to wrinkle that.

Naked but for her underwear, she checked the door. It had no lock, and there was no chair to put underneath the doorknob, but who would come inside? Bard was likely standing watch outside Jissa's room as he did every night, unbeknownst to the brownie, and the Guardian of the Abyss couldn't wait to be far from Liliana.

"Enough," she snapped, annoyed at her self-pity. "Tomorrow, I'll start to push. And push hard." Micah had to remember his destiny soon, or it would all be for naught.

MICAH WASHED AND WASHED, but still, the evil clung to him, a pernicious stain. He couldn't touch Liliana, couldn't taint her with it. Frustrated and angry, he thrust his hands through his hair, his overriding thought to be *clean!*

Magic whispered over him, magic of a kind he'd never before tasted. *No.* That was wrong. He had tasted this magic before. A long, long time ago. It was *his* magic— but not of the Black Castle. It came from inside him, whispering of a place that was both alive…and dying. His body turned rigid, but before he could follow the ominous thought to its root, it was gone. And he was clean.

"Liliana." Now he could go to her. Except the heavy moon, only days away from being full, told him it was late. She'd be curled up in bed fast asleep.

Maybe she'd be naked.

He bared his teeth in a smile and opened the door.

Having put her in a room no one could reach without going past his own, he made the journey with quick steps. No light showed beneath her door, but he hesitated for less than a second, too hungry to taste her again to worry about waking her from her sleep. After all, she knew full well he wasn't civilized.

The room was drenched in moonlight. Liliana lay on her front, her face turned to the side on the pillow, the sheet pulled up to just below her shoulder blades. Those shoulders were bare, glowing with warmth.

Curling his fingers into his palms, he closed the door very quietly behind himself, and simply watched her. Perhaps he shouldn't be invading her privacy in such a way, but he couldn't bring himself to care, not when it was his storyteller. Stroking his gaze down her body, he wished that sheet would disappear…then smiled, because there was no need to use magic to make that happen.

Walking across the floor, he went to—

He froze, having never seen her back close up. It had been hidden by the steamy water in the bath, the marks not as visible under the crisscrossing lacings of the red dress, but there was no impediment to his vision now. Anger roared through him, a ferocious beast. Who had dared lay hands on her? *Who?* Enraged, he tugged down the sheet enough that he could see how far the marks went.

Thick and white and ridged, he knew they'd been made with a whip.

Not a single beating. It would have taken repeated and brutalizing strokes of the whip to create the pattern of scars that went as far as the curve of her waist. He didn't push the sheet down any farther, though rage made him want to examine every inch of the damage.

Shaking, not trusting himself to touch her, he turned away and stared at the moon. But he couldn't leave the room, couldn't go without having his questions answered. Once he could speak without yelling, he sat on the bed beside Liliana's sleeping form. She stirred at once. Wariness stiffened her shoulders, her hand fisting on the pillow.

"Liliana."

"What're you doing here?" Jerking, she went to pull up the sheet he'd tugged down.

He stilled her efforts by the simple expedient of putting his hand flat on her lower back. When she froze, he moved that hand gently over her, his anger a violent thing, but his need to... He didn't have the words. He'd never felt such a rage of emotion. "Who did this?"

She flinched at the ice of his tone. "No one."

"You *will* tell me." And then he would drag the monster into the Abyss.

Her spine went rigid. "He is no one to me. Do you understand? *No one.*"

He heard her own anger, the pulsating ribbon of it threaded through with pain. "You won't speak his name."

"No." A hesitation. "Not until I need to."

He thought about it. He could push her, bully her—and he was quite capable of that—but he had a feeling that might make her cry. He didn't like it when Liliana cried. So he took a deep, deep breath and crushed his anger into a small, tight ball that he hid away deep in his heart. It would be released when the time came, when he knew the name of the man who had dared hurt the woman who lay so still and wary beneath his touch.

Only when he was certain the black rage within was contained, that it wouldn't hurt her, did he bend his head and press his lips to her shoulder. Her skin was warm, silken where unbroken, sleek where the scars cut across it.

"What are you doing?" A high, breathy demand.

"Tasting you." He hadn't gotten a good taste yet, so he placed his hands palms-down on either side of her head and pressed his lips to the curve of her neck, licking out at her skin as he did so.

This time, her jerk was strong enough that she almost clipped his chin with the back of her head.

"Careful," he murmured, nudging her back down with his hand on her lower back. "You'll hurt me."

"I—" She took a trembling breath, her body rising up under his touch. "I *will* hurt you if you don't release me this instant."

"I'm not holding you down." Maybe he didn't know the rules of civilized behavior, but he knew a woman who bore such painful stripes on her back would hate to be restrained.

A pause. Then, "You know I can't get up." It was a hissed accusation.

Deeply satisfied with the situation, he kissed the top of her spine. Hmm… He kissed the next vertebra, then the next. "Why would that be?"

She wiggled. Fascinated by the movement, he thought about moving his hand lower, stroking over the lush curves that tempted him to squeeze and pet—but that might make Liliana panic enough to forget about her modesty.

"Micah."

"Yes?" He continued kissing his way down her spine.

"I'm all but naked," she blurted out at last. "If you'd leave, I can get dressed and then—"

"Why would I want that?" he asked in genuine puzzlement. "You looked pretty in the silver dress, but I like you even better bare and warm."

Heat under his fingertips, and he wished he'd thought to light a lamp so he could see the color creeping over her body. Since he couldn't, he indulged himself by imagining what her breasts would look like, all hot with her blush. It made his body heavy and hard in a way that had him considering if this was torture.

If it was, he'd take more of it.

"You—" She shivered as he stroked his fingers over the curve of her waist, played them over her rib cage. "You didn't want to touch me, remember?"

He stopped, frowned, decided he needed to be in a better position. Kicking off his boots in silence, he got on the bed to her gasp and stretched out alongside her, bracing himself on one elbow. "Only because I was dirty." He replaced his hand on her lower back, nudged just a fraction lower.

A long, long quiet. Followed by, "Dirty?"

"There was much filth in the air, but we won't talk of it while I'm kissing you."

Liliana didn't know which one of his statements to challenge first. Finally, she decided on the least confusing one. "You can't just assume I'm going to welcome your kiss after you snarled at me when you came in."

He stopped making those maddeningly slow circles on her back. "I did not snarl."

She couldn't stand it anymore. Clutching the sheet and pulling it up as she moved, she flipped onto her back, almost surprised when he didn't stop her. But his hand was on her abdomen an instant later—on top of the sheet this time. Thank goodness, because the slightly rough skin of his hand—

Her eyes went wide. "Your armor is gone." *All* of it. And while she could see pants of some tough black material, he wasn't wearing a shirt.

"Of course it is. I needed to bathe."

"But—"

He moved over her, insinuating a muscled thigh between her own, even as he kept his upper body braced above her. "I don't want to talk about anything except kissing now, Liliana."

"You— I—" Snapping her mouth shut before she started babbling, she tried to relearn to breathe.

Micah ran a finger down the side of her face, found a tendril of hair, tugged. "Your hair is curly here. I like it." Twisting that curl around his finger, he lifted it to his mouth, rubbed. "Soft. Smells like Jissa's pretty-making lotion."

"You stole the lotion from Jissa?"

He dropped the curl, picked it up again, rubbed the strands between his fingers. "I borrowed it."

It was near impossible to think with him so close. His shoulders blocked out the world, the muscled thickness of his thigh nudging hard and intimate against the embarrassingly damp heat between her legs. Each time she took a breath, she took the primal scent of him into her body, until it felt as if he was already inside her.

"Micah?" It took all her courage to speak.

"Yes?"

Her heart a drumbeat against her ribs, she said, "Will you come closer?"

Unhidden interest on his face, he dropped his head until strands of thick golden hair stroked across her forehead, his body warm and heavy. Able to feel herself losing her nerve under the impact of him, she tipped up her head and pressed her lips to his jaw.

The wild taste, the rough feel of the bristles on his skin, the sound of his breath so close, it overwhelmed her. Dropping her head back on the pillow, she stared up at him, wondering what he'd do. He settled even more heavily against her, brought his lips to her ear. "Again."

Shivering at the quiet demand made in *that* voice, she dared curl her hands over the naked warmth of his shoulders, even as she gave him what he wanted. When he remained in place, she got bolder, trailing kisses along his jaw, her breasts crushed against his chest as he nuzzled at her neck, the thin sheet the only barrier between them.

It was intoxicating and a little terrifying and so breathtaking that she could hardly think. Caressing his shoulders, she tasted him again. It felt beyond good.

Opening his mouth over her throat, he sucked.

"Micah."

"You're so soft, Lily." A lick, hot and wet.

She melted.

He'd called her Lily. She'd never had a pet name before. It was rather wonderful to have one now.

Then he bit her.

Her body jerked. "You just used your teeth."

He raised his head, a hotly sexual being in her bed. "No?"

"Well…"

"Shall I do it again?"

"Yes." She fisted her hand in the raw silk of his hair after issuing that wicked invitation, her toes curling into the sheets.

Smiling a sinful kind of a smile touched with the dark arrogance of his power, he gave her another sharp nip, then sucked over the spot before lifting his head. "I'll bite you other places, too. This softest place—" a push of his hips as he changed position to fit himself against her "—first of all."

At that, her mind simply hazed over.

CHAPTER FOURTEEN

THAT WAS WHEN MICAH kissed her.

There was no build-up, no little kisses to get her used to the idea. He just took her mouth, all hot and wet and raw—a kiss as untamed and uncivilized as the man himself. One of his hands pushed into her hair, holding her head at an angle that allowed him to explore her mouth with a wild hunger that had her body attempting to arch into him. He was too heavy, too strong. Frustrated, wanting to feel more of him, she spread her legs without realizing it.

Settling more intimately against her, he made a deep sound of pleasure, his hand moving down to her throat, lower. Breaking the kiss, she gasped, "We have to stop." She'd finally remembered she was naked—or so close to it as not to matter.

"Why?"

She couldn't think of an answer.

Which got her kissed again, Micah's hand lying heavy and warm over her chest, just above the curve of her breasts. When he moved a fraction lower, she gripped his wrist. "A kiss." It was a husky reminder.

He smiled, slow and so charming she knew he planned to talk her into every kind of wickedness. She should've told him no, but he felt so good and that smile was so very tempting that she found herself kissing *him*.

MICAH HAD KISSED LILIANA his way and he wanted to do it over and over again, but now she was kissing him her way. She was much gentler than him, her lips lush and bitable, her heart pulsing beneath skin silky and warm. "Use your tongue, Lily," he said when she took a breath.

"Like this?" A shy brush.

As he met her intimate advance with his own, he realized his hand was somehow on her hip, and that she was lush and sweet there, as well. "I like touching you here." He rubbed.

"You can't just say things like that." Whispered against his lips.

"Why?"

She laughed, the sound hushed and intimate. "I don't know."

"Then I'll say what I want." Sucking her lower lip into his mouth, he squeezed her hip, pressing deeper into her. "I want to touch you without the sheet."

A shake of her head. "No."

"Why not?"

"I don't let a man kiss me and...do other things on the first night."

"Tomorrow night?" He petted her hip again, because every time he did, she seemed to soften. And he'd use every weapon in his arsenal to coax her to lie bare and open beneath him. "Say yes."

Her hands stroked down to his back, her response a whisper. "Maybe."

He had the certain thought that he could melt her resistance, but some long-forgotten voice whispered to him of *honor*.

Shaking his head, he lifted it, stared down at Liliana. "Did you say something?"

"No."

Honor is what makes a man.

"Micah." A gentle touch on his face. "What do you hear?"

Looking down into her eyes, he saw an impossible kind of clarity. "Honor is what makes a man."

"Yes." A single tremulous word. "Those are the words of a great king."

"I'll go now, Liliana," he said, not ready to ask the name of the king, to consider why the thought of it made an unknowable pain awaken deep inside him. "Wear the green dress tomorrow."

"I don't have a green dress."

BUT WHEN SHE WOKE, AFTER a night spent in hazy half-forgotten dreams featuring the Lord of the Black Castle and a carnality that had left her soaked with sweat, she found a pretty green dress draped over the end of the bed. Touching it after her bath, she sighed at the feel of the fine wool against her skin. That was when she realized she'd just washed both pairs of her underwear, having forgotten the intimate chore last night after what she'd thought had been Micah's rejection.

It made her blush bright red, but she went without them. They'd be dry in two hours, she thought, checking where they hung on the back of the bathing chamber door. No one would know that beneath her pretty dress, she was bare as the day she'd been born—they'd have no reason to wonder about it.

Pressing her hands to her cheeks, she repeated that reassurance once more before going down to the kitchens to make a cup of chocolate. Flavoring it with cinnamon, she took it to the great hall, but Micah was nowhere to be found. About to leave it there for him, she heard a ghostly whisper in her ear, felt a nudge toward the back right of the hall—where she glimpsed a small door. *Stone garden.*

"Thank you."

Stepping out into the "garden," she found the velvet green grass host to the most graceful dancers formed of stone. There was a woman, one leg raised, the foot of the other arched. She looked as if she would take flight. The sculpture next to her did look as if she had taken flight, the girl's small body held to the earth by a toetip at best.

But the dancers weren't only female. There was a male crouching at the foot of the woman poised on one leg, his hands cupped, as if ready to push her aloft. His face was adoring and filled with mischief at the same time, the woman's with laughter. In front of them, another dancer stood with his hands on his hips, his expression that of a fond friend.

Enchanted, Liliana craned her neck to see the other statues. There were too many to take in all at once, but she noticed one thing. None stood alone. Not like the man at the very edge of the garden, beside a long, rectangular pool filled with water clean and fresh. Several small birds frolicked in it, diving and flicking water at one another, their chatter a bright stream of music.

"Micah."

"Liliana." His slow, dawning smile stopped her in her tracks. No one had ever looked at her that way, as if she was the best thing they had ever seen.

"Is that for me?" he asked when she reached him.

She held out the cup. "Yes." *So is my heart.*

"No, not that."

As she stood there, confused, he stepped even closer. "Hold very, very still so you don't spill the chocolate."

It was difficult to follow the order with him so near. He smelled wonderful—soap and water and warmth. The black armor covered his chest and legs once more, but his arms were bare to the sky, and his skin glowed under the sunlight, making her want to touch, to stroke. "What—"

"Still, Liliana. So still." Curling his hands around her neck, he stroked his thumbs over her jaw. "This smile is for me, isn't it?"

"Yes."

Then she lost her words, because Micah was sipping at her lower lip, his mouth caressing, his hands possessive. The tenderness of it made her tremble.

"Careful." Spoken against her mouth. "I'm kissing you like you kiss me." Another soft sip, the feel of teeth. "I like it, but it's even better when you kiss me this way." Slanting his mouth over hers, he took her with open-mouthed wildness that made her want to push him to the earth and do things no good maiden should even think about.

"You spilled the chocolate," he said, biting at her lower lip.

She glanced unseeing at her hands. "I did?"

"Let me." Taking the cup, he placed it carefully on the edge of the pool. Then he rose, lifted one of her hands to his mouth and stroked her fingers inside one by one. Each hot, wet tug pulled at things low and deep within her, her thighs clenching in darkest need.

"Chocolate tastes better on your skin."

"Don't stop." It was a whisper as he started on her other hand.

But he did so abruptly. "I smell blood sorcery."

Yes. A putrid odor infiltrated the air. That of a corpse defiled, a grave broken.

"Go inside," Micah ordered.

"I'm a blood mage." Never would she leave him to face such malignant power alone. "I can—"

Micah snapped out a hand, closing it over Liliana's wrist when he saw her pick up a sharp stone. "No."

"I must." Determination steeled eyes that had been sultry with pleasure only moments ago. "This is who I am."

"You are not *this*." And he wouldn't allow her to be swallowed by it.

Her eyes flicked up. "Look."

He'd already seen— the sky was turning a fetid brown streaked with red. The spreading color was no shapeless stain. It had the appearance of a skeletal hand tipped with claws. "Who is that, Liliana?"

"My father." Her pulse turned rapid, almost panicked under his hand, but her voice was resolute. "He's found me."

"Not yet." Squeezing her wrist, he made her drop the stone she'd intended to use to cut herself. "But he will if you spill your lifeblood."

"Sorcery of his kind is stronger than other magic. It's created of death."

"I am the Guardian of the Abyss and this is my domain." Releasing her hand, he gripped her chin, looked her directly in the eye. "You will obey me. Do not spill your blood."

"Take care, Micah." Shimmering emotions in those eyes that showed her every mood. "I'm not worth your life. You're meant for far more."

He didn't understand what she meant, but saw a silent promise that she would do as he asked. Dropping her hand and anchoring his feet, he awakened the old, *old* magic that was of this place and that lived in him when he wished it to. Of the Abyss.

The black armor crawled over the exposed parts of

his body at the same time, curving over his fingers and around his neck, into his hair and across his face in fine threads of impenetrable jet.

"Please be careful. My father doesn't play fair."

Things didn't touch him in the depths of the Abyss, but he felt the care in her words wind around his heart, protecting it in armor that was invisible. "Wait for me, Liliana." Then he rose into a sky stained with the malevolence of a dark blood sorcerer.

The magic in that stain recoiled from his black armor, from the kiss of death that was the Abyss. But it didn't retreat. Instead, after a short hesitation, it curved around him, and he knew it had tasted the death, decided that it held no danger. It was wrong. The Lord of the Black Castle stood as the guardian against evil, no matter its form.

Arms down his side, he spread his fingers and said a single word. *"Rise."*

The ghosts of the Black Castle circled into the sky in a wave of cold, the wind vicious and cutting. He knew they wouldn't hurt Liliana where she stood looking up at him, a tiny figure clothed in green.

Around him, the ghosts formed a twisting ribbon of ice, and he knew it was time. *"Hold."*

The ribbon solidified into shimmering white on either side of him. An instant later, the ice coated his armor in glittering shards bright as diamonds.

The dark sorcerer's claw reached out again—only to scrape off the ice with a screech that had Liliana clapping her hands over her ears below. Perhaps he should've warned her, Micah thought with the part of his mind that remained of the man, not the Guardian, but he *had* told her to go inside. The shriek reverberated through the sky, through the dark sorcerer's power, shattering the stain into thousands of lethally sharp pieces. Those pieces began to ricochet back. Hard.

Micah smiled.

CHAPTER FIFTEEN

DEEP IN THE CASTLE THAT HAD once been the heart of Elden, the Blood Sorcerer fell to his knees with a bone-chilling scream, his entire body covered with hundreds of cuts seeping thickest crimson. He hadn't seen this much of his own blood in decades.

A banging on the door.

"Leave me!" He couldn't be discovered in such a weakened state.

Hissing out a breath, he struggled to his feet—it had been a mistake to probe that realm. It was protected by something that had never welcomed the dark magics.

He had ever hated the wall of black that stood between him and the vicious nightmare of the Abyss. Oh, he cared nothing for the sorcerers trapped within, but if he ruled the Black Castle, he would have access not only to wealth incomparable, but also to all that power. Sweet, deadly, beautiful power.

But he couldn't go there. Not yet.

However, there were others who could—because though he called her stupid, his daughter was very smart, smart enough to have found a way to hide in the one place he wouldn't follow. His minions didn't understand why he wanted her back, didn't comprehend that she was his *possession*. None of his possessions had ever dared leave him.

He was going to hurt Liliana a great deal when he

dragged her back. She'd beg him for death by the time he was done. Maybe he'd give it to her...or maybe not. His daughter was his most amusing toy. But before he could indulge himself with her, he had to find her.

Swiping the blood from one of his cuts, he fed it to the palm-sized spider on his desk. "It's time, I think, to awaken your brethren."

CHAPTER SIXTEEN

LILIANA'S EARS WERE STILL ringing an hour later. "Have you ever seen anything like that before?" she asked Jissa as they sat in the stone garden, shelling nuts simply because they wanted to be out in the sunshine after the cold. Goose bumps broke out on Liliana's arms at the memory.

Reaching over, Jissa rubbed at her skin with a tsking sound. "Always here. The ghosts. Always here." She removed her hand after a comforting pat. "Never saw them do that before, never, ever."

"Their power was different." It had tasted of death, but been pure in a way her father's magic never would be. "Jissa," she said, still thinking of death, "does the thought of the Always scare you?"

Jissa gave her a curious look. "Why would it? Happiness and golden magic, that is the Always. I would like to see it, yes, I would."

"Yes." Yet her kind friend remained trapped on this earth because of whatever it was the Blood Sorcerer had done to her when he'd killed her, stolen her life force. "Jissa…I'm sorry."

"Why?"

"You'll know one day." Until then, Liliana would steal a little more time with the first true friend she had ever had. "Here." She handed the brownie a funny-shaped nut. "It matches the rest of this castle's inhabitants."

The other woman laughed, but the sweet sound was

drowned out by the roar of violent rage that came from within the castle. Placing the basket of unshelled nuts haphazardly on the ground, Liliana stood. "Micah."

"Liliana, don't!"

She didn't listen, running headlong toward the house. Huge hands clamped over her arms before she would've raced over the doorstep. Bard's eyes were liquid dark with sorrow, the shake of his head slow, so slow.

"Let me go." She forced herself to sound calm, though her blood thundered through her veins. "Please, Bard, let me go."

"Liliana." Jissa's breathless voice. "You mustn't, no, no. He is a monster, a terrible monster, when the curse is upon him."

Liliana snapped her head toward the brownie. "So am I, Jissa." She was the worst monster of all. "Tell Bard to release me."

"I—" The small woman squared her shoulders. "No, we will protect you."

"Then I'm sorry again, my friend." Liliana bit down hard on her lower lip, spilling blood into her mouth. Power flowed through her, vibrant and strong for not having been woken in days.

Lashing out with it, she broke Bard's hold, sent him swaying. She was gone before he could regain his footing, Jissa's cry echoing in her ears. Slamming the door behind herself, she pulled down the brace to lock it. None too soon. Bard's body crashed up against it a moment later, making the entire thing shake.

Knowing it would hold for now—hopefully giving Jissa enough time to stop Bard from attempting to follow—Liliana took a breath. "Where?" Her heart pounded like a drum in her chest, until she wasn't certain if she would hear the whispering ghosts.

A roar reverberated through the walls.

The feral *power* of it pushed her back a physical step before she shoved it off to run toward the sound as fast as her feet would carry her. The blood from her cut was beginning to slow, but she swiped a small ceremonial knife off the outer wall as she ran into the great hall, dropping it into the pocket of her green dress.

The hall was a place of splintering chaos.

Liliana couldn't believe the carnage—the massive dining table lay tipped on its side, a huge crack running down the middle, while most of the chairs were nothing more than piles of jagged firewood. Stepping around them with care since she wore only soft green slippers, she searched for the author of the devastation.

"Micah?" Pushing aside an overturned chair, she almost stepped onto the broken shards of what might've been a water pitcher. That was when she noticed the weapons embedded in the walls.

There were at least ten, all of them—large and small—having been punched about three inches into solid stone. And they were lined up in two neat rows… as if they'd been released from some enormous catapult. Her heart was in her throat now, but she wouldn't walk away, wouldn't leave him to this. "Micah?"

A snarl.

Whipping around her head, she stumbled and fell back against a chair that was somehow still upright. Only her grip on it kept her from crashing to the floor, onto the shards waiting below. Using that hold to steady herself, she scanned the room again. Curtains lay torn off the huge windows, tapestries had been shredded from the walls and furniture destroyed. There was no place to hide.

A low growl, that of a beast ready to attack.

Mercy.

Swallowing, Liliana dared look up at the one place she hadn't searched. The ceiling.

He crouched along one massive beam, a great shaggy beast on four legs, his claws bigger than the sickles embedded in the wall. They flexed with each breath, his eyes trained on her. And those eyes, they were a murderous red, without any thought or sentience.

This, she understood on a scream of knowledge, was the realization of the spell her father had cast on the night Elden fell. It had caught Micah, tangled him in threads of darkest sorcery.

For how could a prince return if he was not a man at all?

She should have run. But her feet remained rooted to the black stone of the castle. She knew about feeling grotesque, about being alone. She wouldn't abandon Micah now, when he was this monster her father had made him. "Hello," she said, hiding her trembling hands behind her back. "Why are you up there?"

The huge creature cocked its head, its eyes continuing to swirl with menace, its claws flexing and unflexing on the thick beam. Curls of wood drifted to the floor, making it clear his claws were as sharp as any weapon. Fear thumped in her throat, and he growled, low and deep.

A predator would scent fear, would hunger for it.

Straightening her spine, she took a deep, quiet breath, and reached for the sorcery within, her mouth still touched with the metallic scent of iron. The power flooded her body, flowing through to inhabit every part of her, until she wasn't simply Liliana with the ugly face and the hair so rough and hard. She was a blood sorceress who knew her own strength. "Come down," she said, putting a subtle compulsion in the request. "I would admire you."

A considering look.

"You would like to be admired, would you not?" she murmured with a smile. "You are a fierce creature."

He began to strut along the wooden beam, this monster who was as arrogant as Micah. She was amazed at the grace of him when those knotted muscles, those overgrown shoulders too big for the rest of his body, should've left him unable to move. But move he did, with a power that said he could crush her with but a thought. Now, he used that power to jump into the air, twisting around to clamp his claws into the wall at the apex of his lunge.

He walked down that wall as if he were walking across the floor, using his claws to slice into the stone, his mouth open in a lazy yawn to reveal rows of teeth the gleaming ebony shade of the castle itself. Each and every tooth was razored to a lethal point—the same as the spines along the line of his back, black as jet.

"You are strong," she said, using her blood magic to imbue her words with shimmering intensity. "And so very large." That last slipped out past her veneer of confidence. For this terrible creature who was Micah stood taller than her, though he was on four legs, each of his paws so massive as to be able to annihilate her face with a single swat.

He growled, but didn't spring for her throat.

Burying her nervousness with sheer will, she said, "Let me admire you." Again, she threaded compulsion, silken and seductive, through the words—blood sorcery to combat blood sorcery.

Those swirling red eyes followed her every move as she shifted to lay a hand on his mane. "It's softer than my hair," she murmured without stopping to think about it. "I'm jealous."

A huffing growl that sounded almost like laughter. It made her smile, chuckle into his mane as she drew her fingers through the thick brown of it. "So glorious," she said, admiring him in truth in spite of her fear, because he was a creature who demanded respect. "Though I do wish you'd sit down—it would make it easier for me to pet you."

He bared his teeth at her, an aristocrat who was not to be given orders.

She bowed her head at once, understanding that any defiance would likely lead to that head rolling off her shoulders. "Please, my lord. I am only a small thing."

A low snarling sound drifted along the air currents, but he folded himself down at last, his massive head coming to her abdomen. "Thank you." She began to stroke him again. "You are strong, indeed, to break that table."

Turning that head with its too-large jaw to look at where the table had been cleaved almost in half, the beast huffed out an agreement.

"Yes," she said, entangling him in fine, fine tendrils of persuasion. Micah the man would've caught her. Micah the cursed beast didn't appear to understand the subtleties of magic. "Should you not rest after such an action? Every great warrior must rest."

He angled his head and looked at her with eyes of bloodred. It should've made her afraid, but there was something in them… "I will tell you a story," she whispered, "of three princes and a princess who once summoned a unicorn."

The beast shifted forward to lay its head on forearms lumpy with muscle.

"So the heirs," she said, picking up the story from where she'd stopped it the day of the bath, for she knew her Micah existed within this beast, "made their way to the Stone Circle. They were arguing about the best incantation to use when Breena produced an ancient book she'd taken from the library before they set off on their adventure—she was said to mutter that her brothers had likely never seen the inside of the place."

A deep, rumbling sound. Agreement, perhaps.

"In this book, there was a very old, near-forgotten spell. Later it came to be known that scores of sorcerers had tried to work this spell, and failed. Most believed it to be nothing but a chimera."

A pricked ear.

"As you know, my lord," she murmured, stroking his back—being careful to avoid those spines she was certain would take off the skin on her hand, "a chimera is a mythical beast. It doesn't exist except in the imagination. So sorcerers call those spells which they do not believe will ever work, but which people insist on trying, chimeras." She'd always liked that little whimsy. "And this chimera had survived centuries."

The beast's eyes closed, but its large black ears remained alert.

"It required a certain level of innate magic, and a simple calling," she continued. "Nicolai, oldest and strongest, attempted it first—without success."

A snort that might've been a snore.

She checked but he'd opened one eye, was awake and listening. "Breena went next, for they thought perhaps the unicorn would prefer a woman. Nothing. Finally Dayn tried it, certain his brother and sister had done it wrong. Nothing. That was when Micah demanded a turn.

"They smiled at him in that way of older siblings who

are amused by a beloved younger brother. After all, he was so small he could only just read his letters, so how could he possibly summon a unicorn? It took him a long time to read aloud the entire incantation, but he owned his siblings' hearts and so they did not halt or hurry him."

No sound from the ensorcelled beast, but she knew he heard every word.

Folding down into a sitting position in front of him, she went to continue when those massive knotted forearms opened, swept her inside. Instead of fear, she felt only warmth as she laid her head against his neck and listened to the beat of his great heart. "The moment Micah finished speaking, there was a brilliant burst of light, so bright that for an instant they thought they had gone blind.

"However, when the sparks cleared, they found themselves host to a regal unicorn prince who was bemused by them, as such ancient beings are by the follies of youth." The idea of Nicolai, the one they called the Dark Seducer, being considered a "youth," had always made her laugh.

"You see, to call a unicorn, you must have the purest of hearts. All children are born thus, but each day as we grow, we gain small shadows. Not every shadow is bad. A strong man needs his shadows. On that day, only Micah was as he had been born. And so only Micah's voice could reach the unicorn realm," she said, her eyes fluttering shut.

MICAH DREAMED OF UNICORNS noble and gracious, and of deep male laughter. He'd never had family, but in this dream, he ran after two tall men—they chuckled when he fell, and he didn't like that, but he was stubborn, fought to get up. Then there was one of those men, pulling him up and brushing him off. All anger was forgotten as he ran in his brothers' footsteps across the sand.

Nicolai scrambled down the dune first.

Micah wanted to race down after him, but his chest hurt and he stopped to gasp in a breath. But he wasn't left behind. He never was. Grabbing him in his arms, Dayn swung him onto his back. They laughed when they reached the beach to find Nicolai fighting off a territorial red land crab, the water a warm lick of foam against their feet. It was a good day.

The thought lingered as he woke, as he became aware that he lay on the cold stone floor of the great hall in the Black Castle. He was naked, and that told him what had happened before he ever saw the fractured table, the splintered chairs. However, that wasn't the most interesting thing about this waking.

He wasn't alone.

Always before, he'd been alone. The day servants scattered at the first sign of the curse, while Bard and Jissa had strict instructions to bar their doors and keep their distance until he was a man once more. But today, he woke curled around a female body that had the most intriguing curves. Especially down where her bottom snuggled so prettily against the hardness of him.

He rubbed against her because it felt good. When she murmured but didn't move away, he smiled and spread his fingers on her abdomen, holding her to him as he slid his thigh up between the silky skin of her own legs, pushing up the dress as he went. It would be better, he thought, if she was naked, too, but the stone floor was cold. Liliana wouldn't enjoy that.

Her name was dawnlight in his mind, a signal that he was no longer lost. "Lily," he said, rubbing against her again. "Wake up, Lily."

"Mmm." A husky sound that delighted him, pleased him. "Micah?" She tried to turn onto her back, was stopped by his embrace. *"Micah."* Shock colored her tone this time, her thighs squeezing down on the one he'd insinuated in between.

Kissing her neck, he moved his free hand up to cup her breast. "You're so soft, Lily. I wonder what it'd feel like if I lay on top of you."

Her skin grew hot under his lips, her hand rising to grip the wrist of the hand on her breast. "We have to get up. The others could come in."

Ignoring the husky order, he ran his thumb over her nipple through the material of the green dress he'd brought her. She tried to pull away. He growled low in his throat, held her to him. "Mine."

"You're no longer the beast, Micah." Her hand tightened on his wrist. "Don't try to trick me."

Laughing, he played his thumb over her nipple again. "You like this, Lily. I can feel your dampness against my thigh." He pressed that thigh harder against her. "My mouth waters—I think I want to taste you there."

CHAPTER SEVENTEEN

A SQUEAK ESCAPED LILIANA'S mouth. Biting down on it, she tugged away that teasing hand and scrambled up into a sitting position, surprised at her success. Then she turned…and felt every bit of air leave her body.

Micah was naked.

And he was the most sensual creature she had ever seen—all tumbled hair of golden light, eyes of slumberous winter-green and a jutting arousal he fisted without shame. Her own hand flexed and she almost whimpered when he released himself to stand.

Snap out of it, Liliana.

Rising after him on the strength of the command issued by some small sensible part of herself, she tried to find the rest of her rational mind as he closed the distance between them to circle her like the beast he'd been not long ago.

She shivered when he stopped behind her, put his hands on her hips and squeezed. "Mmm." A deep, rumbling sound as he—

"What are you doing?"

Ignoring her attempt at pushing away his hands, he continued to raise the skirts of her dress. The air was cool against her calves, the backs of her knees, moving ever higher. "Micah, we must stop," she said, but it came out holding not the least bit of certainty.

"Why?" Kisses on her neck, wet and open and involving licks that made her melt from the inside out.

"It's not d-decent." The air had reached her thighs now. "We're in the great hall."

Continuing with his sinful game, Micah made no response, not until he said, "You aren't wearing underthings."

Red filling her cheeks, she went to tug away but he braceleted her waist with one muscular arm. "They're drying," she admitted.

"I'll find them and throw them away," he told her, biting her ear. "I like this." Then he pressed his hotly aroused body against her bare curves.

She shuddered at the shock of feeling that hard ridge of flesh nestled so intimately against her, but Micah snarled in frustration. "You're too short for this."

Not sure what to say to that, she'd barely opened her mouth when he swung her up in his arms and made his way to a chair lying on its side, beside the table. Putting her down, he set it upright. Liliana's befuddled brain took that long to figure out what he intended. "I think I better—oh!" He had her in his arms, his mouth on hers before she could finish the sentence.

His tongue pushed past her lips and, oh, it was a very naughty kind of a kiss but she couldn't resist him, especially when he was so strong and warm and hard against her. His skin was like hot satin, his muscles fluid beneath the smooth heat. His jaw was a little rough, making her wonder what that stubbled skin would feel like against her breasts.

The wickedness of her own thoughts scandalized her, but that didn't stop her from sucking on his tongue. He liked that. His hands, those arrogant, wandering hands, told her so. A minute later, he was raising her dress again and she had no will to stop him.

So when he sat down in the chair and swiveled her around so her back faced his front, she went, feeling shameless and brazen and bad. Very, very bad. But Micah didn't pull her down to the dark temptation of his lap. No, he stopped her between his legs. Then, tucking up her skirt into the thin belt that was part of the dress, he ran his hand over the lush curves she'd hated all her life.

Heat burned her cheeks and she wasn't sure whether it was arousal or embarrassment. Whatever it was, it left her immobile, waiting on tenterhooks for his next touch.

A hot breath. "So soft, Lily." His fingers sliding through her slick flesh, heading straight for the little nub that pulsed hot and tight.

"Micah!"

"This place gives you pleasure." It was a satisfied statement. "Like this?" A rough flick.

Her knees crumpled.

Making a low, rumbling sound that seemed to be a remnant of the creature he'd been before they slept, he held her upright using an arm around her waist. His fingers rubbed, slid back, circled the entrance to her body with an exploring touch. Expecting a sensual intrusion, she was taken utterly by surprise when he arrowed his fingers through her intimate lips again, closing the rough pads of his fingers around the nub that made her boneless. "I want to put my mouth here, Lily."

"Don't. You. Dare." She wouldn't survive. Even the thought of it—that beautiful, sensual mouth on her most secret place, a place that he was caressing with a distinctly proprietary touch—made her so hot that her dress was suddenly too tight, her breasts feeling far bigger than she knew them to be.

"I will dare." Continuing to hold her up with that strong arm around her waist, he moved his fingers back down to her slick and sensitive entrance, began to push in a little with one thick finger, halted at her cry. "Am I causing you hurt?"

"No," she whispered, knowing she should've used the opportunity to stop him, keep this from progressing any further—but she wanted this wicked pleasure, would steal it from him.

Taking her at her word, he pushed in slow, so slow.

She cried out again—her body was tight, untried, and it felt too much and not enough at the same time. When he withdrew his finger, she couldn't help her whimper of protest. But he didn't leave her for long. Stroking his hands down the insides of her thighs, he said, "Can you reach the table?"

"Yes." Her hands were already gripping the edge of the fallen wooden table before she realized what she was doing, her thighs parting in an instinctive attempt at balance. Nerves awakened—she'd never had a man within her, and he'd moved so fast, until she was now in position for him to mount her. However, she had no intention of stopping him, not this man who looked at her and saw a woman he desired. Never had she felt as she did in Micah's arms. Never had she wanted this badly.

The hot gust of his breath on her most intimate flesh was the only warning she had before he put his mouth on her. Her brain simply stopped functioning at the crash of scandalizing pleasure, her entire body taut with shock. She had to protest. This was surely not something...

"Oh." It was a shuddering moan as he flicked his tongue over the entrance to her body.

MICAH SMILED AT THE SOUND of Liliana's pleasure. It was good that she enjoyed this, because he had every intention of repeating the act; she tasted unlike anything he'd ever before sipped. Hot and dark but with a delicate feminine musk that intoxicated senses still sensitive after the visitation of the curse.

The reminder made him frown, lift his head from his exploration of Liliana's sweetness. "Was I terrifying?" He didn't scent fear on her, needed to make certain it didn't linger in her blood.

"What?" It was a breathless word.

"When the curse came upon me?" He caressed her with his fingertips, deciding that next time, he'd have her on her back in bed, so he could spread her more fully, see everything he tasted. It would be good. She was so soft and flushed and pretty.

For him.

His smile was probably very uncivilized.

Liliana went as if to rise, but he stopped her by the simple expedient of stroking her with his tongue once more. Trembling, she held her position. "You were terrifying," she said. "But you were rather beautiful, too."

He liked that answer, liked that she'd seen both beauty and danger in him. What he liked even better was that when he reached down and rubbed his finger on that little nub at the apex of her thighs at the same time that he kissed her long and deep in her most secret place, she made a hotly feminine sound before her body clenched and grew even more slick for him. Lapping up the proof of her pleasure, he inserted a finger inside her again.

"Micah!"

Tiny muscles clenched on his finger over and over again as tremors shook her frame. Pleased, he stroked his hand over her hip until she stopped trembling. "No,

Lily," he murmured when she would've pulled away. "I'm not done."

He'd never had a woman, never wanted any of the silly village creatures so rank with fear. After a while, that part of him had seemed to go to sleep, leaving him the perfect Guardian, cold and without need of any kind. Then had come Liliana. A woman who looked at him as if he was wonderful, told him fantastical tales and filled his castle with laughter. He wanted to lick and suck and bite at her until he knew her every pleasure point, her every sensual weakness. "I like the taste of you."

"Micah, if you—" A short scream as he covered her with his mouth again.

This time, he decided to try little flicks and licks using his tongue, rubs with his thumb and sucks with his mouth. Lifting away his lips when she began to buck against him, he played his finger through her slickness before sliding it inside…then adding another. Quivering, she gasped, but didn't ask him to stop. So he pumped his fingers, slow and deep and again. Her body clamped down on his, tight as a fist. Tighter.

His cock surged.

Feeling her spasms subside into shuddering aftershocks, he withdrew his fingers and pulled her down to sit on his lap, ensuring her nakedness met the pulsing rigidity of his own. Soft and wet, she tensed, then folded back against him, boneless. "I gave you much pleasure, Lily."

He saw her lips curve up at the corners as she lay with her eyes closed, her head against his shoulder. "You sound quite satisfied with yourself."

"I am." Reaching forward, he pulled up her dress, ignoring the small attempt she made to slap away his hands. "I like looking at you," he murmured, and her hands dropped. When he'd exposed her thighs, a paler shade than the honey-brown of her skin where the sun had caressed it, he put his hands on them. It made her shift on him, causing his arousal to nestle more snugly into the hot, wet place between her thighs.

His hands clenched on her, his head dropping back.

The feel of it was so raw, it took him long moments to realize Liliana had gone motionless. "Micah?" Her hand closing over his. "Will you come inside me now?"

"No." He wanted to try this first. "Move on me, Lily," he whispered, nuzzling at her throat.

He saw color tinge her skin, but she didn't deny him, sliding along his hard flesh in small, sensual movements that made his arousal throb. Groaning, he shifted his hands up to close over her breasts. She gasped, her nipples tight points against his palms through the dress, but didn't stop the hot little movements of her body over his cock.

Hands tightening on her breasts, he buried his face in her neck and urged her to speed up with harsh murmurs against her skin. When she did, pleasure shot a lightning bolt through his body, so primal and raw that he knew he wanted to experience it again and again and again.

He tensed before he spilled, clenching his jaw until his bones grated against one another. "Stop."

"Did I do something wrong?"

"No." Petting her breasts, he took a deep breath, lay back. "I want to see your face."

Liliana rose to her feet at his urging. Her cheeks were red when she turned around, but it was pleasure that colored them, not embarrassment. When she touched her fingers to his lips in a shy caress, he pretended to bite. Her laugh was husky, only for him.

Pleased, he pushed up the front of her dress and

tugged her forward to straddle him. Her mouth opened in a shocked gasp as their bodies came together, his cock sliding through her delicate folds. *"Micah."*

He smiled and claimed a hot, deep kiss, realizing the position allowed his cock to rub up against that sensitive nub, the one he was going to suck on when he had her naked and spread out on his bed. For now, he clasped his hands on her bottom and began to rock through her folds over and over again with her lush cooperation, feeling pleasure build up hot and dark along his spine. His cock jerked as she whimpered, went liquid around him and then his own release had him in a grip hard and brutal.

"That was good," he murmured afterward, collapsing against the chairback with her limp against his chest. "Next time, I'll be inside you."

CHAPTER EIGHTEEN

LILIANA COULDN'T LOOK JISSA in the eye that afternoon as they began to set the great hall to rights. She could still feel the heat of Micah's breath on her intimate flesh, the shocking wetness of his seed against her thigh, the rough clasp of his hands on her bottom. He'd left marks, he'd held on so tight at the end, but unlike with the scars on her back, Liliana had found herself twisting in front of the mirror to examine these with a sinful lash of heat.

They'd disappear within the next day or so, but until then, they were a physical indication of not only her own pleasure, but of Micah's. There was going to be pain, terrible pain, when she told him her lineage, but nothing and no one could ever steal this truth from her—that she'd brought him to that extremity of need, of desire.

"Liliana," Jissa said, and from the tone of her voice, she'd been trying to get Liliana's attention for a while.

"I'm sorry." An ache in her heart, entangled with memories of a most beautiful sin. "I was woolgathering."

But Jissa didn't smile or scold her. "He is not himself," she said, "not at all, oh, no, when the curse is upon him. You must not blame him." Distress in every word, in those dark button eyes. "Oh, please, don't—"

"He didn't hurt me," Liliana managed to get in when her friend paused to gulp in a breath. "He didn't, Jissa. Please believe me."

"He is so fearsome, big and wild and terrifying."

"Yes," Liliana agreed, putting broken dishes on the cracked but usable table. "But inside, he is still the Lord of the Black Castle." Her father had tried to twist the soul of the child Micah had been, and succeeded only in twisting the physical shape of him. "Kindness and a little flattery will calm him if you ever find yourself alone with the beast."

Jissa's eyes were huge. "Oh, no, never. Not me. I'm not brave like you."

Liliana thought of how she'd cowered under her father's whip, how she'd lain weak and starving in his filthy dungeons, and knew she wasn't brave. But she didn't say that to Jissa, who finally looked more like herself. Instead, sweeping up the remains of what might've been a chair leg, she asked, "Where is the lord, do you know?" He'd been nowhere to be seen when she'd returned from cleaning herself up—and putting on her now-dry underwear.

"The village elder, sharp and pointy man, came here. A scourge of Bitterness in the village, you see." Seeing Liliana's confusion, she said, "Many arms and feet they have, yes, they do, and they are covered in black, so black, fur. Small creatures, so much trouble. Trouble, trouble."

"Are they creatures of the Abyss?"

Jissa shook her head. "Oh, no, they are simply drawn to the Black Castle. Home, it is, home from long, long ago. But rice and potatoes they love, tsk, tsk. Stealing rice and potatoes."

Liliana laughed at the idea of these pieces of "Bitterness" eating their way through potatoes with relish. "What does Micah do with them?"

"He brings them back home," came a familiar male voice from the doorway.

Turning, she found Micah standing there, fully armored again—and surrounded by a small sea of furry little creatures who were making the oddest chittering sounds. Before she could say a word, Jissa put her hands on her hips. "No, no! Pests! No pests in my kitchen!" the brownie said in an unexpected show of temper.

"They've promised to behave." Micah smiled, slow and coaxing, and Liliana all but saw Jissa melt. "They'll only be here for a while. Something scared them and so they've come to hide until the badness is gone."

Liliana felt a chill in her heart. "What is this badness?"

"Bad magic," Micah said. "The Bitterness were created to sense bad magic, and eat it up. But they are too small, and can only eat small bad magics."

And the Blood Sorcerer's magic, Liliana thought, was huge and ever growing. Had she needed one, this was the final sign that there was no more time—she would tell Micah the truth tomorrow, hope he would remember... hope he wouldn't hate her.

THAT NIGHT, WHILE MICAH WAS gone hunting the souls destined for the Abyss, Liliana dreamed of huge spiders as big as horse carts. Their eyes were a malignant red that burned, until she couldn't look at them without tears of blood streaking down her cheeks. And yet she knew she couldn't look away, for their legs were lined with razors, their mouths with knives.

Then she fell, and they were on her, cutting and tearing and ripping.

It was her own scream that wrenched her out of the nightmare.

Sitting up in the huge black bed in the room that belonged to the Lord of the Black Castle, his shirt—the one she had borrowed from his closet, though he had ordered her to sleep naked—stuck to the sweaty film on her skin, she bit the inside of her cheek, creating enough blood magic to open her palm on a ball of light. It floated to the ceiling, bathing everything in a soft glow. There were no spiders in the corners, or if there were, the small creatures were too shy to bother her.

But it wasn't those insects that worried her. "They are coming," she said to the mouse who watched her from the windowsill, his tail twitching as if he sensed it, too. "The Arachdem are coming."

MICAH RETURNED TO THE CASTLE with many shadows this night, all of them so full of evil that he felt drenched in it. Not going to Liliana until he'd washed off their stench, he was most displeased to find his bed empty—though the hunt had been long and dawn touched the sky in a luminous cascade of color. "Where is she?" he snarled at the mouse who had the bad fortune to be sleeping curled up on the bedside table beside the unicorn timepiece he'd shown Lily last night.

The mouse squeaked, stood up on two paws for a second, before dashing down and behind the table and under the bed. Leaving the creature because it was a denizen of the Black Castle, though its magic was very, very small, Micah slammed his way down to the kitchen. Jissa jumped when she saw him; then shook a wooden spoon.

"Look! Look at this!"

Bemused by the sudden aggression from this most sweet and timid of brownies, he walked around the counter to see what had her so upset. By and around her feet rippled a sea of furry black. The Bitterness. Micah scowled. "You promised to behave."

A chittering, squealing response.

"Oh." Raising his head, he said to Jissa, "Have they eaten any of your potatoes or rice?"

Jissa frowned, put down the spoon and went to check the stores, the Bitterness at her heels. They made a mournful, hungry kind of sound when she opened the bins, but didn't swarm. Instead, they followed her back when she returned to stand in front of Micah. "No, they did not." Shocked words. "Not at all."

"Then I believe they must like you, Jissa." Kissing her on the cheek—and enjoying her "eek" of surprise— he left her surrounded by the squealing happiness of the Bitterness.

"Hush, silly, silly," he heard her mutter, but there was no ill will in it. Then, "*Very* hungry you are?"

Smiling because the Bitterness would not be harmed here and Jissa would not be lonely, he was almost in a good mood for an instant. Until he remembered that Liliana hadn't been waiting warm and naked in his bed as she should have been. She was his, after all. Didn't she know the rules? He was scowling again by the time he entered the stone garden, following the scent of her sorcery to the grassy area beside the long reflecting pool that was a favorite with birds.

She'd drawn a blood circle and though he could've crossed it as this was his domain, he didn't. To disturb such magic could cause harm to rebound on her. Instead, he took a seat on an overturned sculpture and watched as she knelt on the cold, hard earth dressed in nothing but her old brown dress and a black jacket.

At least the jacket was his, he thought, mollified.

A tickle at his leg announced one of the Bitterness. Looking down, he saw it was, in fact, four of the creatures. Carrying a cup of chocolate dusted with cinnamon.

"My thanks." He took it, was almost expecting the group that came along with a plate of bread heaped with butter and honey. "Jissa is working you hard."

They all but leaped in joy before running back to their new mistress. That was what no one understood about the Bitterness. They had been created to eat bad magic, and that was how they got their name—for it was said they became bitter with the eating of it. That, however, was not true. When the Bitterness ate bad magic, it lost its badness and became inert. The Bitterness, on their own, were loyal creatures, full of happiness and a desire to help. If not for their unfortunate propensity to raid farmers' stores, they would be much loved.

Eating a piece of the bread, Micah decided to keep one aside for Liliana. He wasn't pleased with her for depriving him of a chance to touch and kiss her naked body, but he didn't like her looking weak. After spilling that much blood—from a wound in her arm, he saw—she'd need sustenance.

Her lips moved, her fingers lifting to make graceful flowing patterns in the air that glowed with light. It was blood sorcery, beautiful and arcane and of Liliana. He watched, enthralled, his own power resonating with hers, as if it was as enamored of it as he was of the woman who wielded it.

"See," she whispered.

A minute later, her hands fell, the glowing patterns disappearing into the ether. "I wasn't wrong, Micah," she said, her eyes flicking open. "He has sent the Arachdem."

Her words were a chill wind. From what he'd heard pass the lips of the condemned, the Arachdem were fed the worst of the dark magics and, as such, were nightmares given form. It was said they could cross the Great

Divide, traverse the ice mountains, lava-filled pools and other obstacles that protected this realm. "When?"

"Soon. Within hours."

"Break the circle, Liliana."

"What? Oh." Standing, she ignited a match and dropped it on the circle. It opened with a "pop" of sound, the magic dissipating. "Is that for me?"

He held out the bread. "I will not share my chocolate." But when she smiled at him, he gave it to her.

A small, quiet moment passed with her sitting beside him, warm and smelling of nothing but Liliana. Then the sun's rays hit the broken circle, caressing the dark ruby stain of her blood. "How many?" he asked.

"I think...an army."

BARD TOOK CARE OF EVACUATING the people of the village to the safety of the Black Castle—which had, according to legend, never fallen. The villagers came in huddled and scared, not simply of the threat of which they had been warned, but of the castle and its inhabitants.

Jissa, shy and afraid of strangers, came out with the Bitterness holding cups of sweet tea and cakes for the little ones. At first, people stared and whispered, but the sight of the Bitterness chittering and obeying Jissa soon charmed them into smiles. Before long, the Black Castle was filled with the sounds of children's laughter as they attempted to catch the Bitterness—who were delighted at the attention, but never wavered from their devotion to Jissa.

"I think," Micah said to Liliana in a rare moment of quiet on the castle roof, "that the Bitterness are here to stay."

"Them, I welcome." She touched her fingers to his

arm. "He has sent the monsters for me. You must know that."

He didn't know why she told him that. Did she think he would turn her away so as to escape the Arachdem? The thought annoyed him. "Good," he said, "then I'll give you to them at the edge of the village and they'll return from whence they came."

A small pause, then an even smaller voice. "I'm sorry."

Frowning at the bloody black of the sky, he shot her a glowering look. "Don't be sorry. Help me halt this army."

"The Arachdem are his greatest weapon," Liliana said, an odd catch in her voice. "He has never been defeated when he has brought them into battle with him."

Micah didn't like the sound of that, but he also knew that this was his domain. The power of the Abyss would respond to no other, and would sing for him. "He has never before attempted to breach the Abyss." Something pushed at him from the back of his mind, an insistent prodding. "Their eyes shine red in the dark—like living embers of flame, and they carry pure poison in the sacs on their legs."

Liliana's expression turned desperate. "Do you remember?"

"What?" Shaking his head, he dislodged the odd prodding.

"*Please* don't fight it."

But he barely heard her, his attention caught by a roiling cloud in the distance. "I must go. They're almost here." Turning, he caught her startled lips in a kiss that warmed him to the core, before he rose into the air on leathery wings meant for hunting shadow prey.

The sky thundered, menacing shades of red and black licking at the horizon. He dived down through the ugliness of darkest sorcery, to see another layer of black. But this one was furred and moving, flashes of gleaming metal catching the light as the huge spiders crawled forward on razor-armored legs; there were so many of them that they covered the bubbling lava pools that had kept out intruders for aeons. He wondered how they did not drown in the agonizing heat of the pools—until he swept lower and saw that they were using the bodies of their fallen as a bridge.

It was no surprise.

The Arachdem were, after all, a creation of the blackest blood magic. It was said that the Blood Sorcerer himself, the one who had done more evil than the others combined, the one who sought to live forever and escape the Abyss, had formed them before— A wicked lance of pain swept through his mind, trying to disgorge thoughts his consciousness wouldn't accept. It had him gritting his teeth as he hovered above the coruscating mass of the Arachdem.

They stopped as one.

Their heads lifted up, their many eyes holding him in their sights.

CHAPTER NINETEEN

HE DIDN'T FLINCH. "YOU trespass," he said, his voice amplified a thousand times over. "Turn back before you fall into the Abyss."

A high keening sound was his only answer, an unintelligible noise from minds that knew nothing but destruction and pain. The Arachdem didn't only kill; they ate the bodies of their victims until not even the slightest sliver of bone remained. But they weren't scavengers. No, the Arachdem were hunters, eating anything living in their path. They didn't mind if it was still screaming as it went in.

He didn't know how he knew that, but he had no doubt of its truth.

Now, their heads lowered and they resumed their relentless march. At this pace, they would hit the perimeter of the village in an hour. Narrowing his eyes, Micah flew back toward the Black Castle, speaking on channels of magic that were of the Guardian as he did so, commanding the land to awaken and protect itself.

The rise to consciousness of that land was a languid stretch at the back of his mind, a near-sentient presence that said, *???*

Trespassers, he said. *Those who should not be.*
!!!

Below him, the ground began to roll and ripple, cracking open to expose huge chasms filled with noxious gases and ropes of liquid magma. Shrill screams pierced the air at his back and he knew some of the Arachdem had fallen prey. Still more fell when the land rose up into mountains, then crashed down on the invading army.

But the Arachdem were creatures of blood magic, and they had their defenses. They stabbed the earth with poisons enhanced with sorcery, tainting its strength. It cried in Micah's mind, and he told it to rest, to hide, to regroup. It had done enough, for when he circled back, the army had been cut in half, the formation straggling and broken, the bridge of bodies having sunk too deep for the survivors to cross the lava pools.

The Arachdem would recover, but the earth's rebellion had brought Micah and his people more time. At least another hour, perhaps even two. It would have to be enough. Diving through the clouds, he made his way back to the castle, where Bard had formed the able-bodied into a last line of defense, their backs to the castle walls.

A small group of men, however, stood apart, on top of the battlements. If Micah fell, they would lower the final gate, sealing the Black Castle from intruders. The defenders had orders to run inside, but some would inevitably be left behind, prey to the Arachdem. It wasn't an outcome Micah would permit.

Landing beside Bard and Liliana, he said, "Send them all through the gates."

"They want," Bard boomed, "to fight. To protect."

But Liliana was nodding. "They possess no offensive magics and thus stand no chance against the Arachdem." A pause. "Though if Micah were my father, he'd send those men out in front—the Arachdem slow when they are feeding."

"Your father doesn't sound like a good man, Liliana."

Micah couldn't imagine such a man having fathered someone like his storyteller—who cried because she'd torn her red dress and kissed him so sweet and tender.

"No." A choked laugh. "He isn't."

"Bard." Micah nodded. "Lead them inside. Tell them they must save the castle from falling, for if it falls, all is lost." The truth was, if the Arachdem reached the castle, it meant Micah was dead, at which point the defenses of the Black Castle would engage on their own. Those defenses were impressive— a shield of black nothing could penetrate—but it took the death of a Guardian to raise them.

However, every man had his pride, needed to know that he could protect his home and his family, and so Micah said this thing that Bard's eyes told him wasn't the truth. "They must," he said to the big man.

Bard finally rumbled his acquiescence and began to head back, but Micah stopped him. "Do not return, Bard."

A silent look that made the air go still.

"You cannot." He held the man's intelligent, scholarly eyes. "If I fall, the next lord will need your guidance."

Bard's expression filled with defiance, but Micah shook his head and, at long last, Bard nodded. His footsteps thundered on the earth, followed minutes later by the sonorous echo of his voice as he gave the villagers their new orders. There were raised shouts, resistance, but Bard was a general. He got what he wanted.

Soon, only Micah and Liliana stood on the edge of the village, the Black Castle looming beyond the Whispering Forest. "If I order you to leave," Micah said, knowing she wouldn't go, not his brave Liliana, but needing to protect her, "what will you do?"

"Hit you with a stick." She followed her words with a gentle Liliana kiss. "I stand with you, Micah."

So soft was his Lily. But that didn't mean she wasn't strong. He didn't attempt to send her to safety again. "They haven't lowered the final gate," he said, having risen into the air to check.

"Of course not. They'll wait until the last possible moment, until they're certain we won't make it."

"Do you believe we won't?"

"Never." Her voice was fierce. "You carry the heart of a kingdom, Micah. This will not defeat you."

He didn't understand her words, though they nudged awake that violent pain in his head once more, stabbing and jabbing. "Your blood is strong," he said, shoving away the excruciating sensation.

"Not as strong as his."

"I give you mine freely." He curved his hand around her nape. "If the time comes, take it and use it to protect my people, my realm."

Her changeable storm-sky eyes filled with power compelling and haunting. "Whatever happens, you *must return.* Do you understand?"

He assumed she spoke of the Black Castle, and so he nodded.

Liliana's expression changed to one he couldn't read. "Micah, I have something to tell you. I thought to do it this morning, but—"

"After, Lily," he interrupted. "I sense them closing in. It's time."

"Wait!" Grabbing his arm when he would've lifted it to call upon the dark strength of the Abyss, she rose on tiptoe to press her lips to his own.

Not at all averse to this, he reached down to squeeze her bottom. Gasping, she broke the contact. "You're not supposed to do that when I give you a kiss on the eve of battle."

He squeezed again, pulling her into a deliciously deep and wet kiss. "More later." With that, he released her and threw his arms wide in a call to power.

Awaken. Arise. Defend.

Again, the earth trembled, but this time, it was not to act against the menace, but to disgorge the inhabitants of this realm that lived in layers deep underground. The kitchari were large sluglike creatures, pale, heavy and slow, their many eyes milk-white with blindness, their legs clawed and stumpy, their mouths wide maws filled with sharp teeth that constantly shifted. Making an eerie screeching sound, the lumbering creatures heaved themselves up onto the ground, their bodies gleaming in the red light that was the sky.

"They're so slow," Liliana said in horror. "They'll be slaughtered."

Smiling, he called a second time. *Fly. Fly and protect.*

A rush of air pushing back his hair and then the sky filled with another kind of darkness. Huge black birds with serrated beaks and clawed wings squawked and screamed their way into battle.

At the same moment, the kitchari met the Arachdem.

LILIANA WANTED TO AVERT her eyes from the slaughter she was certain was going to ensue, but she owed it to the innocent lives about to be lost to stand witness.

The first spider reared up, ready to strike down the awkward creature below. Its poison-tipped leg sliced down into that pale body...to break off with an audible snap. Disabled in one leg, the spider foundered—and found itself being consumed in a rather methodical fashion by the large, clumsy creature with milk-white eyes.

Liliana's own eyes went wide. "Goodness."

Beside her, Micah laughed. "The kitchari can eat for days without stopping, and they aren't picky about what they eat."

However, in spite of the considerable damage the creatures were doing, they were slow and single-minded. So when one spider was being consumed, the other Arachdem climbed over their unfortunate brethren to continue on toward the village. And, it appeared the kitchari did have one weakness—their eyes. A stab from a razored leg into those orbs had them writhing in pain before the poison turned their bodies bruised and rigid in death. "The Arachdem can communicate!" she yelled to Micah, slicing her arm to release her blood.

Using her sorcery, she crushed the spiders back with a gale-force wind she could only maintain for a bare instant. However, it was enough time for Micah to warn the kitchari. Instead of sliding away into their tunnels, they simply lowered their heads, hiding their vulnerability from the Arachdem, who weren't flexible enough to reach under and through to the eyes. And they continued to eat.

At the same time, the birds Micah told her were called the anubi dived en masse toward the army, heading straight for the vulnerable joint between neck and torso. The attack was stunningly successful, leaving the front wave of Arachdem bleeding and paralyzed. Of which the kitchari took absolute and loud advantage, their teeth crunching through bone and flesh and tendon with calm, steady relish.

The back wave of her father's menace halted, waited. When the anubi sounded the next aerial attack, they raised their front legs and sprayed poison directly at the birds. Screaming, half of them fell to the ground, while the others beat frantically up into the sky, scared into keeping their distance. Still, between them, the anubi and the kitchari had given Liliana time to spin a more complex bit of blood sorcery, while beside her, Micah literally hummed with power, so much of it that he was a gleaming blade, covered head to toe in the black armor, his face threaded over by a network of fine tendrils.

Cold whispers along her neck, her sides, and she knew the ghosts were coming to aid them. She couldn't harness their chill power, but she whispered her thanks and felt them flow into Micah, who was a black diamond, a living weapon.

Stepping forward, Liliana completed the line of blood she'd laid down earlier from one corner of the village to the other. A hazy shield sprang up in front of them. By definition, a line couldn't be anywhere near as strong as a circle, for it was open, but it was enough to cripple the spiders who had survived the kitchari and the anubi to slam up against it. Dissolving in the blood acid that resulted when they touched the shield, they fell to their deaths. But her father's creations were not stupid creatures.

That was the Blood Sorcerer's genius—he'd made them just smart enough to comprehend danger and respond to it in a logical fashion. Now, they fell back—waiting rather than wasting time by circling around the line. They knew her blood wasn't as strong as their master's, didn't taste of innocent sacrifice, wouldn't last long.

Already, her arms were trembling. "Micah."

"When I give the word, Liliana, you must let it fall."

She nodded, biting the inside of her mouth to spill blood onto her tongue as she tried to find the strength to hold her ground. When her legs shook, she went to her knees, but maintained the shield.

"Now."

Her arms dropped and so did the acidic haze.

Shrieking, the Arachdem rolled forward. She scrambled backward on her hands, screaming for Micah to run. But he ignored her, standing rooted to the ground as the spiders arced up on their back legs above him, poisonous claws ready to slice down. Sobbing, she scrambled forward, thinking to create a desperate blood-circle to protect him. Her hand had just brushed his calf when a fury of knife-sharp black spikes taller than a man rose up in front of him. The spikes ranged deeper than the width of the Whispering Forest…covering the area where so many of the Arachdem had amassed.

Stunned at the sheer depth of his power, she sat silent, watching as the hideous creatures were impaled, their putrid yellow blood staining the earth.

MICAH PULSED WITH POWER, with the heartbeat of the Abyss. But beyond the roar was another—that of memory. Of seeing the Arachdem advancing on his home. Their eyes had been red embers in the gray time before true dawn, their furred bodies making a susurrating sound as the razors on their legs cut through those who tried so valiantly to defend the castle and its inhabitants. His father was out there, he knew, holding the line. His mother had put him in this room, told him to stay put. She was in another part of the castle, healing the injured, helping those she could. He knew that because Nanny had told him.

"Nanny," he said, his fingers turning white on the windowsill. "Why are the monsters coming to get us?"

Nanny's hands were warm and wrinkled on his shoulders. "Because the Blood Sorcerer wants to steal Elden."

"He can't, can he?"

"No," Nanny said, but Micah heard a hesitation in her voice, and it scared him.

Below them, the horrible monsters crushed the soldiers, and though Micah knew he was supposed to love his subjects as family, he was only a child who knew the man who was the foundation of his world fought below. "Father," he whispered. "Father."

"He'll be fine," Nanny said, her hands tightening on Micah's shoulders. "He is the king and kings do not fall." The absolute conviction in her voice convinced him, but he couldn't turn his eyes from the carnage below, the air filled with screams and scents that made his stomach churn.

It was as the Elden forces began to fall back that Micah saw the man in the center of the chaos of spiders. Tall and spidery thin himself, he held a staff of twisted and blackened wood, his fingers appearing like claws to Micah's suddenly crystal-clear vision.

Magic, he'd realize as an adult; it had been magic that had let him see so clearly, forged from his natural connection to Elden. But that night, all he knew was that he could see the monster within the other monsters, and a chill came into his heart, his young mind comprehending that that one was the worst of them all.

Then the man with the nightmare face looked up, his gaze zeroing in on the window from where Micah watched. It was a child's urge to hide, to turn away, but he locked his eyes with those of dirty ice and saw the bad man's lips form the words, "I'll get you, *boy.*"

"No," Micah whispered. "You never will."

CHAPTER TWENTY

THE MEMORY FRACTURED, BUT it was all there now, just waiting for him to look, to see. As the Arachdem who hadn't been impaled screamed and scuttled away, giving up the fight, he opened the mental doorway a little. Names and places, scents and sounds, and pain, such *pain* rocketed through him. He'd been thrown through time and space itself, his body locked in a spell meant to protect and cast in desperation as Elden fell.

His mother's spell had found unlikely expression in the cool, quiet room below the Black Castle, where it was said the new Guardian always appeared when it was time. But he'd been too young when he arrived, had spent years in sleep, rising only when he could take on the mantle. Of the old lord, he knew only what the ghosts had told him—that he had chosen to return to the place from whence he'd come, to spend the rest of his years far from the Abyss.

But none of that mattered. What mattered were those eyes of dirty ice.

Retracting the spikes formed of the earth's elements once he was certain the spiders wouldn't regain their courage and return, he held up his exhausted body through sheer strength of will as he turned to face the woman who scrambled up to her feet, unhidden concern in her expression. However, he halted her with a palm held flat out when she would've touched him.

Those eyes…those *eyes* looked at him with a dawning comprehension that turned them dull and distant. "You know."

"You lied to me, Liliana." He'd seen storm skies in those changeable eyes, and yet all this time, they had been filled with lies.

She flinched, stayed silent.

"You didn't tell me your father is the sorcerer who stole my parents' lives." He couldn't bring himself to ask about Nicolai, Dayn and Breena.

Swallowing, she fisted her hands. "I needed you to trust me, to remember."

"Why?" Something niggled at him, a half-remembered dream.

"The twentieth anniversary of Elden's fall is almost upon us," Liliana said, hugging herself. "You must be at the castle before midnight on that day."

Micah gripped her upper arms. "Why? *Tell me.*"

"At midnight, Elden will die…and so will your siblings." Instead of attempting to break his rough hold, she touched hesitant fingers to his chest. "After today, there are only two more days left and the road to Elden is long and filled with many dangers. I may be able to take you halfway using the spell that brought me here, but it'll drain me—and I must fight beside you, for my father is an evil man bloated with power."

Letting her go, he stepped away from her touch. Hurt filled her eyes and it made him want to rage, but he was so angry at her, the wildness of it leaving him near wordless.

"I know," she whispered in a broken kind of a voice. "I know what I stole from you. I don't expect you to feel the same toward me now that you know whose blood runs in my veins, but *please,* Micah, you must believe me. You must or your family will be forever lost."

"It's not your blood," he said, rising into the air, rejuvenated by the powerful magic of the Abyss. "It's the fact that you lied to me."

LILIANA WATCHED MICAH disappear into the clouds on those strange leathery wings that had formed from the ether, aware he was chasing the last of the Arachdem to ensure they wouldn't return. But he was also getting away from her—a woman who had lied to him. However, regardless of what he'd said, she knew that couldn't be the sole reason for his fury.

How could he bear to touch her when her visage was an ugly feminine echo of her father's? When her eyes were those of the Blood Sorcerer? When her hooked beak of a nose was a replica of the man who had murdered his parents? There was nothing of her mother in her beyond the color of her skin, as if he'd stolen that, too, when he locked Irina in a spell of haunting blindness to the child she'd borne.

The sky above her began to fill once again with blue, the purity of it mocking her pathetic attempt at escaping the truth of her murderous lineage.

"I'm sorry," she whispered. "I'm so sorry."

But Micah wasn't there to hear her, and when the sun blazed dark orange as it sank toward the mountains, the kitchari having cleaned up the Arachdem corpses and returned to the earth, he wasn't there to hold her...never would be again. Forcing herself not to think of that lest she become paralyzed by the pain, she spent the last half hour before sunset working with Jissa to pack enough supplies for the journey to Elden, though she didn't yet know how they would cross the border between realms, or navigate her father's vicious traps to reach the castle. "We'll find a way," she said. "We will."

"What?" Jissa asked. The brownie was more than a little confused over Liliana's sudden desire to pack supplies, but she was doing everything she could to assist.

"Time," Liliana answered. "We just need enough time, for though he'll lose the power of the Abyss after he leaves this realm, he is an earth mage, and will have not only his personal magic but the strength of Elden at his command once we reach the kingdom." Except his land was crushed and broken, its spirit in tatters.

"Liliana." Jissa's small, warm fingers on her arm. "Why are you crying?"

"Oh," she said, trying to rub off the tears and failing because they kept falling. "I must look a fright. Worse than usual." Grabbing the handkerchief the brownie held out, she slid down into a sitting position in among the bags of apples and flour, the chittering mass of the Bitterness whispering around her, their tone as close to a croon as the creatures could manage. Her oldest friend in the castle snaked in between them to nudge at her with his nose, his small magic sparking in distress.

Their tenderness only made her cry harder for she deserved none of it.

"Liliana." Jissa's concerned voice. "Come, come."

Somehow, she ended up with her head in Jissa's lap, crying her heart out. The brownie stroked a careful hand over and over her hair, murmuring things Liliana didn't really hear, but that gave her some small measure of comfort. The gaping hole that Micah had made in her when he walked away would never heal, but this brittle healing, it would allow her to get through the days to come.

There wouldn't be many—the death spell would ensure it, cleansing the taint of the Blood Sorcerer once and for all.

SHE WAS SITTING IN THE BATH off her room just after sunset, trying to wash off the stink of her own perfidy when Micah walked in. Heart a giant twisting pain, she looked up to find him covered neck to toe in armor. "Are you ready to leave?" she asked, barely keeping herself from begging for something to which she had no right.

"No." A single hard word. "I must remain here tonight to ensure the Arachdem don't return."

"Yes, of course." Her father's creatures had just enough cunning for that, but they wouldn't be capable of waiting beyond that time. "You'll be going out into the night again?"

"There's no need. The land knows to be aware—it'll warn me if it senses their approach," he said in that same harsh tone so unlike the Micah she knew.

And loved. So much.

"Now," he ordered, "you will tell me everything."

So she did, laying out her vision, what she thought would happen, what she knew. "The watch in your room—I think the queen anchored the spell to it, so you'd know when time was about to run out."

Arms folded, he stared down at her. "You didn't tell me this at the start."

"I tried. You weren't ready to listen, to remember."

A scowl. "You didn't try very hard."

She'd thought she had, but perhaps she hadn't. Maybe she'd actually been doing everything she could to extend this fragile fantasy of a life with the man who had become her very heart. "I'm sorry." Putting the soap on the rim, she wished for him to pick it up, hold it away from her, anything the old Micah would've done, the one who hadn't looked at her with that dark judgment in his gaze.

He didn't move.

Biting the inside of her lip, she pushed back wet strands of the hair she'd pinned up and said, "Elden Castle is very well fortified." If she focused on the practical side of their task, then maybe it wouldn't feel as if knives were shredding her to pieces from the inside out. "It stands in the middle of a lake."

"I know."

"The lake," she added, "is now full of fish that like to feed on human flesh."

The Blood Sorcerer enjoyed throwing "scraps" out the window and watching the fish jump and snap—at the hacked-up pieces of magical creatures, human beings. He'd once put Liliana in a thin, woven basket and lowered her so close to the water that she'd felt the snapping teeth of the fish a bare inch from her on every side. She'd been eight years old at the time.

Fighting back the memory of horror with resolve gained from experience, she continued. "There's a connecting causeway to the shore, but it's guarded night and day by large poisonous creatures who were once blue sand scorpions and are now nothing that should exist." A single sting equaled instantaneous death. "There are four of them. Two stand at the gate, while two prowl up and down the causeway."

"Why are you scared of the lake?"

Jerking up her head, she stared at Micah. "What?"

"You're scared of the lake." His eyes pinned her to the spot. "Tell me why."

"My father is an evil man," she said, because what

else was there to say? "I was a great disappointment as a daughter."

When Micah said nothing, simply watched her with eyes of cool winter-green, she began to feel as if she was drowning, though the water only came up to her shoulders. "I'd like to get out now," she said. "I need to prepare dinner."

For a second, she thought he'd refuse to leave and part of her wanted him to do exactly that—because it was something the old Micah would've done, the one who was sly and arrogant and liked to tease her in wicked, wicked ways. But this Micah—the one who had every right to hate her—pushed off the wall and stalked out, slamming the door behind himself. Trying for the ice-cold will that had allowed her to survive her father, she found only the hot burn of tears.

Stupid, stupid Liliana.

Her harsh imprecations didn't assuage the rawness in her throat, but a splash of cold water on her face after she left the bath had her eyes clearing at least. Rubbing herself dry, she once more put on the ugly brown dress in which she'd arrived, though it was dusty from the fight with the Arachdem. It seemed only fitting. She was no longer the woman for whom Micah had brought dresses of chocolate and red, green and silver.

Combing her hair straight, she stared at her face in the mirror.

It's a good thing you're my daughter or you'd be spit at like a mongrel dog on the street. As it is, men beg to come to your bed, even knowing they'll have to do the deed with their eyes closed.

Her stomach revolted at the memory and the only way she kept down what little she'd eaten was because she refused to give her father the satisfaction. Back then, she'd been young, a cowering animal on the floor that he'd kicked at with steel-toed boots to emphasize his words. Now she was a woman who was going to drag him into the Abyss for the basilisks to feed on.

With that in mind, she opened the bathroom door and walked out to face Micah.

He wasn't there.

Her hand trembled on the edge of the door but she shook her head, said, "No more tears." There was no longer any room for self-pity. No room to mourn the loss of something that hadn't been hers to begin with; she'd been a thief, stolen so many moments, moments she'd never, ever thought to have. That stolen hoard would have to be enough.

Except now that she'd touched Micah, been touched by him, been looked at as if she was beautiful even though she knew she wasn't, it hurt much, much more than before, when she hadn't expected anything at all.

MICAH PROWLED THE GREAT hall until his patience ran out, "Where is my meal?" he roared so loudly the walls shook.

Dard turned baleful eyes on him. "Jissa will be scared."

"Find *her!*" If she had tried to run away, he'd throw her in the dungeon and chain her up with cuffs of iron forged in the burning cold of the Abyss.

The door opened on the heels of his command, the object of his anger walking in with a tray. "I'm sorry this is late, my lord." Her words were polite, reserved.

He scowled and went to grab a seat. The food she placed in front of him was some kind of a thick stew with rice, followed by fruit. She set it out and went to leave until he grabbed her wrist. "You will stay here." But he nodded at Bard to leave.

Liliana stood motionless beside him as he ate.

"Why are you scared of the lake?" he asked her once more.

She grew stiff. "I—"

He waited to see if she'd lie to him again.

"Just because," she said at last, "I was his daughter didn't mean I was safe from him."

Pulling her down with his grip on her wrist, he fed her a piece of fruit. "Sit. Eat. I need you healthy if we're to defeat your father."

Her lower lip trembled. He saw it. But she bit it and, tugging away her wrist, sat down at the table, began to force food into her mouth. He watched to make sure she ate what she should. "What did he do to you?"

She pushed away her plate, pressed her hands to her abdomen. "I was his to use, his to hurt in any way he saw fit. After all, he made me."

Micah slammed a fisted hand on the table, causing the plates to jump. "Stop sounding like that!"

Those eyes of no particular color that reflected everything were dull when she said, "I've offended you. I'm sorry."

He should have been happy that she felt so bad about lying to him. He should have made her apologize over and over. Except he didn't like the way she looked, the way her shoulders were hunched up, as if she expected him to hurt her. The realization enraged him. "You think I'll beat you!"

Liliana caught a plate before it would've skittered over the edge of the still-cracked table and crashed to the floor. "No, my lord. You need me to defeat my father."

Her shoulders straightened to reveal the line of her throat. "I'll give you everything I have."

He wanted to bite that throat.

Hard.

And suddenly, he had the answer. "You will make me be not angry."

Her gaze slammed into his. "What?"

"You will convince me not to be angry."

"How?" She shook her head, as if her thoughts wouldn't settle. "I can ask for forgiveness but—"

"No. Words aren't enough. You lied to me with words."

"Then?"

"Come." Taking her hand, he ordered her to leave the dishes and dragged her up the stairs and to his bedroom. "Here," he said, turning to trap her against the closed door. "This is where you will convince me to be not angry."

CHAPTER TWENTY-ONE

LILIANA'S MIND SIMPLY STOPPED working for several long seconds. Because before Micah had shut the door and pinned her to it, his arms braced palms-flat on either side of her head, her eyes had fallen on the massive four-poster bed with black sheets that she'd occupied the night before the Arachdem invasion. A bed in which she'd fallen asleep waiting for the Guardian of the Abyss.

"Liliana."

She scraped up her pride, set her jaw. "What if I say I don't want to?" Being with him again was a temptation almost beyond bearing, but she wouldn't degrade herself, not even to appease this man whom she'd foolishly thought had cared for her at least a little.

"I would touch you between the legs and prove you a liar."

He must truly hate her, to want to humiliate her this much. "Am I your prisoner?" she asked, shame a cold, cold rock on her heart; each and every memory of intimacy stained with an ugliness that made her want to tear out her soul because those memories were her greatest treasure.

Eyebrows lowering, he pushed off the door. "Go. Go, then." Turning away, he folded his arms.

He'd let her go.

Even after the lies she'd told him, and though he was so furious his eyes glittered hard as gemstones, he'd let her go—when he would have been perfectly justified in hurting her. *No,* she thought, *no.* That was the dark reasoning of a woman who had been raised in the house of someone who had treated her like a piece of property, his to break and bloody and beat.

For Micah, a man with honor that ran so deep and true it had survived the Abyss itself, hurting a woman would be anathema. Yet he'd brought her to his bedroom, demanded she defuse his anger. The proximity of the bed led to only one conclusion, but she knew it was the wrong one.

Hurting, confused, scared the hope inside her was a mirage, she took a page out of his own book and just asked, "Why did you bring me here?"

Silence.

Angry and frustrated, but wanting him more than she'd wanted anyone or anything—even her freedom— she stomped around to face him. When he refused to lower his head to meet her gaze, she slammed her fists on his armored chest. "I need to know, you big sulking beast!" It just slipped out.

And it made him glance down, his gaze blade-green, his words snarling with anger. "You wanted to leave. There's the door."

Glaring at him, she barely resisted the urge to kick at his booted foot. "I thought…" …*you wanted to humiliate me.* She bit off the words before they could escape, because to say those words would be to hurt him in a way this man should never, ever be hurt.

No. Words aren't enough. You lied to me with words.

"Liliana, you are not leaving."

This is where you will convince me to be not angry.

"Why are you not leaving?" It was a growl.

"We enjoyed each other in the great hall," she whispered, speaking past her embarrassment because she had to fix this. "On the chair."

His eyes gleamed and she knew, she *knew,* he was imagining her naked flesh on his own as she moved over the hot, hard ridge of his arousal. "I don't think you enjoyed it so very much."

"I did." Swallowing to wet a dry throat, she stood on tiptoe, realization a shimmering rain through her senses. "Please bend down a little."

"Why?"

"I'm trying to convince you to be not angry." There had been nothing brutal or cruel in his demand, in his dragging her to his room. Micah hadn't grown up in the world, didn't think in the ways of a sophisticated courtier or a world-weary seducer, had never had cause to learn to hide lies behind charm or to become jaded in his sexuality. For him, there was only pleasure in this act, only delight…and so he'd used it to give her a way to ask for forgiveness that would cause her no pain.

Sweet mercy but she loved him. "Micah, please."

He dipped his head an inch. Just barely enough to allow her to brace her hands on his shoulders and press her lips to the line of his throat. "Are you still angry?" A whisper.

"Very." He bent a fraction more.

Still on tiptoe, she suckled kiss after kiss along his neck, his folded arms pressing against her torso. When she stopped to go back down flat on her feet, his eyebrows drew together in a heavy scowl. Heart thudding from the taste of him—hot skin and salt and Micah— she said, "If you'd sit down on the bed, I could go about this easier."

Pure suspicion in his expression, but he stalked to sit on the edge of the bed, his thighs spread. Those thighs were thick with muscle and coated in black armor that flowed over him with gleaming faithfulness. Not giving herself a chance to change her mind, she kicked off her shoes and straddled him in an echo of their loving in the great hall, curving her legs behind his back and locking them at the ankles.

He caught her with his hands on her waist but didn't do anything else. Leaning down, she made good on her promise, suckling long, slow kisses down the other side of his neck. She stopped to lick at his pulse before retracing her journey. Still his hands remained locked in place, but his heartbeat pulsed hotter, faster…and his armor disappeared from his arms.

Wanting to moan at the sight, she reached out to shape and caress his bare skin, using her mouth on his jaw at the same time. His stubble was rough against her lips, a decadent sensation, his own lips firm. Moving her hand back to curve around his neck, she kissed him with soft sucks and licks.

It lasted about two seconds.

Fisting his hand in her hair, he angled her head the way he liked and then he devoured her mouth with a carnal intent so blatant that her legs clenched around the intrusion of his body.

"Are you wet between your thighs?" It was a rumbling question as he allowed her to breathe. Not giving her a chance to answer, he began to tug at her dress until it was over her bottom at the back, bunched between their bodies at the front. "Shall I touch you and find out?" Fingers playing over her thigh.

"I'll tell you," she whispered, breath coming in jagged gasps.

"You might lie." His fingers on the inside of her thigh now, so close to her underthings.

"I won't." She nuzzled at him with an affection that felt utterly natural when she'd never had a chance to be affectionate with anyone, having learned never to love anything or anyone after her father murdered Bitty, for the Blood Sorcerer would take that love from her. But she couldn't help it with Micah. "I promise."

The slightly rough skin of his finger stroked along the edge of the fine fabric. Her heartbeat accelerated, her breath coming in soft puffs of air. Part of her wanted him to make good on his silent threat, so starved was she for his touch. But the rest of her…she needed him to believe her. To forgive her.

"I'm still angry." Spoken against her mouth. "But I'll let you tell me."

Shuddering as he moved his hand back down to close over her thigh with stark proprietariness, she swallowed, said, "Yes."

"Yes?" He squeezed her thigh. "I want more words."

They stuck in her throat. Even after everything she'd done with Micah, all of it so scandalous it was obvious she was no respectable girl, she couldn't say such a thing. It was a step too far over the line.

Kisses on her cheek, along her jaw, back up to her ear. "Say the words, Lily." A husky order. "Say them and I'll suck your pretty little nipples for you."

Thunder roared in her ears, her mind overflowing with images of Micah's mouth at her breasts, tugging hot and deep and strong. Rubbing her cheek against the abrasive skin of his jaw as he caught the sensitive flesh of her earlobe between his teeth, licked, she said, "I…I'm…" Her throat dried up, her fingernails digging into his nape.

He released her earlobe. "I'll suck so hard." A coaxing whisper that was all male, as was the rigid cock pressed against her. "Until they're tight and pouty and make me want to use my teeth."

Sliding his hands down to her bottom, he repositioned her so she rode flush against his arousal. So hard and close that she realized the armor was gone. But he remained clothed in black, the fabric a thin barrier between them.

"For me, Lily."

And the words tumbled out. "I'm wet between my legs. Needy and hot and—"

A hand gripping her jaw, holding her in place as Micah took her mouth his way again, demanding entrance and then demanding her full participation. Thrusting her hands into his hair, she gave him everything. The taste of him, dark and compelling and wild, was in her every breath, in her blood itself.

It took a deep masculine groan, his hand squeezing her bottom, for her to realize she was rubbing herself against the hard ridge of his erection in time with the thrusts of his tongue in her mouth. Too needy to be shocked, she continued her wanton actions, not stopping even when he broke the kiss to taste his way down the line of her neck, sucking hard enough over her pulse that he had to have left a mark.

He encouraged her to shameless excess, using his grip on her to urge her to increase her speed, ride against him even harder. But the position wasn't quite right, and she couldn't rub against the spot she needed. Brazen in her frustration, she tried to get closer, was foiled by the bunched-up fabric of her dress. "Please touch me."

"That tiny nub?" Kissing her without waiting for an answer, he inserted his hand down the back of her underwear and touched her not where he'd said...but at the pulsing entrance to her body, pushing in with a single rough-skinned fingertip.

Her entire frame went taut, arrows of sensation spearing out to every extremity. She knew she was dampening his hand, knew she was writhing on him, but she didn't care. An instant later, the tiny muscles low in her body clenched hard.

It left her gasping for breath on his chest, her face buried against his neck. Murmuring in complaint when he removed his hand, she raised her head and watched with passion-hazed eyes as he lifted his finger to his mouth and— *"Micah."*

"You taste good, Lily."

Wrung out from the pleasure that had just torn through her, she should've been limp and crawling. Instead, the place between her thighs tingled in anticipation, her breasts painfully tight against the coarse material of her dress.

"Now I will suck your nipples." With that, he took the front of her dress in both hands and tore.

She didn't protest, and all too soon, the coarse sensation was gone, to be replaced by the heated air. Her bare breasts rose up and down in a sharp rhythm, as if she was inviting his touch, but though he never moved his eyes off the small mounds, he didn't touch her there until he'd torn the upper half of her dress completely off her body.

Only then did he span her rib cage with his hands. The sensation was beyond wonderful, but nothing came close to the impact of those eyes watching her with absolute focus. "They're small," she blurted out, because she couldn't stand it anymore.

Micah's answer was to dip his head and suck one begging nipple into his mouth. Trembling from the hot burn of pleasure, she thrust a hand into his hair and held on for the ride. He sucked and rolled her nipple as if it was a favorite treat, playing and tugging with the unkissed one at the same time before covering her entire breast with his palm and squeezing.

"I like this," he said, raising his head to devour her mouth before glancing down at her breasts again.

Not sure she could take that depth of eroticism, she nonetheless followed his gaze. Shuddered. Her nipple pouted taut and wet from his mouth, her breast flushed and red under the brown of her skin. As she watched, he continued to fondle her other breast with a big, confident hand.

"Don't look away." Switching his focus with that husky order, he began to pet her already pleasured breast with his hand, his mouth closing over the nipple he hadn't earlier sucked. The first decadent tug had her crying out, her eyes locking with those of winter-green as his lashes lifted.

It was a shocking intimacy.

Perhaps that was why she said it. "Harder."

Making a rumbling sound in his throat, he shifted his free hand to her back and pressed her impossibly closer as he obeyed her command, taking more of her breast into his mouth at the same time.

"That feels so good," she said, scandalized at herself, but continuing to speak because Micah liked it. "The other one again. *Please.*"

Releasing her nipple with a wet sound, he demanded a kiss before giving her what she wanted, rolling and tasting her nipple as if it was a lushberry, one he intended to savor.

It made her wonder if he would give the nub between her thighs the same intense attention. "You make me have wicked thoughts."

"Good." He continued to suck and fondle her breasts with open enjoyment.

When she found the strength to whisper, "Are you still angry?" in his ear, he released her nipple with a graze of his teeth, and said, "Yes."

She kissed the spot beneath his ear, made her way down his neck to the seduction of his pulse. "Are you sure?"

"Perhaps once I've licked you between the legs, I'll change my mind."

Every nerve in her body quivered in response. She knew full well he wasn't angry at her any longer, but the Lord of the Black Castle had a way of getting what he wanted. So when he lifted her off him and placed her on the bed, she didn't protest. Neither did she protest when he pulled away the remains of her dress, to leave her clothed only in thin underwear so soaked through it clung to the plump folds between her legs.

Coloring as he spread her thighs to kneel in between, she said, "I want to give you pleasure." Her eyes dropped to his erection, so rigid behind the black material of his pants. "I could...I could suck you, too."

A hard, possessive brand of a kiss. "You will," he said, rising back into a sitting position. "Later."

Her mouth watered. Never had she expected to have a lover, but she was a woman. She'd had dreams. However, not even in her most secret dreams had she dared hope for a lover who would be so unabashed about what he wanted and liked that he turned her bold and sinful, too.

Shifting so she could close her legs, he said, "Turn over."

Surprised, she did as asked. He didn't torture her with suspense, spreading her thighs again and resettling himself. Then he tugged her underwear down to just below the curve of her buttocks, as if framing the sight. Clenching her fingers in the sheets, she forced herself not to wiggle, not to protest, though she was mortified by the spectacle she must present.

Micah's hands on her flesh. "You're soft here, Lily."

She moaned, because his hands, those strong, confident hands, felt exquisite on her.

"I like that sound you make," he said, leaning down to lave kisses on her neck, the heat and weight of him making her feel deliciously trapped.

She protested when he rose back up, but he trailed a single bold finger down the cleft of her buttocks and parts of her mind just hazed over. Then he started talking.

"When I've been inside you two or three times," he said, squeezing and petting, "then I will lie over you thus while we are both naked and rub my cock along here." That bold finger returned. "Would you like that, Lily?"

CHAPTER TWENTY-TWO

Sinful, that question was too sinful to answer. But she did so, anyway, because she wouldn't lie to Micah ever again. "Yes."

"Good." Sliding one hand under her even as he spoke, he cupped a taut, sensitive mound, capturing her nipple between thumb and forefinger. "I like your nipples as much as this." A luxuriant caress over her exposed curves, his hand hot, his skin rough.

She couldn't take it anymore. Bucking against him, she somehow managed to get herself onto her back, her hair sticking to perspiration-damp skin, her legs tangled up in her underwear. Micah tore them off, allowing her to spread her legs around his big body. She tugged at the thin black material that covered his chest. "Take this off." She'd seen but not had the chance to caress him as she'd wanted in the great hall. "I want to kiss you there."

He smiled.

And she realized she'd become as bad as him.

But there was something to be said for being upfront in her demands because he rose up onto his knees and tugged the fabric off over his head to throw it to the floor. Reaching up as he came back down over her, she splayed her hands over the heated silk of a chest that would have surely sent her to ruin if he hadn't already taken care of that several times over. Lightly covered with curls of golden hair that arrowed down in a thin line to the waistband of his pants, it made her want to lick and bite and do things she'd never, ever considered doing to a man.

When she curved her hands over his sides, tugged him down, he lowered himself until she could reach him with her mouth. Oh, but he felt good against her lips, her tongue. The satin of his skin, the crisp roughness of his chest hair, the salt of his scent. She went to hook a leg over his waist, but he shifted, taking her with him so she ended up on top.

Too delighted at her new ability to explore him as she wished to worry about the wandering hands that stroked along her back to close over one of his favorite parts of her body, she kissed her way down to a flat male nipple. When she opened her mouth over it and sucked as he'd sucked hers, he fisted one hand in her hair. "Again, Lily."

Melting at the growl she could feel beneath her palm, she obeyed. When she lifted her head, he said, "Why are you stopping?" The hand fisted in her hair nudged her back down.

She resisted. "The other side."

He didn't stop her as she tasted and explored him as she'd wanted to do for so long. Rubbing her cheek against his chest, she stroked her hand down his body, so hard and muscled and strong and beautiful—because he was Micah, who saw beauty in her, too, until she could almost see what he saw.

Pressing kisses down his chest, past the ridged muscle of his abdomen, she nuzzled at the line of hair that disappeared into the black of his pants. When she lifted her head to find him braced on his elbows, eyes of wintergreen locked on her, she licked down the line. He made a rough, impatient noise deep in his chest. "I want your mouth on me."

Oh, yes. Scrambling off the bottom of the bed, she undid the closures on his boots and pulled. It almost sent her tumbling to the floor but she got the left one off, then the right. But before she could crawl back up to undo his pants, he swung off the bed to take care of the task himself.

Four seconds later, he was all bare skin and muscle. Only her grip on the bedpost kept her upright. Especially when he reached down to fist the long, thick pulse of his erection. Not consciously thinking about her actions, she climbed back onto the bed and knelt on the edge, waiting. Micah's fingers circled tight around the base of his cock as he walked to her.

"Doesn't that hurt?" she asked, resting her palms on the rock-hard strength of his thighs, the crisp hairs on him a delicious friction.

"A little." His breathing was rough, his skin hot. "But if I don't do this, I will spill in your mouth."

She clenched her thighs to quench the ache between. "I won't mind." Because this was Micah, the man she loved, the man who made her want to try everything and anything to see how it would feel. "You've tasted me," she whispered, her breath gusting over the engorged head of his cock. "It's my turn."

His groan was deep as she fit her hand below his and took him into her mouth. She didn't know what she'd expected, but loving him this way was better than anything she could've imagined. Though he was hard as rock, rigid and demanding, the skin against her tongue was almost delicate, the taste of him a dark musk that made her his slave.

"That feels good." The guttural statement was followed by the removal of his hand.

He began to move in shallow thrusts against her

tongue an instant later. Moaning, she sucked harder, wanting to give him the same pleasure he'd given her. When his hand tangled in her hair, she expected a push, got it an instant later.

She just barely grazed him with her teeth.

He snarled. "Lily!"

Stroking her mouth off him in a slow, teasing motion, she looked up. "You were trying to take over."

The Guardian of the Abyss stared down at her. "And you are trying to make me be not angry."

She smiled, blew a breath over the hot length now gleaming wet from her mouth. "You're not angry."

Growling in pleasure, he pulled on her hair. "Suck me."

So wet between her legs that she might've been embarrassed by it had she not been so aroused, she held still as he slid between her lips, both of them craving the sensation. Except Micah's patience was on a short leash—he began to speed up his short, shallow thrusts. His hands moved to cup the sides of her face at the same time, his thighs going rigid beneath her palms. Taking him as deep as she could, she heard him groan. And then he was spilling into her mouth.

MICAH LAY SPRAWLED ON HIS back on the bed, his chest still heaving from the intensity of the pleasure that Liliana had wrung from him. When she came to cuddle up next to his body, he wrapped an arm around her and tucked her to his side where she should be. They lay like that for a long time—until his blood no longer pounded, and his body began to stir again.

Taking her hand, he slid it down to his cock. "Stroke me until I'm hard," he murmured, showing her what he liked best with his hand on top of hers. "I want to push inside you."

Her skin heated up against him, but she didn't hesitate in her caresses. "Are you never shy?"

Removing his hand because hers, soft and small, felt so much better, he said, "No." He didn't see the point of it. But Liliana was sometimes shy; he allowed it because he could tell what she wanted by her little cries and the way she twisted, and how damp she got, the scent of her earthy and erotic.

Making a rumbling sound deep in his chest, he gripped the back of her neck as she worked him with her hand. "We'll do this often when we're married."

She stopped her long, hard pulls of his cock. "You can't marry me, Micah."

Reaching down, he urged her to continue. It felt so good. "I'm the Lord of the Black Castle. I can do whatever I want."

Liliana jerked up and onto her knees, his erection sliding through her hand to jut into the air. "You're also a prince of Elden and my father is the Blood Sorcerer."

"So?" He decided he liked her in that position, her legs tucked under her, her heels resting against her bottom. Maybe he'd push into her from behind. That way, he'd feel her lush bottom against him, be able to play with her breasts and the sensitive nub between her thighs at the same time. Cock jumping at the idea, he reached out to stroke the plump lips he could see though the dark curls at the apex of her thighs.

Jerking, she gripped his wrist. "The people," she gasped out, "of Elden would hardly accept me."

"I'm the youngest prince," he pointed out, continuing to tease her with his finger. "I won't sit on the throne—

and even were I the eldest, I would still choose my own bride. Stop arguing."

She made as if to pull away so she could do exactly that, but Micah didn't want to speak anymore of something that wasn't a problem even if she thought it was. Shifting, he pressed her onto her back and spread her thighs in a single motion. He covered her with his mouth a second later.

"Micah."

He liked the way she said his name, all trembly and wanting. Finding the taut bundle of nerves that gave her much pleasure, he sucked on it. This time, her cry held an edge of desperation. Lifting his head, he saw that her eyes had gone dark as her pupils dilated, her chest rising and falling in a jagged rhythm.

He knew what she needed, what she wanted. Rising above her, he fit himself to the entrance of her body, driven not by experience, but by primal instinct. Then, dropping his mouth to her own, he began to push inside. A liquid-hot furnace gripped his cock. Groaning he broke the kiss to catch a breath—and found she'd wrapped her legs around him, was urging him to move faster with impatient rolling movements of her lower body.

"Lily." Shuddering, he thrust deeper. Deeper still.

Until she cried out, her nails digging into his back. "It hurts."

He froze, would've pulled out except that her legs remained locked around him. "Lily?"

"It's because I haven't done this before," she gasped. "I just…need a minute."

She felt so luscious that Micah wasn't sure he had the willpower to give her that minute, but then he remembered her cry of pain and knew he did. He wouldn't hurt

Lily. Even when he was very angry with her, he wouldn't hurt her. Maybe he'd growl at her a little, but she seemed not to mind that very much.

The thoughts were good ones, but they didn't help in keeping his mind off the fact that he was half-buried inside her, his entire body poised on the brink of the most delicious sensations he'd ever felt.

Sweat broke out along his spine.

She spoke against his lips. "Now, Micah."

Not asking her if she was sure, he pushed deeper. She made another sound, but this one didn't have any hurt in it. Kissing her, stroking his hand down to grip her bottom, he sank in to the hilt. *"Lily."* It was a groan.

Liliana's response was softer but no less passionate, her thighs clenching around him. "Don't stop."

He moved out of her slow, pushed in as slow. It felt even better. So he did it again. Hot and tight and wet around him, her body soft where he gripped her, she was perfect. He found he was moving faster, thrusting into her in hard pulses, but she was with him, murmuring at him to hurry, kissing his jaw, his face, her nails digging into his sweat-slick shoulders. A last hard thrust and he spilled inside her with a low, deep sound of pleasure, able to feel her muscles spasming as she bucked, gasped and went liquid around him.

Later, after they'd both managed to find enough strength to bathe, she snuggled up next to him and called him "darling." Micah decided he liked it. He'd allow her to call him darling, but only when they were alone. The Guardian of the Abyss couldn't be called darling, after all.

It was his last thought before slumber crept over him in a stealthy wave.

THEY LEFT THE BLACK CASTLE at first light.

Liliana finished organizing the food and other supplies, while Micah armed himself with knives and a long, lethally sharp sword that he carried in a sheath down his back—because once they left this realm, he would no longer be able to call on the power of the Abyss. He and Liliana would have to rely on the magic that resided within their bodies until they reached Elden—but to use too much of it would leave them weak and vulnerable.

"You will watch over the castle," he said to Bard. "The kitchari keep their eyes on the perimeter, and the anubi the skies. But the Arachdem shouldn't return." He'd sensed them leaving the realm when he woke with Liliana so warm and soft beside him.

Bard's soulful eyes were dark. "Be safe."

Nodding, Micah looked over at where Liliana—dressed in another one of those footmen's uniforms Jissa kept digging up—was saying goodbye to the brownie who owned Bard's heart. Jissa was distressed but not crying. The women hugged, tight and fierce, and then Liliana was by his side. "It's time," she said, glancing at the watch she carried for him on a chain around her neck, the one with a unicorn prince on its face.

The hands were almost to midnight.

Leaving without further goodbyes—though he did catch Liliana waving surreptitiously to a tiny twitching nose that appeared in the doorway—Micah walked them out to the stone garden and gathered her up in his arms.

AS MICAH ROSE INTO THE AIR ON wings of leathery brown, Liliana distracted herself by attempting to work out how they were going to get to the castle once they reached Elden. The lake was impassable—her father's specially bred fish didn't hunger only for flesh, they would also devour any boat or raft not enspelled with the Blood Sorcerer's personal protections.

As for the walkway, the guards with the arms and tail of a giant scorpion and the teeth of a screaming banshee might once have been small, relatively harmless creatures, but no longer. Their lurching size meant she and Micah might possibly be able to move fast enough to avoid the whipping sting of their tails—but the risk would be a terrible one, not only because of the deadly nature of the creatures' poison, but also because they would be out in the open on the causeway, easy prey for any guards on the castle battlements.

A scorching wave, on the fine border between bearable and painful.

Glancing down, she glimpsed bubbling lava pools belching heat. Dark red and angry, the pools were rumored to be so hot that should a man fall into one, he'd be so much liquid between one breath and the next. Something moved below the viscous surface of one and when it pulled itself to the ledge with four-clawed hands, she saw it was a giant salamander, its brimstone eyes watching their progress with a greed that said should they come too near, it would reach out with its fiery tongue and drag them down to its lair for a slow and torturous devouring.

Micah's arms tightened. "Don't be frightened, Lily. Nothing can touch us here."

Not taking her eyes off the salamander, she said, "My father burned me with a salamander once. I'm so afraid of them." She'd never before shared her fear with anyone, never before had anyone whom she'd trusted not to use that fear to torment her.

Micah's wings made batlike flapping sounds as he

flew faster over the lava pools. "I will kill your father, and then you won't be afraid anymore."

The order—and it was that—made her want to laugh, even as fear lingered in her veins. Then they were leaving the bubbling pools behind to traverse a barren stretch of desert, the sand appearing to glitter with shards of precious gems. "Micah," she said some time later, frowning at what she saw, "your wings."

"I know." Descending on hot gusts of air, he landed on the brilliant desert sands flecked with red and blue and aquamarine.

She put down the small supply pack she'd been holding and asked him to spread his wings, checking the places where the leathery material had gone translucent. A fine webbing continued to hold muscle and tendon together, but it was fragile, easily damaged. "It must be because you're carrying me," she said, frowning. "The strain—"

"No." Dropping his sword to the sands, he angled his head into the blistering desert winds. "There is a subtle poison in the air. It's been weakened by entry to this realm and won't harm our bodies, but my wings, it appears, are vulnerable."

"Me," she whispered, knowing the poison spell was anchored to her blood. "This poison attacks us because of me."

CHAPTER TWENTY-THREE

"STOP THINKING ABOUT HIM, Lily." Micah scowled at his wings. "Focus on how we will thwart the poison, because without my wings to carry us to the Great Divide, we won't make it in time."

Shaking off the cold inside her, she touched one of the translucent patches. "Does it hurt?"

"Yes."

Her head jerked up, hand dropping. *"Micah."*

"It's all right." Reaching back, he poked a hole through the damaged patch. "It's no use. They're disintegrating."

As Liliana watched, the edges of his wings began to curl inward. Horror roiled into her stomach. "You mustn't take the wings back into your body."

"I don't know where they come from, but yes, if they do return to my body, then the poison may succeed in attacking me from the inside. I shouldn't die while in this realm, but your father's magic is twisted." Reaching into his boot, he pulled out a large hunting knife. "You must cut them off, Lily. I can't reach."

Her stomach threatened to revolt at the idea of it, but she didn't hesitate, because if she knew her father, the poison would cause Micah excruciating pain before it killed him. Taking the blade, she shut out everything else, and then, for the first time in her life, took a knife to a living being by choice.

The material of his wings was tough, and she nearly sobbed in grateful joy when the first cut didn't bleed. But she knew it was hurting Micah, though he didn't make a single sound. "Almost there," she whispered, throat raw. "Just a little longer, darling."

The second curled-up wing fell to the glimmering sand so hot it was starting to sear the bottom of her boots. "There." Checking the two thin ridges of tissue that remained on his back, she couldn't see any sign of the poison, but biting down on her lower lip, she used a smidgen of blood magic to make certain. "You can retract those pieces."

He collapsed to his knees even as the stubs of his wings disappeared into his flesh, black armor closing over the slits. Dropping the knife, she knelt before him, uncaring of the sands burning through her tights. "I'm sorry, Micah. I'm so sorry." Wrapping her arms around him, she kissed and petted and stroked until he stopped shivering and stood, taking her with him.

"Without my wings," he said, once more the Lord of the Black Castle, "we'll need another way to reach the border between realms."

Now that she could think again, she became aware of the blazing heat once more. "I could use my blood," she said, beads of sweat trickling down her spine, the valley between her breasts.

Micah shook his head. "No, we need to conserve as much of our strength as possible. Your father is a powerful adversary."

"Is there another way to use the magic of the Abyss to get us to the border?" Putting her hand up to shade her eyes, she looked around, saw nothing but endless sand in every direction, shimmering and rolling with waves of incandescent heat.

"Yes." Micah gave her a solemn look. "I can call one of the giant salamanders to carry us the rest of the way."

Bile rose up in her throat. "It'll burn us alive." The creature's very skin was fire.

"I will protect us," he said with a gentle caress on her cheek. "You must trust me, Lily."

The child inside of her, the one who had smelled her flesh sear to the sound of her father's cruel laughter, scrabbled in panic, but she nodded. "Do it."

He was already covered by the black armor, but now it swallowed him until only his face remained exposed. Throwing up his arms, he roared to the heavens. A responding roar sounded an instant later. All too soon, the sands began to ripple in a strange wind. When she looked up, it was to meet the hungry gaze of a salamander as it flew on wings of fire to land beside Micah.

Flicking out its forked tongue, it licked at the air, its multifaceted eyes locked on her as if on a particularly tasty snack. It took every ounce of courage she had to allow Micah to lead her to the beast, the heat of which was a burn against her senses. Dropping her hand, Micah jumped onto the back of the creature, sword once more on his back but angled now. "Touch only me, Lily," he said, reaching down for her.

It wasn't easy, but he was strong, and he got her—and the supplies she carried—onto his lap without allowing any part of her to come into contact with the salamander. Curling up against him, she held on tight as he used one of his gauntleted and gloved hands to grip several of the thin, flexible spines that grew from the creature's scaly head. "Rise!"

With a bellow that belched flame, yellow and lethal, the salamander leaped into the air, its wings created by pure fire and thus unaffected by her father's curse of poison. Terror chilled the blood in her veins, made her teeth chatter, her chest twist to painful tightness.

The salamander continued to bellow with fiery breaths. "It's not happy," she managed to get out past the fear.

"It is an elemental creature. As with the wind, you cannot tame it." Angling his body to the left as the salamander banked away from a roiling spurt of sand that punched up from the ground, he tucked her impossibly closer. "It flies faster than I do. We'll reach the border in plenty of time."

It was, Lily knew, from that point on that their journey would become more difficult. Once they crossed the boundary between the realms, they would be in the kingdoms, but far from Elden. Covering the remaining distance on foot would take too long, so they'd have to find some other way, but that was a problem for another time. Right now, she had to focus on keeping her sanity.

Later, she would remember the hellish heat, the noxious scent of sulfur, but most of all, she would remember Micah's arm holding her, implacable and strong as steel, his body her haven. They flew for hours, over the glimmering sands, over the eerie marshlands filled with flickering lights and six-legged animals that loped and cackled, over the waving red grasses that hid the cunning predators with the sharp teeth, over the mountains of ice so cold a man without magic would freeze before taking a breath, until finally, they came to the rolling plains of verdant green.

The Great Divide lay on the other side.

Sweeping down, the salamander bellowed again, scorching the grasses to nothingness and burning the earth to black on landing. Alighting as quickly as possible, Liliana somehow managed to stay on her feet, though her legs were cramped, her muscles stiff. Heart in her throat, she fought not to scream for him to get away as Micah walked around to face the beast, so near that mouth that could easily belch flame. "I thank you, friend," he said, rubbing that huge scaly head with a gloved hand.

To Liliana's shock, the salamander dipped its head to the side, as if shy. Suddenly unable to bear her own cowardice, she forced her legs to move forward until she was close enough to look into one of those multifaceted eyes. "My thanks," she whispered, her voice hoarse.

Coming around to stand beside her, Micah said, "Fly home."

Wings of flame shot out on either side of the salamander and then it was ascending with a roar of yellow flame against the darkening sky. Tracking its blazing progress, she was forced to admit that it was a magnificent being—one that would forever scare her, that much she knew, but at least now the terror wouldn't debilitate.

"Come, Lily." Taking her hand in his, Micah led them to the very edge of the Great Divide.

A crossing such as this, she thought, must only exist in the Abyss and the Always. It offered passage to all of the realms, but the shimmering wall of magic could not be passed by most mortals. However, Micah, as the Guardian of the Abyss, had the right to cross it at will. "The ability is, I think," he'd said when she'd brought up the point, "a fail-safe lest one of the condemned manages to slip into another realm." Now, he touched his fingers to the rippling sparks of color, and it was as if the magic sighed in welcome. "Yes, this part of the crossing will take us to the kingdoms."

She came into the protection of his arms and he stepped through the barrier. The experience was… Like being kissed with magic, if such a thing was possible. Yet there was a subtle menace to the sensation—if she hadn't been held in Micah's arms, the shield would've repudiated her with wrenching violence.

"It's done."

Liliana saw that they were in a night-dark wood. "What is this place?"

"The path to a borderland village."

"Micah." She touched his left cheekbone—where he was now marked by the symbol of a sickle and a sword crossed. "The sign of the Abyss."

"To ensure no one forgets who it is who walks among them." He took her little pack. "Come—the screaming pines mark the village boundaries."

The trees lived up to their name as they approached, keening and wailing, their arms waving in agitation. As a result, the villagers beyond were waiting for them armed with scythes and pitchforks. A single look at Micah and they dropped their weapons, turning as pale as ghosts. A few ran. However, a sturdy man with a peg leg and a tremor along one side of his face walked forward. "My lord. Do you come for us?"

Micah put one gauntleted hand on the brave man's shoulder. "Your soul is not black. I seek the services of Esme."

A whispering sounded from the gathered villagers, but the shoulders of the man who'd spoken were suddenly set with pride. "She be my wife, then—I'm her George." A beaming smile. "Come with me, honored lord."

Liliana heard the words *ugly* and *hook-nosed crea- ture* as she passed, and though it hurt, it was a hurt she could shrug off. Because Micah didn't think she was ugly even though he knew about beauty, had seen the stunning women in the village below the Black Castle. "You didn't tell me about any Esme," she whispered.

He angled his head to stare curiously at a fat tabby cat that watched them from beyond the bubbled windowpane of some prosperous tradesman's house. "I didn't know if the wind mage lived here still. Bard has been gone from this realm for many moons."

"A wind mage." *Bard, I think I adore you.*

"Here we are," their guide said at that moment, leading them to a small cottage surrounded by cheery blossoms closed up for the night. "Esme! We have guests! Put on the stew!"

Suddenly realizing how hungry she was, Liliana said nothing to counteract the man's order as they followed him inside—to come face-to-face with a round dumpling of a woman with red cheeks that turned white as soon as she glimpsed Micah. "Now look here," she said, though her voice shivered with terror, "I don't do no evil."

"Bard sent us," Micah said before Liliana could attempt to assuage the woman's fear.

Esme's mouth fell open. "Bard?" Collapsing into a chair, though the Lord of the Black Castle stood in front of her, she gaped. "I did save his life once and he promised to repay me, but to send the Guardian…"

Micah retrieved a velvet pouch from their pack of supplies. "Payment."

Esme watched as her husband opened the pouch to pour a tumble of rubies, emeralds and diamonds onto his palm. He, too, collapsed into a chair. Not waiting for an invitation, Micah took a seat, and so did Liliana.

"For this much wealth, my lord," Esme said in a quiet, worried voice while her husband ignored what was a king's ransom to close his hand over her own, "ye either want my soul or my life."

"Neither. Lily."

Aware of the couple looking at her with stark curiosity, this odd creature who walked with the dread lord, she said, "We need to reach the heart of the kingdom of Elden before midnight tomorrow. You speak to the winds?"

Esme swallowed. "I'm no powerful mage, milady. I can only whisper."

Her husband shook his head, pride in every sinew and tendon. "My Esme can get you halfway to that godforsaken kingdom—pardon my words, my lord, but that's the way it is—and from there, ye ask for two night-horses from her sister Emmy's husband." He paused. "Night-horses be temperamental."

"I'm sure we'll be fine." She knew the powerful animals would serve Micah, for he was as pure of heart as any creature of the land. As for her, oddly enough, most animals seemed to accept her, in spite of her tainted blood.

"Right, then." George rubbed his thumb over Esme's knuckles. "With the night-horses, you'll be in Elden proper by tomorrow eve, well before midnight."

Liliana nodded. "Thank you." Perhaps her actions in going to Micah had changed the future so events wouldn't come to pass as she'd foreseen, but she could not—would not—take that chance. Nothing would be certain—Micah's land, his siblings not safe—until her father was dead.

NOT LONG AFTERWARD, HAVING eaten a simple, hearty meal, they stood in the flickering shadow of a torch held by George as his rose-cheeked wife said, "If ye would stand closer to one another." She twisted her hands together.

"Close as ye can. Otherwise, the wind might tear ye apart."

Micah wrapped his arms around her, strong as iron, as she slipped hers around his waist, his armor warm under her touch. Its presence confirmed her theory that the armor was created from his own innate magic. As such, it would protect him against her father—but not forever, for the Blood Sorcerer was a man malignant with the life force of innocents.

"Good journey, my lord and lady," Esme said, and lifted her hands.

Her face and that of her husband was obliterated by a tornado of wind an instant later, a tornado that ripped them from the earth and made them fly. If she hadn't been locked tight around Micah, she might well have been torn asunder in a spray of blood and flesh. As it was, she was aware of his body curving over her own in an effort to protect her from the punishing might of the wind.

Her Micah.

Strong.

Honorable.

Wonderful.

Liliana couldn't have said how long they traveled trapped within the windstorm, but she would've crumpled to her knees in the empty courtyard of what looked to be a small inn when the journey ended, had Micah not been standing solid as a stone wall beside her.

"Now maybe," he said, a touch of wickedness to him, "the salamander doesn't look so bad."

"I wouldn't go that—" She broke off as a couple, their nightclothes flapping at their ankles, clattered out of the inn, torches held aloft. "Micah, if they do indeed have night-horses, I think we should rest here," she said to him before Esme's sister—and with those cheeks, it was surely her—and her husband came within earshot. "It'll be the only chance we have before Elden."

Micah gave a single nod as the couple reached them. Emmy proved not as stout of heart as Esme—she took one look at the Guardian of the Abyss and fell into a dead faint. Scowling, Micah bent down, picked her up without effort and glared at her gaping husband. "Take us inside."

"Yes, my lord!" The man hurried ahead, his torch bobbing wildly above a head covered by a long white nightcap.

"Yes," he said when Liliana asked about the nighthorses while Micah placed the man's wife on a table, "we host a pair. My Emmy is a healer of beasts—they come to see her, stay awhile, help the travelers they like. Magical creatures, you know, can't force them to do anything."

The inside of the inn explained why they'd caught the couple so unprepared—the place was empty but for the four of them. "We used to be busy as bees, we did," the innkeeper muttered, his long face mournful. "Then *he* came and now everyone's too scared to pass this way. He's got monsters guarding the roads into Elden, hasn't he? And most folks, they passed this way toward the kingdom, didn't they? Such a wonderful place it was— sad what's become of it. Sad, indeed."

He continued to mutter away under his breath, not realizing he'd driven a spike of ice into Liliana's mind. She hadn't known about the monsters, hadn't prepared for them. What were they going to do? The time—

Fingers closing around the back of her neck, a small squeeze. "We will consider it in a few hours, Lily."

"Lord." The innkeeper bobbed his head. "Here we are. One room for the lady and one room for yo—"

"*One* room." Micah's tone left no room for argument.

The innkeeper's eyes swung to her, but instead of the scandalized reproach she expected, she saw only pity. Her first response was to ignore it, so used was she to that look…but then she caught the fear behind the pity and realized the poor man thought Micah was going to eat her alive or something else horrendous—after all, he was the Guardian of the Abyss.

Rather than disabusing the trembling man of his erroneous notions, she did her best to look fearful when the innkeeper gave her the keys and showed them to the simple but large room. The Guardian's reputation did as much to protect the Abyss from encroachment as the dangers of the badlands.

Kicking off her shoes and tights the instant they were inside, she pulled off her tunic, pushed down the sheet and crawled in. A naked Micah followed at almost the same moment, hauling her against him and throwing a heavy thigh over her own. Safe, she fell into darkness.

CHAPTER TWENTY-FOUR

MICAH WOKE TO THE REALIZATION that dawn remained at least an hour away. Heading out into the dark wasn't an option—light would be their friend when facing the monsters the Blood Sorcerer had created. Which meant he'd have to use that hour some other way.

Glancing down at the woman curled up against his side, he told himself she was tired, that he should let her rest. It would be the right thing to do. Unfortunately, the good part of him was totally overwhelmed by the part that wanted to roll her onto her back, part her thighs and slide into her deep and hard.

Extricating his arm from under Liliana's head, he nudged her gently onto her back. She mumbled something but didn't wake. The depth of her trust in him made a quiet, fierce happiness hum through his blood. That trust, the wicked part of him murmured, should make removing her underthings so much easier.

Peeling down the sheet until it lay at her feet, he smiled in satisfaction as her tight, bitable breasts were exposed to his gaze. Warm and relaxed in sleep, one arm thrown over her head, and with only a whisper of fine cloth hiding the curls between her thighs from his gaze, she presented a luscious picture. He thought about sucking her nipples to wake her up, but he was enjoying the view too much.

Bracing himself beside her, he looked his fill, running

his gaze over those firm little peaks with the dark nipples and wide areole. His cock, already hard, pressed insistent and demanding against her thigh, and she made a restless movement before settling. But she'd cocked her leg, the thin fabric that covered her mound stretching tight.

Stroking his hand oh-so-gently over her thigh, he got her to straighten up her leg again, and then, not wanting to lose the opportunity, inched down the tease of clothing that covered her until he could pull it off and discard it over the side of the bed.

Now, she was naked. And all his.

Braced beside her again, he insinuated his hand between her thighs, waiting until she settled before rubbing one finger along the seam of her flushed folds. A tiny sound, her body arching into the caress. Liking that, he repeated the act. Her breathing altered, and he froze... but she remained asleep.

He touched her again, so slow and stealthy, felt a slick of dampness.

Removing his hand, he spread her thighs and moved over her, fitting his cock to the entrance that was so wet and hot for him. Her eyes snapped open as he began to push into her, her hands fisting in his hair when he dropped his head to suck at her nipples, doing that thing with his tongue that had made her clench around his hardness the previous night. It did so now, too. Groaning deep in his throat, he reached down to spread her wider, and then he shoved in all the way.

A cry muffled against his chest, but it held only pleasure, no pain. He would never hurt his Liliana. Pumping into her in short, hard thrusts, he lifted his head to claim her mouth. She wrapped a leg around him at the same time, attempting to brace herself against the bed with the other.

Laughing at her frustration at being unable to control the rhythm, he squeezed one breast with a surely proprietary hand—after all, she was his—before flipping them so that she was on top, with him below. "There, Lily. Am I not generous?"

She brought herself up into a seated position with her palms flat on his chest, moaned. "You're very hard."

Gripping her hips, he urged her into a slow rotating movement that felt very, very good. "It's morning. You're naked. There is no mystery here." The last words were a groan because she was starting to squeeze him with her inner muscles as she moved and, oh, he liked that.

"Micah, wait." She pushed at his hands when he would've urged her to increase the pace.

Deciding to occupy himself elsewhere, he cupped her breasts in the curve created by thumb and forefinger, squeezed in to pinch her nipples. "Come closer," he said, her breasts sweet temptation. "I want to use my teeth."

"Horrible, teasing beast." Pulling his hands off her breasts, she used their handclasp to brace herself and lift up off his cock.

The exquisite silken suction bowed his back. Then she slid down and the shock of liquid heat had his balls drawing up tight to his body. Knowing he was going to spill sooner rather than later, he broke her hold and reached down to flick that tiny nub between her thighs.

"*Micah.*" She shuddered around his cock on her second downward stroke, and after that, there really was no hope for either of them.

FINISHING HER BATH IN THE shallow tub, Liliana pulled on fresh underwear, part of a set of two that Micah had made a predawn trip into the village to get for her the morning they left the Black Castle. She'd never be able to face the shopkeeper again, but at least she felt decent. That done, she was bending over to grab her tights when she found herself being pulled backward and into Micah's lap where he sat half-dressed on the bed. Settling in, she wrapped an arm around his neck. They had time yet—the light hadn't touched the horizon.

He slid his hand up her rib cage to cup her breast, and while it was a lusty act, as he was an unashamedly lusty man, it was also affectionate and comforting. "Don't be afraid," he said, winter-green eyes clear and free of deception, yet no less strong for their purity. "Your father won't win."

"I just…" Drawing in a deep breath of the morning air, she nuzzled her face against the solid warmth of his neck. "He hurt me," she said, telling him because he was Micah, who would never betray her. "Part of me is still that scared little girl, hoping my door won't open at night, that I won't be dragged screaming, sweat-soaked and shivering to—" a huge knot in her throat "—to witness him slit the throats of innocent men and women, watch their blood drip along the channels carved into his killing bench and into the enspelled pots that keep the blood ever-fresh."

Micah's hand clenched tight on the back of her head. "For that alone, I will make him suffer before he dies."

"No, Micah." She couldn't bear the thought of him becoming tainted in any way by the Blood Sorcerer. "I needed you to know in case I freeze up during the fight." It was a humiliating and horrifying thought, but she had to consider it. "If I do, please don't show any mercy in trying to wake me. Slap me if you have to, but *get me out of the nightmare*."

"I won't slap you, Lily." A brutal line to his jaw. "I might just kiss you, though—and use my tongue."

That suddenly, her worry transformed into a need so intense it scared her. "Save yourself, Micah," she whispered. "Whatever happens, please don't let him kill you." He was someone unique and wonderful and she couldn't bear to think of the world without him.

"If you die, Lily," he said, fondling her breast, "I'll steal your soul and take you to the Abyss, where I will keep you in my magical dungeon so you can never escape." The threat was sealed with a Micah kind of kiss. Hot and dark and possessive.

The pleasure drugged her until she could almost not taste the guilt. Because she'd broken her promise and lied to him again—a lie of omission, but that had been her sin the first time, too. Yet how could she tell him about the death spell when she knew he wouldn't allow it? No, dishonorable as it was, she couldn't bring herself to confess her secret—not when it might mean Micah's life.

NIGHT-HORSES WERE CREATURES of legend, rare and fierce. Her father had never been able to trap one, though he coveted their proud blood—and for that mercy, she could only thank the heavens. Standing beside Micah, she looked at the two huge beasts he'd brought forward—both were as black as pitch, with eyes of a startling amber that sparked with temper.

Huffing and pawing at the ground, they showed her their teeth, as if they would take a bite out of her. Micah, strapping his sword to the saddlebag, tapped the nearest one on the nose. "She is my mate. Treat her with respect."

Liliana didn't know what shocked her more—Micah's words, or the way the horses dropped their heads as if in shame. Staring at Micah, who seemed oblivious to the turmoil he'd engendered within her, she reached forward to cautiously pet first one velvety nose, then the other.

"You are very magnificent," she said with complete honesty. "I'm sure you are the fastest creatures in all the realms."

Their heads lifted, manes flaring in pride. In those eyes of amber lightning, she saw magic that sang to her blood. "You must run," she whispered. "When you have taken us to our destination, turn around and promise me you will *run*." Her father, if he caught these amazing beasts, would brutalize them—to imagine them broken and bloody in razor chains made her heart ache.

The horses neighed in rebellion.

"They are creatures of great pride, Liliana," Micah told her, "warriors in their own right. We must treat them as comrades."

It was hard for her to do that, to accept that she might be riding these glorious animals to their deaths, but there was no arguing with the sentient eyes looking back at her. "Thank you, friends." With that, she swung herself onto one of the horses and waited for Micah to do the same.

The innkeeper and his lady wife—both considerably richer—waved them goodbye with tearful eyes, aware of their destination. They were good people, had promised Liliana and Micah that there would always be a bed for them at the inn regardless of what may come.

Taking a last look at the cheery building, Liliana met eyes of winter-green. "Ready?"

His response was a wicked smile and a, "Whoa!" that sent his night-horse racing ahead.

Laughing—an unforeseen gift—she raced after him, her own magical partner ready for the chase. They raced each other until the inn faded out of sight, then settled into a steady run of such furious speed that Liliana expected to see wings. Exhilarated in spite of the evil to come, she allowed herself a moment to remember the time before dawn.

Waking in such a way, to see Micah with that playful, sensual smile on his face, his body so big and hot around her, inside her…it was something she wanted to experience a million times over. But even if, by some inconceivable miracle, she survived this, she knew that was never going to happen. Micah believed what he said, of that she had not a single doubt, but she also knew how royal houses functioned.

A prince, regardless of his position in line for the throne, was expected to marry a certain kind of woman, a woman with an unsullied past, one who could carry the crown of princess with elegance and beauty.

Everything Liliana was not.

You could be his mistress.

The sly suggestion came from the part of her that had no honor where Micah was concerned. She was sure she would do any terrible thing to be with him—but she didn't think she could stand to share him, to know that another woman had the right to bear his name and his children, to love him and hold him. It would break her.

No, when the time came, she would quash this selfish need and let him go, allow him to embrace the destiny that had always been his.

"Liliana!"

Looking up, she followed the line of Micah's raised hand. She couldn't see anything at first, but then realized the ground not far in front of them was moving. "What is that?"

"Snakes."

Horror uncurled within her—the writhing sprawl went on at least five lengths deep, in every direction as far as the eye could see. There was no way to circle or jump it. Then she saw the glittering red scales on the snakes' backs. "Get back!" Touching Micah's arm, she urged him to move back with her. "Their poison," she said when they were at a safe distance, "it's enough to bring down the horses."

The night-horses shook their heads and stamped their feet, as if in violent disagreement. Proud, temperamental creatures. Rather like the man in front of her, who scowled. "Snake fangs can't penetrate their skin."

"These snakes aren't natural," she told him, having been chained naked in the tower room when her father created them, her wounds seeping. He'd needed powerful blood, but the Blood Sorcerer rarely spilled his own. "Their fangs are made of steel. However, I can use my sorcery to make them move."

Thick and gleaming, the snakes' hissing was a continuous susurration in the air as they stroked and rolled over one another—when they weren't devouring each other. Strange how her father's creations had a way of turning out cannibalistic. Thicker than Micah's forearm and at least ten feet long, each could crush a human being. The only good news was that they appeared to be restricted to moving within a defined boundary—likely a sorcerous safeguard to ensure they wouldn't spread across the land.

"We won't use your magic," Micah said after a moment. "Your father may have laid further traps tied to your blood. As we are now in a realm in which he holds power, there is a good chance the effects will be more virulent."

Though it galled, she agreed. There was also no point in giving away her presence when the element of surprise was the only real advantage they had. "They're afraid of fire," she said, remembering her father's anger at that flaw. "But it'd have to be a big one to scare a swarm this large."

"We don't need to scare them all." Turning his night-horse so that he was positioned behind her, he said, "When I tell you to go, you take your horse and fly. *Understood.*" It wasn't a question.

"I'm ready."

"Promise me."

Thinking he needed to be sure because the escape would require split-second timing, she nodded. "I promise." Stroking the mane of her night-horse, which was too intelligent to fuss, but clearly didn't like being near the snakes, she waited. And almost screamed in horror as she turned back to see Micah jump off his horse and to the ground. "No!"

"Remember your promise." With that, he dug his fingers into the earth. The strain across his shoulders and on his face was obvious, beads of sweat trickling down his temples. But his eyes, they were focused forward. Following his gaze, she saw the swarm grow agitated, hissing in a nonstop chorus, sharp and fractious.

An instant later, they began to slither rapidly away in two directions, opening a narrow—too narrow— corridor in between. That's when she saw thin runnels of magma forcing their way out of the earth, burning the snakes bellies, making them squirm to get away. Heart thudding, she went to turn to look at Micah again when she heard, *"Run!"*

Every part of her wanted to rebel but she'd promised, and so she bent over the long neck of her night-horse, spurring the valiant creature across the magna, its feet flying so fast she hoped its hooves would be spared from harm. It wasn't until she was almost to the other side that she realized she couldn't hear anyone behind her.

CHAPTER TWENTY-FIVE

MICAH DIDN'T KNOW THIS LAND. It wasn't his. Rather than speaking to it, he had to force his power into the earth, literally pull up the magma. It was difficult, leaving his muscles rigid. Knowing the thin streams of molten liquid would retreat the second he broke contact, he waited until Liliana was safely on the other side before rising and jumping onto his night-horse in a single smooth motion.

The intelligent creature leaped at the same instant and they were off, the earth's heated tears already retreating. Hissing, the snakes began to arrow back, their goal the legs of his horse. He saw Lily jump off her own steed, caught the light glinting off the blade in her hand and knew she was ready to use her blood magic. *Not yet, not yet.*

He bent down flat over the night-horse's nape. "Ready, my friend?"

A powerful leap, muscles bunching, and the night-horse cleared the final snake to come to a scrabbling stop on the slight rise beyond. Dropping her blade, Liliana ran to him as he jumped off the horse. He expected an embrace. She thrust at his chest with both of her hands instead. "How could you do that to me!" Fury colored her cheeks, brightened her eyes. "You could've been lying there dead with those horrible snakes biting into you!"

Micah grabbed her wrists, but she just started kicking him instead. So then he crushed her in his arms, tangling her legs with his own. "Liliana," he began, but she wasn't listening. Having never had an enraged woman in his arms before, he wasn't quite sure what to do, but it seemed reasonable that pleasure might mute her anger.

So he kissed her.

She bit his lip.

Jerking away, he glared at her. "I saved us!"

"By putting your life in mortal danger!" She tried to push at his chest again, her breath coming in jagged spurts. "How would you have felt if that had been me? *How?*"

Ice down his spine, through his veins. "I'm sorry, Liliana." He'd never before said such a thing to anyone--the Lord of the Black Castle need not apologize to a soul. Except, it seemed, the bad-tempered creature in his arms, the one who had bitten him hard enough that it stung.

She blinked at his words. "Sorry?"

"Yes."

Her lower lip quivered and then she was throwing her arms around his neck and squeezing him tight. "If you die, my heart will break. You mustn't die, Micah. You mustn't." Wet against his skin.

She was crying.

"You are using up all your chances for the year," he growled. "Don't think I'm not keeping track."

A sniff, a hiccup and then she was lifting away her head to touch her finger to his lip. "Does it hurt?" Remorse in those storm-sky eyes that had become his lodestar.

"Terribly."

"Oh, Micah." Rising up on tiptoe, Liliana sucked that lip into her mouth, suckled gently before going back down flat on her feet and taking a deep breath. "I have to tell you something." He'd be so angry, but after what she'd just lived through, she understood what a staggering hurt she'd be doing him if she sacrificed herself to save him.

Her heart still ached from the pain of that instant when she'd thought he wouldn't make it, her mind tortured with images of him helpless under those slashing fangs. The nightmare sight wasn't one she would ever forget, and it made her take a grim look at the consequences of her plan. To make Micah helpless while she died...it would do more damage to him than any of her father's traps, savage that proud heart.

A heavy scowl on his face. "You've lied to me again."

"It wasn't a real lie," she said, knowing she was only digging the hole deeper.

"I can read your guilt. Tell me."

Knowing there was no way to dress up the cold finality of the act she'd been contemplating, she just spit it out. "I know how to kill my father. However, the spell requires a death."

Rage turned the winter-green molten. "And *you're* angry at *me?*" He'd obviously realized exactly whose death would've been involved.

"I didn't know you when I came up with the idea."

Wild fury, his eyes never shifting off her.

"I'm sorry."

No effect.

Baring her teeth, she pushed at his chest. "I accepted your apology."

"I didn't *plan* to die and forget to tell you."

Guilt stabbed but she folded her arms, because if she gave in now, he'd bully her into doing everything exactly as he wanted. "You also didn't warn me. I just did." And in so doing, had ended their best hope of defeating her father—because there was no way Micah would allow her to go through with it.

Snarling, he kissed her. "If you even think about using that spell, I'll chain you up to a tree while I go meet your father alone."

Fisting her hands against his chest, she bit at his jaw. "You dare do that and I'll use blood sorcery to send you to another kingdom."

He threw her up on her clearly bemused night-horse with a growl. "I'll punish you later."

"Vengeful man."

"Remember that."

With that, they were on the road to Elden once more.

It was perhaps noon that they came upon the giant bridge troll with a stone mallet so big it would've crushed both man and beast should he have brought it down. But in this case, no violence was needed.

The troll, a creature who had something of a magpie's nature, was appeased by a gift of pink sapphires and rough-cut topaz. Micah scowled at losing so much of his treasury, but Liliana glared at him and so he didn't say a word—not until they were past the gloating creature, who was currently holding his jewels up to the sun. Then he muttered about the wisdom of giving such precious gems to a troll who would only hide them in his cave.

Liliana turned to argue with him since, at least now, he'd calmed down enough to talk to her, but never got the chance to speak a word—because that was when the arrows began flying.

A sharp pain.

Crying out, she fell over the neck of her horse, an arrow embedded in her left arm. Desperate for her blood not to touch the earth—her father might not have bothered to tie warning enchantments to the air as that took

much power, but he *would* most certainly have tied them
to the land—she clamped her hand over the wound and
tried to keep her seat as her night-horse followed Micah's
to a small ridge behind which they could take cover.

Grabbing her from the saddle the instant they were
stationary, Micah sat her down. "We must pull this arrow
out."

Nodding, she bit down on the gauntleted arm he held
against her mouth as he removed the arrow with his other
hand. Tears rolled down her face, but she forced herself
not to use her sorcery to stitch up the wound. Any trap
her father had laid would spring at the confluence of her
blood and magic.

Slapping a wadded piece of cloth over the wound and
telling her to hold it there, Micah wrapped the arrow in
another cloth and thrust it into a saddlebag to ensure
none of her blood touched the earth.

"Brave girl," he murmured, cupping her face. "I am
sure I would've roared with displeasure and threatened
to throw you in the dungeon."

His words made her smile through the pain. "I'm sure
you would have." Squeezing his wrist when he went as
if to call on the power he carried within, she said, "You
already used it with the snakes. You must conserve your
energy," and tugged at the bottom of her tunic. "Rip off
a piece of this and tie it over the compress. It'll do—I'm
not bleeding much now."

A scowl. "Lily—"

"You must listen to me on this." Arrows thudded into
the rise behind them. "I know my father's strength—
and we'll need everything we have if we aren't to use
the death spell."

"We'll talk about this later." Ripping off a strip of her
tunic, he tied it around her arm.

More arrows thudded home.

"Do you know who's shooting at us?" she asked.

"A pod of gremlins."

Liliana winced. The small, thin creatures with their pointed brown teeth, corpse-gray skin and thirst for blood were natural allies of her father, feeding as they did on carrion. But it appeared they had turned from scavengers to hunters after years of unparalleled freedom. "They won't give up now."

"Then we'll have to get rid of them." Going to his saddlebags, he returned with both the arrow that had hit her and a number of small, sleek knives.

He touched the arrow to a blade, murmured low deep words under his breath. "A small magic, Lily. Child's play." Rising, he threw the blade in the general direction of the gremlins. A scream of pain sounded, followed by a hail of arrows landing around them.

Smiling, Micah began to pick them up.

The gremlins ran off screaming after their arrows kept returning— to unerringly find living targets. "That was very clever," she said as he helped her back onto her horse. Her arm hurt, but she could still use it and that was what mattered.

"It's from a game my father taught me." Micah pulled himself up onto his own horse, looking no more drained than he had after dealing with the snakes. "To find things."

And what Micah had found, they saw when they looked into the bushes where the gremlins had been hiding, were the hearts of the shriveled and hairless creatures who had the two legs and arms of man, but the intelligence of a rat. The only things they wore were their weapons. Before running away, their "friends" had hacked off an arm and a leg each—to snack on, most likely. Gremlins didn't care what they ate as long as it was dead.

"Nothing here, Lily. Let's go."

It seemed like forever before they reached the border to Elden, the sky turning from blue to orange to dark red as the hours passed. There were other obstacles in their path, including a hungry ensorcelled bear and a fleet of crows with venomous beaks. The bear they'd been able to simply fool, but Micah had had to use his magic the other times…and he was getting weaker with each incident.

It was on the edge of sunset that they finally crossed an invisible line that had him saying, "Elden." The wonder in his voice quickly turned into rage and sorrow as he saw the state of the land around them, unmistakable even under the shadow of oncoming night—the trees stunted and browned, the ground cracked, no birdsong in the air, though it was early yet.

Jumping to the earth, Micah touched his hands to it. "We have come," he whispered. "We have come."

The ground rumbled, but it was broken, almost dead. *No, no.* A tear fell in her heart. *Without the earth's strength, Micah was now too weak to battle the Blood Sorcerer and live.*

He lifted his head at that instant, his eyes incandescent with a chaos of emotions. "Give me a knife, Lily."

"No, Micah." Jumping down herself, she blocked him from going to his saddlebags. "If you bleed yourself here, my father will win and the land would die, anyway."

His body vibrated against her palms and she knew that should he decide to shove her out of the way, she'd be unable to stop him. "Please listen to me. You are here now—the earth will heal. *It will heal.*"

The eyes that looked down at her were of the deadly

Guardian…and also of a prince of Elden, blazing with strength and incredible raw *power*.

"How?" she whispered, for around them the land lay dying.

"The power is ancient," he said, his voice resonating with the force of it. "It lay hidden, slumbering until it sensed my presence. The price was this sickness—the land sacrificed itself to protect that power."

She staggered under the weight of the magic in the winter-green, but didn't back down. "My father tried to end your lineage two decades ago," she said, forcing herself to hold that terrible, beautiful gaze. "You do this and he succeeds. Your parents' sacrifice, that of the land, will have been for nothing."

His fingers gripped her jaw. "You know nothing of my parents."

"No," she said, taking the emotional blow because she was the daughter of the Blood Sorcerer, the reason why Micah was an orphan.

"I hurt you." His hand dropped from her chin, his expression losing its stony edge.

"There was no hurt." She tapped the unbruised skin where he'd held her. "See?"

"Not there—" a big palm settling below her breast, over her heart "—here."

That heart clenched in need, in sorrow, in love. "It's all right—"

"No, it's not." He shuddered, dropped his forehead to hers. "This land, it sings to me in a broken voice until I can't hear my own thoughts."

Trembling, she reached up to hold his head against her, stroking her fingers through the thick silk of his hair. "It is only happy that you have come, Micah." So long had Elden waited for its blood to return.

Kissing the tip of her nose with a tenderness she didn't expect from the Lord of the Black Castle, he brushed his thumb over her cheek. "If I promise not to growl at you anymore, will you believe me?"

She shook her head, touched her fingers to his lips. "I'm keeping track, too, you know," she teased. "Perhaps I'll ask you to give me your best jewels in recompense."

"You can have them all."

"Oh, Micah." Though she wanted nothing more than to stay in his arms, she forced her mind back to the task they couldn't afford to leave incomplete. "Ask the land to be quiet until you've dealt with my father. It will understand."

Going down to his knees, Micah touched his fingers to the dry and cracked earth, murmured his plea for quiet. *Not forever,* he promised. *Just until the bad blood is gone. I am here now—I will sing to you as you need.*

The earth sighed, answered with a caress of peace.

"Come, Lily. It is time."

Mounting their night-horses in silence, they began the last leg of the journey to the castle that had once been the heart of Elden and was now the seat of such evil it had shattered the earth itself. They rode until they reached a place Liliana called the Dead Forest.

"I used to play here," he said, remembering the shimmer of the aseria blooms, the bright green of the dew-honey trees heavy with their tulip-shaped flowers, the symphony of birdsong.

Now it crawled with plants the shade of rotten flesh, blackened trees shooting their diseased branches out into the sky. The living things that roamed its murky depths, Liliana told him, were akin to the gremlins—nasty creatures who lived only for death.

And who would delight in bringing down a night-horse.

"Go," Micah told the proud beasts after they'd dismounted and unburdened the night-horses of their gear. "We thank you for your help."

The horses shook their heads.

Gripping their manes he looked each in the eye. "You must go. The things that roam here will hurt you, and if they do, Liliana will cry. I don't like it when Liliana cries." He put all the menace he was capable of—and the Guardian of the Abyss was capable of a great deal—into his voice. *"Go."*

The night-horses reared and turned, neighing loudly as they raced away.

Going to the saddlebags, he removed the knives and strapped them to Lily's body so that she would have physical weapons, before picking up his sword.

"Wait." Liliana took out the food Emmy had packed and forced them both to eat to further armor themselves with energy.

Prepared as well as they could be, they stepped into the hungry jaws of the Dead Forest. Things jeered and skittered at them from above, but nothing came close.

The strange plants that smelled of decaying meat, however, tried to lick out, as if they would wrap their enormous tongues around Micah and Liliana and drag them into the teeth-filled maw of their "flowers." Micah sliced out at one aggressive tongue and the plant screamed, its appendage gushing black blood. The others snapped back at the warning. Walking past without pause, Liliana used her knife to hack away a vine that had attempted to wrap itself around her arm.

That was his mate, he thought, fierce and strong.

Teeth bared in a smile of pride, he walked beside

her as they cut, sawed and sliced their way through this once-lush forest become a nightmare. It took too long, time slipping through their fingers at an inexorable pace. Bones crunched underneath his boots sometime later, hours after full dark.

"My father," Liliana said, flinching at the sound, deep grooves around her mouth, "disposes of his enemies here or in the lake." A hollow statement. "He used to ask his minions to bury them, but he no longer cares, as long as there's no stench from the rotting flesh."

Micah stepped with more care after that, for though some of these bones might be of men who had once served the Blood Sorcerer, many would be those of innocents. It was as he was making his way around a skull gleaming white in the night air that he caught his first glimpse of what had once been Elden Castle.

CHAPTER TWENTY-SIX

IN HIS MEMORIES, THE CASTLE was a proud structure of glimmering stone standing in the middle of a pristine lake. At night its windows had been filled with golden light, while during the day the colorful pennants that spoke of the Royal House of Elden and their allies had flown high overhead. Music had rolled out over the lake more often than not, and the causeway that connected the castle to the mainland had been filled with the bustle of movement as the people came and went.

What he saw before him was a desecration.

He and Liliana had come out of the forest on the opposite side of the lake to the causeway, but even from this far he could see the foul creatures moving about along the narrow stretch. They appeared agitated, their anger vicious. But their presence was, in many ways, the easiest to bear. As for the castle itself...

Enough sickening yellow light spilled from within that he could discern the black slime mold crawling up the sides of the stone, see the monstrous vegetation. His mother's gardens, her fruit plants, were all gone, dead. To be replaced by putrid plants akin to those in the forest behind them.

The lake was in no better condition—slow moving and polluted, with a thin film of grease overlaying the surface, it appeared lifeless. But it was not untenanted.

"What are those?" he said, catching the eager movements beneath the slime.

"The flesh-eating fish I told you about," she said with a shudder before nodding to a small wooden boat that lay pulled up on the verge not far from them. "If we try to take that out into the water without my father's sorcery to protect us, the fish will eat through the hull to get to us." Staring at the water, she said, "I've been thinking. My blood is close enough to his that I may be able to fool the fish, get us safely to the castle—otherwise, we'll have to breach the causeway."

He tasted her fear, knew her father had terrorized her with the bloodthirsty fish in the lake. But they weren't the only beings beneath the water.

You must always treat them with respect, Micah. They are the guardians of this place.

His father's voice, stern and yet kind to a young boy who'd been flushed with his own power after summoning one of those great guardians from the deep, for his was the magic that spoke to the earth and its creatures, whether on the land or in the water. Perhaps the guardians were long dead, poisoned by this filth, but Micah didn't think so. They were beings of vast and ancient magic who slept far, far below, under the silt of the lake bottom itself.

"No, Lily," he murmured. "Save your strength, your blood." Heading to the boat, he told her to get in. "You must trust me."

It didn't surprise him that she entered the boat without another word. She was his. Of course she should trust him; he would've likely growled at her if she had not. Putting his sword in with her, he knelt beside the boat, his hand braced on the bow, and went to brush the water with his fingertips.

Liliana pulled his hair. *Hard.* "Those fish can swim in the shallows. They'll bite the tips of your fingers right off."

He glared at her. "That hurt."

"It'll hurt more when they're nibbling on you."

Scowling because she was right, he considered the situation. "I must touch the water to do this."

Liliana scrambled out of the boat to run into the forest without a word. Spinning, he ran after her to see her sawing away at one of the "tongues" he'd hacked off near the edge of the trees. It infuriated him that that black blood was touching her, but he helped her in her task and, together, they dragged the piece back to the lake.

"If you put this in front of your fingers," she said, sliding away her knife, "the fish will go for it first. It'll last perhaps ten heartbeats at most."

"Are you sure? I quite like my fingers."

"So do I." A sinful smile so unexpected it made his own lips curve. "The plant is a delicacy to them—my father uses it as a reward after they take care of another enemy."

"Back in the boat," he ordered, and waited until she'd scrambled inside before taking the hunk of dead plant and dropping it in the water. As the hideous white fish, their eyes a dull pink, swarmed in a frenzy, he dipped his fingers into the shallows and whispered, *"Your help I ask, one guardian to another. It is time to wake."*

Teeth grazed his fingers just as he wrenched them out of the water. Liliana cried out in dismay when she saw the blood running hot and slick down his—still whole—finger. "You may kiss it better later," he told her, his eyes on the lake.

The surface remained placid, the fish having calmed.

"Micah," Liliana whispered, her eyes on the watch she wore around her neck. "It's almost midnight."

"Patience." *There.* A bubble of water too big for a fish.

Running to the back of the boat, he began to push it into the lake, jumping in right before it would've been too late. "Row, Lily!"

TINY CRUNCHING SOUNDS CAME from all around them and Liliana knew the revolting fish with the pink eyes were eating away at the boat. A cold sweat broke out along her spine as she lifted her oar out of the water to dig it in again and one of those foul creatures appeared, teeth clamped on the wood as it flopped in the night air. "Micah."

"We're almost to the deep."

That didn't reassure her, since it ruled out any possibility of escape. But she'd promised to trust Micah, so she continued to row with frantic determination…and almost dropped her oar when a giant tentacle appeared, curling over the side of the boat. Another gleaming tentacle appeared on the other side.

She felt a tug, realized Micah was taking her oar and putting it on the bottom of the boat. "Hold on," he warned, just before the water began to churn and they crashed over the lake at a speed that had her fingers going white-knuckled from the force of her grip. Around the lake, other mysterious creatures rose with a haunting song, their bodies so immense as to be incomprehensible, their jaws massive as they swallowed up her father's evil creations with slow dives that rippled throughout the polluted water.

Exhilarated, she wiped away the filthy water spraying onto her face and held on tight as they headed straight for the shore—and the back of the castle. The tentacles slid away as they reached the shallows, but their momentum crashed them right onto the rocky edge, the boat falling apart on impact.

Scrambling onto the rocks with Micah behind her, she looked out over the churning surface of the lake. "My father's creatures are vicious," she said, able to see the flesh-eaters clamped on the tentacles that waved in the air. "They'll hurt the guardians."

Micah was already leaning back down to touch his fingers to the water, the fish too distracted to pay him any mind. *"Sleep once more,"* he said. *"Wake when the lake is pure. You have my thanks."*

The lake began to calm an instant later, the guardians diving to the deep, where the flesh-eating fish could not follow. "They survived," she whispered. "All this time while my father thought he had this land cowed, they survived," A fierce happiness bloomed in her heart. "If they survived, so must others."

Micah grinned at her, and it held the lethal chill of the Abyss. "It's time to destroy the monster, Lily."

A screeching cry overhead interrupted her response. Looking up, she saw the scorching form of a firedancer. It dropped flames as it flew, and only then did Liliana become aware that parts of the island were ablaze. "The menagerie!" she called to Micah as they began to scale the rocks to the castle. "The bird must've escaped!"

She heard the trumpet of a great tusked mammoth an instant later, followed by the stampede of smaller creatures. "My father trapped them to bleed," she said, wiping her damp face with her equally damp sleeve. "They aren't creatures of evil."

Nodding, Micah raised his arm.

And the firedancer arrowed down to rest on his gauntlet, its entire body flaming, from the long fanned-out tail of flickering red, to the equally bright crest on its head, to the inferno of its eyes.

Mouth agape, Liliana stared. "How?"

"I called and it came," was his simple answer, before he leaned closer and murmured something to the bird.

Liliana swore the bird cackled before flying off toward the Dead Forest—which began to burn not long afterward. Giving in to a smile, she continued on toward the narrow back entrance almost no one ever used. "I can sense his blood here. He must sense me, too."

"It seems he has other problems so he may not be paying attention."

The door was unlocked—and guarded by a spitting three-headed serpent.

Micah sliced the beast in half before she could reach for her magic. Stepping around the remains leaking blood as black as the plants, she continued down the passageway. She could hear trampling feet overhead, cries and yells, and hoped that part of her vision had held true. If the other heirs had arrived this night, dividing the attention of her father and his forces, then Micah and Liliana might have a hope of defeating him.

Exiting from the passageway, Liliana found herself face-to-face with a tiny snapdragon, so-called for its liking for biting. "Duck!" She and Micah both fell to the ground as the creature—the size of a five-year-old child—belched fire before making a scared sound and running in the other direction.

Micah was grinning when she glanced back. Shaking her head at him, she proceeded with care down the corridor littered with paw prints and the debris from crushed tables and broken vases, heading for the stairs that led to the tower room. The guard on the second step wasn't an escapee from the menagerie—he was one of her father's own creations, a giant yellow centipede that he'd fed with his own sorcerous blood until it grew to a monstrous size, its pincers like two enormous knives slicing in the air.

"No blade will penetrate its skin," she whispered as they came to a halt several feet away—the centipede wouldn't leave its post to attack; its only task was to guard the stairs.

She sliced a gash across her palm before Micah could stop her. "This is the easiest way to bypass it." Because her father had fed her blood to the creature, too. Many times.

Micah's eyes glittered with anger. "This is one more thing we'll discuss later." In spite of his fury, he allowed her to paint lines on his cheeks with her blood, to touch it to the backs of his hands.

"I'll go ahead," she said, flexing and unflexing the hand that she hadn't cut.

"No." Micah pushed her behind him, sword held out in front. "If it's a question of blood, I'm now covered in yours."

"But—"

"Do not tell me that you want to go ahead because you aren't sure the plan will work?" A silken question. "I'm very definitely locking you up in the dungeon when we get back home."

"Stop threatening me with the dungeon," she muttered, though the word *home* was one that made her throat burn. "Or maybe I'll lock you in there myself."

"I have the only key." He prowled across to face the centipede, Liliana protected behind his armored form.

The creature's malformed antennae waved with eagerness as they came close, one tendril reaching out to brush against Micah's cheek. Liliana was sure she saw the vile thing open its maw in anticipation of a feed, but it allowed Micah to pass. However, when Liliana would've followed, it blocked her path. Hearing Micah's sword whisper through the air, she shook her head. "Wait."

The centipede curved its long body down to suck at her wound, a horrible sensation that made her want to vomit, but it was a violation she could bear. Pulling away her hand after it had had a taste—with a firmness she'd learned during the times her father had thrown her into the pit with it as it grew—she curled her fingers into her palm and walked past.

Micah's body was a stone wall, his eyes pinned on the centipede. "If that creature doesn't die when your father does," he said in a tone that whispered of the Abyss, "then I will take it home and feed it to the basilisks myself."

No one had ever stood up for her. No one but Micah.

Heart a knot of pain and love, she wiped off the blood from his face and hands using a damp but not wet part of her sleeve. "The tower room, where he does his magic, is at the top of these stairs."

"You sense him?"

"Yes." They scaled the steps at top speed—if she knew her father, he wouldn't have bothered with booby traps, secure in the knowledge that nothing could get past the centipede.

She was wrong.

The sharp metal spikes exploded out of the wall three steps from the door to the tower room, skewering her to the opposite wall. Micah, a step ahead, roared, shaking the stone of the castle itself as she looked down at herself to see massive spikes through her stomach, her chest, her thighs, arms and shoulders. It didn't hurt. But it would.

Blood seeped slow and dark against the damp black of the footman's tunic.

Her. The trap had been tied to the blood of the *only* other person who could control the centipede. If she hadn't wiped the blood off Micah, this would've been him. "Thank you," she whispered to whatever fate had saved him, saved the man who was her heart.

Hot, rough hands on her face. "You. Will. *Not.* Die." An order.

Blood bubbled into her mouth. "Go," she whispered, so happy he was alive. "Don't let him win." It was getting difficult to breathe, to speak, but she had to make him move. "If he wins—" liquid trickling down her arms and to the floor "—everything is lost. Your brothers. Your sister."

Micah didn't care about anything, anyone, else. Only Liliana. But then her eyes flickered to his back, and the mute horror in them was enough to have him turning around in time to slam up his armor over his neck and face as a skeletal-thin man with cadaverous skin threw dozens of carnivorous beetles at him. They fell off him, headed toward Liliana's vulnerable, broken body.

No!

He crushed them all, but it took time, allowing the Blood Sorcerer the opportunity to throw up his arms, and chant an incantation that swept chilling cold through the staircase as twisted souls were ripped from where the sorcerer had trapped them.

"Kill him!" the Blood Sorcerer screamed.

Fighting the souls with his power, Liliana protected at his back, Micah tore apart their shadow selves, but there were many and he was far from the Abyss. Their icy fingers penetrated his armor to touch his heart and he had to use every ounce of his strength to keep them from closing those fingers around the organ.

Then he heard, *"Leave."*

Screaming, the ghosts were sucked back from whence they came, Liliana's blood sorcery powerful…because so much of her life's fluid stained the ground, stained the wall. The Blood Sorcerer screamed in rage and whirled back inside the tower room. Not following, Micah turned to cup Liliana's face. "Do not do the death spell. Trust me one more time and do not cast the spell."

Tears shone, turning her eyes into a shimmering mirage. "I won't let you die." Blood-soaked words.

"One more time, Lily," he repeated. *"Don't leave me."*

"Go," she whispered. "I won't be able to stop him until the moment of death."

No. "Not unless you promise."

"Elden—"

"Means nothing without you. *Promise* you won't do the spell."

A tear rolled down her cheek. "I promise."

Turning, Micah slammed into the door to the tower room, breaking it to pieces as, from the corner of his eye, he saw the snapdragon crisp the centipede to help out two mountain trolls who were currently bashing it with hands heavy as hammers. The tiny being began to scamper up the steps.

Watch over her.

It was instinct to issue the command, to reach in and touch the snapdragon's mind. For it was of Elden, and Micah's magic knew it. Not waiting to see if it obeyed— he knew it would—he walked into the magic room, the feared Guardian of the Abyss once more, with his armor that covered every inch of his flesh but for his eyes.

The Blood Sorcerer lifted his glistening red hands

from the body of the man he had just butchered—one of his minions from the look of it—and laughed. "You'll get no power from the land. It's mine!"

Micah strode forward, only to slam into an invisible wall. No matter how hard he hit it, it refused to break. Reaching for the ancient power that had slumbered where the Blood Sorcerer could not reach, the power that was of his blood, he drew it to his armored fists and began to pound at the invisible wall. Cracks appeared, sizzling red across the surface. Hissing, the Blood Sorcerer began to chant an incantation.

Micah punched through—to find himself assaulted by a tornado created of blades so sharp they cut through his armor, drawing blood. Slamming aside the blades with a snarl, he reached for the sorcerer who had hurt his Lily.

Liliana's father, drenched in the lifeblood of the man he'd killed, smiled and pointed with a hissed command... and Micah's armor disappeared, leaving him acutely vulnerable to the blades that began to whirl again. As his blood flew to speckle the air, he continued to stride forward, but the man who had eyes as reptilian as his Lily's were warm, laughed. "You'll be cut to pieces before you ever touch me—and I will bathe in your blood. Such powerful blood. Like your mother's."

Micah's rage was such he almost didn't hear the whisper in his mind. *Still, Micah, still.* The voice of a ghost. Liliana's voice.

CHAPTER TWENTY-SEVEN

THE BLADES DROPPED.

The Blood Sorcerer's rage made his eyes protrude, his veins bulge. "I should've strangled that whelp in her crib!" Overturning a table of magical potions in front of Micah, he backed away. "She'll be dead soon enough, anyway. Then I'll lick up her blood."

The taunt had the opposite effect from the one intended—it told Micah Liliana was alive. All he wanted to do was finish this so he could return to her. But in one thing the Blood Sorcerer was right—bloated as he was by his most recent sacrifice, his sorcery was too strong for Micah to defeat.

Not alone, Micah. They are here.

Liliana's voice again, showing him things he'd forgotten, reminding him that the land, the animals, weren't the only things he knew here. Reaching out with something inside him that had no name, no form, he searched for the blood that called to his own.

Nicolai.

Dayn.

Breena.

The ties of his lineage soared through him, filling him to the brim with power, and it didn't matter that the Blood Sorcerer called in an army of tiny insects that acted like sandpaper across his skin, peeling the flesh from his arms, his face. Shoving through the virulent swarm and then the sorcerer's blood shield as if it didn't exist, he gripped the monster's neck, and dragged him to the window. "Look," he said, forcing the man's eyes to the forest that was a blazing conflagration. "By the time we are done, there'll be nothing left of your legacy."

A laugh bitter with evil. "Then you will have to kill Liliana."

Micah slammed the Blood Sorcerer's head against the stone, cracking his skull. "She is not your legacy," he whispered in the man's ear before he snapped his neck. "She is her own."

The insects disappeared with the Blood Sorcerer's death, but Micah wanted to make sure the evil wouldn't rise again. Picking up the sword he'd dropped by the door, he hacked off the man's head and gripped it by the hair as he ran back to Liliana. She lay with her chin slumped on her chest.

"No!"

Her chin lifted, her eyes struggling to stay open—but she saw his trophy. "He's dead." A red smile.

Throwing the head at the snapdragon, who caught it in an eager mouth—crunching it down with greedy glee before waddling past for the rest of the body—Micah wiped off his palms on his thighs and cupped Liliana's face. "You must not die, Lily." He tried and *tried* to close her wounds with the deep magic within him, but his power it became clear, was not one that was of healing.

"...all right." A whisper.

"No, *no*." Feeling wet down his cheeks, he realized he was crying. "You've made me cry, Lily. I will throw you in the dungeon for many days."

When her lashes fluttered shut, he growled at her. "Help me! Tell me what to do!"

The earth, Micah. I read about...

The thought seemed to hold the last of her strength, because her head dropped forward and then was motionless. Refusing to believe that she was dead, he began to wrench the spikes from her body. When another man thundered up the steps, past the dead centipede, Micah turned only long enough to see—to recognize—silver eyes streaked with gold before returning to his frantic task. "She can't die."

Nicolai began to pull out the spikes with him, both of their hands drenched in blood within seconds. Grabbing Lily from the wall the instant they'd removed the last spike, Micah ran down the steps, past a startled woman with soft brown hair, and outside into the twisted gardens. This earth was too broken, too polluted, to heal as it had once done for the royal family, long ago. But he had to try. Laying Liliana on the ground, he cut his palms, pressed them to the land.

The earth began to green under his palms, but too slow, too slow. Then another pair of bloodstained hands appeared on Lily's other side. A third pair—that of a green-eyed man with dark hair. A fourth, feminine and delicate as the blond hair that haloed his sister's face. And the land grew green around Liliana. *"Save her,"* he whispered to the earth. *"Save the one who helped save you."*

The earth tried, but it was too damaged and Liliana was not of Elden blood.

"No, no!"

"Micah, I'm sorry."

Ignoring his sister's voice, so full of sorrow, he gathered Liliana's limp body into his arms, refusing to let go. "Help me, Lily," he whispered again, burying his face in her hair. It ignited a memory, of another time when he'd held her in his lap, her hair brushing his chin…blood perfuming the air.

"Slit my wrist." He shoved it at his sister's face, and he would always love her for the fact that she didn't hesitate. "Take, Lily," he said, pressing his wrist to her mouth, the wounds on her body, every part of her he could reach. "You have no need to murder me in my bed. I give you this freely."

An endless pause before her body jerked, the sorcery within her taking control. Because Liliana, sweet, gentle Liliana, who kissed him so soft and touched him as if he would break, was a far greater sorceress than her father had ever been. That was why the evil man had hated her so—even using only her own blood, she had traveled to the Abyss itself, a feat beyond extraordinary.

To repair her body, all she'd needed was the fuel to ignite her power.

Liliana's blood stopped flowing, her hand spasmed… and finally, she opened her eyes. He wanted to yell at her, but he waited until he was certain every one of the holes in her body had been repaired before dragging her to his chest and telling her all the terrible things he was going to do to her.

Arms wrapped around him, she kissed him, halting the flow of his words. He decided he would allow the kiss, but since he couldn't make her naked here, he had to stop it. "Why did you change your face, Lily?"

Liliana lifted her hands to her face at that quizzical question, terrified her father had cast a final vengeful spell. "Is it very bad?" she whispered to the man who held her in arms of steel.

"I suppose I'll get used to it," he muttered, then kissed her again using his tongue and squeezing her bottom—

as if his brothers and sister, and other people, weren't standing right there.

An instant later, she decided she didn't care.

EPILOGUE

I SUPPOSE I'LL GET USED TO IT.

Liliana stared at her reflection for the thousandth time since the day that had changed the fate of Elden. The woman she saw in the mirror was Irina's daughter, with a face of such luminous beauty that it had made Micah's siblings and their mates stare, and hair so silken it was a mirror. It seemed her father's death had *broken*, not created, a spell, one he must have put on her as a child.

Why, she would never know. Perhaps it was as Micah said—he'd feared her power and so had tried to break her. Or perhaps he had enjoyed the control it gave him over her and others, too. He would've gained cruel pleasure in watching men stumble over one another as they tried to win the hand of such an ugly woman. But in the end, the joke was on him.

Because Micah had loved her then, and he loved her now. He was the only one who didn't stare—because to him, she was simply Liliana. Liliana, whose eyes remained a nowhere color that Micah called storm-sky and had decreed were nothing like her father's. Liliana, whose body hadn't changed much where it mattered. While her legs were now the same size, her back remained a mass of scars and she still had small breasts and a large behind, both of which Micah liked to see naked as much as possible.

Blushing at the thought of how he'd woken her this

morning, so big and demanding between her thighs, she
played with the emerald-and-diamond ring on her left
hand, the central stone the color of a certain lord's eyes.
It was one of his mother's, he'd told her, part of the hoard
they'd found beneath the castle.

He had given it to her because he was going to marry
her.

"It is customary to ask," she now said as she turned to
watch him button up a black shirt over that chest she'd
licked and sucked and kissed not long ago.

"Why?" He shrugged. "I'm not giving you a choice."

She surely shouldn't encourage him, but when a
woman loved a man so very much, it was difficult to be
stern. "Let me." She did up the buttons, shaking her head
when he slid his hands down her back to curve over her
bottom. "So your brother Nicolai is to take the throne?"

This was the third time they had returned to Elden—
Micah couldn't remain far from the Abyss for long, for
it would unbalance the realms, glut the badlands with
shadows. Yet he also had a deep, unquenchable need to
heal the earth here, though the presence of his siblings
meant he didn't need to stay on a permanent basis.

So they came and went, the journey far easier now that
her father's spells had unraveled, his monstrous creations
dying without his sorcery to sustain them. They most
often traveled overland—the night-horses had claimed
Liliana and Micah as their own, biting the nonmagical
horses they'd been about to mount when they arrived at
the inn the second time. The temperamental creatures
were awfully possessive—much like the man she adored
with her every breath.

"Yes," he said, answering her question about Nicolai.
"He will rule with his mate, Jane."

Jane was tall and slender and appeared fragile, but she

would make a strong queen. She was also not a princess. Neither was Alfreda, Dayn's chosen. Breena's mate was a berserker, quite wild and as uncivilized as Micah she was sure. Not a one had turned a hair at having her become part of the royal family. "I think," she murmured, "your brother will be a great king."

"Yes." Petting her, he bent his head to kiss a line down her neck. "Dayn and his mate will be staying in Elden and taking over the guard."

She shivered, stopped buttoning and began unbuttoning. "And your sister?" His sister, who had become a warrior, something that had caused her older brothers intense astonishment. Micah, of course, had simply offered to let her borrow his weapons.

He sucked over her pulse. "She travels with Osborn and the boys to his homeland, so that her mate can teach his brothers what it is to be an Ursan warrior."

"Yes." She wove her fingers into his hair, holding him to her. "The berserkers are needed still."

"Hmm." Continuing to kiss her, he began to walk her backward, toward the bed. "They will not be strangers to Elden, as we are not."

Allowing him to press her down onto the bed, she waited for him to shrug off his shirt and prowl up to cover her. But instead of kissing her once there, he braced himself above her, his expression solemn. "I am the Guardian of the Abyss, Liliana. I will never abandon my duty."

"Of course." She caressed his chest. "You can keep your promise to the land by visiting regularly." Short, intense bursts of working with the earth, they had discovered, had the same impact as if he stayed continuously in Elden.

"Will you mind living in the Black Castle?"

"Living there was the first time in my life that I was happy," she whispered. "The place where I found you. You're my heart. Jissa and Bard and Mouse are family."

To her gratitude, Jissa had not blamed her for her father's evil, and remained her very best friend.

"You—Bard, too—can die in truth now, if you choose," she'd told the brownie, though it caused her terrible pain to think of a world without Jissa. "Leave the Black Castle for a day and a night and you will wake in the Always."

Jissa had shaken her head. "The Bitterness would cry, cry. And without me, you will get into more, much more trouble with the lord. Dungeon you will live in." A laughing look. "And…I would like to play more games of chess with Bard, he with me. Together we play."

"Is it only chess you two play?" Liliana had jested, overjoyed at Jissa's choice.

Except the tips of Jissa's ears had turned pink.

"Jissa."

Lips curving at the memory, she met eyes of wintergreen. "The Black Castle is home."

Micah's smile shattered her, it was so very bright, and for her alone. "There are less servants there, too," he muttered, referring to the people of Elden who had begun to come out of hiding in droves to help set the castle to rights for Nicolai's wedding, "which means I can make you naked far easier."

Laughing, she stroked her hands into his hair and tugged him down for a long, lazy kiss that ended with his hand on her breast and her leg cocked around his hip. "I will be planting some flowers, though."

He reared back. "At the Black Castle? *The gateway to the Abyss?*"

Kissing his jaw, she nuzzled him. "And I want more

comfortable furniture—my mother will be visiting, after all." Irina, too, had been freed from her ensorcellment. She did not know her daughter, but had touched Liliana with love from the first. The bonds would only grow deeper in time.

Micah groaned, began to pull up the red, *red* gown he'd brought her, so very pretty and dusted with gold. "As long as you don't try to make the dungeons appealing. That I will not allow." His hand on her thigh, rough and proprietary.

Shivering, she tugged him closer. "Done."

Micah rocked against her. "Lily?"

"Yes?" she said against lips firm and sinful.

"We're getting married in an hour. I already spoke to Nicolai."

Her mouth fell open, and then she began to laugh. "My beautiful, arrogant, wonderful lord," she said, kissing his jaw, his cheeks, his neck. "I can't wait to be your wife."

"Now tell me you love me."

"I love you." She kissed the spot she'd once bitten on his lip. "Shall I say it again?"

A delighted look. "Yes."

He made her repeat it ten times. Then he said, "Your name is written on my heart, Lily."

It made her cry. He yelled. Then he kissed her.

By the time the day was done, she was married to the Guardian of the Abyss, in the gardens of the Royal House of Elden that had come back to life. The snapdragon behaved and didn't fry any of the guests.

THE ASERIA FLOWERS ARE blooming again in what was once the Dead Forest and is now a young, green playground, with saplings reaching for the sparkling blue sky. The firedancers have returned to circle above the castle at twilight, providing a show to which nothing can compare, and the lake runs clean and sweet once more.

There is still much to be done, but laughter fills the castle and the land, for the time of darkness is past and the blood of Elden walk its roads once more. This truth I write with untrammeled joy.

—From the Royal Chronicles of Elden, on the one hundred and seventy-eighth day of the Reign of King Nicolai and Queen Jane

* * * * *

DESERT WARRIOR

To Mum, Dad and the Amazing FMP,
for Everything

CHAPTER ONE

"Do not put even one foot on Zulheil soil unless you are ready to stay forever. You will not get past the airport gates before I kidnap you!"

Hands trembling, Jasmine skirted around the small groups of people in the waiting area and headed for the glass doors that would lead her out of the airport, and into Tariq's land.

"Madam." A dark hand fell next to hers on the handle of the luggage trolley.

Startled, she looked up into the smiling face of a man who appeared to be an airport official. "Yes?" Her heart started to pound in a mixture of hope and fear.

"You are going the wrong way. The taxis and hire cars are on the other side." He gestured toward a long corridor leading to another set of glass doors. Desert sands glittered in the distance.

"Oh." She felt foolish. Of course Tariq wouldn't complete his threat so literally. He'd been angry enough to scare her when he'd warned her against coming to his land. Now, Tariq was a cool, controlled man, whom she'd seen a number of times on television, leading peace talks between warring Arab states. Her Tariq was now Tariq al-Huzzein Donovan Zamanat, the Sheik of Zulheil, the leader of his people.

"Thank you," she managed to say. When she began

to move again, the pale blue fabric of her ankle-length dress swished around her legs in time with her steps.

"It is my pleasure. I will escort you to the vehicles."

"That's very kind. What about the other travelers?"

The corners of the stranger's eyes crinkled. "But madam, you were the only foreigner on this flight."

Jasmine blinked, thinking back over the trip. All she could remember were lilting vowels and flowing hands, beautiful sloe-eyed women and protective Arabian men.

"I didn't realize," she admitted.

"Zulheil has been closed to visitors."

"But *I'm* a visitor." She stopped, wondering if it was too much to hope that Tariq would actually kidnap her. No sane woman would want to be captured by a desert sheik who held her in contempt, but she was long past logic and sanity.

Her guide paused, and she could have sworn that he blushed under his golden skin. "It...Zulheil began letting in people again this last week."

At his graceful wave, she started to push the cart down the marbled floor once more. "Was it closed because of mourning?" Her voice was quiet, respectful.

"Yes. The loss of our sheik and his beloved wife was a tragic blow to our people." His eyes momentarily darkened with pain. "But we have a good sheik in their only son. Sheik Tariq will lead us out of the darkness."

Jasmine's heart skipped a beat at Tariq's name. From somewhere she found the strength to ask, "He's ruling alone, your new sheik?"

If the man told her that Tariq had taken a wife during the period of media blackout since his parents' deaths, she'd get on the next plane out of Zulheil. Even now, her lungs protested every breath she took, and she hung on the edge of control.

The look her guide threw her was assessing. He nodded sharply, but waited until they were outside before speaking. The harsh heat of the desert hit Jasmine like a physical slap, but she stood firm. Wilting was not an option, not when this was her last chance.

There was a black limousine parked at the curb. She'd started to move away from it when her guide halted her.

"That is your taxi."

"That's definitely not a taxi." Hope, she understood, came in many forms. Hers had arrived in the shape of a long, sleek piece of gleaming machinery.

"Zulheil is rich, madam. These are our taxis."

She wondered if he expected her to believe that. Biting her lip to muffle the slightly hysterical urge to giggle, she nodded and let him put her cases into the trunk. She waited, heart pounding and mouth dry with anticipation, until he came around to the back passenger door.

"Madam?"

"Yes?"

"You asked if our sheik rules alone. The answer is yes. Some say it is because his heart has been broken." His voice was a low whisper.

Jasmine gasped. Before she could continue the conversation, he swung open the limo door. Her mind in a whirl, she stepped inside the luxurious air-conditioned interior.

The door shut.

"You really did it," she whispered to the man sitting across from her, his long legs encroaching on her space.

Tariq leaned forward, his hands on his knees. The

darkness inside the limo threw the sharp lines of his face into vivid relief. None of the softness she'd seen in her Tariq was present in this hardened stranger.

"Did you doubt me, my Jasmine?"

Her body went into delayed shock at the sound of his voice. It was deep and compelling. Beautiful and dangerous. Familiar yet…different. "No."

Tariq frowned. "And yet you are here."

She bit her lower lip again and drew in a ragged breath. His eyes, deceptively dark in the confines of the vehicle, were fixed on her like those of a predator waiting to pounce. The opaque partition between passengers and driver was raised, further collapsing the space, leaving her nowhere to turn.

"Yes. I'm here." The car moved off at that moment, unsettling her precarious balance. She fell forward and barely caught herself on the edge of the seat. Tariq's arms came around her anyway and he lifted her into his lap.

Jasmine clutched at his wide shoulders, the fine material of his white tunic crumpling under her fingers, but she didn't fight, not even when he gripped her chin with his fingers and forced her to meet his gaze. He was so angry. She could see the turbulence in his vivid green eyes.

"Why are you here?" He tightened his hold around her when the car bounced over something on the road. His muscled body was so much bigger than hers that Jasmine felt surrounded, overwhelmed. But still she didn't fight.

"Because you needed me."

His laugh was a harsh, ragged echo of pain that hurt her inside. "Or have you come to have a liaison with an exotic man, before you marry the one your family has chosen?" With an oath, he dumped her unceremoniously back into her seat.

Jasmine pushed her fiery plait over her shoulder and lifted her chin. "I don't have liaisons." His distrust of her was clear, but she refused to let that silence her.

"No," he agreed, his voice cold. "You would have to have a heart to experience passion."

Her already fragile confidence was shaken by the direct hit. All her life she'd struggled to be special enough to deserve love and acceptance. Now it appeared that even Tariq, the one person who'd ever treated her as if she were worth cherishing, found her wanting.

"You can't hold a man like Tariq. He'll forget you the minute some glamourpuss princess comes along."

Uninvited, Sarah's spiteful words from four years ago burst into Jasmine's mind. Back then, they'd delivered the last emotional blow to her belief in herself, coming from an older sister who knew so much more about men. What if it hadn't just been spite? What if Sarah had been right?

When Jasmine had made the fateful decision to find Tariq again, she'd been uncertain of her ability to reach the man she'd known. How could she hope to reach the man he'd become? Buffeted by doubt, she turned and stared out the tinted windows. There was nothing to see but endless desert.

Strong fingers on her jaw forced her attention back to the panther lounging opposite her. His green-eyed gaze caught her own and held her in thrall. "I will keep you, my Jasmine." It was a statement, not a question.

"And if I don't wish to be…" She paused, unable to think of the right word.

"Owned?" Tariq suggested in a silky whisper.

Jasmine swallowed. A part of her was terrified of the dark fury she saw swirling in his eyes, but she'd come too far to fall victim to her fears now. "Like a slave?" Her voice was husky, her lips parched. However, she didn't dare moisten them with her tongue, afraid of how Tariq would react.

He narrowed his eyes. "You think I am such a barbarian?"

"I think you're going out of your way to give me that impression," she retorted, before she could caution herself not to bait the panther.

The corners of his lips tilted upward in a slight curve. "Ah, I had forgotten."

"What?" She lifted a hand to his wrist and tried to break his hold on her jaw. It proved impossible. Under her touch, his pulse beat in a slow, seductive rhythm that promised her both exotic pleasures and darkest fury.

"That the fire of your hair does not lie." He moved his thumb over her lower lip and frowned. "Your lips are dry. Moisten them."

Jasmine scowled at the command. "And if I don't?"

He lifted one brow in response to the defiance in her tone. "Then I shall do it for you."

Betraying color stained her cheeks at the erotic image of Tariq moistening her lips. His intense gaze made her feel like a tasty morsel he'd be only too happy to devour. Breathing in shallow gasps, she flicked out her tongue and wet her lips.

"Better." His approval was apparent in the deepening timbre of his voice and the way his thumb slowly swept over her lower lip, now soft and wet. When he abruptly set her free, surprise kept her perched on the edge of her seat for a moment, leaning toward him. Sanity returned with a shock. Face flushed, she scrambled back and across the seat until she was in the opposite corner of the car.

"Where are you taking me?"

"Zulheina."

"The capital?"

"Yes."

"Where in Zulheina?" She refused to back down despite his repressive monosyllabic replies.

"To my palace." He lifted one foot and placed it next to her right hip, effectively caging her against the door. "Tell me, my Jasmine, what have you been doing these four years?"

It was clear that he wasn't going to answer any more questions. Jasmine bit back her frustration, wanting to push but aware that she was on very shaky ground. "I was studying."

"Ah, the business management degree." His words were a soft taunt, a reminder of the times she'd cried on his shoulder, sobbing out her dislike of the subject.

"No." *There,* she thought, *let him suffer for a minute.*

He moved and suddenly he was sitting next to her, his shoulders blocking her vision, his legs caging her in the corner. He wasn't the one suffering.

"No?" His deep voice evoked memories of huskier tones and sensual laughter. "Your family let you change?"

"They had no choice." She'd followed their dictates and cut herself off from Tariq, but it had almost destroyed her. Her weak state had alarmed even her family, and no one had commented when she'd switched studies. By the time they'd tried to change her mind, she'd grown up. Disillusionment with the selfishness of those she'd trusted had followed fast on the heels of her sorrow.

"What did you study? Hmm?" He curved one big hand round her neck in a blatantly possessive gesture. The heat from his body swirled around her.

"Do you have to sit so close?" she blurted out.

For the first time, he smiled. It was a smile full of teeth, the smile of a predator tempting his prey to venture out into the darkness. "Do I bother you, Mina?"

He'd called her Mina. She remembered the way he'd always shortened her name to Mina when he'd been coaxing her to do something, usually involving kissing him until she felt like liquid honey inside. He hadn't needed to coax much. One look of sexy invitation, the husky whisper of her name against her lips, and she'd softened like a sigh in the wind.

When she didn't answer, he leaned down and nuzzled her neck, his warm breath seeming to burrow through her skin and into her bones. He'd always loved to touch. She'd relished his affection, but right now it was making her more off balance than she already was.

"Tariq, please."

"What do you want, Mina?"

Jasmine swallowed. He traced the movement down her throat with his thumb. "Space."

He raised his head. "No. You have had four years of space. Now you are mine."

His intensity was almost frightening. As an eighteen-year-old, she'd been unable to cope with his sheer, charismatic power. Though he was only five years older than her, his strength and determination even then had been enough to command unswerving loyalty from his people. Now, four years later, she could see that he'd grown impossibly stronger, impossibly more charismatic. However, she was no longer a sheltered young girl, and she had to learn to cope with Tariq if she wanted a future with him.

Holding his gaze, she lifted her hand and placed it over the one curled around her neck. When she tugged, he released her, his curiosity apparent in the quizzical look in his green eyes. Raising his hand to her cheek, she turned her face to drop a single kiss on his palm. His breath grew harsh, loud in the confines of the car.

"I studied fashion design." His skin was warm against her lips, his masculine scent an irresistible aphrodisiac.

"You have changed."

"For the better."

"That remains to be seen." His eyes narrowed. The hand against her cheek tightened. "Who taught you this?"

"What?" Shivers threatened to whisper down her spine at the sound of that dark, rough tone.

"This play with my hand and your lips." His jaw could have been carved out of granite.

"You did." It was the truth. "Remember the time you took me to the Waitomo caves? As the canoe floated in the glowworm grotto, you picked up my hand and you kissed it just so." She moved her head, and he loosened his hold enough to allow her to repeat the soft caress.

When she looked up, she knew that he'd remembered, but his features remained stony and his eyes boiled with emotions she didn't have the experience to identify.

"There have been others?"

"What?"

"Other men have touched you?"

"No. Only you."

He curved his hand around to tug at her plait, arching her neck and making her vulnerable to him. "Do not lie to me. I will know," he growled.

He was threatening to overwhelm her. In response, she relaxed into the exposed position that he'd engineered and slid her arms around his neck. "I will know, too," she said quietly. Under her fingers, his hair was soft, tempting her to stroke. Below that was the living heat of his skin.

His jaw firmed. "What will you know?"

"If you've let other women touch you."

Tariq's eyes widened. "When did you become fierce, Mina? You were always so biddable." She knew he was taunting her with the way she'd let her family control her life, even to the extent of ignoring her heart.

"I had to grow claws to survive."

"And am I supposed to be frightened of your puny claws?" He raised one dark brow, daring her.

Deliberately, Jasmine sank her fingernails into the back of his neck. She forgot that she was goading a panther. To her surprise, her panther didn't seem to mind her claws. He smiled down at her, a dangerous, tempting smile.

"I would like to feel those claws on my back, Mina," he whispered. "When you are in your place—flat on your back, under me—then I will."

"In my place?" Jasmine jerked out of his hold. When he continued to loom over her, his body crowding her against the door, she pushed at his chest. Masculine heat seared her through the fine fabric. "Move, you... you male!"

"No, Mina." He put one hand against her cheek and turned her toward him. "I will no longer follow your commands like a dog on a leash. From this day forth, you will follow mine."

He held her in place as his lips descended over hers. He needn't have bothered. Jasmine was transfixed by the raw pain she'd glimpsed on his face, before his shields had risen. She'd done this to her panther. It was, she acknowledged, his right to demand restitution.

CHAPTER TWO

TARIQ COULDN'T FIGHT THE driving, primitive urge to taste Mina, to claim her in this small way. Not even the knowledge that she was feeling overwhelmed and trapped could halt him. He tried to be gentle in his possession, but he hungered too much to stop. Then small, feminine hands clutched at his nape, holding him to her, inciting him. The painful craving he'd leashed for years battered at his control, pleading for freedom. He wanted to gorge on Mina. To feast on Mina.

Not now, he decided.

When he took her, he wanted hours, days, weeks in which to linger over her. But that long-suppressed craving had to be fed something, or it would shatter the bonds he'd imposed in order to keep from being eaten alive. Anger threatened to flame at the edge of his consciousness as he crushed her soft lips under his. He'd kill any man who'd dared to touch her. He would never forgive her if she'd allowed a single caress.

Mina was his.

And this time, he wouldn't let her forget.

In his arms, she shivered, and the simmering need inside him threatened to take complete command. He stroked his tongue across the seam of her lips. She opened at once. The taste of her was an elixir, a drug he'd starved for for years. His feelings for her were as wild and chaotic as a desert storm. How dare she leave him? How dare she take four years to return? When she gasped for breath, he breathed into her mouth, feeding her even as he took from her.

"No one else has touched you." He found some peace in that. Not much, but enough to rein in the beast.

"And," Jasmine responded in shocked surprise, "no one else has touched *you*."

He smiled that predator's smile. "I'm very hungry, Mina."

Jasmine felt her body begin to react as it always had to Tariq's dark sensuality. "Hungry?"

"Very." He was stroking her neck with his thumb in an absent fashion, feeling the vibration as she spoke.

"I need time." She was unprepared for the reality of the man he'd become. Dark. Beautiful. Magnificent. Angry.

He raised his eyes from his perusal of her throat. "No. I am no longer willing to indulge you."

She had no response to that flat statement. Four years ago, Tariq had delighted in letting her have her way. She'd never had to fight this warrior. Back then, he'd been careful with her innocence, but when he'd touched her, Jasmine hadn't felt like an outcast. She'd felt cherished. Today, she didn't feel that beautiful but fragile emotion. Tariq wasn't acting like a lover, but rather a conqueror with his prize. The true depth of what she'd lost was only now becoming clear.

He moved and set her free, but remained on her side of the car, one arm slung negligently over the back of her seat. "So, you have been studying fashion design."

"Yes."

"You wish to be a famous designer?" He threw her a look full of male amusement.

Jasmine bristled. Though used to her family mocking her dreams, she'd never expected it from Tariq. "Why is that funny?" She aimed a scowl at his savagely masculine features.

He chuckled. "Sheathe your claws, Mina. I simply cannot see you designing those ridiculous things on the catwalks. Your dresses wouldn't be see-through, hmm, displaying to the world treasures that should only be viewed by one man?"

She blushed at his heated gaze, ridiculously pleased that he wasn't laughing at her.

"Tell me," he commanded.

"I want to design feminine things." Her dream was real to her, no matter what anyone said, but until this moment, no one's opinion had truly mattered. "These days, the male designers seem to have an incredibly macabre idea of the female form. Their models are flat boards with not a curve in sight."

"Ah." It was a wholly male sound.

She looked up, suspicious. "Ah, what?"

Tariq spread one possessive hand over her abdomen. She gasped. "You're full of curves, Mina."

"I never pretended to be a sylph."

His warm breath close to her ear startled her. "You misunderstand. I'm delighted by your curves. They'll cushion me perfectly."

Biting hurt turned to red-hot embarrassment and shocking desire. Blinded by longing, she barely finished her explanation. "I want to design pretty things for real women."

Tariq regarded her with a contemplative expression. "You'll be permitted to continue this."

"I'll be *permitted* to continue my work?"

"You will need something to do when I'm not with you."

She gave a frustrated little scream and shifted until her back was plastered against the door, making it possible for her to glower up at him. "You have no right to *permit* me to do anything!" She poked him in the chest with her index finger.

He captured her hand. "On the contrary, I have every right." The sudden chill in his voice stopped her.

"You are now my possession. I own you. That means I have the right to do with you as I please." This time there was no hint of humor in his expression, not even the shadow of the man she'd once known. "You would do well not to provoke me. I have no intention of being cruel, but neither will you find me a fool for your charms a second time."

When, after a frozen moment, he released her and moved back to the opposite side of the car, she gathered the shreds of her composure around her and turned to the window. Had she done this? she asked herself. Had she with her cowardice so totally destroyed the beauty of what had once been between them? She wanted to cry at the loss, but something in her, the same something that had urged her to come to him when she'd heard of his parents' deaths, refused to surrender.

Unbidden, she remembered the way he'd held her so protectively in his arms when she'd run to him, frightened by the suffocation of her home.

"Come home with me, my Jasmine. Come to Zulheil."

"I can't! My parents..."

"They seek to capture you, Mina. I would set you free."

It was a bitter irony that the very man who'd once promised her freedom was now intent on caging her.

"I was only eighteen," she exclaimed abruptly.

"You are no longer eighteen." He sounded dangerous.

"Can't you understand what it was like for me?" she pleaded, despite herself. "They were my parents and I'd only known you for six months."

"Then why did you—what is your phrase?" He paused. "Yes…why did you lead me on? Did it amuse you to have an Arab royal at your beck and call?"

He'd never been at her beck and call. At eighteen, she'd had even less self-confidence than she did now, but he'd always made her feel…important. "No! No! I didn't…."

"Enough." His voice cut through her protests like a knife. "The truth is that when your family asked you to choose, you did not choose me. You did not even tell me so *I* could fight for us. There is nothing further to say."

Jasmine was silenced. Yes, it was the truth. How could she even begin to make a man like him understand what it had been like for her? Born with a mantle of power, Tariq had never known how it felt to be crushed and belittled until he didn't know his own mind. Shrinking into her corner, she thought back to the day that had changed her forever. Her father had forbidden her to see Tariq, threatening to disown her. She'd begged on her knees but he'd made her choose.

"The Arab or your family."

He'd always called Tariq "the Arab." It wasn't racism,

but something much deeper. At first she'd thought it was because they expected her to marry into another high-country farming family. Only later had she understood the ugly reality of why they'd crushed her small rebellion under their feet.

Tariq had been meant for Sarah.

Beautiful Sarah had wished to be a princess, and everyone had assumed it would happen. Except, from the moment he'd arrived, Turiq's eyes had lingered on Jasmine, the daughter who wasn't a daughter, the daughter who was a cause for shame, not celebration.

The huge spread in the hills, which had been Jasmine's home, had been in the Coleridge family for generations. As the beneficiaries of that heritage, Jasmine's parents had been used to controlling everything in their high-country kingdom and they had feared Tariq's strength of will. Added to that, his choice of Jasmine over Sarah had made him anathema. To let Jasmine have him when their darling Sarah couldn't, would have meant being continuously faced with both their failure to manipulate Tariq *and* the wrong daughter's happiness. It was ugly and it was vicious, but it was the truth. Jasmine was no longer a needy child, and couldn't pretend that they'd had her best interests at heart.

"Did you implement that irrigation system?" Her voice was softened by pain. They'd met when he'd visited New Zealand to learn about a revolutionary new watering system discovered by a neighboring family.

"It has been operating successfully for three years."

She nodded and laid her head against the seat. At eighteen, she'd made the wrong choice because she'd been terrified of losing the only people who might ever accept her, flawed as she was. A week ago, she'd turned her back on those very people and ventured out to try and recapture the glorious love she'd had with Tariq.

What would he say if she told him that she was now alone in the world?

Her father had carried out his threat and disowned her. But this time she hadn't compromised her soul in a bid for acceptance. She'd walked away, aware that she'd made an irrevocable decision. There would be no welcome back.

The only things Jasmine had in the world were her determination and a soul-deep love that had never died, but she couldn't tell Tariq that. His pity would be far worse than his anger. She'd chosen him and completely forsaken everything else. But was it too late?

"We are approaching Zulheina, if you wish to look."

Grateful for a chance to escape the distressing memories, she pressed a button by her elbow and the window rolled down. Warm air floated in, caressing her cold cheeks. "Oh, my," she whispered, distracted from her emotional agony.

Zulheina was a city of legend. Very few foreigners were ever allowed into the inner sanctum of Zulheil. Business was usually carried out in the larger town of Abraz, in the north. She could see why the people of Zulheil guarded this place with such zeal. It was utterly magnificent.

Fragile-seeming minarets reached for the heavens, illusions that touched the indigo-blue sky. The single river that ran through Zulheil, and eventually fed out into the sea, passed by in a foaming rush. The white marble of the nearest buildings reflected its tumbling, crystalline beauty.

"It's like something out of a fairy tale." She was fascinated by the way the water flowed under them as they drove over the bridge and entered the city proper.

"It is now your home." Tariq's words were a command.

Strange and wondrous smells drifted to her on the warm breeze. Sounds followed, then the vibrant living colors of the people as the limousine passed through a busy marketplace.

Hard male fingers encircled the soft flesh of her upper arm. Startled, she faced Tariq. His green eyes were hooded, hiding his emotions from her. "I said that it is now your home. You have nothing to say to that?"

Home, Jasmine thought, a sense of wonder infusing her. She'd never had a real home. Her smile was luminous. "I think that it will be no hardship to call this place home." She thought the panther opposite her relaxed a little. In the next moment, she saw something out of the corner of her eye that made her gasp. "I don't believe it. It can't be true." Ignoring the firm but strangely gentle grip on her arm, she stretched her neck to peer out the window.

Rising in front of her was the most fragile-looking building she'd ever seen. It seemed to be formed out of mist and raindrops, the artistry in the carving magnificent beyond imagining. The crystal-white stone of the building seemed to glow with a pale rose luminescence that had her transfixed.

She turned to Tariq, wide-eyed, forgetting his anger

in her amazement. "I could swear that building is made of Zulheil Rose."

Though Zulheil was a tiny desert sheikdom, enclosed on three sides by bigger powers, and on the fourth by the sea, it was a rich land, producing not just oil, but a beautiful, precious stone called Zulheil Rose. The striking, clear crystal with the hidden fire inside was the rarest gem on the planet, found only in Tariq's land.

"If your eyes get any bigger, my Jasmine, they'll rival the sky," Tariq teased.

Jasmine forgot the stunning building the moment she heard the quiet humor in his tone. Tariq had apparently decided to put aside his anger for the moment.

"That is your new home."

"What?" She lost any composure she might've attained.

He eyed her flushed features with amused interest. "The royal palace is indeed made of Zulheil Rose. Now you see why we do not let many foreigners into our city."

"Good grief." Earnestly, she leaned forward, unconsciously putting her palms on his thighs for balance. "I know the crystal is harder than diamonds and impenetrable, but don't your people, um, get tempted to chip off pieces?"

His voice was rough when he answered, "The people of Zulheil are happy and well cared for. They are not tempted to lose their place in this society for money.

"And the palace is considered sacred. It was carved where it stands by the one who founded Zulheil. Never in the history of our land has anyone discovered another such concentration of the crystal. It's believed that as long as the palace stands, Zulheil will prosper."

Hard male muscles flexed under her fingers. Jasmine jerked up her head. Blood rushed through her veins to stain her cheeks bright red. Flustered, she removed her hands and scrambled back into her seat.

"That, Mina," Tariq said, as they came to a stop in the inner courtyard of the palace, "is something you're permitted to do at will."

Hot with a combination of embarrassment and desire, she muttered, "What?"

"Touch me."

She sucked in her breath. It was clear that while Tariq had been prepared to wait for intimacy when she'd been eighteen, he was no longer so patient.

They stepped out into the heart of the palace complex—a lush garden protected from the outside by curving walls of Zulheil Rose. From where she stood, Jasmine could see a pomegranate tree heavy with fruit in one corner of the garden. A fig tree dominated the other. Bright, luxuriant and glossy flowers spread like a carpet in either direction.

"It's like a page of the *Arabian Nights* come to life." Any second now she expected a peacock to come strutting out.

"These gardens are opened every Friday to my people. At that time I meet with those who would talk with me."

Jasmine frowned. "Just like that?"

Beside her, Tariq tightened his clasp on her hand, his big body shifting to dominate her field of vision. "You do not approve of my meeting with my people?" The bright sunlight made his hair glitter like black diamonds.

"Not that. From what I've read, your people adore

you." Pausing, she turned her head to avoid his penetrating gaze. "I was thinking about your safety."

"Would you miss me, my Jasmine, if I was gone?" The question escaped Tariq's iron control, betraying emotions he refused to acknowledge.

"What a thing to ask! Of course I'd miss you."

Yet she'd walked away from him without a backward look, while he'd bled from the heart. "It has always been done this way in my land. Zulheil is small but prosperous. It will only stay that way if the people are content. None would hurt me because they know I will listen to their concerns."

"What about outsiders?" Her hand clenched around his.

He was unable to restrain his smile, seeing in her intent expression echoes of the bright young girl who'd claimed his soul. "The minute a foreigner enters our borders, we know."

"Your driver tried to convince me this was a taxi." Her gentle laughter was as light as the desert dawn.

At the happy sound, something deep inside Tariq was tempted to awaken. He had ached for her for so long. Ruthlessly, he crushed the urge. This time, he would not give Jasmine either his trust or his heart. Not when the scars from the hurt she'd inflicted in the past had yet to heal.

"Mazeel is a good driver, but not the best of actors." He looked up at the sound of approaching footsteps.

"Your Highness." A familiar pair of brown eyes regarded him with barely veiled disapproval. Tariq wasn't worried. Hiraz might let him see his anger, but his loyalty would keep him silent on what mattered.

"You remember Hiraz." He nodded at his chief advisor and closest friend, allowing the woman in his arms to turn.

"Of course. It's nice to see you again, Hiraz."

Hiraz bowed, his manner stiff and formal. "Madam."

"Please, call me Jasmine."

Under Tariq's hand, her back felt incredibly fragile. He didn't fight the surge of fierce protectiveness that thundered through him. However angry he was with her, Mina was his to protect. *His.*

"Hiraz does not approve of my plans concerning you, Mina." His words were a subtle warning.

"Your Highness, I would speak with you." Hiraz blinked in understanding, but his stance remained stiff. "Your uncle and his entourage have arrived, as have all the others."

"And he only calls me Your Highness when he wants to annoy me," Tariq murmured. "It is not the address of our people." It took an effort to keep his tone even after the blithely delivered message. The arrival of those who would stand witness to the events of this night, brought his plans one step closer to fruition.

Hiraz sighed and relaxed, unable to continue on in such an unfamiliar way. "So you actually did it." His gaze settled on Jasmine. "Do you understand what he has planned?"

"Enough." Tariq made the words an autocratic warning.

Hiraz merely lifted a brow and moved aside. He fell into step beside them as they entered the palace.

"What have you planned?" Jasmine asked.

"I will tell you later."

"When?"

"Jasmine." His quiet, implacable tone usually commanded instant obedience.

"Tariq." At the unexpected echo, he paused and turned, to find Mina scowling up at him.

Hiraz's chuckle provided welcome respite from the sudden shock of recognizing that Jasmine was no longer the fragile girl of his memories. "I see that she has grown up. Good. She will not be easy to control. You would crush a weak woman."

"She will do as I say."

Jasmine wanted to protest at the way they were ignoring her presence, but Tariq's dark expression stole her faltering courage. He'd humored her in the final minutes of the journey, but the man in front of her was the Sheik of Zulheil. And she didn't know this powerful stranger.

Inside, the palace was surprisingly comfortable, with nothing ornate or overdone. Light came in through lots of tiny carved windows, bathing the rooms in sunlight lace. Though beautiful, it was very much a home. Jasmine was still admiring her surroundings when a woman dressed in a long flowing dress in a shade of pale green materialized at her elbow.

"You will go with Mumtaz," Tariq decreed. He lifted their clasped hands and kissed Jasmine's wrist, his gaze locked with hers. Her blood raced through her body, frenetic with the effect of the simple caress. "I will see you in two hours." Then he was gone, striding down the corridor with Hiraz.

CHAPTER THREE

MUMTAZ SHOWED HER TO HER rooms—a suite in the southern end of the palace. While one room she was shown into had a very feminine feel, the others in the suite were full of masculine accoutrements. She commented on the fact.

"I...do not think there was enough warning of your arrival." There was an odd catch in Mumtaz's voice.

Jasmine attributed her faltering explanation to embarrassment over discussing Tariq's business. "Of course," she agreed, wishing to put the friendly woman at ease.

"Where do these doors go?" she asked, after they'd put her clothes away in the huge walk-in closet.

"Come. You will like this." Mumtaz's ebullient smile was infectious. With a flourish, she flung open the doors.

"A garden!" Under Jasmine's bare feet, the grass in the enclosed garden was soft and lush. A small fountain in the middle of the circular enclosure sent arcs of water tumbling over the Zulheil Rose carvings at its base. Benches surrounded the fountain, and were in turn encircled by millions of tiny blue flowers. A haunting fragrance drifted to her from the huge tree in the corner, which was covered with bell-shaped, blue-white blossoms.

"This is the private garden of..." Mumtaz stumbled over her words. "I am sorry, sometimes my English..."

"That's okay." Jasmine waved her hand. "I'm trying to learn the language of Zulheil, but I'm not very good yet."

Mumtaz's eyes sparkled. "I will teach you, yes?"

"Thank you! You were saying about the garden?"

Mumtaz frowned in thought. "This is the private garden of the people who live behind these...entrances." She pointed to Jasmine's door and to two other similar ones to the left. Together, they encircled three quarters of the garden. A high wall overrun with creeping vines completed the enclosure.

Jasmine nodded. "Oh, you mean it's the guests' garden."

Mumtaz shuffled her feet and gave her a smile. "You like your rooms and this garden?"

"How could I not? They're stunning."

"Good, that is good. You will stay in Zulheil?"

Jasmine looked up, surprised at her tone. "You know?"

Mumtaz sighed and took a seat on a bench near the fountain. Jasmine followed. "Hiraz is Tariq's closest friend, and as Hiraz's wife—"

"You're Hiraz's wife?" Jasmine choked. "I thought you were...never mind."

"A maid, yes?" Mumtaz smiled without rancor. "Tariq wished for you to be with someone you felt comfortable with when you arrived. I work in the palace and will be here every day. I hope you feel you can ask me for anything you need."

"Oh, yes." A little spark of warmth ignited inside Jasmine. Tariq had cared enough to arrange for this lovely woman to welcome her. "But why didn't he say anything?"

"Both he and Hiraz are terrible when they are in a temper. Tariq is angry with you, and my husband with me."

"Why is Hiraz angry with you?" Jasmine's curiosity got the better of her.

"He expects me to agree with something he and Tariq are doing, even though he himself does not agree with Tariq." Before Jasmine could question her further, Mumtaz continued, "Hiraz told me the story of what happened in your country. But it is common knowledge in Zulheil that Tariq had his heart broken by a red-haired foreigner with blue eyes."

Jasmine blinked. "How?"

"Hiraz would go to his grave with Tariq's secrets, but others in that party were not so…loyal," Mumtaz explained. "You are a mystery, but it is good you have come now. After his parents' deaths, Tariq is much in need."

"He's furious with me," she confessed.

"But you are in Zulheina. It is better to be near him even if he is angry, yes? You must learn to manage your h—"

The sudden look of distress on Mumtaz's exotic face alarmed Jasmine. "What is it?" she asked.

"I…I have forgotten something. Please, you must come inside."

She followed, bemused by Mumtaz's sudden change in mood.

"A bath has been drawn for your comfort. Afterward, please wear these." Mumtaz pointed to clothing that had appeared on the bed.

Jasmine touched the soft and incredibly fine fabric with her fingers. It was as weightless as mist and the color of Zulheil Rose—pure white with a hidden heart of fire. There was a long flowing skirt sprinkled with tiny shards of crystal that would catch the light each time she moved. The top was a fitted bodice bordered with the same sparkling crystals. Though the long sleeves would end at her wrists, the garment itself was short and would leave her midriff bare. Multiple strands of fine gold chain lay beside the top. Clearly, they were supposed to go around her waist.

"These aren't mine," Jasmine whispered.

"There is a special…meal, and your clothing is not correct. This is for you as, uh…"

"A guest?" she suggested. "Well, I suppose if this is normal practice, then it should be okay. I just wouldn't feel comfortable wearing something so expensive otherwise."

She had to repeatedly ensure Mumtaz that she'd be fine before the other woman would leave. "It's something formal, this dinner?" she asked, just before Mumtaz walked out.

"Oh yes. Very formal. I will return to do your hair and make sure you look beautiful."

As Mumtaz left, Jasmine was certain that she heard her muttering under her breath, but the delicious promise of the scented bath distracted her.

"I FEEL LIKE A PRINCESS," Jasmine whispered, almost two hours after she'd entered the palace. She touched her hand to the gold circlet that Mumtaz had insisted on placing about her head. Her deep-red hair had been brushed until it shone. Now it flowed in riotous waves to the middle of her back, the fine gold strands within it complementing the simple circlet.

"Then I have done my job." Mumtaz laughed.

"I thought flesh wasn't meant to be shown?" Jasmine put her hand on her abdomen. The fine gold chains about her hips were lavish and utterly seductive.

Mumtaz shook her head. "We are reserved in public only. Zulheil has no strict laws, but most women prefer modesty. In our homes with our men, it is acceptable to be more…" She waved her hands at her own clothing. She was wearing wide-legged harem pants in a pale shade of yellow, cinched at the ankle, and a blouse fitted much like Jasmine's. However, her clothing didn't glitter with sparkling crystal shards.

"I won't be overdressed?" Jasmine didn't want to change. She'd been imagining the look in Tariq's eyes at her appearance. Maybe he'd think her beautiful, because for the first time in her life, she felt that way.

"You are perfect. Now we must go."

A few minutes later they entered a room full of women, all dressed in stunning costumes bursting with color. Jasmine's eyes widened. At their entry, conversation stopped. A second later, it started again in a chaotic rush. Several older women came over and invited her to sit on the cushions with them. With Mumtaz acting as a translator when necessary, Jasmine was soon laughing and talking with them as if with old friends. Something about them seemed familiar, but she couldn't put her finger on what.

The innate tensing of her body was the only warning she needed half an hour later. She looked up and found

Tariq standing in the doorway. Unbidden, her legs uncurled and she stood. Silence reigned again, but this time
it was full of expectancy, as if everyone was holding their
breath.

He looked magnificent, dressed in a black tunic and
pants, the only ornamentation being gold embroidery
on the mandarin collar of the tunic. The starkness of
his clothing set off the dark beauty of his features. He
walked across the room and took her hand. She was
vaguely aware of other men following him inside, and
the rustle of cloth as the women around her stood up.

His eyes blazed with heat when he gazed at her. "You
look like the heart of the Zulheil Rose," he whispered,
for her ears only, his eyes on her hair. He drew back, but
she felt as if she was in the center of an inferno.

"I have a question for you, my Jasmine." This time the
words were crystal clear in the otherwise silent room.

She stared up at him. "Yes?"

Green fire met her. "You came to Zulheil of your own
free will. Will you stay of your own free will?"

Jasmine was confused. Tariq had made it clear that
he wasn't going to let her leave. Why ask her this now?
However, she instinctively knew that she couldn't question him in front of witnesses, not without doing damage
to his pride and standing among his people. "Yes."

Tariq's smile was quick and satisfied. He reminded her
of a panther again and she suddenly felt stalked. "And
will you stay *with me* of your own free will?"

The question was the trigger her mind needed. She understood what was happening, but the knowledge didn't
change her answer. "I will stay," she said, and sealed her
destiny.

The savage satisfaction in his eyes burned unfettered for one bright second. Then his lids lowered and hid the fire. He lifted her hand to his lips and turned it over, to lay a single kiss on the pulse beating rapidly under her skin. "I take my leave of you, my Jasmine…for now."

Then he was gone, leaving her standing, her mind in shock at what she'd just done. Giggling women came to her side and directed her back to her cushion. Jasmine caught Mumtaz's worried expression as the other woman took a seat next to her.

"You know?" The whisper reached only her ears, muffled by the buzz of conversation in the room.

Jasmine nodded. Aware that she was the center of attention, she tried to appear calm, even though her heart beat so hard she was afraid that it was going to rip out of her chest. The secret that she'd successfully buried under her love for Tariq raised its head, like a cobra readying itself to strike, taunting her with its inevitability. Unable to face his rejection, she'd planned to tell him once she was certain of her welcome in his life. Now it was too late. Much too late. How could she tell him the truth now?

"Jasmine?" Mumtaz interrupted her thoughts, reminding her of the act that had just taken place.

"When he asked me those questions…"

"I wished to tell you the truth, but they forbade it."

"And your loyalty is to Tariq." Jasmine couldn't hold the omission against Mumtaz. The other woman had done everything she could. "I thought the country was in mourning?"

"One month we have mourned, but it is part of Zulheil's culture that life conquers death. Our people would rather live joyously as an offering to those who are gone, than shroud ourselves in darkness."

Someone put a plate of sweetmeats into Jasmine's hands. She nodded an absentminded thanks at the woman, but didn't attempt to eat. Her stomach was in knots. Suddenly, she knew why the guests around her seemed so familiar. All of them had an unmistakable regal bearing that reminded her of Tariq—of course his family would be in attendance on this night.

"Do you know what happens next?" At the negative shake of her head, Mumtaz explained. "The questions are the first step in the marriage ceremony. Second is the binding, which will be performed by an elder. The final part is the blessing, which will be sung outside. You will not see Tariq again until it is over."

Jasmine nodded. Her eyes went to the lacy window set in the middle of the dividing wall. Her future awaited on the other side. "I've never heard of such a ceremony."

"Zulheil's ways are not those of our Islamic neighbors. We follow the ancient paths," Mumtaz explained. "You truly answered him knowing the consequences?"

Jasmine drew in a deep breath. "I stepped off that plane with only one goal. I didn't expect this, but he's the only man I've ever wanted. I could never say no to him."

Mumtaz's smile was understanding. "He is angry, but he needs you. Love him, Jasmine, and teach him to love again."

Jasmine nodded. She had to teach him to love her, or she was going to spend her life as the possession of a man who didn't care about her love. A man who, unless he loved her, would reject her once she revealed her shameful secret.

By the time she stepped out of this room, she would be married to the Sheik of Zulheil.

"It is time for the binding." Mumtaz nodded toward an aged woman, clad head to toe in vibrant red, who had just entered the room.

Coming to kneel next to Jasmine, the elder smiled and picked up her right hand. "With this I bind you." She tied a beautiful red ribbon with intricate embroidery around Jasmine's wrist.

Leaning close, Jasmine saw that the embroidery was writing—flowing Arabic script. When the elder raised her wrinkled face, there was power in those dark eyes. "You will repeat my words."

Jasmine nodded jerkily.

"This binding, it be true. This binding, it be unbroken."

"This binding, it be true. This binding, it be unbroken." Her voice was a whisper, her throat clogged with the knowledge of the finality of her actions.

"With this bond, I take my life and put it in the keeping of Tariq al-Huzzein Donovan Zamanat. For ever and eternity."

Jasmine repeated the words carefully and exactly. She'd made her choice, and she would see it through, but a deep shaft of pain ran through her at the thought that her parents weren't present on this day. They'd cut her adrift with a callousness she still couldn't comprehend.

Once she'd finished, the elder picked up the other end of the ribbon and fed it through the lacy window halfway up the wall. A minute later, Jasmine felt a tug on her wrist.

Tariq had just been bound to her.

For ever and eternity.

The haunting chant that began outside seemed to echo in her soul.

TARIQ STARED AT THE SMALL aperture that was his only window into the room where his Jasmine sat. As the blessing chant grew in volume around him, he kept his eyes trained on the opening. Images raced through his mind, competing to hold his attention.

Mina, wearing the dress of his land. He felt fierce pride in the way she'd carried herself. A princess could not have been more regal.

Mina, her red hair a fall of sunsets that beckoned him with promises of warmth. Soon he'd collect on that promise.

Mina, looking at him with eyes that betrayed her awakening sensuality. Yes, Jasmine had grown up. It would be his pleasure to teach her the secrets of the bedroom.

His need to possess her clawed at him, but underlying it was a deeper need and an even deeper hurt, things he refused to acknowledge. He allowed only a sliver of hunger to escape his control. Mina had always belonged to him, but in a few more minutes, the ties between them would become unbreakable.

Then he would claim his woman.

HE WAS VERY HUNGRY.

Tariq's words in the car refused to leave Jasmine's

mind. How was she supposed to relax, knowing that a hungry panther was coming to lay claim to her? With a groan, she sat up in the huge bed in the room next to hers. Tariq's masculine presence was everywhere.

The flimsy nightgown that she'd found on the bed was scandalous as far as she was concerned. The superfine white linen fell to her ankles like a sheet of mist. It was laced with blue ribbon down to her navel, and had long sleeves tied with the same ribbon at the wrist. Thigh-high slits on either side bared her legs with every movement she made. The sleeves were also slit from wrist to shoulder, exposing her skin. All that wasn't as bad as the fact that the material was almost sheer, her nipples and the darker triangle between her legs far too visible.

"They might be reserved in public but they could give lessons in eroticism," she muttered, standing beside the bed.

Uncomfortable in the sensual clothing, she crossed to the closet, with the intention of finding a robe to throw on over it. She found a large blue silk one that was clearly Tariq's. It would have to do, she thought, and pulled it out.

"Stop."

Startled, she swiveled around. She hadn't heard him enter. Hadn't heard him move across the room. Tariq was almost upon her, his eyes hot as they skated over her body. Her gaze fixated on his naked chest. He was magnificent. His shoulders were wider than she'd imagined, the muscles thick and liquid when he moved. The ridges on his abdomen appeared hard and inflexible, pure steel under skin. The only thing saving him from nakedness was a small white towel.

"I did not give you permission to cover yourself."

Jasmine bristled at his autocratic tone. "I don't need your permission."

With a single flick of his wrist, he pushed the robe from her nerveless fingers and captured both her hands in one of his own. "You forget that I now own you. You do what I wish."

"Rubbish."

"If it comforts you, feel free to disagree," he said, magnanimous in victory. "But know that I am going to win."

Jasmine stared up at him. Not for the first time, she wondered if she'd taken on more than she could handle. Maybe Tariq really was the despot he was acting. Perhaps he did consider her a possession.

"I wish to see you, Mina." He turned her with such speed that she would've lost her balance had he not clamped an arm around her waist. His other arm came to lie under her breasts.

When she looked up, she found, to her shock, that they were standing in front of the full-length mirror in the corner. Her hair was exotically red against the white of her nightgown, her pale skin a stark contrast to the darkness of his arms. His big body was curved over hers, his shoulders blocking out the night.

"Tariq, let go," she begged, unable to take the erotic intimacy implied by the reflection. She turned her face to one side, so her cheek pressed against his chest. Her worries about him were buried under the river of need that flooded her body.

"No, Mina. I wish to see you." He nuzzled her neck,

brushing aside the strands of her hair in his path. "I have fantasized about this for years."

His rough confession made her tingle from head to toe. It no longer felt wrong to know that his eyes were on the mirror, seeing everything she attempted to hide. It felt completely right, as if she had been born for this moment. Born to be the woman of the Sheik of Zulheil.

"Watch me as I love you." He nipped at the side of her neck, then suckled the spot.

She shook her head in mute refusal. Despite the feeling of rightness, she was too innocent, too untouched, to easily accept this level of sensual discovery. Tariq kissed his way up her jaw and over her cheek. Her earlobe was a delicate morsel to be sucked into his mouth and savored. He ran his teeth over her skin in a gentle caress. Jasmine shivered and stood on tiptoe in an unconscious attempt to get closer.

"Look in the mirror," he whispered, spreading his fingers across her stomach and under her breasts. "Please, Mina."

His husky "please" broke through her defenses. She turned her head and looked. And met his burning green-eyed gaze. Holding her eyes, he moved the hand under her breasts until he was cupping one full globe. She gasped and gripped the arm at her waist. In response, he squeezed her aching, swollen flesh. It wasn't enough. She needed more.

"Tariq," she moaned, shifting restlessly against him.

"Watch," he ordered.

She watched.

He moved his hand up until his thumb lay near her nipple. Under her wide-eyed gaze, he rubbed his thumb over the throbbing peak once, twice, and again. She was panting for breath. Behind her, she heard his own breathing alter, felt his body harden, muscles and tendons settling into unyielding lines. She cried out when he stopped caressing her, only to sigh and whimper when he repeated the teasing stroking on her other breast. His hands were big, sprinkled with dark hair, and Jasmine ached to feel them everywhere. When he moved, she dropped her hands to her sides.

He left her breasts aroused and hot. His hands moved over her stomach, smoothing their way to her hips. There, he very carefully spread his hands so that his thumbs met in the middle across her navel. She dug her fingers into the rigid muscles of his thighs behind her when she saw the way the action framed the shadowy curls between her legs. He murmured in approval against her ear and rewarded her with another teasing nibble of her sensitive earlobe.

Then he smiled at her in the mirror, a very male, very satisfied smile. Still holding her gaze, he moved his thumbs. The curving arc rubbed the top of her curls. Jasmine tried to shift but his upper arms held her shoulders pinned to his chest. She watched in helpless fascination, her heart thudding in her throat, her knees losing their strength, as he slowly, deliberately pushed his thumbs down and inward.

The sudden pressure on the tiny bundle of nerve endings hidden under the fiery curls made Jasmine scream and bury her face against his chest. He let her recover before repeating the intimate caress again and again, until she was arching into every touch, urging him on. Dazed, she met his gaze. His eyes were hooded and dark, but the flush high on his cheekbones assured her that he was as affected as she was.

"No!" she cried, when he removed his hands.

"Patience, Mina." His breathing was irregular, but his control intact.

Jasmine squirmed in an effort to make him return. Instead, he gripped her gown at her hips and started to gather the soft material into his big hands. She was bare to her thighs before she registered his intent.

"No!" She tried to lift her arms but he squeezed with his biceps, trapping her. Unable to watch as he claimed her so blatantly, she pressed her eyes shut. And felt his lips on her neck, on her temple, on her cheek. He stopped raising the nightgown.

"Mina." It was an invitation into sin. Jasmine couldn't resist. She opened her eyes and watched him bare her to the waist, mesmerized by the rich sensuality of his voice.

"Oh, God." She felt like a complete and utter wanton, standing there unveiled, her legs parted for balance, Tariq a dark masculine shadow behind her.

His thigh muscles moved fluidly under her hands as he changed position. To her shock, she felt one thickly muscled thigh slide between her legs. He began to rub it across her aroused flesh, a gentle abrasion that set her senses reeling. There were no barriers between his heat and her moist warmth. Her hands were free but she no longer wanted to stop him.

"Ride me, Mina." He shored up the gown with one arm and slid his other one between her legs. Jasmine thought she would lose her mind when she saw his fingers part her curls. He shifted his leg again, inciting her to do what he wanted. Jasmine moaned and, almost without volition, began moving her hips. His fingers stroked her pulsing flesh even as his leg pushed harder and lifted her toes off the floor.

Lost in his touch, she closed her eyes and rode. Desperate for an anchor, she curled her hands around his biceps, but it was too late. She felt the explosion building, and then suddenly, she crashed. It was as if every part of her had broken apart and then reintegrated. Sobbing with her release, she lay against Tariq, trusting him to hold her up.

"Mina, you're beautiful." His voice was reverent.

Jasmine lifted her head and found herself looking at her image in the mirror, her legs spread apart, Tariq's thigh holding her up. Too full of pleasure to blush, she raised her head and met his eyes. "Thank you."

Tariq shuddered, almost undone by her surrender. "I haven't finished yet."

The gown whispered down her lovely legs as he released it. Her fever-bright eyes watched him untie the laces. He took his time, enjoying the culmination of years of erotic dreams. When she moved, he felt the faint shivers that rocked her. Pleased, he flexed his thigh against her sweet heat, knowing it would send shards of pleasure rocketing through her.

"Tariq, don't tease." She tilted her head toward him.

He dropped a kiss on her lips, enchanted by the feminine complaint. "But you are so teasable." He finished with the ribbons and the gown gaped open, baring her breasts. His arousal became almost painful in its intensity, at the sight of a reality that outstripped his every fantasy. Closing one hand around the taut flesh, he squeezed gently.

Mina's eyes drifted shut and she arched into his touch. He nudged her hips, needing her to feel him, to understand this claiming. This branding. He wanted to mark her so deeply that she'd never think of walking away from him again. The urge was primitive and uncivilized, but when it came to this woman, his emotions had never been polite or bland.

Opening her eyes, she smiled at him in the mirror, a smile full of newly realized feminine power, and then began to move her body up and down. The slow dance was an unmerciful tease, but the feel of her was indescribable.

He growled in warning. "Witch."

"Tease," she accused.

He started to fondle her breast again, rubbing her nipple between his fingertips. She was so exquisitely sensitive, it was a temptation he couldn't resist. "Perhaps," he agreed, "but I'm also bigger than you."

Before Jasmine could take another breath, Tariq lifted the gown and tugged it over her head. Her arms came up of their own volition, her mind unable to defy the compulsion. She heard him throw the garment aside at the same time he withdrew his thigh from between hers. Only his arm around her waist kept her upright.

Jasmine pushed aside the hair in her face and gasped at the sight of her naked body displayed so openly for him.

"You are mine, Jasmine."

This time, the blatant possessiveness of his words didn't scare her. No man could touch a woman as tenderly as Tariq was touching her if he only saw her as a possession. Somehow, she had to reach the man she knew existed behind the mask.

She'd hurt Tariq more than she could've imagined when she'd ended their relationship. Now she had to love him so much that he would never doubt her again. Her panther had to trust in her loyalty before he'd allow himself to trust in her heart. And he would, because she had no intention of giving up. She couldn't allow herself to think that there was no hope of winning him back. That was a nightmare she couldn't face.

His eyes met hers in the mirror, daring her to deny him. Instead of answering the silent challenge, she took a deep breath and said, "I want another ride."

CHAPTER FOUR

TARIQ'S ARM TIGHTENED convulsively around her waist and the fire in his eyes blazed out of control. "No, this time *I* will ride." He turned her in his arms and picked her up without effort. "A long, slow ride. You can have another turn later." A hard kiss on her lips sealed the rough promise.

He laid her on the sheets after pushing aside the blanket. For the first time, Jasmine saw him completely naked. He was big. She hadn't thought about just how much bigger than her he was, until that moment.

His eyes met hers and she knew he understood her apprehension. "I won't hurt you, Mina." He moved onto the bed and covered her body with his own. The heavy weight of him was like a full-body caress, a feast for her senses.

"You always call me Mina when you want to get your own way." She spread her thighs for him and wrapped her arms around his neck.

Tariq rewarded her trust by slipping his hands under her waist and cupping her buttocks. "I'll always get my way from now on." His statement was uncompromising, as was the blunt tip of his erection against her.

Then he kissed her, his tongue mimicking the ultimate sensual act. Jasmine knew she was ready; she'd felt herself slick and moist against his thigh. She knew it, but it took his kiss on her breast, his huskily uttered, "I'll take care of you, Mina," to make her believe.

"Now," she whispered.

He gripped her hips and pushed. At the same time, he captured one strawberry-pink nipple into his mouth and suckled. Hard. Jasmine screamed and bucked under the onslaught of feeling, inadvertently easing his way. He surged inside her, tearing through the thin membrane that had protected her innocence. She gasped, her body taut.

"Mina?" He was frozen above her.

She dug her fingernails into his shoulders. "A long, slow ride," she reminded him in a breathless murmur, still adjusting to the feel of his heat inside her.

Three torturously slow strokes later, she was begging him to go faster.

"You are too impatient," he reprimanded her, but his body glistened with sweat and she could feel him trembling with the effort to hold back.

She tightened her legs around him and drew her nails down his back. His eyes flashed as his control fractured and then he slammed into her. Jasmine bit his shoulder when her desire reached a crescendo, and then she felt herself explode for the second time that night. Above her, Tariq went rigid as his own climax roared through him.

His body was heavy when he collapsed on top of her, but she was so exhausted she couldn't move. Instead, she nestled her face in the crook of his neck and fell asleep.

JASMINE AWOKE SOMETIME in the twilight hours when her stomach growled. Only then did she realize that, as a consequence of her nervousness, she hadn't eaten since she'd left New Zealand. She attempted to shift, and found she couldn't. One heavy male leg pinned her lower body to the bed and the arm curved possessively under her breasts immobilized her torso. Her stomach growled again.

"Tariq." She turned her head and kissed his neck. Under her lips, his skin was warm and tasted faintly of the desert and the salt and spice of their loving. "Wake up."

He groaned in his sleep and tightened his embrace. Sighing, Jasmine put her hands on his shoulders and shook him.

"You wish for your ride already, Mina?" His sleepy question made her turn bright red. Now that she wasn't in the grip of passion, she couldn't believe her boldness.

She frowned. "I wish for food. I'm starving."

He chuckled and rolled over, taking her with him. She ended up sprawled on his chest. His eyes glinted at her from behind half-closed lids. "What will you give me if I feed you?"

Her stomach growled again. Loudly. "Peace."

This time he laughed, his chest rumbling under her hands. "Ah, Mina, you are never what is expected." He gave a long-suffering sigh. "I'll see if I can find you food."

He put her aside with careful hands and slipped out of bed. Jasmine couldn't help watching him. The well-defined muscles of his back bunched as he stood up and bent over to pick up the robe he'd pushed out of her hands.

"Like what you see?" he asked, without turning around.

Jasmine felt herself blush again. "Yes."

He was pleased by her answer. She saw his smile when he turned to walk out, shrugging into the robe.

"Where are you going?"

"There is food in the dining area. I'll bring it to you."

After he left, Jasmine quickly found her rumpled gown and slithered into it. She was sitting cross-legged on top of the blankets, hoping the shadows hid the sheer quality of the gown, when he came back. Not saying anything, Tariq put the tray of food in the center of the bed and lounged on the other side like a lazy panther, watching her eat.

"So, what's my name now?" she asked, once the sharp edge of her appetite had been dulled to something bearable.

"Jasmine al-Huzzein Coleridge-Donovan Zamanat."

Jasmine's eyes widened and her hand stopped midway to her lips. She stopped chewing. "Good grief. What a mouthful! I didn't know that I got to keep my maiden name."

"Zulheil's women have always been cherished." He stretched lazily. "It's why we do not ask them to convert their religion upon marriage. The choice is yours."

The words sent a warm glow through her. Yes, she thought again, there was hope. "So Donovan was your mother's name?"

A flicker of darkness seemed to shadow his eyes, but his response was easy. "You know she was Irish." He plucked a fig off Jasmine's plate and put it into his mouth. For a minute, she just stared at the sensuous shape of his lips, reminded of the things he'd done to her with that clever, clever mouth.

"When we have a child, he or she will have al-Huzzein Coleridge Zamanat as their name. Al-Huzzein Zamanat is the name of the ruling family, but their mother's name is also always carried by the children."

He glanced curiously at her when she didn't reply. She blushed and transferred her attention back to her food. The thought of carrying Tariq's child caused bittersweet pain. She knew she had to tell him her secret…but not now.

"You have her eyes."

"Yes. And…" He paused. When Jasmine looked up, he smiled his dangerous smile. "Some would say I have her temper."

"They're obviously bright people." She picked up a dried apricot and fed it to him. He caught her wrist in a lightning-fast move and licked her fingers clean, like a great big cat lapping at his meal. His eyes never left hers.

"You must miss them." Swallowing, she fought the sensual promise in the air to address something far more important.

He looked away from her, into the shadows. "They are gone. I must lead my people now. I have no time to mourn."

Jasmine hurt for him. Everyone should be given the chance to grieve. Even a sheik. She'd opened her mouth to offer her support when he took the tray of food and put it on the floor. "Enough talking." He tumbled her to the bed.

Tariq did not wish to talk of his parents. The pain of their deaths had been intense. What he'd discovered afterward had almost driven him mad with grief. His beautiful, loving mother had been dying of cancer. His parents had been on the way back from a clinic when the car crashed.

The woman he'd trusted most in the world had kept a secret that had stolen her from him before her death. He'd had so many things to tell her, but because she hadn't had enough faith in him to share her secret, he would never get the chance. And he'd never know if there was something he could've done that would have averted tragedy.

Shaking off the memories, he pressed Jasmine into the mattress, pleased by her instant acceptance. Here, there would be no lies between them. There would be no secrets in the pleasure their bodies found in one another. He shoved aside the errant thought that there couldn't be such passion without emotional consequences, unwilling to concede that this tiny woman, with her gentle smiles and lush sensuality, might have already found a foothold in the lost places of his soul.

"You are sore?"

He could tell that she blushed by the hotness of her skin under his palm. Her heart's ragged beat became even faster.

"No." She hid her face against his neck.

"I won't force you, Mina. Never will I take what is not freely given." He stroked her back and pressed a line of kisses down her throat, luxuriating in her softness. Mina's delicious curves made him want to conquer her feminine secrets with slow, languorous enjoyment.

"Can I force you?"

He was startled for an instant by the suggestive whisper, and then he smiled. "Do you want me so much then, my wife?"

"You know I want you." Those eyes of hers flashed

fire at him, unexpected and delightful. Again he had to acknowledge that this Mina wasn't the same girl who'd almost destroyed him four years ago.

He leaned down and tasted her lower lip. Her teeth scraped gently over his in return. Yes, he thought, this Mina was no tame kitten to be ordered to heel. This Mina had claws. Would she use them to fight him or fight for him?

New excitement flickered through his bones.

TWO DAYS LATER, HE WALKED into a turret room at one end of their suite, just in time to see Mina raise her arms above her head and say, "Perfect!"

Surrounded on three sides by clear glass, the room was bathed in sunshine. As Mina danced across the floor, dust motes whirled with her, as if excited by her laughter. His whole body clenched. Buried feelings shook off their bindings. So easily, she could once again hold his heart in her hands.

Shocked by the knowledge of his susceptibility to a woman whose loyalty had never belonged to him, he fought off the tenderness she'd aroused.

"What's perfect?" he asked at last.

Startled, Jasmine froze and met Tariq's dark gaze. His power and charisma seemed to have increased in the hours that they'd been apart. "This room," she managed to answer. "I thought I'd use it for a workroom. Is that okay?"

Tariq moved farther inside. "This is your home, Mina. Do as you wish."

His generosity gave lie to his harsh words in the car. Jasmine smiled and hugged him. He didn't react, and she drew away before he could think to push her away. Affection was something completely different from touching in bed, and Tariq had given no sign that he wanted anything from her outside of that sensual arena. The knowledge hurt, but she was determined to break through the barriers between them.

"Thank you." Walking over to one of the windows, she found that it looked out into their private garden. "This room would be perfect for your painting. Where's your studio?"

The vibration of the floor beneath her bare feet warned her of his approach. Seconds later, he put his hands on her shoulders and turned her around. "I am a sheik, Mina. I don't have time for such things."

Jasmine frowned. "But you loved painting." She treasured the painting he'd done for her in New Zealand. It had become a talisman of sorts, keeping her focused on her dream.

"We do not always get to do what we love."

"No," she agreed, shaken by the implacability of his statement. Her Tariq, who'd been gentle enough in his heart to truly love, was now buried under the stoney facade of this sheik. Doubts about her ability to reach him surfaced once again, though she tried to fight them. For a woman who'd never been loved by those who were supposed to treasure her despite her faults, it was a task that required a mix of defiant courage and desperate hope.

Tariq closed his hands around her neck and caressed the sensitive skin with his thumbs, his eyes hooded and mysterious. "We do not have the time for a wedding journey, but I am scheduled to visit one of the desert tribes tomorrow. You will come."

He was giving her no choice, but Jasmine didn't want one. She'd spent four years apart from him. It was enough. "Where are we going?" Her skin felt as if it was on fire.

Tariq rubbed his thumb over one particular spot. "I marked you this morning."

Her hand flew to her throat and touched his hand. "I didn't realize when I chose this blouse."

He looked at her, the green of his eyes altered by emotion to something close to black. "You are mine in every way, Mina."

She didn't know what to say to the possessiveness in his tone. It was a little frightening to be the wife of this dangerous man. Sometimes her Tariq appeared, but mostly, all she saw was this cold, glittering mask.

"Such soft, white skin, my Jasmine." His throaty words made her relax. Tariq's desire she could cope with, but when he retreated behind his shields, she wanted to scream with frustration. "You mark so easily."

"Tariq, what—" she began, surprised when he started to undo the buttons on her scoop-neck blouse.

He ignored her fluttering hands. Eyes wide, Jasmine watched his dark head dip and then felt his mouth on her breast. *Sizzling.* It was the only word to describe the sensation of his lips against her skin. She clutched at his silken hair as he began to suck at the soft flesh. Her body felt like one big flame, his touch the fuel. A minute later, he moved away.

Picking up her hand, he touched one finger to the

small red mark on her breast. "See this and know that you are mine."

She stared at him, stunned by the possessive act. Yet she was also aroused beyond comprehension, her body reacting to the primitive maleness of his actions.

"Keep thinking those thoughts." He kissed her once, a kiss calculated to keep her aching. "I will satisfy us both tonight." Then he turned on his heel and strode out.

Jasmine felt her knees begin to buckle. She grabbed the window ledge behind her for support. Unbidden, one hand rose to her breast. He'd deliberately marked her as a gesture of possession, of ownership. She remembered the glittering satisfaction on his face, the harsh lines of his cheekbones, the lush sensuality of his lips, and shivered. Part of it was desire, but the other part was a painful uncertainty. She didn't want to believe that Tariq felt only lust for her, not when he treated her so tenderly at times, but this act of branding had been driven by something darker than love or affection. Something that she instinctively knew could destroy their relationship if she didn't find and confront it.

THE NEXT DAY DAWNED WITH skies of crystal clarity and beauty so pure and pristine it made Jasmine's heart ache. Such glory humbled her and yet gave her courage.

They left Zulheina in a limousine for the five-hour journey into the hinterlands of Zulheil. From there, they would have to go by camel to the important, though small, desert holding of Zeina.

"Who are the others following us?" she asked Tariq, after they had pulled out of the palace.

"Three of my inner council are coming." He crooked

a finger. Jasmine smiled and moved to sit beside him. He cradled her against his body. Unlike the steely intensity of his passion the night before, today he was relaxed, content to just hold her. "At the end of the road, we'll be met by two guides sent from Zeina to lead us to the outpost."

"It sounds isolated."

"It is the way of our people. We are not like the roaming Bedouin tribes, because we settle and set up cities. But for the most part, our cities are small and isolated."

"Even Zulheina isn't that big, is it?"

Tugging off the tie at the end of her plait, he unraveled her hair. Jasmine laid her head against his chest and basked in his unexpected affection. Just yesterday, she hadn't believed it possible that he'd enjoy this gentle touching.

"No. Abraz is the biggest city, the city we show to the outside world, but Zulheina is the heart of the sheikdom."

"Why is Zeina important?"

He moved his hand to her nape and began to rub his fingers over the sensitive skin in a slow caress. She arched into his touch like a cat. "Ah, Mina, you're a contradiction." His amused words made her tilt her head back to meet his gaze.

"In what way?"

He touched her parted lips with his fingers and said, "So free and uninhibited in my arms and yet such a lady in public. It's a delightful combination."

"Why do I know you're going to add something else?"

"I find I relish stripping away that ladylike facade in my imagination. It's very enjoyable to spend time planning exactly how I will make you cry out."

"Now every time I look at you, I'll think you're thinking that." She blushed.

"You would probably be correct." His laughing eyes warned her of his intention before he covered her lips with his own.

Jasmine wrapped her arms around his neck and relaxed into the slow and lazy loving. Tariq was in no hurry. Pulling her into his lap, he caressed her breasts with hands that knew every inch of her, and gave her a lesson in the pleasures of kissing. He tasted the inner sweetness of her mouth and nibbled at her lips when she needed to breathe, then returned to tempt her with his tongue, seemingly willing to do this forever. She was the one who got so heated she began to wriggle.

"No more," she gasped, and broke the kiss, aware of the hard ridge of his arousal under her bottom.

His eyes were slumberous, his desire clear, but he pulled down her tunic and settled her beside him on the seat again. "You're right, Mina. I would need hours to finish this."

Flustered and aroused, she scooted to the other side of the car. "Tell me about Zeina before you start your work."

His smile was very male as he gazed at her heaving breasts. "Zeina is one of the major suppliers of Zulheil Rose. For some as yet unknown reason, the gem only exists alongside deposits of oil. It is a strange crystal."

Jasmine whistled. "Talk about double dipping."

"It could be like that, but over centuries, the tribes of Zulheil have set up an interconnecting system that means that not just those people living near such bounty will benefit. For example, the Zulheil Rose leaves Zeina in a condition close to its raw state. It then goes out to two tribes in the north, who train the best artisans in the world."

Jasmine knew Tariq's pride was justified. The artisans of Zulheil were considered magicians. "Wait a second." She frowned in thought. "If the crystal is only found next to deposits of oil, why isn't Zulheina an oil center?"

"Zulheina is odd in more than one sense. Contradictory as it seems, our engineers and geologists insist there is not an ounce of oil in the area," he informed her. "So we think of the palace crystal as a gift from the Gods."

"I can't argue with that. It's so beautiful." She sighed in remembrance. "What's the purpose of this trip?"

"We're a scattered people. I make it a point to visit each tribe at least once a year." He stretched out his long legs, taking up even more of her space. "I'm afraid I must read these reports now, Mina." He gestured to some papers that he'd slipped into one of the pockets lining the limousine doors.

She nodded in acquiescence, thinking over everything he'd said. It was clear that while Tariq didn't yet trust her with his love, he had no qualms about sharing the business of his sheikdom with her. For the first time in her life, she felt a part of something greater, not just an outside observer. With hope renewed in her heart, she plucked a small sketchbook out of her purse and began to design a dress of moonlight and silver.

TARIQ LOOKED UP FROM HIS papers to find Mina's hand flying in graceful strokes across the page. Her face was intense in concentration, her mouth set in a way that suggested something had caught her attention. He was fascinated.

When they'd first met, she'd been a student, but her studies hadn't captured her interest. Today, she was fully absorbed in her thoughts. This was, he realized with a sense of wonder he couldn't fight, the first time he'd truly come face-to-face with the woman his Mina had grown into.

"May I see?" he asked, wanting to learn about this new Jasmine, this woman who threatened to catch him in a net far stronger than the one that had ensnared him four years ago.

Startled blue eyes looked into his, but then a slow smile bloomed. "If you like." At the shy welcome, he moved to sit beside her, his arm along the back of the seat.

He looked over her shoulder. "An evening gown."

"I thought that I'd use material shot with silver."

Her hair was soft against his fingertips as he leaned down to study the clean lines of the drawing. "You're talented. This is lovely."

Her cheeks flushed with color. "Really?"

There was hunger in the need she tried to hide. He recalled her defensiveness about her designing when he'd first questioned her—the reaction of someone whose dream had never received support. Distanced from the rapier-sharp pain of the past, he began to see a glimmer of the forces that had shaped this woman and her decisions. A kind of furious tenderness for her rose inside him. The urge to punish those who had hurt her while she'd been lost to him was so strong, he had to exercise conscious effort to control it.

"Yes, really. You might find some material to your liking in the shipment that comes from Razarah in the next month." In fact, he'd make sure that bolts were delivered for her perusal. "Tell me about your designs."

Eyes bright, she did. The journey passed in easy companionship that surprised him. Since he'd ascended to the throne, he'd never been free to simply "be" with anyone. Now Mina, with her laughter and her dreams, was tempting him to relax. To play. Did he trust her enough to unbend that much?

CHAPTER FIVE

"I'm scared," Jasmine blurted out.

Tariq turned to face her. "Scared?"

She nodded. "They're so big and…"

To her surprise, he walked over and pulled her into a gentle embrace. "Don't worry, Mina, I'll take care of you."

"Promise?" Her voice was shaky. She hadn't thought through the idea of what a trip on the back of a camel would entail. It had been something vague and slightly exotic.

"What is this?" Tariq moved back, his hands on her shoulders, eyes dark with concern. "You're terrified."

She nodded, miserable. "I can't stand heights and their backs are so high."

"There is no other way to reach the tribe or we'd take it." He cupped her cheeks in his palms.

"It's okay. I can handle it," she lied.

"So brave, Mina." He rubbed his thumb over her quivering lower lip. "The car is still here. You may return home."

Jasmine's head jerked up. He'd been so domineering in his demand that she accompany him that this concession was a real surprise. "You don't want me to come anymore?"

"I would not have you suffer."

She bit her lower lip. "How long will this trip take?"

Tariq dropped his hands to her waist. "It'll take three days to reach Zeina. With the time I must spend there and the return trip, a week and a half is an optimistic guess."

A week and a half! She couldn't bear to be parted from him for that long. "I'll come. Can I ride with you?"

He nodded. There was approval in the soft kiss he dropped on her lips. "You can snuggle your face against my chest and close your eyes, just like you do in bed."

She blushed. It was true that she liked to sleep with her head on his chest, her arms and legs spread over him, but she hadn't realized that he'd noticed her preference. She raised her hand and stroked his jaw, which was shadowed by his white head covering. "Thank you, Tariq."

"You are welcome, my wife. Come, it is time to go."

Sometimes, Jasmine thought, as Tariq helped her mount the sway-backed creature, her husband could be the most thoughtful of men. He mounted behind her before she could begin to panic. For the ride, both of them were in wide-legged pants and tunics, their heads and necks also covered from the harsh sun.

Her stomach lurched at the camel's first step, but she kept her eyes resolutely forward, determined to conquer this fear if it killed her. The endless desert vista was an unexpected ally, tranquil and beautiful. By the time they stopped for the day, she was watching everything with wide eyes. The camel's rolling gait was a little disconcerting, but as long as she didn't look directly at the ground, no nausea arose. And in truth, her husband's strong grip around her waist almost gave her the confidence to do that, as well.

However, she understood that even he couldn't help her with a sore rear. They had stopped at a hidden desert oasis for the night when she discovered just how bad it hurt. After they arrived, she excused herself and walked until she was out of sight of the men. She quickly took care of her needs and then stood in the shadow of a small tree, rubbing her sore behind.

Tariq's low chuckle made her spin around, face flaming. He was standing less than a foot away, his arms crossed over his chest, a wide smile on his aristocratic face.

"What are you doing here?" She dropped her hands and started to walk past him, embarrassed.

He caught her around the waist with one arm and swung her against his hard body. She turned her face away. Tariq nuzzled her neck affectionately. "Don't be angry, Mina. I was worried when you didn't return to camp."

Mollified, and melting from his warm touch, she decided to be honest. "It hurts." For the first time since she'd arrived in this land, she felt ill at ease, a foreigner unused to the ways of these exotic people. She needed Tariq's comfort. What she got was something totally unexpected.

His hands dropped to her bottom and began to massage her aching flesh with soothing strokes. "It will get worse before it gets better. I believe that's a Western saying."

She groaned, too relieved to be embarrassed. His hands felt like magic, but she knew that if he kept going, she'd do something silly like ask him to make love to her. Shoving at his chest, she backed away, her legs shaky.

NALINI SINGH 333

"We, um…better return or we'll miss dinner." She didn't look him in the eye, afraid of her own hungry desire.

His disappointed sigh was loud in the silence. "You are correct, Mina. Come." He held out his hand. Jasmine slipped her palm into his and they made their way to camp.

Her wicked husband leaned over and said, "I promise to soothe your sore muscles tonight, my Jasmine. I wouldn't have you so aching from riding that I couldn't ride you," just as they reached camp. A blazing blush stole over her.

The other men took one look at her and smiled knowingly. Ignoring them, Jasmine sat down next to Tariq. He sat to her left and a little in front of her, protecting her from the curious looks. Jasmine almost smiled at his possessiveness, but didn't challenge him. Aside from the fact that she was relieved she didn't have to face everyone in her current state, she would never dishonor Tariq in front of his people. In private, she felt free to question him, but deep instinct told her it would be a betrayal to do so publicly.

It wasn't just that Tariq was sheik in a desert land, where men possessively protected their women even as they cherished them. It was him. He was a very private man, a man who met the world wearing a mask. His pride was tied to his inherently private nature.

To his people, Tariq was approachable and kind, but he maintained an aristocratic reserve that was appropriate to his role. However, in New Zealand, he'd utterly frozen out her family, his contempt for their manipulative games completely undetectable. Yet with Jasmine he'd been warm, playful, teasing and, most of all, loving.

Four years later, she understood that only she had seen the man behind the mask. He'd trusted her. Even now he was really himself with her only occasionally— times when he seemed to forget the past. The rest of the time, he wore a mask for her, that of a man who would "own" his woman. It *was* a mask, she told herself. Her Tariq was hidden behind it.

After the evening meal, there was a short discussion in the native language of Zulheil. It was a beautiful language, but one she hadn't yet mastered.

"You were discussing sleeping arrangements?" she asked Tariq, when he turned to her. His eyes were hooded by the edge of his headgear, but she could see the campfire reflected in their depths. Her body began to burn with an inner blaze that was hotter than anything the desert could create.

"Yes. We carry tents with us if you wish to use one."

Jasmine shook her head. "No, I want to see the stars."

He smiled, as if she'd made him proud. "We will sleep away from the rest of the men."

Remembering his promise, she blushed. "Won't that be a problem?"

He raised an aristocratic eyebrow. "No man would let his woman bed down where other men may look upon her sleeping face."

"That sounds very…"

"Primitive? Possessive? I am all those things where you are concerned, Mina."

With the wild desert surrounding them and the night sky sparkling overhead, his words sounded exactly right.

He was a warrior into whose keeping she had given her life, and she knew that he would always protect her.

"What, no arguments?" he asked, when she remained silent.

"How can I argue with a man who has promised me a massage?"

For once, her controlled husband looked disconcerted. It only lasted a moment, but it was enough. The desire between them was mutual, a living, breathing thing. Unlike the loneliness of her love, when he took her in his arms, they were very much partners.

"I think it is time to retire." As he spoke, Tariq's eyes glowed with inner fire, not reflected flames.

They left the others soon afterward, carrying their own bedding. Tariq waved off offers of help, saying that if he couldn't make a bed in the desert, he wasn't worthy of being sheik. His men nodded solemnly, pleased with their leader.

He made Jasmine wait while he lay the bedding on top of a thick patch of some springy vegetation that would cushion their bodies from the hard ground. Then he held out his hand. "There is one thing, Mina."

"What?"

"Tonight, you cannot make a sound. We are too close to the others." He'd already removed his headgear. Now he took hers off and put it aside, before tangling his hands in the heavy fall of her hair. A rough sigh betrayed his pleasure. "Not a single sound, my Jasmine."

"Not a single one." Her promise was softly whispered.

She didn't make a sound when he stripped her and then himself. She managed to remain silent when he kept his promise to loosen her muscles, his powerful hands tender on her abused flesh. She even bit back her cries when his mouth enclosed her engorged nipples. Then his hand moved between her legs.

Jasmine bit his shoulder. He continued to play with the soft, moist folds between her thighs until she couldn't breathe. She sank her teeth farther into firm muscle in an effort to control her scream. Finally, after tormenting her for what seemed like hours, he lifted her hips and thrust into her in one smooth stroke. This time, she muffled her cries against his neck. He gritted his teeth against his own cry of satisfaction, his face a study in restraint.

They lay with arms and legs tangled until their skin began to chill from the cool night breeze. Tariq rolled off her and sat up to zip the attached sleeping bags closed. When he propped himself beside her, Jasmine saw what she'd done.

"Oh, no." She was horrified at the deep, red marks.

"What is it, Mina?" His concern was clear.

"I bit you." She touched the evidence of her crime with her fingertips.

He grinned. "Thank you."

"I'm really sorry."

"I do not mind. There are two more nights we must spend in the desert. Perhaps you will give me another two souvenirs?"

She remained concerned. "Are you sure it doesn't hurt?"

"Why don't you kiss it and see?" he invited.

Jasmine immediately reached over and laved the spot with her tongue and then pressed a tender kiss over it.

"*Now* I hurt," he growled against her ear. The hardness pressing impatiently against her thigh explained why.

"But we'll travel far tomorrow. You must have your rest. Turn around and stop tempting me."

Jasmine laughed at how disgruntled he sounded, but she fell asleep in seconds, despite the embers of desire glowing between them. When she wakened, Tariq was already dressed, which was probably just as well. The look in his eyes said that if she'd wakened a few minutes earlier, he'd certainly have delayed the entire party.

"Good morning, Mina."

"Morning." She sat up and rubbed at her eyes.

"I let you rest as long as possible, but we must be away soon if we are to make the next oasis by the time daylight fades." Tariq's deep voice was a caress in itself, full of sensuous memories.

Fighting off her blush, she replied, "I'll be quick. Give me ten minutes."

"Ten minutes." A hard kiss sealed those words.

Jasmine watched him stride away into the lush foliage, her body craving his touch. Hurried along by the cool wind, she shook off the desire that lay heavy upon her senses, and rose. The morning air was crisp, almost chilly, with no hint of the fire and heat that would descend as the sun rose higher. As she completed her toilette, Jasmine was struck by the way her husband reflected the hidden glory of his land.

Tariq could be ice, and he could be fire. Since arriving in Zulheil, she'd experienced both. Four years ago, she'd never seen the ice. Had she known only half the man? Four years ago…four years lost. Suddenly, she was starving for knowledge of Tariq's life in those lost years. The longing was a physical ache inside of her. Tariq had rebuffed her attempts to discuss the past, but she knew that until they did, they'd never truly be at peace.

"Mina! Are you ready?" Tariq's call cut through her unwelcome thoughts. The warmth in it was an arrow to her heart. Despite her hunger to know, she couldn't bear to disrupt their new harmony by bringing up the past.

She parted the branches protecting her from his view. "Are we leaving?" Other than a few bent shoots of grass, nothing revealed that they had camped in this desert haven.

"I would not starve you. Not when I am the cause of the hunger you must be feeling." The rumble of his voice washed over her. She smoothed her pants, inexplicably shy.

Straightening from his leaning position against the trunk of a tree heavy with dark green, glossy foliage, Tariq skated his eyes over her modestly garbed form with a possessiveness she couldn't mistake. Her breath hitched. When he looked up, she thought she might just beg him to take her.

He crooked a finger.

Some feminine instinct protested that arrogant action, even as the needy part of her wanted to run over and say yes, please. Instead, she stuck one hand on her hip and copied the gesture, with a boldness that, around her husband, felt right.

Tariq's smile was a slash of white in the duskiness of his face. To her surprise, he obeyed her command and walked over to stand in front of her, so close that her breasts brushed his chest with every breath she took.

"What would you do with me, my wife?"

Now that she had him where she'd wanted him, she couldn't think of what to say.

Mina's sudden shyness surprised Tariq. He traced a finger down the cool smoothness of her cheek. She ducked her head, but brought her hand up to cover his. He smiled and bent his knees to bring himself to her level. He surprised her with his sudden descent, and that was the only reason he saw the shadows in her eyes.

He rose to his full height, thunder pouring through his veins. She was hiding something. "What is worrying you?"

She jerked her head up. Hair the color of shattered rubies tumbled over his hands. Blue eyes displayed her distress at being found out. "What do you mean? I'm fine."

Her small lie only made him more determined. What was she thinking that she had to hide it from him? Where she was concerned, he'd learned to trust his instincts. Mina called to the part of him that was wild, primitive, untamed, a part that could be dangerous if he didn't keep it leashed. Complete possession of Mina was the payment demanded by the wildness for four years of imprisonment.

"I am your husband. You will not lie. Answer me." He thrust his hands through the fiery silk. The last time she'd hidden her thoughts from him, she'd been convincing herself to walk away. It had almost destroyed him. He didn't think he would survive if she ran from him a second time.

"We'll be late," she protested.

Time was no longer important. "They will wait." His

voice was made rough by his knowledge of his vulnerability to her.

"This isn't the place." She put her hands on his chest,
as if to push him away.

"You *will* answer me."

The small hands on his chest curled into fists. "You
are so arrogant, sometimes I want to scream!"

The explosion almost made him want to smile. Mina's
temper delighted him. Only the knowledge that she was
hiding something from him curbed the urge. His mother
had hidden her illness and it had cost him his chance
to say goodbye…and maybe more. Mina's secret could
cost him his wife. "I am simply willing to go after what
I want."

"So am I." Her voice was fierce. "I came to you."

"And you will stay." He would not give her a choice.
"Is this primitive land starting to lose its charms?"

She rolled her eyes, impertinent in her anger. "No, but
you're driving me crazy with your questions."

"Answer me and I will ask no more." His logical response made her grit her teeth. Those magnificent eyes
flashed lightning at him.

"I'll tell you later."

"Now." He kept her in place with his hands in her hair,
clenching thick handfuls of the luminous strands.

She looked away from him. Her body was poised for
flight but there was nowhere for her to go. In its blinding
starkness, his land was his greatest ally. As he watched,
the realization of her weakness dawned on her.

"You're taking advantage of your strength." Her
hunted expression accused him.

"I will use every advantage I have." He would not, could not, lose her. She was as vital to him as breathing.

For a second, their eyes met. Silence hung between them, his implacable words almost visible in the air.

"What does it matter what I was thinking?" He knew she was clutching at anything that might offer a reprieve. The hint of victory sharpened his hunter's instincts.

"You belong to me, Mina." This time she'd have no secrets from him. Perhaps, he acknowledged, her youth had made her vulnerable to the pressures she'd been put under four years ago. But if he'd known of those pressures, he would have been ready to fight for her and might not have had his heart ripped to pieces.

Her sigh signaled defeat. "I was thinking of the past."

Some of the chill that had retreated under the fire of their heated conversation returned with a vengeance. "Why do you think of such things?" The past held only pain and betrayal.

"I can't help it. Not when it stands between us." Her expression was earnest, her words passionate.

As Jasmine had feared, the mention of the past blighted the incipient joy of the day. Tariq's smile was only a memory now, this hard-visaged desert warrior the reality. He didn't deny her statement and the silence grew until it pressed heavily upon her. Wary of the stranger he'd become, she lay her hand on his left biceps. The muscle was inflexible.

"Four years, Tariq." Her emotions were naked in her voice. "Four years we were apart, and you refuse to share even a crumb of your life during that time."

His expression grew even darker. "What would you know?"

The question stunned her. She'd been expecting a harsh reprimand or perhaps cold dismissal. For a moment, shock kept her silent, but then words tumbled out of her. "Anything! Everything! Not knowing about those years is like a hole inside me, a part where you're missing."

"You made that choice."

"But now I've made another choice!"

The infinitesimal turning away of his face was his only response.

"Please," she begged.

He released her. Startled, she swayed before regaining her balance. Stepping back, he regarded her with eyes darkened to the color of ancient greenstone. "I was the subject of an assassination attempt by a terrorist organization on my way back from New Zealand."

"No! Did they…?"

He shook his head in a sharp negative as an answer to the question she couldn't bring herself to ask. "They had no chance." When he returned to his position by the tree, her sense of isolation almost overwhelmed Jasmine.

"Are they still active?"

"No, they were supported by their government, which was overthrown two years ago. The new government is friendly and will sponsor no more such attempts."

She thought that he was trying to soothe her obvious pain. That gave her the courage to continue, even though the ice in his voice was an obvious command to withdraw. She almost expected to see the air fog with her breath.

"But even one!"

That was when he delivered a blow so staggering that

he might as well have backhanded her. "They thought me weak and an easy target, because a woman had brought me to my knees."

Jasmine wanted to scream in agony. To have almost lost him…and to finally comprehend that her mission would be a thousand times more difficult than she'd believed. Maybe even impossible. The night before, she'd begun to understand the depths to which her husband's honor and pride were intertwined with his private nature. Today, it was painfully clear that Tariq's pride had been savaged by the reason behind the attempt. His strength as a leader, as a warrior, had been questioned because he'd allowed himself to feel. He would not forgive the woman who had been the cause of the insult.

A call from one of the guides interrupted the heavy silence. Tariq replied without shifting his gaze from her, his eyes dark, impenetrable. The syllables sounded brusque and guttural, as if he, too, were keeping strong emotions in check.

"We must go."

She nodded, numb from shock. Unable to trust herself not to break down, she followed him to the main area. He put food in her hands, and when she didn't move to feed herself, he leaned down and whispered in her ear, "Eat, Mina, or I will put you in my lap and feed you."

She believed him. As quickly as possible, she forced the food down. She had her pride, too.

TARIQ CAREFULLY PICKED UP Jasmine and placed her on the camel, once she'd bolted down the meal. He could see her fighting the urge to bring up the food, but he was ruthless in his protectiveness. She would need her strength to survive the desert journey. He would not let her mistreat herself.

When he mounted behind her, he made sure not to jostle her. She'd been silent since his revelation about the assassination attempt. He didn't like her stillness. His Mina was fire, life, joy. Yet he knew his harshness had caused her withdrawal. He had spoken to his wife in anger, and now that it had passed, he did not know how to bring her back to him.

"Hold on," he said, as the camel stood up, even though there was no need. His arm was a band around her waist. He would never let her fall, never let her be hurt.

She clutched at his arm, but let go the minute the camel was up. Her white headgear gave her a hiding place and frustrated him. He needed her to talk to him. The discovery made him scowl. A sheik didn't need anyone. A man would be a fool to need a woman who'd proved incapable of loyalty. He'd merely become used to her presence and voice over the past day. It was nothing more than that.

"Will you sulk all day?" He knew he was being unfair, but was unable to stop himself. He wanted her to fight back, wanted her to feel as much as he did, even if it was only anger.

"I'm not sulking." Her response held a hint of her customary fire.

Something he didn't want to acknowledge inside him eased at her response. She hadn't been beaten or broken. "It's better that you know the truth."

"That you'll never again allow me close to your heart?"

Her blunt question threatened to unsettle him. "Yes. I will not be such an easy target a second time."

"Target?" It was a husky whisper. "This isn't war."

His mouth twisted. "It's worse." After her rejection, he'd barely been able to function. He had loved her more than he loved the endless deserts of his homeland, but it had been the desert wilderness that had helped him heal the wounds she'd inflicted.

"I don't want to fight with you."

Her words calmed him and made him gentle in his response. "You belong to me now, my Jasmine. There's no reason for us to fight. This is forever." He would not trust her with his heart again, but neither would he let her go.

Forever. Jasmine lay her head against Tariq's chest and swallowed her tears. At one time she would've crawled on her hands and knees across broken glass for the promise of forever with Tariq. Now that wasn't enough. Forever with a Tariq who didn't love her and would never love her wasn't enough.

The obstacles in her path had grown to almost insurmountable proportions. Convincing Tariq of her loyalty would not be enough. He might eventually forgive her for not fighting for their love against her family, but she doubted it would be easy. But would he ever forgive the second staggering blow to his warrior's pride?

And what if she caused a third, with the secret that had broken a child's heart?

Panic threatened to choke her. No! No one would know about her illegitimacy! No one would shame her husband. Only her family knew, and they valued their position in society too much to let the truth slip out.

*You think your prince would marry a girl who can't
even name her father? Keep dreaming, little sister.*

Four years ago, Sarah had picked at her most vulnerable spot and then kicked hard. Jasmine still hadn't recovered from the blow, because she knew her sister was right. How could Tariq accept her, much less love her, if even her adoptive parents hadn't been able to?

He wouldn't believe that she'd been so overwhelmed by the marriage ceremony, she'd forgotten the one vital fact that made her the wrong choice to be his wife. As a girl of eighteen, she'd planned to tell him…until Sarah had bluntly thrown the consequences in her face. Believing her sister, Jasmine had kept her hurtful secret, and her family had used it to batter her down when they'd asked her to choose.

"You will speak to me." The rough order jerked her out of her maudlin thoughts. He liked her speaking to him, did he? Yesterday, he'd teased her that she chattered like a magpie.

Allowing a smile to escape, she let hope fill her heart about her ability to inspire love in this complex man. So the fight would be harder. So what? She'd almost died living apart from him. As long as there was the slightest hope, as long as her panther liked to talk to her, as long as he touched her body like he was starving for her, she'd persevere.

Maybe one day he'd trust her enough, love her enough, to accept all of her. Until then, she'd keep the secret she desperately needed to share, the anguish she needed to fight with his love, deep within her. And she'd make up for that one lie by fighting for other truths, however much it hurt.

"Tell me." Her tone was quiet but determined.

"What?"

"Tell me exactly what they tried to do."

"Mina." Tariq's annoyance was clear. "I have said that the past is the past. If you do not wish to fight, we will not speak of this." His hard body moved behind her as he made an adjustment to the reins held negligently in his left hand.

"And I'm supposed to obey your decree without question?" She was unable to let such an arrogant presumption pass.

He was silent for a long moment. "No one challenges the sheik when he has spoken."

"You're my husband."

"Yet you don't act as a submissive wife should."

His tone was so neutral that she almost missed the wry undertone. He was teasing her, no longer cold, as he'd been after the revelation in the oasis. Jasmine decided to continue her quest for the truth, despite his implied forgiveness for the pain she'd reawakened that morning. If she let it go now, Tariq would always refuse to discuss the past. An incredibly strong man, he needed a woman who would challenge him when required, not buckle under his demands.

"If you wanted submission, you should've gotten a pet." She didn't add that a submissive wife would bore him out of his aristocratic skull within a week.

His arms tightened around her. "No, Mina, I need no pet. Not when I have you to pet."

The wordplay made her blush. "You speak English just fine when you put your mind to it," she noted. "But I'm not going to be distracted."

"No?" Under her breast, his arm suddenly came to life. Muscle flowed and shifted, caressing her without any visible movement.

"No." Her voice was firm, though desire crackled through her like white lightning.

He slid his hand down to press against her stomach. Then, without warning, he said, "We stopped in Bahrain on our return, for diplomatic reasons. On the way from the airport, my car was separated from the cavalcade by two large trucks."

"Hiraz?"

"I was not good company at that time." Tariq's quiet response drove another nail into the bruised flesh of her heart. "Hiraz was riding in the foremost car with two guards. Another two were in the following car."

"You were alone." Instinctively, her hands left the pommel and pressed over his.

"I am never alone, Mina." His words were as close to a complaint as she'd ever heard. Even a sheik, she understood, needed privacy. A man like Tariq would need it more than most. "My driver is always a trained guard."

"What happened next?" She was caught in the destructive grip of a past that could have physically stolen Tariq from her. As it was, the emotional damage caused by the attack was profound.

He leaned down and moved her headgear aside so he could whisper into her ear. The intimate gesture made her glad that they were riding at the back of the group.

"We took care of them." His masculine scent surrounded her, his warmth an experience she didn't want to escape.

"That's all you're going to say?" she protested, dis-

turbed by the way he seemed to be withdrawing once
again.

"There isn't much else. They were religious zealots
from a troubled nation who sought to kill me with their
bare hands. I disabled three, my driver two." He nuzzled
her neck, a gesture so achingly familiar that tears threatened. The tone of his voice belonged to an exasperated
man tired of a topic, rather than one bent on rebuilding
an impenetrable wall.

"And the other guards took care of the rest after
breaching the barrier of trucks?" she guessed.

Tariq drew back from her and pulled the covering
close around her face. "You are too fair," he grumbled.

"Maybe I'll tan." There was always hope.

His response was a disbelieving snort. "Enough of
this. We will talk of other things."

She might've argued with him, but he'd already re-
lented a great deal after his initial refusal to speak about
his life. Pushing her luck could backfire. "All right."

"I don't believe you." He sounded so male, so put
upon.

"Drat." She fell back into the relationship as it had
been before she'd learned the awful truth about how
Tariq had been targeted for assassination because of his
perceived weakness in loving her. She needed to feel his
happiness, to find hope in his laughter.

"How are you feeling?" he asked.

She thought he was referring to their fight. "This is a
beautiful day. It's a day to be happy."

His chuckle startled her. "I was asking how your sweet
bottom was feeling."

She blushed and elbowed him. "Behave." The last

traces of frost were long gone. Fire surrounded her. She swallowed tears of bittersweet happiness. There would be no more pain this gorgeous day. She'd pretend that the world was perfect and that the man holding her so carefully loved her, too.

HOWEVER, THAT NIGHT, Jasmine couldn't keep pretending that everything was okay. Not when her heart was threatening to break under the strain. "Would it be okay if I retired early?" she asked Tariq. The firelight, which had seemed so romantic the night before, now made her eyes feel dry and achy.

From his protective position slightly in front of her, Tariq glanced over his shoulder. "You do not wish to remain?" His voice had a dark edge that she couldn't decipher.

"I'm tired. This is new for me," she confessed, hiding one truth behind another.

Her husband moved until he was sitting next to her. Then, to her surprise, he pulled her against his seated form. Tariq rarely touched her in public. She hadn't yet found the courage to ask him whether it was because he didn't want to, or because of the circumspection demanded of his position.

"I apologize, Mina. You don't complain, so I forget that this journey must be hard for you." Deep, sensuous, caressing, his words washed over her like soft, welcoming rain.

She nestled her head against his shoulder, finding that some of her inner ache had disappeared. He held her as if she mattered. "Am I expected to stay because I'm your wife?"

His muscled arm firmed around her as he shifted her a tiny bit nearer, eliminating any hint of space between their bodies. "Your intelligence is one of the reasons you are my wife," he murmured. "My people judge those not of our land. It's a flaw in us and yet it's so much a part of Zulheil that it may be our saving grace. We do not trust easily." Jasmine had known that the first moment she'd met him.

"Even though they've accepted you because you are my chosen wife," he continued, gazing down at her up-turned face, "and you'll receive obedience, the amount of respect you receive will be determined by a thousand things, among them your ability to endure this harsh land."

She understood what he would never articulate. His honor was now bound inextricably to hers. It was a fragile link that could shatter as it had once before, and rip even this shaky relationship from her grasp. "I'll stay. Just hold me?" She winced at the neediness of her voice.

He answered by touching her cheek with his free hand, his dark eyes fierce with what she wanted to believe was pride. Another knot melted inside her. When he looked away, she watched the play of the firelight on his face. He was at once beautiful and dangerous. A panther momentarily at rest. A warrior at home among his people.

Jasmine smiled. Her earlier frustration and pain had faded to a dull ache. Strangely content now, she stared up at the jewel-studded night sky, wondering if within those pinpricks there was a candle to light her way into her husband's heart.

CHAPTER SIX

BY THE TIME TARIQ RETURNED from a last-minute consultation with one of the guides, Mina was curled up and half-asleep. No light from the campfire reached their bed and neither did the voices of the men. He stripped down to the loose pants designed by his ancestors to offer respite from the unrelenting heat of the desert, glad for the small lagoon that had allowed the entire party a chance to bathe.

Memories of watching over his wife while she swam sent familiar need racing through him, but it was clear that Mina was exhausted. Tenderness overwhelmed him. She looked so small and fragile, and yet she made him feel so much. Too much. Heart clenching with emotions he didn't want to accept, he lay down beside her, wrapped her in his arms and let her rest. For a while.

Unfortunately, he didn't get to wake her with slow, sensuous caresses as he'd wanted, because deep in the night she jerked upright beside him, and he could almost smell her fear. He reached up to pull her back into his arms.

"Tariq!" She turned blindly toward him.

"I'm here, Mina." He succeeded in trapping her fluttering hands and held her tight against his body, disturbed by the too-fast thudding of her heart.

"Tariq." This time her voice was a husky whisper, but

no less desperate than her first fearful cry. She clutched at his shoulders with small hands.

"Hush. You are safe, my Jasmine." He stroked the curved line of her spine, trying to calm her. When she continued to shiver, he flipped her over onto her back and pressed his body along the length of hers. Some of her tension seemed to seep out of her at the full-body contact. "Mina?"

"They hurt you."

"Who?"

"The men in the trucks. I thought they took you from me."

He hadn't thought that his revelation would have this effect. "I am safe. They did not succeed. You did not lose me." When she looked as if she disagreed, he held her tightly. "You will not worry about these things."

Wrapped in Tariq's strong arms, Jasmine felt her fears start to dissipate. "I'll try. It was probably because I was tired."

"We will not talk of it anymore."

"Wait—" she protested.

He squeezed the breath out of her. "I have decided. You may sulk if you wish, but we will not talk more of it."

"You can't just decide that on your own," she snapped.

"Yes. I can." His voice was neutral, but she heard the steely determination. When he closed his eyes, she knew that any further words would only strengthen his resolve. Sighing, she conceded defeat…for tonight.

Wide-awake, she thought back over her nightmare. Unlike the dream, the real assassins hadn't succeeded in killing him, but they'd broken the connection between her and Tariq, torn the emotional threads. Their taunts had destroyed whatever had been left after she'd walked away.

A man's pride was a fragile thing.

A warrior's pride was his greatest weapon.

A sheik's pride upheld the honor of his people.

She had to learn to deal with the power of all three.

"WE'RE GOING TO FINISH what we started last night."

"No. I will not have you disturbed." Though Tariq wasn't surprised by Mina's stubbornness, his first duty was to protect her. The memory of how she'd trembled in fear made him hug her against his body as the camel picked its way across the golden sand.

"I'm a big girl. I can handle it."

"No." He would *not* allow her to be hurt.

"Tariq! Don't do that. Don't protect me by keeping me in ignorance." In his arms, her small body was stiff with anger and frustration. "I'm not eighteen anymore."

Her perception about his motives startled him, proving the truth of her words. "Perhaps not," he allowed.

"Then the assassins—"

"You know all there is to know, Mina." This time he acknowledged the quiet pain of the memories. "You *know*."

After a small silence, she leaned back in his embrace. "I'm sorry."

Unable to bear her sorrow, he held her close and told her stories of the desert and his people, and after a long time, she smiled again. And as they rode, he considered her persistence. Four years ago, she would never have challenged him. Since she'd returned to him, she'd never stopped fighting him. Some men would have been dismayed by the change. Tariq was intrigued.

ON THE MORNING OF THE fourth day, they rode into the small industrial city of Zeina. Despite their functional nature, the steel-and-concrete buildings of the city had been designed with curved edges and flowing lines. Overlaid with the omnipresent sand, the low-rise structures almost blended into the desert. The two-lane highway snaking out of Zeina in the opposite direction from their route showed how oil was moved out of such an isolated spot. To Jasmine's surprise, they continued through the city and a good distance beyond, to where a number of huge, colorful tents sprawled across the desert sand.

"Welcome to Zeina," Tariq whispered against her ear.

"I thought that was Zeina back there." She jerked her head to indicate the city they'd passed.

"It's part of Zeina. This is the heart."

"No houses, just tents," she mused out loud.

"Arin and his people prefer it this way. As they are happy, I have no right to question."

She pondered that for a moment before asking, "I assume many of them work in the industrial section—how do they get there?"

Tariq chuckled. "There are camels for those who prefer the old ways but also several well-hidden all-terrain vehicles."

"Why didn't we travel in those?" She scowled at the thought of the abuse her rear had suffered.

"Some of the areas we passed through are too treacherous to trust even those vehicles. They also cause much damage to the delicate ecosystems of the desert.

But, for commuting the distance to the metal city, they are useful," he explained. "Arin's people may be old-fashioned but they are also eminently practical. See the pale blue tents?" He pointed.

"There's quite a few."

"They appear the same as the others, but look closely."

Squinting, she did. "They don't move with the wind! What are they, plastic?"

"A durable type created by our engineers," Tariq confirmed. "Each houses sanitation facilities for use by four closely related families."

Given the dimensions of the tents and the typically small size of Zulheil's families, the allocation appeared generous.

"How ingenious." Jasmine was impressed by the way old and new had been merged so creatively.

"Arin is certainly that."

She met the intriguing Arin minutes later. He was a huge bear of a man with a short, neatly trimmed beard, but his warm smile took the edge off his menacing appearance.

"Welcome." He waved them both inside his large tent after exchanging greetings. "Please, sit."

"Thank you." Jasmine smiled and sat down on one of the luxuriant cushions arranged around a small table.

"I forbid you to smile at this man, Jasmine."

Jasmine stared at her husband in shock. "Did you just forbid me to smile at the man in whose home we are guests?"

Her subtle reprimand made her husband's lips curve in an inexplicable smile and Arin howl with laughter. She looked from one to the other, belatedly aware that she'd missed something. When Tariq continued to smile with that hint of mischief in his eyes and Arin to howl, she threw up her hands. "You're both mad."

"No, no," Arin answered, his shoulders shaking with mirth. "This one is just afraid of my power over women."

Intrigued, Jasmine turned to Tariq for an explanation, but he just grinned. Shaking her head, she busied herself trying to follow their conversation, which could not be undertaken in English, as their host wasn't fluent enough for the subtleties required.

"My apologies." Arin seemed discomfited by that fact.

"Oh, please don't say that," she said earnestly. "This is your land. I should be the one to learn your language. While I'm learning, it would be better for me to be surrounded by it."

The big man looked relieved. Tariq squeezed her fingers once in silent thanks. Warm, strong, male, his hand represented so much of who he was.

If she concentrated, she could follow the bare bones of their talk. They appeared to be catching up with each other's news but there was an undercurrent of seriousness. The sheik was asking after the health of his people.

As she listened, the changes in Tariq struck her again. When they'd first met, he'd been every inch a royal, but more relaxed, having the support of his parents, a much-loved royal couple. Now the mantle of authority sat on his shoulders alone, and he wore it as if it had been made for him.

He'd always been touched with the promise of greatness. Before her eyes, that promise was being fulfilled.

"Enough," Arin announced at last in English. "I am a poor host to keep you so long even before the dust is gone from your clothes." He uncurled his legs, incredibly graceful for such a big man, and began to stand.

"Terrible," Tariq agreed, but his eyes were full of laughter as he followed their host's example. Jasmine's guess that the two were good friends was confirmed by the back-slapping embrace they exchanged, before Arin led them toward the much smaller tent that had been prepared for them. Members of Arin's council had greeted Tariq's advisors upon arrival, and it was likely that they'd all settled in by now.

"Your tent should be larger. I would give you mine but your husband, he is not wanting to be treated like royalty." Arin scowled at Tariq over Jasmine's head. The two men had bracketed her between them as soon as they'd exited. She felt like a shrimp between two very large carnivorous beasts, but one of the beasts was hers and the other appeared friendly.

"If I am in that cavern you call a tent, people will not come to me as willingly as they do if I am in something approximating their own homes." Without breaking his stride, Tariq reached over and tugged Jasmine's headgear around her face, protecting her from the sun. "With you it is different. They have known you their whole lives."

With a sigh, Arin abandoned trying to get Tariq to change his mind. "This—" he waved to a small dun-colored tent "—is to be your home for the next three or four days."

Despite the dull exterior, the interior was beautifully appointed. Colors created bright splendor through the room, in cushions scattered about and gauzy silk hangings decorating the walls. Delighted, Jasmine peeked around the partition dividing the space and discovered a sumptuous sleeping area.

"Thank you. It's beautiful," she exclaimed, bestowing a dazzling smile upon Arin. He looked taken aback.

Tariq scowled. "You will go now," he ordered. "I wish to talk to my wife about the smiles she gives away so easily."

Arin laughed good-naturedly and left, but not before he threw Jasmine a wink. She ran to her husband and tugged his head down for a kiss. He picked her up off her feet to facilitate the soft, urgent caress.

"That is permissible, Mina." He set her down on her feet. "You are welcome to kiss me at any time."

"Gee, thanks." She stepped back to escape him but he was too quick. Tariq held her against him, his hands splayed over her bottom. When she wiggled, he took mercy on her and slid his hands to her waist. "Why did you forbid me to smile at your friend?"

"Because women like him too much. It is very provoking." His complaint was without heat.

"I think he's nice." Her husband's playful mood was a rare treat, one she fully intended to enjoy.

He lifted her up until they were eye to eye. "Really?"

"Mmm." She wrapped her arms and legs around him. "But I think you're the nicest of all."

Tariq's grin was pure male. Her reward for her honesty was a kiss that was so hot, she felt singed.

THEY ATE DINNER WITH ARIN and other members of the camp in Arin's huge tent. Jasmine liked being able to watch her sheik among his people. He was magnificent. Charisma flowed from him like a physical substance, bright and clear and utterly seductive. People listened when he spoke, and answered his questions without hesitation, basking in his attention.

"Your accommodations are suitable?" Arin asked.

She had to force herself to look away from her husband, aware that the moment she did so, Tariq glanced at her. His obvious awareness of her, even in the midst of a busy dinner, warmed her to her toes.

"They're lovely. Thank you." She smiled. "I've been forbidden to smile at you because women like you too much."

Arin stroked his neat beard. "It is a curse I must bear. It makes finding a wife difficult."

Jasmine thought she'd misunderstood. "Difficult?"

"Yes." He looked mournful. "How can a man pick one lovely fruit when every day he is confronted with an orchard?"

She clapped a hand over her mouth to muffle her laugh at his outrageousness. No wonder he and Tariq were friends. Right then, her husband tugged at her hand. Though he was talking to someone else, it was an unmistakable sign that he wanted her attention on him. She knew that he wasn't really worried about Arin's affect on women, so his possessiveness puzzled her.

"He is like a child, unwilling to share you," Arin whispered, leaning over. "He is correct in this."

She ignored the last part of that statement and concentrated on the first. It was true. Tariq was unwilling to share her—sometimes. He liked having her interact with his people and make friends such as Mumtaz, so he was no controlling oppressor. However, he seemed to want to keep her close.

What she didn't know was whether he wanted her near because he needed her, or because he didn't trust her out of his sight. She swallowed her hurt at the possibility that it was the latter, and smiled brightly at the woman sitting across from him. Taking that as a sign of encouragement, the woman drew Jasmine into conversation.

"TODAY, I INTEND TO VIEW several Zulheil Rose mines." Tariq finished his breakfast the next morning and stretched. The power and beauty of his impressive musculature made Jasmine catch her breath. "It will require hard riding, so unfortunately you cannot accompany me."

She scowled in disappointment. "Maybe next time. After we get back home, you have to teach me to ride those beasts."

He smiled at her mock shudder. "I'll do that, Mina. While you are here, you may wish to...I do not know the word, but it would be good if you would walk among the people."

"Oh, you want me to mingle?"

"Yes. Especially with the women. Out here in the desert, a lot of them tend to be shyer than their city counterparts."

"So you want me to talk to them and make sure they're doing okay?"

He nodded. "You are a woman and you are friendly, especially as you continue to smile at everyone." His tone was disgruntled but his expression approving. "Most of the Zeina citizens will try to come to meet us. It is the way we strengthen the bonds that tie our land together. The men tend to wait for me, but the women will feel easier with you."

Jasmine bit her lip in sudden indecision. She felt more than saw Tariq's relaxed body tense.

"You do not wish to do this?"

"Oh, I do. It's just that…do you think I can? I'm just an ordinary woman. Will your people talk to me?" All her life, she'd never been good enough. Sometimes the past threatened to overcome her hard-won self-esteem.

"Ah, Mina." Tariq tugged her into his lap and held her close. "You are my wife and they have already accepted you."

"How do you know?"

"I know. You will trust your husband and do as he bids."

His autocratic command made her want to grin. If he trusted her with this, then he had to have some faith in her. Perhaps it was even the beginning of a deeper kind of trust. The flame of hope inside her, which had been threatening to go out ever since he'd revealed the assassination attempt, started to flicker with fiery life.

"Aye, aye, Captain." She adopted a meek expression that made him laugh and kiss her.

He rode out ten minutes later into the crisp desert morning. After waving him off, Jasmine took a deep breath and began to walk toward the heart of the camp. Within moments, she was surrounded by Zeina's women, surrounded and welcomed.

It was only as dusk began to descend in purple strokes across the desert that she returned to their quarters. After washing the grit and dust of the day from her body, she dressed in an ankle-length skirt and fitted top in a beautiful shade of gold and lay down on one of the low couches to wait for her husband. Lulled by the soft chatter outside, she closed her eyes, intending only a moment's rest.

ONCE AGAIN, TARIQ FOUND Mina asleep. This time he needed to wake her, to satisfy not carnal hunger, but something far more dangerous. "Wake up, my Jasmine." His voice was rough.

"Tariq." With a wide smile she opened her eyes and her arms and tempted him into her embrace. "When did you return?"

"Perhaps forty minutes ago. Now you must awaken so we can eat." Nevertheless, he leaned toward her and let her put her arms around him. Spending the entire day apart from her for the first time since their marriage had brought old pain to the surface—raw, jagged pain that mocked him for pretending he didn't need her. The truth was that he needed her far more than she would ever need him.

"With Arin?"

"No." He smoothed the tangled strands of her hair off her face. "Just me. Tomorrow we'll dine with our people again."

Not wishing to face the emotions she aroused, he started to leave. She held him tight. "Don't go. I missed you."

"Did you, Mina?" He couldn't keep the edge out of his voice. He needed her, but would never again chance entrusting her with that knowledge.

"Yes. I kept looking for you all day." Her eyes were soft, her body warm from sleep.

"Show me how much you missed me, Mina. Show me." He clasped her to him possessively, the wounded

beast inside him unsatisfied with less than complete surrender.

He stripped her so quickly that she gasped, but made
no protest. He laid her down on the thick rug on the floor,
inflamed by the sight of her creamy skin and fiery hair
against the scarlet-and-gold material. She was like some
pagan fantasy, a dream designed to drive men wild.

Wrapping his hand around her neck, he kissed her,
claimed her. He tasted every corner of her mouth while
his free hand roamed her body, then covered the soft
mound of one breast, making her whimper. Finally
breaking the kiss, he bent down to take a tightly beaded
nipple into his mouth. He sucked. Hard.

She bucked under him and her hands clenched in his
hair. "Please…please…"

The broken sounds urged him on. Nudging apart her
legs with his knee, he settled in between them, opening
her to him. One hand flat on the rug beside her, he raised
his head and looked down at her as he moved his other
hand to her stomach and inexorably lower. Sky-blue eyes
bled into indigo and lush lips parted in a fractured breath
as he found the small nub hidden in her curls.

Though he was careful not to hurt her, this woman
of cream and fire, his strokes were firm. Mina clutched
at his arms and he could feel pleasure exploding inside
her. He stroked harder, leaving her only for the instant it
took to lift her right leg and place it over his hip, giving
him full access to her secret places.

Her moan when he touched her again wasn't enough.
He needed more. He needed Mina's utter and total submission. He needed her to hold nothing back from him.

Needed her to need him like he needed her. Needed her to love him so much she would never leave him again.

Reaching lower, he slipped a finger inside her. Her body jerked. Her skin dampened. Then he lowered his head and lightly, carefully, bit the underside of one plump breast. Around his finger, her muscles clenched in an intimate fist so tight he was drenched, surrounded. It was at that moment, as she shoved a fist in her mouth to muffle her cries, that he removed his hand, released himself from his pants and surged into her. Unable to control the spasms overtaking her, she held on to him, biting his shoulder to silence her gasps and moans.

He welcomed the sweet pain. Mina had fallen over the edge and he could feel it beckoning, but he wouldn't surrender. Not yet. Gripping her hips, he thrust hard. Fast. Deep.

Branding her.

"You're mine, Mina. Only mine." The words were wrenched out of the part of him that raged to claim her for all time.

Only when she lost the battle to muffle her pleasure and her cry rode the night air did he allow himself to fall into the beckoning void.

IT WAS AT THE FINAL DINNER with Arin that Jasmine learned about the relationship between the two men. While Tariq was deep in conversation, Arin answered her questions.

"Tariq spent time in each of the twelve tribes after he turned twelve. This was to teach him about his people."

Jasmine thought that the experience must have been unutterably lonely. He would have been one of them but also, as their future leader, set apart. Her heart ached for the boy he'd been, but she could see the results of his training. Tariq mixed as effortlessly with these desert dwellers as he did with his people in the city.

"He came to Zeina at fifteen and we became friends."

Arin's words were simple, but she understood the depth of that friendship. Her husband didn't bestow his trust lightly. And once that trust had been breached...

"And you've remained friends." She swallowed her sudden apprehension and turned a bright smile on Arin.

The big man nodded. "He is my friend, but he is also my sheik. Make him just your husband, Jasmine, not your sheik."

His advice echoed her thoughts of not so very long ago. She knew that Tariq needed freedom to lay aside the heavy burden of leadership, even if only for a few hours each day. It was easy to say but hard to put into practice, especially where her stubborn husband was concerned. Without warning, he could change, seeing in her the shadows of the past.

A memory of the bittersweet glory of their lovemaking yesterday flickered through her mind. The complex man she'd married, a man even more fascinating than the prince who'd been her first love, would give neither his trust nor his love into her keeping, unless she proved herself worthy. But she refused to quit trying to breach the walls around his heart. She could be just as stubborn as him.

THAT NIGHT, JASMINE SAT cross-legged on their silken bedding and watched Tariq undress in the warm glow of the lanterns. He turned and motioned her over with a tilt of his aristocratic head. She rose and walked toward him. Without words being exchanged, she knew what he wanted. She began to help him remove his clothing. His back was golden heat under her light touch, his body beautiful to her.

"You'd make a perfect harem slave," he commented, tongue in cheek.

She bit him on his back for that remark. "I don't think this primitive desert atmosphere is good for you."

He chuckled at her response. She drew back when he was dressed only in loose white pants. To her shock, he held her gaze and pulled them off in one smooth motion. She couldn't move as he threw the last piece of his clothing aside and stalked to her. It wasn't as if she'd never seen him naked, simply that he had never acted with such sexual aggressiveness. Even his furious loving last night hadn't been this...blatant.

He was a sleek, muscled warrior, rippling with strength kept in check for his woman. She knew that Tariq would never physically hurt her, which only made his maleness more compelling. Lips parted with sensual longing, she raised her head to meet his green eyes, shadowed in the dim light from the lanterns.

"You're overdressed for a harem slave," he murmured, and tugged her nightshirt over her head, leaving her naked.

"What about women?" she managed to ask, though her throat felt dry with need and her thoughts were scattered like tangled skeins of thread.

"Hmm?" He nuzzled her neck. It was, she was beginning to realize, one of his favorite preludes to lovemaking, as well as a gesture of affection.

"Did they have harems?"

He raised his head to meet her laughing eyes. "You wish for a harem, Mina?"

She frowned as if considering it. He squeezed her tightly. "Okay! Okay! I think I can handle only one of you at a time," she stated.

"You will only ever handle me," he said with a masculine growl.

Jasmine smiled and, without stopping to consider her words, said, "Of course. You're the only one I love."

Tariq turned to stone. She wanted to take back her hasty declaration. He wasn't ready; she knew he wasn't ready. But the words had welled up in her heart and escaped before she could control them.

"You do not need to say such things." Under her hands, liquid silk turned to steel and his warm flesh was suddenly searingly cold.

"I mean it. I love you." There was no going back. Throwing away her pride, she gazed at him, silently begging him to believe her.

Tariq's eyes were midnight dark in the lantern light. "You cannot love me."

"How can I make you believe I do?" She ached for the loss of their joy, their laughter, their blindingly beautiful love.

Too late. She was four years too late.

He shook his head, answering her with silence. In the past, his control over his emotions had fooled her into thinking that his feelings didn't run as deep as hers. Only now, when it was too late, did she understand that she'd hurt him more than she could have believed possible.

He'd given her his warrior's heart and she'd thrown it away in her ignorance of its value.

How could he possibly believe the truth after such a betrayal? And yet the truth existed. Her love for him was deeper, richer, more intense now. The child-woman who'd first loved him had matured into a woman who loved him so much she sometimes thought she'd die from the sheer intensity.

When he kissed her, she gave herself up to his embrace, swallowing her tears. Tariq played her like a well-tuned musical instrument, drawing every note of pleasure out of her. But he didn't give her his heart. Her warrior didn't trust her not to hurt him again.

Long after he'd fallen asleep, Jasmine lay awake, thinking of the past and how it had indelibly marked her future. Her husband's distrust was like a razor in her chest, making each breath incredibly painful. Even worse was the knowledge that he believed love weakened him.

"...You'll never again allow me close to your heart?"

"Yes. I will not be such an easy target a second time."

The memory of his implacable expression and his determination to never again fall prey to love haunted her. How could she fight her warrior's pride and his distrust in her loyalty at the same time?

JASMINE WOKE TO FIND Tariq gone. She missed him. Missed his smile, his morning caresses, his body sliding into hers, completing her in a way that she'd never known was possible between a man and a woman. When their bodies were one, it was as if she could see into his soul for one blinding instant. But only sometimes. Last night he'd shut her out, loving her body with exquisite care but giving her nothing more than his physical passion.

She stood up and quickly ran through her toilette when her musings threatened to make her teary. Then she pulled on a long skirt in a soft peach fabric over her naked skin. She felt exposed even in the confines of the tent and wanted to get covered before she worried about underwear. In her rush to dress, she forgot that they were traveling today and she would need to be in pants.

Her fear was justified. She was reaching for a bra when the tent flap opened behind her and a warm breeze touched her back. Apprehensive, she glanced over her bare shoulder.

"Oh." Relief flowed through her.

Tariq raised a dark eyebrow. "You were expecting someone else?" The flap closed behind him, hiding the incipient brightness of the day.

She blushed. No one would dare enter without his express permission. "I just can't get used to the openness of these tents." With a shake of her head, she turned and picked up the bra.

"Leave it." Husky and rough, Tariq's unexpected command startled her into dropping the piece of lace and satin.

The feel of his naked chest against her back startled her even more. He'd been fully dressed when he'd entered, and she'd turned her back on him only a few seconds before. Unlike last night, this morning his hands were impatient, cupping her breasts and teasing her nipples with more heat than expertise, while he kept her trapped in front of him. He was a little rough and most possessive.

She felt a hot rush of liquid heat between her thighs.
It was as if Tariq knew. He slipped one hand under her
skirt. Continuing to caress her breast with the other hand,
he slid a single finger through her curls.

"You are ready." His husky voice held a note of satisfaction, as if he was pleased at her responsiveness.

Before she knew what was happening, he pushed her
skirt up her back and bared her buttocks to him. Too
needy to be embarrassed, she gripped his thighs when
he put both hands around her hips and pulled her onto
him, sliding her down so slowly she thought she would
go mad.

"Tariq, please, please," she moaned. "Oh, please."

From the way he growled in approval and gave her
what she wanted, she knew that he liked her obvious
need, liked the way she wriggled on him and urged him
to go faster. Out of nowhere, an image of what Tariq had
to be seeing as their bodies joined in wild surrender burst
into her mind. It was the final erotic stroke. Her climax
was thunder and lightning. She knew that she took him
with her, his throaty cry mixing with her scream of release.

Afterward, he held her in his lap, their bodies still
joined. She tilted her head back against his firm shoulder
and tried to get her racing heart to calm down. A long
time later, she swallowed and wet her dry lips. "Wow."

Tariq chuckled against her ear and nibbled on the soft
flesh of her earlobe. "Not too fast? I hear women like it
slow." His tone was pure provocation, daring her to deny
the way she'd burned like wildfire in his arms.

She nudged him with an elbow. "You're a horrible
tease, but I'm too sated to argue with you."

She heard his smile in his reply. "So this is what I must do to get your complete cooperation. It could become exhausting."

Jasmine laughed. Tariq closed his hands over her breasts in a final sweet caress before he reluctantly pulled away. "We must prepare to leave, my Jasmine. It is time to go home."

Just before they left the tent, she took a deep breath and put her hand on his muscular forearm. Under the white material of his shirt, skin and muscle moved over bone, seducing her with their effortless flow.

He gave her an indulgent smile, still enjoying the aftereffects of their wild mating. "What is it? I promise you we can play when we get home."

His sensually teasing response made her blush. It was as if last night had never happened. She had her husband back. The shields had dropped, but only as far as they had been before her declaration. It wasn't enough. If she let him deny her love, then this half-life would be all she ever had. And she was tired of never being good enough. Tired of never being loved. Perhaps her flaws made her unworthy of love, but until there was no hope, she would try. This time, she wouldn't let anyone, even Tariq, keep her from fighting for their love.

"Your eyes are getting bigger and bigger." He raised one finger and ran it across her lips.

"I meant it. I love you."

His face underwent a sudden change, from open and teasing to totally reserved. "We must go." He turned away without another word and preceded her outside.

She sucked in a breath of air that felt like a knife blade slicing across her heart. Oh, it hurt so much to have her love not even acknowledged. But her struggle would be worth it if she succeeded in getting back what she'd lost so carelessly in her naïveté.

TARIQ WAITED FOR JASMINE outside their tent, careful to keep his emotions from showing on his face. It would not do for his people to see their leader in turmoil.

Why did she do this?

Did she truly believe that she could control him with a declaration of love? Words so easily said...promises so easily broken. He'd offered her his very soul four years ago, and she'd thrown it back at him as if it were a worthless token, after promising him forever. Though he would never let her know it, he still hurt from that emotional blow.

Part of him wanted to believe her, whispering that she was no longer the scared girl who'd crumbled under the slightest pressure, but a woman strong enough to fight him at his angriest. However, Tariq refused to listen to that voice. His heart was still raw from her rejection, not yet convinced of the depth of her commitment.

More than once, when she'd thought him occupied, he'd glimpsed shadows in his wife's blue eyes. His pride had stopped him from hounding her, as he had in the desert, but the knowledge ate away at him. Even now, even after he'd told her so much, she kept her secrets, and that he could not forgive. Women's secrets had always caused him pain.

By force of will, he buried that part of him that had become entranced by her. It shocked him just how close he'd come to laying his heart at her feet once again, even when it was clear that she didn't trust him. He wouldn't make that mistake twice. He couldn't. Not when his vulnerability to her ran so deep it had become his greatest weakness.

CHAPTER SEVEN

THE NEXT FEW DAYS FELT AS if they'd sprung fully fledged from Jasmine's worst nightmares. Tariq had withdrawn so completely from her that it scared her. No matter what she tried—humor, anger, pleas, protestations of love—none of it reached him. The strength of will implied by such total emotional excision was a huge blow to her fragile confidence. Tariq could apparently cut her out without a thought.

"Tariq, please," she said, in the car on the way back to Zulheina, "talk to me." She was frantic to make him respond.

"What do you wish to talk about?" He looked up from his papers, his eyes holding the mild interest of a stranger.

"Anything! Stop shutting me out!" She was close to tears, which horrified her.

"I do not know what you mean." He bent his head again, dismissing her.

With a cry torn from deep inside, she pulled away the papers and threw them aside. "I won't let you do this to me!"

His eyes flashed green fire as his hand snaked out and gripped her chin. "You have forgotten the rules. I no longer follow your demands." No anger, no fury, only calm control. Even his touch gentled and then he let her go.

"I love you. Doesn't that mean anything?" she asked in a broken whisper.

"Thank you for your love." He picked up the papers she'd hurled aside, and sorted them. "I am sure its worth is the same as it was four years ago."

The subtle, sardonic barb delivered in that smooth, aristocratic voice hit home. "We're not the same people as we were then. Give us a chance!" she begged.

He met her gaze with eyes so neutral they were unrecognizable as her panther's. "I need to read these."

He'd beaten her. Tariq's anger she could deal with, but she had no defense against this cold, inaccessible stranger. It was clear that he regretted the indulgences he'd allowed her in Zeina, the small things that had caused her guard to slip. She could imagine his thought processes. He probably thought that she believed she could control him now, because he'd allowed her so much, been so open.

Despite that knowledge, she didn't buckle. Tariq was stubborn, but she'd realized that when it came to loving him, she was obstinate beyond belief.

Their first night back, she was tempted to sleep in her own room, hurting and unsure of her welcome. Instead, she brushed her hair in front of Tariq's mirror and lay down in his bed. And when he reached for her, she went to him. In this place, they connected. Their loving was always wild, always passionate. It gave her hope, because how could he touch her like that, how could he whisper, "You're mine, Mina. Mine!" as he moved inside her, if only lust was involved?

A WEEK LATER, JASMINE pinned some silver cloth in place and picked up her scissors.

"I wish to talk to you, my wife."

Startled by the deep rumble of Tariq's voice, she dropped the pins she'd been holding in her mouth. "Don't sneak up on me like that!" She put one hand on her T-shirt, above her heart. "And stop looming."

He frowned, and she knew he was about to remind her that he gave the orders around here. Since their return from Zeina, he'd been more autocratic than usual, and colder. It was hard to battle this warrior every day, but his anger strengthened her resolve. Anger this powerful had to spring from deep emotion.

And, she realized, she was willing to fight the warrior because he was a part of the man she loved. The ice that tempered the fire.

Mentally rolling her eyes, she raised her arms and smiled in invitation. Loving him was the only way she knew to prove that she'd changed. For a moment, she thought that he would refuse, and her heart clenched in anticipation of another bruise. But then he came down on his haunches beside her.

She wrapped her arms around his neck and kissed him. He let her be the aggressor, remaining quiescent in her arms, but Jasmine couldn't forget the power humming just under the surface. He could have taken over at any second, but he let her control the kiss, seemingly content to taste her.

When she drew back, he removed her hands and clasped them between his own. "I am going to Paris for the week." Any fire that her kiss might have aroused was carefully hidden, if it existed at all.

"What?" She couldn't conceal her surprise. Her hands curled into fists in his grasp. "When?"

"Within the hour."

She blinked. "Why didn't you tell me sooner?"

His jaw firmed. "I have no need to tell you such things."

"I'm your wife!"

"Yes. And you will stay in your place."

The unexpected verbal reprimand hit her like a slap. She bent her head and took a deep breath. "You know some of the French designers are putting on shows this week. If you'd told me earlier, I could've gone with you." She'd come to expect his need for control, could even understand it, but he'd never treated her so harshly, as if he cared nothing for her feelings. She hadn't known that he regretted what had happened in Zeina that much.

He released her hands and gripped her chin between his thumb and forefinger, forcing her to face him. "No, Jasmine. You cannot leave Zulheil."

She frowned. "You don't trust me, do you? What do you expect me to do—run away at the first available opportunity?"

"I may have been a fool once, but you will not make me one twice," he nearly growled.

"I came and stayed of my own free will. I won't run."

"You did not know what you faced when you came." His features were expressionless as he brushed aside her words. "I am not wrapped around your little finger, as you no doubt expected, and I do not intend to be. Because you know this, you will wish to escape. I do not intend to lose you."

She shook her head in denial, but he didn't release her.

"I love you," she repeated firmly. "Don't you know what that means?"

"It means that you can turn your back and walk away at any time." Rapier sharp, his jabs made her bleed. But she still wasn't beaten.

"How long are you going to act this way?" she asked him in desperation. "How long are you going to punish me? When is your revenge going to be complete?"

His green eyes had darkened to the color of the deepest sea. "I do not do this to punish you. To want to take revenge, I would have to feel something for you beyond lust, which I do not. You are a possession, prized but not irreplaceable."

She felt the color leave her face. She couldn't speak. Her heart felt as if it was bleeding. In a desperate attempt to hide her grief, she bit the insides of her cheeks hard enough to taste blood, and waited for him to finish.

"I will be involved in matters of state. Hiraz knows how to get in touch with me."

She remained silent, barely able to hear him through the painful buzzing in her ears. When he bent his head and placed a possessive kiss on her lips, she accepted it dully, too stunned to respond. Tariq seemed to take her reaction as subtle defiance because he moved his hand to her hair and tangled his fingers in the long ponytail, gripping her head.

"You will not deny me," he growled against her lips. Because he knew her every sensual weakness, he was right. She couldn't deny him. Not when she'd been starving for him for so long.

When he drew back, cold satisfaction gleamed in his

eyes. "I can make you pant for me anytime I wish, Jasmine, so do not try and manipulate me with your body."

The sensual fires he'd aroused were doused instantly by his taunt. Thankfully, he didn't continue the lesson.

"I will be leaving in forty minutes." With that, he rose and strode out the door of her workroom.

Jasmine didn't know how long she sat there, unable to function. She felt as if he'd ripped out her heart and then laughed at her agony. She hurt too much to feel the pain. When she finally rose and made her way to the wide glass doors that led out to a balcony overlooking the main gardens, it was to see Tariq walking to a royal limousine.

He was dressed in a black suit, his tie the vivid green of his eyes, his beautiful hair brushed back. She saw him stop and look up at the balcony. Quickly, she stumbled back into the room. From this far, she couldn't make out the expression on his face, but she knew he hadn't seen her. Then he stepped inside and the car drove off.

It was as if his departure released the paralysis that had protected her from her own anguished emotions. Suddenly close to an emotional breakdown, she scurried through the corridors, praying she wouldn't meet anyone along the way. Once safely behind the locked doors of the exquisite room that was her own, she walked out into the private garden and hid under the spreading tree with the blue-white flowers. The branches were so heavy with blooms that they almost touched the ground, providing her with a scented cave of darkness in which to let go of her torment.

Her sobs came from somewhere deep inside, wrenched out of her body with such force that she didn't have breath enough to make a sound. She was destroyed by the sudden insight that she'd been fooling herself. She'd believed that she could love Tariq enough to make him love her, a girl who'd never been loved. She had allowed him every liberty, going so far as to tie herself to him for life. She'd given him her body and her soul, keeping nothing back.

And now he'd rejected her gift in the cruelest of ways. She was nothing but a possession to him, prized but not irreplaceable. He felt nothing but lust for her. Lust! Her illusions of time healing the wounds of the past shattered under the realization that his actions weren't born out of pain. He just didn't care if he hurt her.

Had he married her only to humble her? Crush her?

She curled into a ball at the base of the tree and wrapped her arms around her shaking body, trying to breathe through the pain that lay like a rock in her throat. Dusk fell outside but she didn't notice. She'd cried all the tears she had inside, but her pain was so great she couldn't move.

Freed, the demons that she'd drowned in tears descended upon her, wanting their pound of flesh. In Tariq's land, in Tariq's arms, she'd almost managed to forget the lack in her. The missing part that made her incapable of being loved. Suddenly, the memories of that terrible day in her childhood when she'd understood the truth flooded over her.

"DOES IT BOTHER YOU THAT you demanded half of Mary's inheritance before you'd adopt Jasmine?" Aunt Ella had asked the woman Jasmine had thought was her mother. "After all, Mary is our baby sister."

"No. She should've known better than to get pregnant by some stranger in a bar. I don't know what possessed her to have the child." The sound of ice cubes hitting crystal had penetrated the library door. *"We aren't some charity. How else were Jasmine's expenses going to be covered?"*

"You got a lot more than that," Ella had persisted. *"Mary's inheritance from Grandpa was twice the size of ours."*

"I think of it as adequate compensation for having to accept bad blood into my family. Lord only knows what kind of a loser Jasmine's father was. Mary was so drunk, she couldn't even remember his name."

LATER, WHEN JASMINE HAD forced herself to ask, Aunt Ella had taken pity on her and told her about Mary. Apparently, in order to avoid any hint of scandal, Mary had moved to America after Jasmine's birth. She'd never returned. The people who'd raised Jasmine, Mary's older sister, Lucille, and her husband, James, had already had two children, Michael and Sarah, and had been unwilling to take on another, until they'd been given a financial incentive. Yet they'd gone on to have another child of their own—a beloved younger son named Mathew.

That day, Jasmine had been slapped in the face with the fact that any care she'd ever known had been bought and paid for. Searching for someone to love her, she'd written to Mary, saying hello. The response had arrived on her thirteenth birthday, a cool request to make no further contact because Mary had no wish to be associated with a past "indiscretion."

An indiscretion. That's all Jasmine was to her birth

mother. And to her adoptive mother she was bad blood. Neither Mary nor Lucille had been able to love her. Today, she was forced to accept that the lack hadn't magically disappeared. She was still unloved. Still unwanted.

THE NEXT DAY, JASMINE decided there was nothing to be gained by crying over something she couldn't change. Despite the hurt that existed inside her like a living, breathing creature, she forced herself into her workroom and picked up the scissors she'd dropped the day before.

She had to do something until she figured out how to handle the situation with Tariq, the man whom she'd married in a blind haze of love. Perhaps she'd made the biggest mistake of her life, but she didn't want to think about that now. Neither did she want to think about the way her old fears and insecurities had tormented her last night.

An hour into her work, she heard a telephone ring, but ignored it. There was a knock on her door a minute later.

"Madam?"

She looked up to find one of the palace staff at the door. "Yes, Shazana?"

"Sheik Zamanat wishes to speak with you."

Jasmine's throat locked. About to ask Shazana to tell Tariq that she was busy, she recognized the possible consequences of asking a loyal staff member to lie, and nodded.

"Please transfer the call to this phone." She indicated the one near the door of the turret.

Shazana nodded and left. The phone rang seconds later. Jasmine stood up and walked over. She picked up the receiver...then hung up. Heart thudding, she hurried down the hallway, into her bedroom and out into the garden. The phone rang again just as she escaped. She hid under her tree.

It was cowardly to hide from Tariq but she couldn't bear to talk to him, couldn't bear to hear the voice that she'd dreamed about for years rip her to pieces with the painful truth about her inadequacy. Last night, she'd believed that all her illusions had been destroyed, but today she realized she couldn't face the total loss of hope. Not yet. Not yet.

Perhaps an hour later, she emerged and made her way back to her workroom. There was a message on the table by the phone. She picked it up with shaking hands. It instructed her to call Tariq at a given number.

"Go to hell!" She crunched the note into a ball and threw it into the wastebasket, then began to work on the top she was making. Her movements were jerky and uncoordinated, as for the first time, anger began to simmer under the hurt and sorrow. So Sheik Zamanat expected her to come to heel when he hollered? She almost stabbed the material with her scissors. He was about to learn that his wife was not some toy he could throw aside and pick up whenever he felt like it.

TARIQ HUNG UP THE PHONE for the fourth time. He was annoyed by his wife's subtle rebellion, but another, more dangerous emotion threatened. That emotion would not let him forget the naked pain in Mina's eyes when he'd last spoken to her.

After so long, the anger and hurt he'd ruthlessly controlled for years had shattered its bonds and lashed out. When Mina had voiced her love, he'd felt as if she'd torn open wounds that had barely begun to heal. The almost unbearable pain had sprung from a need that he didn't want to accept. It had caused him to say things he shouldn't have.

Guilt was not something he was familiar with, but pangs of it had been stabbing him since the moment Mina hadn't appeared on the balcony to bid him good-bye. His sense of loss had shaken him. He felt as if he'd damaged something fragile between them. Only angry pride had kept him from returning to her.

But Mina didn't hold grudges. Once he spoke to her, she would return to normal. And the next time he picked up that phone, he *would* talk to her.

JASMINE FELT AS IF SHE was getting ready for a knock-down, drag-out fight. She'd ignored Tariq for two days. At first, it had been blind instinct, an attempt to save herself from rejection. She'd had enough of that in her lifetime. Later, when she'd calmed down, she'd realized that she needed some time and distance to sort out her feelings. Tariq had given her a rude shock, waking her up forever to the fact that the man she loved was not the man she'd married.

Did she love this Tariq?

Her mind wasn't completely made up, but her anger refused to be ignored any longer. This time, Tariq would get an answer to his call. A call that came as soon as dawn was breaking over Zulheil. She picked up the phone on the second ring.

"Prized possession speaking." It slipped out without thought. She was horrified, but just a little proud of herself.

There was complete and utter silence on the other end of the phone. "I am not amused, Jasmine," he said finally.

"Well, since I'm not a comedienne, my ego isn't too badly wounded." Sitting in bed, her legs hanging off the edge, she felt the simmering anger start to bubble. "Did you have anything to say or did you just ring to remind me of my place?" Where had that come from?

"You are being obstinate."

"Yup."

"What did you expect when you returned?" A thread of anger crept into his so far calm tone. "That nothing would have changed? That I would lay my trust in your lap?"

"No. I expected you to have forgotten me." It was a cruel truth. "But you didn't. You took me and you married me, giving me a place in your life. How dare you now treat me like…like an object? Like something to scrape off the bottom of your royal shoe? How dare you?" Tears threatened, riding the crest of her anger.

"Never have I treated you as such!" His response was a harsh reproof.

"Yes, you have. And you know what? I don't want to talk to a man who treats me like that. I could almost hate you. Don't call me anymore. Maybe by the time you get home I'll have calmed down. Right now, I have nothing for you. Nothing!" It was the raw pain of her emotions speaking.

"We will talk when I return." His voice held a note she'd never before heard, a note she couldn't understand.

Jasmine hung up the phone with shaking hands, surprised by her own outburst. She'd planned belligerence, but had ended up ripping apart the shields protecting her heart. She hurt. And yet it felt cleansing. She *was* worth more than this treatment. She might not be loved but she was worthy of respect.

Something her husband might never give her.

I COULD ALMOST HATE YOU.

Tariq stared out at the cobbled streets of Paris, Jasmine's words ringing in his head. He was used to being adored by her, being the center of her attention, as he'd been since their first meeting. He'd never considered being with a Jasmine who didn't treat him that way.

He didn't like the sensation. Not when his need for her ran so deep that he missed her every moment she wasn't by his side. He'd only survived the four years without her by working night and day, striving for mindless exhaustion. Her laughter and affection since her return had been a balm to the hunger inside him. Now she was furious with him.

He'd underestimated the woman she'd become. A woman who apparently felt things more deeply and wildly than he'd given her credit for. She'd always had quiet feminine courage, but this was the first time she'd dared to rebuke him for his actions with such blunt honesty. He finally listened to the inner voices he'd been ignoring, accepting that she'd changed dramatically from the Jasmine he'd known.

That Jasmine would never have hated him.

That Jasmine had also walked away from him.

If he opened his heart just a little, what would this Jasmine do? Would she treat him with the same disregard she'd shown four years ago or…? The possibilities were as intriguing and as tempting as the evocative scents borne on the Paris winds.

But first, he'd have to win Mina back. She was his. She wasn't allowed to hate him.

CHAPTER EIGHT

"WHAT DO YOU MEAN, HE'S in the courtyard?" Jasmine cried, shoving her hands through her tumbled hair.

Mumtaz shrugged her delicate shoulders. "I persuaded Hiraz to delay him so I could warn you."

"But it's Friday night. He wasn't supposed to be back until Monday!"

Heavy footsteps sounded in the hallway. Mumtaz's eyes widened. "I must go. I wish you luck." She slipped out the door. Jasmine heard her say something to Tariq.

With a muted cry of frustration, Jasmine secured the azure silk robe around her waist. It was too late to change. She didn't want to greet Tariq wearing a robe that hit her midthigh, with her hair loose around her shoulders, but the doorknob was turning. Quickly, she settled onto the stool in front of her dressing table and picked up her brush. At least this way, if her legs collapsed, he wouldn't know.

She heard Tariq enter the room and close the door. Her fingers tightened convulsively around the carved wooden handle of the brush, but she continued the smooth, full-length strokes, ignoring his presence. She felt him move until he was standing behind her. He leaned forward and put both hands on her dressing table, one on either side of her, effectively caging her with his body. She kept brushing her hair, though she couldn't feel her fingers anymore because they were shaking so hard. She didn't look in the mirror, avoiding the trap of green fire that awaited her.

"How's your throat infection?" He reminded her of one of her earlier excuses, not referring to the last painful call.

"Much better."

"I can hear that. And you're feeling well?"

"Yes." She tried to avoid touching her head to his chest. Every time she moved an inch away, he leaned closer, until she was on the edge of her stool with nowhere to go.

"Good. I was worried, as you seemed to be sleeping so much when I called." Though his tone was calm, she knew he had to be furious. He wasn't a man used to being reprimanded.

And she wasn't ready to face his anger. Despite her bravado, she didn't hate Tariq. Her feelings for him were raw and undefined, but they didn't come close to hate, and their depth and promise scared her. What if she began to love him even more deeply than she had all these years?

The heat of his body seemed to surround her. She wondered if he'd subtly moved. It was becoming difficult to continue to brush her hair, because with every stroke, she touched him. She chanced a peek at his arms and saw that he'd lessened the gap between them. He was wearing a blue shirt, his jacket discarded.

He reached out, took the brush from her nerveless fingers and put it on the dresser. Then he tucked her hair behind her ears, baring her face. She froze as he stroked the knuckles of one hand down her cheek in a simple but powerful caress, reminding her of the times he'd done that after they'd made love. She curled her fingers into fists and gritted her teeth against the response he could call forth so easily. The memory of his parting gibe helped, but it wouldn't hold up forever against this gentle persuasion.

"Will you also refuse to talk to me now that I am home?" He continued the lazy caress.

"I'm talking to you right now." She was overjoyed when her voice didn't break.

"No. You are answering my questions and hiding yourself from me."

She didn't say anything.

"You are very angry with me, my Jasmine?" The husky timbre of his voice was close to her ear, his body almost totally enclosing her. "You have not calmed down?"

"I'm not angry." Her heart thudded hard against her ribs. The anger had long since burned out, leaving behind a residue of hurt so deep she felt ravaged.

He kissed the lobe of her ear. A shiver raced through her. She couldn't disguise the instinctive reaction, but neither did she do anything else.

"Ah, Mina, you cannot lie. Come, look at me. Welcome your husband home."

His words were an unwanted echo of his commands before he'd left. "Do you wish to have sex? If you'll move, I'll get on the bed." Dark and violent emotions rose in her throat, daring her to release them. She stifled the urge, refusing to let Tariq see just how badly he'd hurt her when he'd brought her deepest fear to the surface and given it form.

His body turned to stone around her. She could feel his muscles tensing as if to strike. He drew back so fast that she nearly fell off the stool, unbalanced. She'd barely got herself grounded when he lifted her and stood her in front of him. In bare feet, she only came halfway up his chest. Startled, she almost met his eyes but managed to fix her gaze on his shoulders.

"Mina, do not do this. You know you will turn into liquid fire in my arms." He curved one hand over her hip and used the other to cup her cheek, but didn't force her to look up.

"Yes, I know you can make me *pant* at any time." She swallowed the lump in her throat as she repeated his taunt. A taunt so true it made her cry inside. If he touched her much longer with those sensitive fingers, she'd shatter like fine crystal. Something wild and needy in her recognized his touch and wouldn't let her pull away. "I'm not going to fight you."

He growled at her response and pulled her into a bruising embrace, holding her head against his chest. Jasmine had to fight every instinct she possessed not to respond. Her hunger for him was a clawing being inside her. She reminded herself that she was prized but not irreplaceable. *Not irreplaceable.* He felt only momentary lust when he touched her. When she remained stiff, arms at her sides, he released her.

"Go to bed, Jasmine." He sounded tired and defeated. Leaving her standing in the center of the bedroom, he pushed through the connecting door and into his room.

The door shut with a quiet click.

Out of nowhere, exhaustion slammed into Jasmine. Dreading this confrontation, she'd barely slept the past five nights. Still wearing the silk robe, she crawled under the blankets. However, a sense of loss kept nudging her awake. She knew it was a lie. She'd never had anything to lose. Still, she wanted to go to her husband and hold him…soothe him.

"No." No, she wouldn't give in to the need, when he clearly saw nothing wrong with his treatment of her. Respect, she repeated to herself. She was worthy of respect.

TARIQ THREW HIS BALLED-UP shirt across the room. She'd denied him! He'd never expected that from Jasmine. He had relied on her generous nature to forgive him. Time and distance, and Jasmine's passionate anger, had made him regret his cruel words. That day in her solar, he'd allowed the wounded beast inside him to speak, full of years of pent-up anger and pain. It would have been better to keep that uncontrollable part of himself locked up.

He'd been feeling instead of thinking, and the words that had slipped out had been weapons aimed at his wife. More than that, they'd been untrue. He had four years of midnight awakenings to attest to the fact that she was irreplaceable.

What if the damage was irreversible? What if Mina did hate him? Her body had been so stiff in his embrace, her lips so silent. She'd been like a small creature frozen in front of a predator. The painful image forced him to accept that what he'd felt from Jasmine hadn't been anger or a need for revenge, but…hurt. His temper vanished in the face of that truth. He had hurt his wife, his Mina. There was no satisfaction in that knowledge, only disgust at himself. She was his to protect. Even from himself.

For the first time in an eternity, Tariq was uncertain about his next act. A sheik could rarely indulge in indecision, but it appeared that a husband had plenty of opportunity to do so. He knew he'd acted badly, but he wasn't a man accustomed to asking for forgiveness. With a sound akin to a growl, he stalked into the shower, his mind on the small woman with big blue eyes next door.

FAMILIAR HANDS, ROUGH BUT gentle, stroked the naked line of her spine. Jasmine frowned, sure that she'd been clothed before sleep, but in this dream, skin touched skin. A kiss on her nape, on each vertebra, possessive hands grasping her hips… She moaned and turned onto her back, welcoming her lover. When he pressed his lips to her breasts, she arched into him. Waking thoughts merged with hazy dreams as her fingers tangled in thick silky hair. A beard-roughened jaw angled across her breast. She shivered and the spot was immediately kissed.

"Tariq," she whispered, awake and aware. It was too late to stop her response. Her whole body was open in invitation. Jasmine sighed and gave in to the inevitable. Whatever he said, whatever he did, he was hers. How could she possibly deny him when he touched her as if she was precious?

When he kissed her, she returned his kiss joyously, unable to hide how much she'd missed him. He shuddered against her and broke away to drop kisses across her breasts. Under her fingers, his shoulder muscles bunched as he moved down her body, dropping a line of kisses across her stomach and flicking his tongue over the indentation of her navel.

Shivers racked her body as he found an unexpectedly sensitive spot. Her reaction made him repeat the quick caress. Her stomach muscles clenched and her hips jerked upward without conscious control. Pressed so close, she could feel his heartbeat in the pulse of his body.

She parted her thighs for him without prompting, but he didn't rise to possess her. He lifted her left leg and placed it over his shoulder. Her sensitive skin burned from the heat of his body. Then he rubbed his rough jaw across the tender skin on the insides of her thighs.

She gasped. "Tariq, please."

He soothed the roughness with his tongue, sending her nerves into further disarray. Then he repeated the whole process with her right leg. Just when she thought that she could feel no more pleasure, he dipped his head and bestowed the most intimate kiss of all upon her.

She screamed and would've squirmed away, but his hold on her hips kept her in place as he slowly, and with great care, introduced her to this shatteringly intimate form of loving. His only aim was her pleasure.

With the tiny slice of her brain that was functioning, she knew this was Tariq's apology. Her warrior was adoring her body, cherishing her response. He couldn't say the words, but he was showing her that she was more than an object to satisfy his lust. How much more, she didn't know, but even the depth of her hurt couldn't survive against this kind of tenderness.

She clutched handfuls of the sheets and gave herself up to his caresses. Once more, she gave her heart and soul to Tariq, her vows to keep him at bay disintegrating into dust. She felt the change in him immediately. His intense, concentrated caressing continued, but his shoulders were no longer so tense under her thighs, and his hands were anchors rather than vices forcing her to stay in place. And then she couldn't think. She found the kind of freedom that she could only find in his arms and splintered on the wings of pleasure. He held her until the tremors subsided and then gently entered her, as if unsure of his welcome.

Tears pricked her eyes at his hesitation. He wasn't acting the autocratic despot now. The silent question delivered the final blow to any lingering hurt. She deliberately clenched her inner muscles and held him prisoner, telling him without words that he was wanted, needed, loved. At the same time, she curled her arms around him and dropped kisses across his shoulders. With a groan, he began to move.

"Welcome home," she whispered, just before she crested the highest pinnacle of desire for a second time that night.

A long while later, she gathered enough confidence to ask, "Why did you return early?"

Tariq spooned her deeper against him and dropped a kiss on the curve of her shoulder where it met her neck. "The trade agreement was completed earlier than expected."

"Did you…" She began to ask him about the agreement, then stopped, unwilling to be rebuffed. He'd loved her with fire, but she was afraid that she'd be waking up beside the cool, reserved stranger he'd become after Zeina.

"What, Mina?"

"Nothing."

He was silent for a while and then said, "Zulheil now

has a contract with several Western states that will allow our artistic products to cross their borders without duty."

She took the olive branch, prepared to meet him halfway. "Why artistic products?"

"Zulheil's jewelry and other artistic products are highly prized. They are our third biggest export. The agreement goes both ways." He chuckled, warming her heart. "They think their goods will flood our markets, but they're wrong."

"How do you know that?"

"Because, Mina—" he squeezed her with unexpected playfulness "—we have had such an agreement with the United States for years."

"Really? But there's no mass-market stuff in your streets." She snuggled into him, her head pillowed on his arm.

"My people are used to the best handcrafted goods. The riches of the land are shared by all. The cheap things they send are never bought."

"You're snobs."

Her husband shrugged. "But we are rich enough to be so."

His unrepentant reply made her laugh. She couldn't temper her responses to him when he let his shields fall. "So you're getting the best of this bargain? Why don't they know about the experience of the Americans?"

"Nobody likes to admit their mistakes. What would it look like if the world's biggest power had been… I have lost the word." He paused, waiting for her.

"Conned?" she suggested cheekily.

"Yes. It would not look good for them if they were

seen to have been *conned* by a tiny sheikdom from the desert. A poor, primitive people."

She laughed so hard that she cried. "Primitive!"

When she'd stopped giggling, Tariq bit her lightly on her shoulder to catch her attention. She turned into his arms, aware that she'd capitulated too easily, without waiting for words of apology to banish her heartache. But she'd always known that Tariq would never humble himself in such a blatant fashion. He was too much the desert warrior for that. For now, his incredibly tender loving was enough.

It was a start.

EARLY THE NEXT MORNING, Jasmine sat on the edge of her Zulheil Rose fountain, listening to the cool splash of the water and the quiet sounds of the birds. Kept awake by her newly reinvigorated demons, she'd made the decision to leave Tariq sprawled in bed, and face them. Face them and defeat them.

First, she accepted that she'd never truly been loved. Not the way she needed to be loved.

Perhaps if she'd chosen Tariq four years ago, he might have learned to love her like that. Perhaps. However, back then, she'd been young and needy compared to Tariq's strength and confidence. While he'd cherished her, he'd also been her caretaker. Her love for him had been deep and achingly true, but it had been the love of a girl growing into womanhood. Tender. Easily bruised.

Though her hurt had made her doubt her feelings, since she'd come to Zulheil her love had matured and grown, fed by her awakening emotions for the man Tariq had become. All vestiges of the youth were gone, but in his place was a man of integrity, power and charisma. A man who touched her with tenderness that turned her heart inside out. A man who was, quite simply, magnificent.

She loved this Tariq with an intensity that even his anger couldn't destroy. This love was tougher and gave her the courage to look behind his remarks, to the pain she'd caused. This love gave her the strength to fight for her lover.

From the first day she'd arrived, Tariq had been demanding. Now, she saw that as a gift. He no longer thought of her as a girl to be protected, but as a woman who had to confront her mistakes.

That was the first truth. The second was that she still wasn't loved. And that terrified her. Her naive belief in her ability to reach Tariq with her love had been smashed beyond repair that day before Paris, and she couldn't face that kind of torment again. She'd been rejected so many times in her life that once more might break her. So, while she would continue to fight for her sheik's trust, she wouldn't do it by offering him her heart…or betraying her hunger to be loved in return.

"I THINK WE'RE GETTING somewhere," Jasmine said to Mumtaz two weeks later. They were browsing in an art supply store in Zulheina. "He's talking to me."

"Talking about what?"

"Business, mostly." She was drawn to the easel in the corner.

"Hmm, that is good, but what about your relationship?"

Jasmine ran her fingers down the polished wood of

the easel. Perfect. Leaning down, she picked up several prepared canvasses and stacked them on the easel. Tariq had always liked to prepare his own, but these would do for a start.

"I don't want to ruin it by pushing." She wandered over to the oil paints and began selecting tubes. Phthalo blue, burnt umber, viridian hue...

"You are waiting for something?" Mumtaz absently added titanium white to Jasmine's collection.

"I want some sign that... I can't explain it." Ever since his return from Paris, Tariq had treated her with kid gloves, keeping an emotional barrier between them. He didn't hurt her with his anger any longer, but conversely, she couldn't breach his shields to teach him to trust in her again.

This lukewarm companionship was simply wrong.

Nothing had ever been lukewarm between them. Their love had been a blaze and their separation pure pain. Even the anger and hurt between them was jagged and sharp enough to draw blood. The sudden change in his behavior mystified her.

"Do not worry about explaining. Simply do what you must." Mumtaz squeezed her hand.

"Good advice, I think." But, Jasmine thought, what *could* she do to breach the wall her enigmatic husband had erected?

"ARE YOU BUSY?" SHE PEERED into Tariq's office. At the sound of her voice, he looked up from his desk.

"You are always welcome, Jasmine."

She ignored the desire to rile him just to get him to respond with more heat. What sane woman would prefer an angry, simmering lover to a friendly, warm one? She had to be insane, because she definitely favored honest fury over a gentle illusion. At least then she knew his emotions ran deep.

Pushing aside those disturbing thoughts for the time being, Jasmine ducked out and picked up the pile of purchases and put them on his desk. The easel she left outside, unwilling to spoil his surprise.

"What is this?" He tugged at the string around the brown paper wrapping.

"A present. Open it!" She moved around to his side and perched on the arm of his chair.

He frowned and immediately curved one arm around her waist. "You will fall in such a position."

"Here." She wiggled and fell into his lap. "Now open it."

He seemed nonplussed by her unexpected cuddling. When she pushed at his hands, he picked up his letter opener and cut the string. His body stilled around hers when he saw the canvasses, paints and brushes.

"I know you're busy," Jasmine began, before he could talk himself out of it. "But surely you can find an hour each day? Think of it as doing something for your sheikdom."

He raised an expressive eyebrow at that.

She smiled. "A workaholic sheik will become stuffy and stressed out, and of no use to his people." She ignored his snort of disbelief. "You used to paint as a way to relieve the stresses of the day. Why not try that again?"

"My responsibilities—"

She stopped him with a hand on his lips. "An hour. That's not too much to ask. And I'll help you."

"How?"

"I'm sure I can do something to lighten the load for you. Filing? Summarizing reports? I'm smart, you know."

He chuckled at her earnest words and his shoulders subtly relaxed. "I know you are smart, Mina. I've always known that. All right. You may assist me and you must also sit for me."

"You're going to paint me?" She sat up on his lap, excited. "Will it be a nude?"

He frowned at her impudence. "Such a painting would never be seen by the world and would be burned upon my death."

Jasmine kissed his cheek, delighted by his acceptance, and scrambled off his lap before he could stop her. "There's an easel, too." She collected the materials. "I'll put this in a corner of my workroom and come back to help you."

She ended up spending the rest of the day with him, reviewing reports. He told her she could leave at any time, but when she saw the amount of work that required his attention, she was more than happy to sit down and dig in.

One of the reports gave her an unwelcome shock. "Tariq?"

He raised his head at her sharp tone.

"It says here that the sheik can have more than one wife." Her brow furrowed.

Tariq's lips twitched a little. "That is an ancient law."

"How ancient?" She didn't intend to share her husband. *Ever.*

"Very. It is a historical oddity. Both my grandfather and my father had only one wife."

"Your great-grandfather?"

"Four." It seemed to her that his eyes were bright with withheld amusement. "Do not worry, I believe I have only enough stamina for one wife."

"I'm going to get this law repealed," she declared.

"The women of Zulheil would salute you. It only applies to the sheik, but the law seems to threaten Zulheil's modern image, some say."

Jasmine nodded, her fears soothed by his practical words. At least another wife was one problem she wouldn't have to contend with. She settled back to work. There was, she discovered, a kind of quiet satisfaction in helping her husband bear some of the burdens he carried on his shoulders.

"Enough, Mina." He stood up and stretched, his powerful body drawing her attention.

She'd been sitting on the sofa in one corner of his study, curled up. Putting aside a report, she stood and stretched as well, loosening tight muscles.

"You may regret your offer." He came to stand by her. "I find your summaries excellent. I will conscript you often."

Pleased by his compliment, she smiled and put her hand in his. "Good. Now let's go before someone else catches you."

Today, for the first time, she'd realized just how many people thought that Tariq was the only one who could possibly provide an answer to their problems. Often they turned up in person. Hiraz and Mumtaz deflected a lot of them, but some were insistent. The relaxed system of government in Zulheil astounded her. However, it appeared to work fantastically well for the small and sparsely populated land.

"Would you protect me, Jasmine?" His smile said he found that a ludicrous idea, given that he was twice her size.

"I think you need someone to run interference. Mumtaz and Hiraz have trouble because they're not seen as royal." She was serious about her observations. "But I am. I could deal with most of what they came to you for, leaving you free to take care of bigger matters."

Tariq was ominously silent. She looked up to find him staring at her, his expression thoughtful.

"I mean, if you want me to." She was suddenly uncertain. A lifetime of never being good enough tended to overcome her efforts at self-confidence. "I know I'm a foreigner…" With a corner of her mind, she shoved aside the secret that threatened to float to the surface. She didn't want to think about that now, not when her husband was looking at her with eyes that held something close to tenderness.

Tariq stopped her with a finger on her lips. "You are my wife. I have told you that my people have accepted you as such. What about your designing?"

"I wanted to speak to you about that," she said. "Would my having business interests damage the royal image?"

He shook his head. "I have many such interests. You wish to develop your designs?"

"I was thinking of a small fashion house. One that markets to the retail sector, but has no shops of its own."

"You will do well." His answer was just a simple statement of confidence in her abilities, yet it filled her with immense joy. No one had ever believed in her.

"But, much as I'll miss not giving the majority of my time to design," she ventured, "I think it'll have to slip into second place."

"Second place?"

"As your wife, my place is here, with you." She didn't betray the love driving her decision. Until she was sure of Tariq's feelings for her, she'd keep that beautiful emotion to herself. Another rebuff, even a gentle one, would tear her to pieces. "My designing will have to be like your painting. Something I do for myself, after serving our people." It was a sacrifice, but one she made willingly. By marrying Tariq, she'd accepted that the country's needs would sometimes come before her own. And Tariq needed a partner who could bear some of the many duties of a leader.

Approval glimmered in his eyes. She was encouraged. It was time for her to grow up and accept the responsibilities that came with being the sheik's wife. He hadn't pushed her, allowing her to do as she wished, but her place was with him.

"If you wish to do this, then I accept."

Jasmine smiled and leaned closer. The slight tensing of his body was his only response. By the time they got to her workroom, he was relaxed again. She frowned in thought.

"I'll work here," Tariq announced.

She looked up, her introspection momentarily interrupted. Tariq was gesturing to the semicircle of windows in the southern end of the room. The light was brilliant in that corner. She nodded and helped him set up.

"Now, you'll recline on this."

Jasmine dutifully stretched out on the plush red chaise longue that he'd dragged opposite his easel. Before beginning to paint, he put a cushion under her elbow to prop her up. She knew that he never bothered with sketches, preferring a light watercolor outline on the canvas itself.

He was, she thought with pride, very, very talented. She cherished the tiny painting that he'd given her a month before they'd separated. It was a Zulheil seascape that he'd painted from memory to show her his homeland.

"You're frowning."

She smiled. "Better?"

"Hmm."

For some reason, his masculine murmur reminded her of her earlier thoughts. Tariq appeared to find physical affection from her somewhat disconcerting. No, perhaps that wasn't the right word, she thought, stopping herself from frowning again. It was more that he seemed to be taken by surprise. He didn't reject her touches, he just didn't seem to expect them. She carefully thought back over the past weeks, and then over the six months they'd spent together four years ago.

Tariq had always loved touching her. Though a highly sensual man, he liked to touch as a gesture of tenderness, as well. He'd been autocratic and reserved with everyone else, but with her, he'd been very affectionate. Conversely, she'd been used to the repressive formality of her own home. It had taken him months to make her comfortable enough in his presence to risk even the simple touches that he'd taken for granted.

"Mina." Tariq's disapproving look made her aware of her frown. She shot him another cheerful smile and waited for him to return to his paints. Once he did, she relaxed.

Since she'd come to Zulheil, he'd touched her often. For the first turbulent weeks, it had mostly been sexual and erotic. She'd understood that he wasn't ready to trust her with his affection. But in Zeina, it had been like being in heaven. After spending so much time pressed together on the back of a camel, their casual touching had merged seamlessly into their lives.

However, since his trip to Paris, their tiny instinctive gestures of togetherness had disappeared. Now it seemed that Tariq was controlling the intensity of their lovemaking. Though he made love to her without fail, and took care to make sure that she always reached her peak, something was missing. The heady eroticism of their earlier encounters had been dampened.

Why? Jasmine asked herself. Why would he seek to limit their sensuality, the one place where they'd always been in perfect accord? Surely he wasn't holding against her the fact that she hadn't welcomed him with open arms the minute he'd returned? She almost shook her head to dismiss that idea. Tariq had apologized to her in his own way, she was sure of that. They'd made their peace.

Then why? The answer flitted just out of her reach.

"That is enough for now, Jasmine."

CHAPTER NINE

STARTLED, JASMINE BLINKED. Only when she attempted to get up did she comprehend how long she'd been in the reclining position. Reaching over her head with her hands, she stretched in a luxurious curve, feeling muscle after muscle relax.

"I'm going to head off to the shower. See you at dinner," she murmured.

Tariq looked up. Desire burst into life in the green fire of his eyes. He stifled it almost as soon as it arose, but answering heat rushed over her in reaction to that single searing glance. So, his passion ran as deep as ever. He'd just decided to hide it from her. Relief that he wasn't truly indifferent to her made her almost dizzy.

"But why would the thought of a shower set it off?" Jasmine muttered to herself. She was in the shower before she figured it out. "Idiot." She laughed at herself. Tariq was the man who'd made love to her in front of a mirror. The sultry possibilities presented by soap and water would be tantalizing to him. They were already affecting her.

It stunned her that she wanted to be in a shower with her husband. She could imagine the darkness of his hand against her sudsy skin, and almost feel his big body pressing her against the wall. As a result of her imaginings, she stepped out of the shower hotter than when she'd entered. Her predinner preparations were under-taken in a state of sexual anticipation.

"I have to entice him into a shower with me," she decided. "Otherwise this fantasy is going to drive me crazy." She would much rather be driven crazy by Tariq himself.

Midway through brushing blush onto her cheekbones, she paused, hit by a thought that she'd earlier rejected as implausible. Her hair was already secured on top of her head in an elegant knot, with a few loose tendrils around her face. Those tendrils now framed her startled eyes.

"What if he thinks our passion doesn't affect me with the same power it does him?" One simple fact that she'd always known was that her husband desired her deeply. His hunger was palpable, or it had been until he'd begun to withdraw. Even at his angriest, Tariq had made love to her until she screamed. She tapped her nails on the wood of her dresser in a staccato beat. "I did manage to resist him after Paris, but that was because I was hurt-ing so much, and even then . . . he could've seduced me if he'd stayed another minute."

However, Tariq didn't know that. To him, it would appear as if her need was nowhere near the strength of his. To a warrior like him, that would be a blow. It wouldn't just affect his masculine pride, but would be hurtful. He stubbornly refused to believe in her love, but he'd accepted her passion as real and unfeigned. Jasmine wondered what it would be like if someday she began to believe that Tariq didn't want her with the same fervor that she needed him. It would rock the one solid founda-tion in their relationship.

"Goodness." Her eyes widened in the mirror, bright

with realization. "I have to convince him that I want him, or he'll just continue to withdraw and I won't even have our passion to build on." However, the idea of seducing her husband was daunting. He tended to take charge in bed, and his control was amazing. It was annoying, too. If she was going to lose control, then he could damn well do so, too.

"Hmph. Any ideas?" she asked her reflection.

"Do you always talk to yourself?" The amused question had her spinning around in her seat. Tariq lounged in the doorway between their rooms. For a second, she thought he might have heard too much, but his expression was the by-now-familiar warm and extremely irritating one.

"It's good for the soul," she quipped. Out of habit, she went to secure the tie on her robe. Then she noticed the way he was looking at her under his eyelids. If she hadn't been concentrating, she would have missed it. She changed direction, picked up the blush again and turned to the mirror.

When she leaned forward, she was well aware that her robe parted in the middle, offering an enticing view of the rounded curves of her breasts. Or at least she hoped it was enticing. It would kill her if the reason for him keeping his distance was that he no longer found her sexually compelling.

"Ridiculous," she muttered. Tariq's fires were the kind that would burn forever. That was what made him so precious.

"What is?" He moved to stand behind her, hands in the pockets of his slacks. While he normally wore traditional garb, sometimes he preferred Western dress. Today he was wearing a blue silk shirt and black pants, the solid colors setting off his rugged masculine beauty in vivid relief.

Her nape prickled with awareness of his nearness, supremely sensitive to his presence. The urge to lean back and rest her head against his firm stomach was so enticing that she had to issue a firm reprimand to herself to behave. If she gave in now, her beautiful, arrogant, sexy husband would once again have her screaming in ecstasy while he remained in control.

With that thought to spur her along, she leaned forward a bit more. It seemed that a lot of seduction in her life went on in front of mirrors, she thought, in an effort to fight her anxiety over her sudden decision to seduce a man who'd proved so capable of controlling his physical passion. Ignoring the voice of fear, she crossed her legs in a movement that looked unconscious. As she'd expected, the robe parted over her thighs and slid off the leg on top, leaving her practically naked.

"Oh, I was just thinking about some of the recent designs on the catwalks." She waved airily and put down the brush, then picked up the lipstick. Curving her lips into a softer-than-normal pout, she began to smooth on the pale bronze with deliberate slowness. It was more of a gloss, which left her lips looking wet and full, rather than a rich hue. She knew her husband preferred to kiss her lips devoid of lipstick, and tonight was about her husband. By the time they got through dinner, the gloss would be gone, but she hoped that by then she wouldn't need its seductive qualities. Right now, the glistening sheen looked like a brazen invitation.

Tariq coughed and shifted behind her, but didn't move

away. Jasmine took that as a good sign, but wondered how far she could go. She didn't want him to guess her plan before she had him safely in bed and at her mercy. She grinned.

"What is so funny?" His voice was rough. She recognized that timbre. Anticipatory heat blossomed in the pit of her stomach. Her heart's beat turned ragged and needy.

"Homosexual male designers and their ideas about the female body," she stated with a decisive nod, proud of herself for being able to keep her head while her hormones were in full riot mode. "I mean, look." She swept her hand over the curves of her breast and hip, lingering just a millisecond too long. "As we discussed before, women are rounded, right?"

"Yes." He sounded as if he was strangling.

"Then why—" she spread her hand on her bared thigh, drawing his attention to the way the fiery curls at the apex of her thighs were barely covered by the blue satin "—are the latest trends going toward boxes and flat, jagged edges?"

When he didn't reply, she looked up into the mirror. Before he met her eyes, she gleefully noted the flush along his cheekbones and the heavy-lidded gaze on her thigh. She thought he'd forgotten what they'd been talking about. Wonderful.

"I am sure you are correct in your view," he said at last.

Nodding in vigorous agreement, she returned to her makeup, aware that he was watching her in the mirror. Keeping a straight face was difficult, but her need to make him feel the same sensual hunger as her gave her the strength. She took her time finishing her makeup and then stood up and crossed to the wardrobe. To her pleased surprise, Tariq lay down on the bed to wait, his arms crossed behind his head. He reminded her of a lazy panther, all liquid muscle and barely contained strength.

Her scowl only surfaced once she was inside the closet. How was she supposed to seduce him with artless ease if he couldn't see her? The bed was placed parallel to the dresser and faced away from the closet behind it. That meant Tariq's eyes were on the bedroom door and she was behind the headboard. Frowning, she pulled an almost-sheer blue skirt off its hanger. The two thin layers of chiffon were just opaque enough for decency, and she'd never before worn the skirt, but today, it was war.

The matching top had tiny cap sleeves trimmed with fine silver braid, and was cut to fit snugly under her breasts, leaving her abdomen bare. She didn't bother to grab a bra because the top was tight enough, and every time she bent forward, the scoop neck would hint at that revealing fact. Walking out of the closet, she put her clothes down on a nearby chair. She almost shimmied into them in haste, before she suddenly understood exactly how sneaky Tariq was.

Far from not being able to see her, her husband had a perfect view of her in the mirror. Her hands went to the knot of her robe. She heard Tariq shift on her bed, and out of nowhere, a belated wave of nervousness hit her. Playing with him was one thing, but could she actually do a striptease?

Before she lost her courage, she undid the robe and shrugged it off. When she leaned forward to throw it across the top of the chair, she thought she heard Tariq's breath hitch. Her own wasn't too steady, but she kept going. She picked up her panties and forced herself to speak.

"Where are we having dinner?" Jasmine slid on the fragile creation of lace and satin, smoothing it over her bottom with fingers that trembled. She snatched them away before he could notice in the mirror, and grabbed the skirt.

Instead of dropping it over her head, she bent over to step into it. She could imagine the picture she presented, and it was making her blush. She hoped the dimness of the light near the closet concealed that betraying fact.

"I had thought the main dining room with Hiraz and Mumtaz, but I've changed my mind. We'll eat in our private dining area." Jasmine didn't miss the possessive edge in his voice. She hadn't heard it for two weeks. At one time, she'd believed it meant he thought of her as an object. She was beginning to understand that Tariq would always be possessive about his woman, even if he loved her. He was simply that kind of man. His possessiveness and protectiveness were traits that she could get used to, she decided. In fact, they made her feel almost cherished.

"Hmm." She buttoned her skirt at the side, picked up the top and turned a little so that her breasts were displayed to him, though her face remained in shadow. She decided that she deserved a medal for bravery. Who would have believed that shy, quiet Jasmine would be trying to entice her virile, sexy husband with such an audacious exhibition? Certainly not her.

The top buttoned down the front, so she slipped it on and then did up the row of five tiny buttons made of white crystal. It was unexpectedly tight across her breasts, which surprised her. However, when she looked down, the line of buttons wasn't distorted, so it appeared that the design required that final snug fit.

Finally, she stepped into a pair of Arabian sandals that she could easily shuck off. Their private dining area was in essence a room full of huge cushions.

"Almost finished." She was thankful that the breathy quality in her voice wasn't too evident.

"There's no hurry." He sounded at ease.

Jasmine wondered if she was mistaken and he hadn't been watching. Walking over to stand beside the bed, she put her hands on her hips and twirled around.

"What do you think?"

He unobtrusively bent his leg at the knee, but wasn't quick enough to hide the arousal straining against the material of his pants. She swallowed a sigh of relief.

"Perfect." His mild tone didn't fool her.

"Hmm, but I think I need some jewelry."

The stroll to her dresser took every ounce of nonchalance she possessed. She didn't even glance in the mirror to check her appearance, not wishing to meet Tariq's eyes and give herself away by accident. From inside the built-in jewelry drawer, she pulled out the fine gold chains that she'd looped over her hips on her wedding day, and put them on. Then she clasped a necklace around her neck. It was pretty but unremarkable, except for the fact that the long spherical Zulheil Rose pendant fell between the globes of her breasts.

"Come on, lazybones, I'm starving." She beckoned to him and pushed through the connecting door to his room. She could have reached the dining room through the corridor, but she couldn't resist the temptation of leading him past the huge double bed. The one in her room had never been used, except for the week that he'd been in Paris.

She heard him mutter, "Me, too," as he rose from the bed. His tone was distinctly bad tempered. She smiled. A starving panther was more to her liking than one attempting to play at being a pussycat.

Her hand was on the knob of the door that led into the dining area when Tariq gripped her waist. Burning heat sizzled through her nerve endings where his hands touched bare skin. His big body pressed her against the door.

"You will wait here while the servants finish."

"It's okay, I don't mind helping them."

His fingers tightened on her skin. "You *will* wait here." Spinning her around, he sealed her next protest with a hard kiss. Giving her a warning glance, he opened the door. It shut with a click behind him.

Jasmine lifted her hands to her tingling lips. He hadn't kissed her like that for weeks. She leaned against the wall because her knees felt as if they'd crumple at any moment. The imprint of his hands on her waist was a living touch that continued to burn her skin.

"I guess I can put up with the arrogance this once," she said out loud, a smile wreathing her face. But she couldn't figure out why he hadn't let her enter the room. Then she happened to glance at the mirror. Her jaw dropped.

She almost ran into the other room to cover herself. The skirt wasn't *almost* sheer. It was absolutely, utterly, scandalously sheer. The outline of her legs was visible with stark clarity, and when she moved, the cloth revealed more than it hid. To make matters worse, the lace front panel of her flimsy panties didn't exactly hide anything, either. The gauzy blue of her skirt granted any watcher blatant hints of the dark red curls at the juncture of her thighs.

The top, which she'd thought sexy but not too revealing, was outrageous in its eroticism. The fabric hugged her breasts with loving care, outlining them with clear precision; her nipples were visible, shameless points of desire against the thin silk. The tightness of the top controlled her breasts, but it also lovingly plumped them up. Soft, white flesh overflowed the neckline.

"Oh my God." She clutched at the wall behind her. No wonder Tariq had forbidden her from entering the other room. She looked like a houri. She felt like a woman dressed to please her master in any way he chose. A wave of apprehension hit her. In desperation, she took a deep breath. In and out. In and out. The added oxygen must have revived her brain cells, because a bright ray of hope stood out from the chaos in her mind.

"He didn't tell me to change," she whispered. "In fact, he said I looked perfect." If Tariq had been put off by her sexy outfit, he wouldn't have been so insistent on leaving her in his bedroom to wait, wouldn't have agreed on her choice, and surely wouldn't have kissed her.

Grinning, she skipped over to the huge bed and perched on the end, away from the mirror. She pasted a bored expression on her face just as Tariq opened the door. He stopped. She saw him swallow, and for once she knew exactly what her husband was thinking. He wanted to throw her on the bed and teach her not to tease him.

Except he wasn't sure that she was teasing. And, Jasmine decided, he was too much in control if he could resist that primitive urge.

She jumped off the bed and walked over. "Ready?"

He nodded but didn't seem to remember that he was blocking the door. Successfully fighting the urge to tease him, she pushed at his chest. He obediently moved aside to let her pass, then followed.

Once inside, he didn't take a cushion on the other side of the low table set with food. Instead, he sat down beside her, propping himself up with one hand flat on the cushion behind her. His shoulder and chest pressed against her and when she leaned back a little, his arm provided a hard masculine backrest.

Jasmine tried to steady her breathing, and picked up a plateful of small tarts of some kind. She offered the plate to Tariq. He lifted one dark eyebrow in invitation. With a blush she couldn't control, she picked up a tart and fed it to him. He almost caught her fingers on his second bite. Laughing, she pulled away just in time.

Her husband had a definite glint in his eye, but she was determined that she wouldn't be the only one losing control tonight. He was coming with her. However, attempting to ignore the way the panther by her side was throwing her body into chaos was proving to be difficult.

With a forced smile, she picked up a tart and took a bite. "I've never eaten anything like this." The savory pastry was spicy, with a hint of unfamiliar herbs, but delicious. To her surprise, Tariq reached out and filched the rest of it.

"Hey!" Surprise overcame her inner trembling.

"I told you I was hungry. Feed me quickly."

Jasmine told herself she was imagining the double entendre in his words—surely he hadn't meant that he was *hungry?* She was getting ahead of herself. She mock-scowled at him, but picked up a kebab and fed it to her sheik. He sprawled beside her, seemingly content to eat whatever she chose, as long as she offered it to him. Tariq had never done this before and Jasmine found that she enjoyed cosseting him. Today, for the first time, she'd begun to understand precisely how enormous his duties were. It made her want to fill his life with pleasure, so that those duties wouldn't burn out the bright light inside him, though that same light threatened to make her love for him impossibly stronger.

"I don't think I can eat dessert." Some time later, she put a hand on her stomach. It wasn't terribly full, but she was aware that she might be engaging in some strenuous exercise soon.

Tariq's eyes traveled in a slow journey from her lips to her breasts, to the curve of her stomach. This time she couldn't fight the glow that tinged her skin the color at the heart of Zulheil Rose. The instant he became aware of her response, he ran a finger across the top of her breasts. The fleeting caress made her feel weak and tingly inside.

"We'll leave it here." Tariq rose to his feet and held out a hand to help her up. "In case you get hungry later."

Jasmine almost stumbled when she caught the meaning of his husky words. However, when she looked up, she saw that he continued to exercise rigid control over his expression. If she surrendered now, she wouldn't be any closer to breaking through the sensual barriers between them than she'd been at the start of the evening.

What now? she thought, frantic at the prospect of failure. He wasn't aroused enough if he wasn't ripping off her clothes. She was sick of being gently undressed each night. She wanted her passionate, insatiable and teasing lover back. He led her into their bedroom, stopped by the bed and lifted his fingers to the buttons on her blouse.

Jasmine took a deep breath and pushed Tariq's hands away. They dropped at once, but he'd already half unbuttoned her blouse, leaving her breasts in imminent danger of falling out.

"You do not wish to proceed?" He was painfully correct in his speech.

"Tariq, would you grant me a boon?" The old-fashioned words seemed appropriate. She was dressed like a princess from a fairy tale, or perhaps a sensual goddess from myth, and in front of her stood a dark warrior she had to woo to her side or all would be lost.

"You do not have to ask a boon, Jasmine. I accept your desire not to…" He began to back away. Only the way he clenched his fists at his sides revealed his true feelings.

She gripped his shirt in desperate appeal. "I want you."

His hands went to her buttons again. She shook her head.

"What is it, Mina?" He sounded impatient, more like the lover she'd known before he'd started to withdraw. And he'd called her Mina.

"I just…" She bit her lip. "Would it be okay if I touched you tonight?" This time, she went for *his* buttons.

He groaned. "I've told you, touching me is permitted at any time."

"But I want you not to touch me."

"I do not understand." He was wary again.

"I lose my mind when you touch me, and for once I want to be able to explore you. Please?" She knew asking him to give her control was a risk. But if he said no, she'd just keep trying, she decided. He was already acting with more heat than he'd shown for the past two weeks. She undid the button she'd been toying with and moved on to the next one.

His hand touched her hair in a light caress before he pulled out the pins. The soft curls tumbled to her shoulders in a fiery waterfall. "And what am I to do while you...explore me?" She didn't miss either the slight hesitation or the abrasive roughness of his voice.

CHAPTER TEN

JASMINE UNDID ANOTHER BUTTON. "Just lie back and enjoy it. I'll do all the work."

Silence filled the room, broken only with the sounds of their breathing. Jasmine bit her lip again and stopped herself from pleading.

"I'll allow you to do this." His hands settled on her exposed hips, his skin warm against hers.

Jasmine smiled and reached up on tiptoe to press a soft kiss to his lips. "Thank you."

He appeared startled by her open enjoyment of the situation, but was willing to do as she wished. She drew back and finished unbuttoning his shirt, then pulled the tails out of his pants to complete the task. His beautiful chest felt as hard as steel under her questing fingers. Delighted by the freedom to explore, she ran her fingernails down the center line of his chest. He sucked in a breath.

"I love your chest." She threw caution to the winds. "Every time I see you come out of the shower, I want to pull you into bed and kiss you everywhere." She moved her fingers to his flat male nipples and then ran her nails over both. His groan was music to her ears.

Emboldened by his response, she wrapped her arms around his rigid body and put her hands flat on his back. His skin was so hot it almost burned. Then she flicked her tongue over one of his nipples. His hand moved up

her back to clench in her hair. Delighted, she continued
to kiss his chest, alternating soft warm kisses with wet
openmouthed ones. She kissed her way down to his abdomen until she was kneeling in front of him. When she
reached the waistband of his pants, he tugged on her hair
with innate gentleness and pulled her back up.

"Mina," he whispered, against her mouth. "Have you
had enough exploring?" His voice was heavy, sensual,
encouraging.

She gasped when he sucked her lower lip into his own
mouth. He took his time kissing her, bestowing nibbling
love bites on her lips before urging her to open. When
she did, his tongue swept in and proceeded to taste her
with arrogant thoroughness. It was a long, lazy kiss that
left her feeling as if she belonged to him. When he released her, she shook her head, breathless and aroused.
"I've just begun."

She trailed her fingers down the bare part of his arms.
His golden skin strained to contain the pure strength of
the muscles beneath. Lifting his hand to her mouth, she
sucked one finger into the moist recesses. He released
his breath in a forceful hiss. One by one, she sucked each
of his fingers and then repeated the hot, sweet caress on
his other hand, before moving to undo the buttons on the
cuffs.

By the time she finished, Tariq's vivid green eyes
echoed the perfect clarity of shattered emerald shards.
"Would you like this off?" He motioned to his shirt.

"Yes." Walking behind him, she helped tug it off.
The skin of his shoulders was hot and smooth. Jasmine
molded her hands over them, captivated by the way they
tensed.

The shirt fell to the floor. After pushing it aside with one foot, she shucked her slippers. When he would've turned, she wrapped her arms around his waist and plastered herself against him. "Stay. I want to touch your back." The shudder that went through him vibrated against her sensitive nipples and reached deep within. It was as if a part of Tariq was inside her, touching her in the most intimate way.

Pressing her palms against his chest, she drew back just far enough to appreciate the sculpted planes of his back. Muscles moved like liquid steel under his skin when he raised his hands and put them over her own.

"You're so strong." She blew a warm breath onto his skin, entranced by the way he groaned and leaned backward. His reaction was the strongest of aphrodisiacs. "So beautiful."

His chuckle was hoarse. "It is you who are beautiful. I am a man."

She bit him just under his shoulder blade. "Absolutely, utterly beautiful."

He squeezed her fingers. "I am pleased you find me beautiful, Mina. However, you are not to tell this to anyone."

Jasmine laughed at the mock warning and tugged her fingers from his grasp. Once free, she began to trace the defined muscles of his back with slow deliberation. His breathing hitched, then restarted in a shallower rhythm.

"Would it damage your reputation as a tough, macho sheik?" She began to kiss her way down his spine. Her half-exposed breasts pressed against him, exciting her as much as she hoped the contact was stimulating him.

He took a deep breath. "I do not know this word *macho*."

She started to undo the remaining buttons of her blouse, while continuing to caress his back, pressing urgent kisses against his slightly salty skin. "Macho means you." She grazed his ribs with sharp little teeth. "Strong, manly, very masculine." The blouse came undone. She pulled it off her shoulders and then licked her way back up his spine with her tongue. There was a swish as the blouse fell behind her. Her mind spinning with the extravagant sensuality of the moment, she plastered herself against him once more.

Electricity sizzled between them as skin touched skin.

Tariq's groan was a rumble deep in his throat. Sensing that her panther was reaching the end of his tether, she moved to stand in front of him. Her lover's expression was devoid of disguise, his eyes so dark they were almost black, his desire etched in stark lines.

Aroused beyond bearing, Tariq had to touch Mina. He raised one hand and cupped the warm weight of one breast. She gasped and her fingers pressed into his chest.

"No, please." It was a husky whisper, a sensual plea.

"You will kill me with this exploring, Mina." He picked her up and put her on the bed, aching to claim her. The disappointment that flickered in her eyes at having her exploration cut short fanned the flames of his passion as nothing else could have done. Keeping his eyes on her body, he kicked off his shoes and unzipped his pants.

"Yes?" He paused, waiting for her instruction.

Eyes wide, she nodded.

He peeled off his underwear with his pants. Jasmine

stunned him by reaching out and trailing her finger down the length of his erection. His body was racked with tremors. "Move aside, Mina, or I will be on top of you and this will end."

She shifted with an alacrity that made him feel like the most desired of men.

He lay down on the bed on his back, his arms folded under his head. "I think you have about five more minutes," he warned, his gaze skating possessively over her body. He'd thought he could manage the beast inside him, dictate what he felt for this woman, but all he'd done was starve himself. The weeks of enforced calm disintegrated, and the primitive urge to take Mina ate away at his control.

As he watched, Jasmine straddled his thighs. Her gauzy skirts settled around them like curtains of mist.

"In that case, I'll get right to the crux of the matter." Without warning, she wrapped her fingers around his erection.

Swamped with ecstasy, Tariq growled low in his throat and pushed into her hands. Her fingers were delicate and feminine around him, her expression utterly fascinated. Seduced by her delight in his body, he surrendered and let his wife have her way with him.

Encouraged by Tariq's unhidden enjoyment, Jasmine increased the pressure and began to move her hand up and down. Velvet over steel. Burning fire and searing heat. A soft moan escaped her lips. She could feel herself being seduced by his reactions. Tariq's face was a study in raw passion. His cheekbones stood out against his flushed skin and his teeth were gritted against the pleasure. Aching with the need to give him more, to give him everything, she dipped her head and replaced her hands with her mouth.

Tariq's thighs went as hard as rock under her. He jerked up into a sitting position and clenched his hands in her hair. When he shuddered under her inexpert caresses, Jasmine's fear of not pleasing him evaporated. Exhilarated by his hoarse cries, she settled into the task she'd set herself.

Mina's attentive exploration snapped the threads of Tariq's control. "Enough." He pulled her up, his hands rough.

Her heavy-lidded, passion-hot face inflamed him further. With another throaty groan, he hauled her up his body, until she was almost astride him. Then he reached under her skirt and found the lace of her panties. The sound of lace and satin ripping was drowned out by the loud panting of their breaths. Tariq threw aside the torn pieces and touched her with his fingers. Creamy heat welcomed him.

"You're so wet, Mina." His voice shook with the discovery.

Sensitized beyond bearing by their erotic play, Jasmine moved demandingly against his fingers. "Now. Now!"

Tariq didn't argue, sliding her onto his hard length. He was too slow for her. She gripped his sweat-slick shoulders and pushed down, surprising him. He lodged to the hilt inside her and groaned in satisfaction. She saw the look on his face and knew that this time, her lover would be coming with her on the incandescent final ride. He had, after all, ripped off her clothing. With a smile, she gave in and rode him to surrender.

TARIQ DREW A LINE DOWN Jasmine's breastbone with his finger. She squirmed under the light caress. Tariq let her capture his hand in her own and place it over her heart. She was almost asleep, apparently exhausted by their wild mating.

"You were aroused just by touching me," he commented.

"Tariq," she murmured, her cheeks red.

"So shy now?"

Opening her eyes, she made a face at him. "Tease." But she wriggled closer and wrapped her arms around him.

He stroked her back, as if petting a cat. "Always?" Under his hand, she was warm and smooth.

"What?" she asked sleepily, burrowing into his chest.

"Are you always aroused by touching me?" he persisted, even as he cuddled her close to him. The need he'd hidden deep within rebelled against being ignored any longer.

Eyes closed and body relaxed almost totally, Jasmine muttered, "I get aroused just by looking at you. It's because I love you. Now go to sleep."

"Mina, when you touch me like that, I could almost believe you." He knew she didn't hear him, because she'd already fallen asleep. Stroking her hair off her face, he wondered if she would remember her declaration tomorrow. It didn't matter, because he would. The fist that had been clenched around his heart loosened. Maybe being unable to control his feelings wasn't the disaster he'd thought. Not if this was the outcome.

While she slept, Tariq couldn't help but compare the woman he'd seen over the past week to the girl to whom he'd given his heart, only to have it rejected. In his arms, she was fire, unafraid of her sensuality. Yet in the desert, though her persistence had angered him, she hadn't given up probing for the truth of the past. The autocratic part of him that expected instant obedience bristled at her audacity. But there was a bigger part of him that was awed by her feminine strength. This was a woman with whom he could rule.

Since Paris, he'd wanted to take a chance on his wife. Tempted by the promise of the last few days, he found that the urge to let his barriers fall was almost irresistible. He wanted to give her his trust. Except the last time he'd done that, she'd almost destroyed him. Did he dare to try again, even knowing that she still hid something from him?

SHE HAD HER PANTHER BACK.

"You will follow my orders. You will not venture into Zulheina today." Tariq slammed the flat of his palm on his desk, the sound as loud as a pistol shot in the quiet study.

Jasmine put her hands on her hips and scowled. "Why not? I've always been able to do so before."

"I have given an order. I expect it to be obeyed."

She blew out a breath through pursed lips. And she'd wanted this fiery, hot-tempered creature to come back? "I'm not a servant to be given a command!" She lost her temper for the first time. After the powerful intimacy of the last few days, he could act with a tad more consideration. "Give me an explanation that makes sense and I'll stay."

Tariq stalked around his desk and put his hands on her

waist. Then he picked her up until they were eye to eye. Her feet dangled off the floor. Jasmine placed her hands on his shoulders and refused to be intimidated.

"Has a terrorist organization infiltrated Zulheina?" she guessed wildly. "No, I've got it. Today is the annual Kill-the-redhead Festival. No, no wait, is it Tariq-is-going-to-act-like-a-dictator Day? Am I right? Come on, am I even close?" She pushed at his shoulders, furious at the way he was demonstrating his greater strength.

His shoulders started to shake. She squinted at his face. "Arrgh! Let me go, you… No, I can't call you an animal because that would insult the animal." Tariq laughed harder, his eyes sparkling. "Stop it you…you husband!"

"Mina." His smile was blinding. "Mina, you're magnificent."

That made her pause. It had sounded like a compliment. She looked at him suspiciously. "Are you going to tell me?"

"It seems I have been insulted into submission."

"Hah! Your hide is as thick as a rhinoceros's. Anything I say just rolls off," she muttered under her breath. "Put me down." He wrapped his arms even tighter around her and walked through the door, into the corridor.

"Tariq, what are you doing?" She glanced around, hoping against hope that no one else was around. His official study was in the main wing of the palace. "My feet are bare. My slippers fell off when you picked me up."

"Then it is just as well I am carrying you." His reply was insufferably male.

She gave up. Wrapping her arms more firmly around

his neck, she hung on, realizing that he was taking them back to their rooms. "Are you planning to lock me in our suite?"

He paused and then resumed his ground-eating stride. "I had not thought of that. It is an excellent idea."

Jasmine shook her head and tipped her head back, but she couldn't catch his eye. "Bad idea. Very bad idea." When he didn't reply, she narrowed her eyes and tried to shake his shoulders. "You wouldn't…would you?"

"I must have a way to deal with the bad-tempered hellcat I've married." He pushed through the doorway to their suite and headed for their bedroom.

"Bad tempered!" She scowled. "Me? I think you've got your wires crossed."

"At least it's not my eyes."

"Eyes? What…I can't believe it. You made a joke?" She gave a theatrical gasp that turned into a cry of surprise when he dropped her onto the bed. "Be still my heart."

Tactile pleasure shimmered over her when he lowered his body full length over hers. He started to stroke her with his talented hands. "Is this supposed to be a distraction?" she demanded.

"Would it be successful as one?"

"Oh, yes," she sighed. "But tell me the truth, please?"

"Persistent little creature," he complained, but his tone was affectionate. His eyes were heavy with sensual promise when he looked at her. "Today is the festival…"

Jasmine's giggles caught her completely by surprise. Tariq tried to frown her into submission. When that didn't work, he kissed her until she was boneless.

"As I was saying, it is the festival of the virgins." He kissed the side of her neck. "If you'd arrived a few weeks later, you could have joined it. No, that's a lie. You would not have remained a virgin long enough. I almost took you in the car as it was."

"Stop that," she ordered.

"What?"

"Making me crazy."

"I like making you crazy." Satisfaction simmered in those green depths when she shivered under his stroking. His lips curved into a grin.

Jasmine didn't know what to do with him in this mood. In the end, she decided that the safest option was to ignore the gleam in his eye and bask in his attention.

"So tell me." She traced a design over his chest with her fingertip, enjoying touching him through the fine linen. Tariq had never once curtailed her sensual explorations after she'd shown him just how much she adored his body.

"It's a day when female virgins of a certain age make a pilgrimage to a sacred place."

"Where?"

He looked chagrined at her question. "No man knows."

Her interest was piqued. "Really?" At his nod she asked, "How old is this festival?"

"As old as Zulheil."

"And why couldn't I go outside?"

Tariq pressed his forehead to hers and spoke against her mouth. "If you would let me finish, Mina, I will tell you."

Jasmine pursed her lips and slanted him an encouraging look. He continued to speak against her mouth, lips on lips, sorely tempting her to open up.

"I do not know what they do and that is probably just as well. No man is allowed on the streets at the time."

Jasmine frowned, the question stuck at the back of her throat. Tariq read her mind.

"Patience, little hellcat. There is no danger because the married women go with them, including the police-women."

She couldn't keep her mouth shut. "Policewomen? Zulheil allows its women such occupations?" Once more, the way the people of Zulheil guarded their privacy so zealously left her feeling at a loss. She had so much to learn. And a lifetime in which to learn it, she reminded herself, ignoring the dart of fear that threatened to ruin the moment. Tariq would trust her again and wouldn't denounce her when he discovered her illegitimacy. Maybe, her heart whispered, if she wanted his trust, she should begin by giving him hers?

"I have told you our women are cherished. We protect but do not cage." He ran his tongue over the line of her lips in a teasing stroke. The urge to surrender almost overcame her.

"Why couldn't I go then?"

"Because—" Tariq took advantage of her open mouth to sip from her lips "—aside from the virgins, only married women who have borne children or been married for five years can do so." He spread his fingers over her stomach in an unmistakable message. "When you have borne my child, then you may go."

Jasmine swallowed. The thought of bearing Tariq's child was a dream she hadn't dared consider. And still couldn't, so long as she hid the truth of her own birth. She had to tell him. But not now, not when he sounded as if he cared for her. "How do you stop foreigners from disturbing the pilgrimage?"

"Zulheil annually closes its borders the week prior to this journey. Those already inside have visas that expire that same week. Recalcitrant visitors are escorted out."

"You closed your borders after your parents passed away, didn't you?" She'd spoken without thinking, but as soon as the words were out, she braced herself. Tariq had remained staunch in his refusal to talk about his loss.

He kissed her. It was a gentle kiss full of warmth, but without overt sexual overtones. Jasmine returned the caress, though she didn't understand what was happening.

"Yes," he whispered into her mouth. "For two months, Zulheil was closed to foreigners. Our people needed to come to terms with the grief and I needed time to heal the fractures."

"Two months? Don't you mean one?" Jasmine stroked his cheek. She wanted to cry with joy. He was trusting her with something important, something that had hurt him to the core. "I came one month afterward, remember?"

CHAPTER ELEVEN

TARIQ'S LIPS CURVED IN A smile. "You were granted a very special visa."

She stopped breathing. "You knew. You knew all along that I was coming."

He shrugged. "I am the Sheik of Zulheil. I knew. Why did you come, then?"

It was the one question that he hadn't asked before, and the one that she couldn't answer without giving away almost everything. Jasmine stroked her fingers into his hair and knew she'd tell him the truth. Four years ago she'd been a coward and it had cost her his love. Perhaps she could win it back with bravery. There would be no more hiding the strongest emotion in her heart because she was afraid of being rejected.

"I came because I heard about your loss and I thought that maybe you might need me." Tariq's body tensed against hers. She understood his silent rejection of the thought of needing her. He wasn't ready to make himself that vulnerable. Perhaps he never would be, his pride having been savaged too badly the first time. She swallowed the feelings of hopelessness and continued. "But more than that, I needed *you*. I'd already decided to come long before. I'd laid the groundwork."

"Why, Mina?" His eyes were dark and impenetrable. His fingers dug into the soft skin of her upper arms hard enough to leave bruises, but she was heartened. If he cared enough to lose control over his strength, then she had to have a chance.

She felt tears rise in her eyes. "Because I couldn't live without you anymore. I just couldn't bear it. I woke up each day thinking of you and fell asleep with your name on my lips. I love you so much, Tariq, you can't even imagine."

He didn't answer in words. His kiss was tender and almost forgiving. She didn't force the issue. It would take time to heal the wounds of the past, but she hoped her bravery would buy her that time.

Tariq rolled onto his back and fitted her to his side. "I miss them."

Jasmine took a deep breath and just let him speak.

"I was brought up with knowledge of the responsibilities that awaited me, but my parents made sure I had a childhood and a relatively free young adulthood." He cuddled her closer, as if needing her warmth. "I traveled and I learned. I was given a chance to grow into a man without being shaped by my role. For that, I'll always be in debt to my parents. Any child of ours will have the same chance."

"They sound like they were wonderful people," she dared to murmur, though not wanting to break this fragile rapport.

"They were." He paused, as if debating whether to continue. His next words shocked her to the core. "My mother was dying and she did not tell me."

Jasmine sucked in a breath. "Dying?"

"Cancer." His voice was harsh. "They were on their way back from a treatment when the crash occurred."

Unable to imagine the depth of his suffering, she blinked back tears and asked, "Do you blame her for their deaths?"

He shook his head. "I blame her for not trusting me, for stealing my chance to try to help her. And to say goodbye."

"She was protecting her son." Jasmine understood his mother's actions instinctively, but she could also understand her warrior's pain. His mother's secrecy had rendered him helpless and he would hate that feeling. "It wasn't about trust. It was about a mother's love."

"I have almost come to accept that, but part of me remains angry with her for making the choice for me. Perhaps there was something I could have done. Now I will never know." His voice was haunted. "When they died, I was ready to assume my duties, but not to lose my parents. I felt adrift, lost emotionally. You have to understand, I was an only child, and despite close friendships, no one except my parents understood the demands of our position in this land.

"We are the rulers and guardians of our people. It's an honor and the gravest of responsibilities. For my people I had to be strong, but I felt as if I was enclosed in a cave of ice, unable to feel, until…"

"Until?" She held her breath, waiting for words that she knew might never come, but couldn't help hoping for.

"Nothing." Quick as lightning, he changed their positions, so that she was pressed under him.

She didn't protest. He'd given her far more than she'd expected. His mother's secret explained so much. It hurt Jasmine to think what damage it would have done to the proud and loyal man she'd married, to know that his mother had not trusted him with the truth of her health. Her reasons had been born out of love, but they'd wounded her son. Jasmine bit her lip, unable to escape the inevitable conclusion. What would her cowardice in keeping her secret cost him?

It was her last thought before Tariq pulled her into the heat of his passion.

TARIQ HELD MINA IN HIS ARMS after their loving, deeply affected by her confession of need. The raw honesty of it was undeniable, but it was hard to trust her completely. While he'd begun to let down his shields, his wife kept secrets that turned her blue eyes dark without warning. Though he'd vowed to have nothing but honesty between them, he wouldn't beg her for this secret. He wouldn't humble his pride for her. Not again. Never again.

He'd thought that she'd fallen asleep, but suddenly, she spoke, "I...have to tell you something."

Keeping his sudden tension from showing in his body was a struggle. He merely moved aside the hair covering her face from him. "Yes?"

She kept her eyes on the bedspread, her fingers playing with the embroidered swirls. "When we first met...I was so frightened of losing you. That's why I never told you."

"What?" He felt a mixture of hope and despair. Was she going to try and give him more excuses? He'd begun to believe that she'd matured, become someone he could trust, but that woman wouldn't try to ease her way with excuses.

"Promise me something first?" she asked.

It was the naked vulnerability of her voice that made

his response gentle. "What would you have of me, Mina?"

"Don't hate me for this." Her tone was ragged, as if she no longer had any protective walls, and suddenly, he knew that there were going to be no excuses from this woman.

Hate her? Though he'd walked close to the line, he'd never hated Mina and couldn't imagine doing so. "On my word of honor as your husband." He gathered her closer, tenderness for her overwhelming him. He did not like to see her hurting.

On the sheets, her graceful hand clenched into a fist so tight that cream turned to white and tendons stood out across her wrist. "I'm illegitimate."

She'd given him no warning, no sign of the strength of her secret. "Illegitimate?" In his arms, she shivered. He reached over and covered them with a blanket, tucking her close to him, almost able to see her need to be touched.

"My...parents are really my aunt and uncle. My birth mother, Mary, had me when she was a teenager." Jasmine swallowed. "I found out when I was a child that my parents only adopted me because they received part of Mary's inheritance. They n-never loved me. To them I was...bad blood." The words came out on top of each other, like a flood bursting its banks. Her fist loosened and then curled again.

Reaching out, he covered her hand and uncurled her fingers, smoothing them out. Her hurt was almost palpable. He'd never liked her parents, but at this instant he could have done physical violence to them. How dare they not treasure his wife, his precious Jasmine? "And you think this matters to me?" He was a little hurt by her distrust.

"You're a sheik. You should've married a princess or at least someone who can claim royal blood. I don't even know the name of the man who fathered me." Her breath was ragged.

That was shameful, he acknowledged, but the shame was not hers, *never* hers. The shame was of the man who'd given his seed to create this lovely woman and then walked away, of the woman who'd borne a child and abandoned her, and of the people who'd asked payment for the priceless gift of this woman.

"Look at me." He turned her in his arms. Jasmine raised her head and met his gaze, vulnerable but willing to face whatever he had to say. Pride in her courage burned in him. "Our people have barbarian roots. Chieftains still occasionally give in to the urge to carry off the women of their choice." He ran his finger over her lips, reminding her of his actions. "A desert male's choice is what is important. And I chose you to be my wife."

"You aren't angry that I didn't tell you?" Her blue eyes shimmered with moisture.

"Of course I'm not angry with you, my wife. I would that you had told me earlier, but I am not such a barbarian that I can't understand your reluctance." He kissed her again, knowing she needed to be physically reassured. Her body felt incredibly fragile under his hands, needing exquisite care.

When she started to relax, he asked, "Why didn't you tell me this when we first met?" Back then, he'd been open in his adoration of his flame-haired girl.

She bit her lip and took a deep breath. "I…just

wanted... I didn't expect Mary to keep me...but I thought after I was older she might want to get in touch. I wrote to her." She swallowed. "She told me never to contact her again. I was...an indiscretion." Her breath had become ragged again, her tears barely held in check.

"Then you... I wanted to...to not be an outcast." Those eyes of hers brightened with tears, but his brave little Mina didn't let them fall. "I just wanted to be accepted."

He heard the important words in that emotional confession. "Then have no fears. You are accepted. As my *wife, Jasmine*. What you were before only matters if you wish it to." Any hurt and anger he might have felt died a quick death under the overwhelming need to shelter her from further pain.

His Mina, his gentle, sensitive wife, had grown up in a place where she had not been nurtured, where her softness had been mocked. It made him furious that this lovely woman in his arms had suffered so much pain and rejection. Knowing what she'd been through, he could forgive her for trying to protect herself. And yet she'd told him her secret. She'd laid her heart at his feet, and then given him the weapons to destroy it. It was an offering of immense trust and courage, and he intended to treat it with the care it deserved.

Slowly, almost shyly, she wrapped her slender arms around his waist. "Truly?" At that soft sound, his heart clenched in a wave of tenderness as fierce as the desert sun.

"Are you saying that the Sheik of Zulheil would lie to you?" He saw a tremulous smile edging her lips and was proud he could make her smile. Mina was his to care for.

"Maybe. If he thought it would get him his own way." Her voice was less teary, her smile wider.

He grinned at that. "I think you are right, but in this thing, never doubt me. You are now equivalent to a queen. No one has the right to make you feel an outcast." He would destroy any man or woman who tried to make his Mina a lesser being. "No one. Do you understand, my wife?"

Finally, she nodded, and her smile was glorious. Tariq kissed her, knowing that she'd just shattered the strongest barrier keeping him from loving her, heart and soul. How could he continue to fight his feelings for her, now that he knew what had driven her? How could he hurt his Mina as her family had hurt her, by not loving her as she needed to be loved?

JASMINE CLOSED THE DOOR ON the last guest of the day and headed to Tariq's study. Since she'd started to spend her days helping her husband, her pride in herself had grown. All her life she'd been told that she didn't measure up, but the people of Zulheil thought she was doing a fine job. And, she thought with a smile, the look in her husband's eyes as he helped her pick up the reins of royalty was magic itself.

"You are looking pleased with yourself."

"Tariq." Jasmine flowed into his arms. Her need to touch him grew daily. "I thought you'd be in your office."

"I have completed my work for today. You make my duties much easier to bear." He cupped her cheek and tipped up her face. His expression was unexpectedly serious. "You are not taking on too much, Jasmine? I would not have you become ill."

She smiled and turned her face into his palm. "Do I look ill or tired?"

He shook his head. "You glow like the crystal of this palace."

"That's because I've found a place where I can belong at last." She was struck by the truth of that statement.

Tariq didn't stop her when she began to walk toward their apartments. He slipped his fingers into hers and shortened his stride to accommodate her steady pace. The ageless beauty of the tapestries and carvings lining the hallway didn't hold her attention while her mind was on things past, but she was constantly aware of Tariq's protective presence. She led them out into the private garden behind their rooms.

"It's like the sun is smiling at the world." When she held out her hands, the thick yellow-orange sunlight shot through her fingers like warm, liquid satin. In the sky, red, orange and yellow vied for prime position in the soft pink glow of sunset, and all seemed at peace.

Tariq tucked a wayward strand of hair behind her ear. "You belong in the sun, Mina."

She turned and smiled at him. "I belong *here.*"

"Yes." He curved his arm around her and cradled her against him. One arm around his back, she rested her head on his muscled chest. They didn't speak until there was more red than yellow in the sky and pink was segueing to violet.

"I know you did not feel you belonged in your parents' home. Was there any reason aside from your birth?"

The question was unexpected, but she welcomed the chance to make Tariq understand the girl she'd been.

"I've never talked to you about this. I think I was afraid you'd begin to feel like everyone else."

"No one can control me, my Jasmine. Tell me."

She knew his words were supposed to comfort her, and to a certain extent, they did. However, they also reminded her of the divide that existed between them. Tariq was treating her like a partner as far as running Zulheil went, but in their personal relationship…would he ever trust her again?

"You know my sister Sarah is a stunning beauty." Sarah had the kind of beauty that made people stand in the streets and stare, something Sarah certainly knew. She'd been using her beauty her entire life to bewitch and control those around her. Even her parents could deny her nothing.

"She is cold. She does not have your fire," Tariq stated, as if it were a simple truth.

Jasmine's eyes widened. "Do you really think so?"

"A man would be a fool to be captured by the glitter of false gold, overlooking the quiet, ageless beauty of purity." He wasn't looking at her and Jasmine didn't know if his words were a compliment or merely a statement.

"Sarah never liked me. I don't know why, but it hurt so much when I was younger. She's my big sister and I wanted her to be my friend."

Tariq was compelled to ease the bewildered pain in Jasmine's voice. "She was jealous of you. I could see it when I first met her. As you grew older, you became competition, and Sarah is not one who would countenance such a thing."

Jasmine snorted. "Thanks for the flattery, but I'm no-where near her in the beauty stakes."

He hugged her tightly. "Your fire burns not only in your hair but in your spirit. Your sister was aware that she would grow colder and colder until she felt nothing. She knew you would burn hotter with each passing year, your beauty growing apace with the unfurling of your wings." He hadn't meant to admit that much, wasn't sure enough of Jasmine to show her that she was gaining a foothold in his heart.

"That's the most wonderful thing anyone's ever said to me." The shimmering joy in her eyes soothed him. If letting Mina see that she mattered to him healed her hurts, then he would risk giving her this insight into his heart.

"Your sister...what is the word?...propositioned me, after I had made my interest in you clear." He frowned at the memory. "She placed her fingers on my chest."

Jasmine's eyes widened. "No."

"I found it distasteful. I simply removed her hand." Implicit was the fact that he'd chosen her over Sarah.

Jasmine remained silent for a moment, mulling over that information. It put a new slant on Sarah's utter vi-ciousness while Tariq had been in New Zealand. She'd known that Sarah wanted Tariq, but not that he'd rejected her advances.

"Tell me the rest, Mina."

Still unsettled, she continued, needing him to know. Needing him to love her despite her flaws. "Because of Sarah and how my parents always took her side, I never felt like I fit there. Then there were Michael and Mat-thew."

"Your brothers hurt you?" Tariq's dangerously calm voice startled her.

"Oh, no. Michael's a certified genius. He's older than me, and spent most of his life in his lab or with his head in his books. He was kind to me when he remembered my existence. Matthew's just turned twenty-one. We were born..." she paused "...over a year apart. Matthew is the baby of the family. He's also a natural athlete. He's been studying in the United States on a football scholarship for the past three years."

"I don't see what you're trying to say." Tariq turned her around. She saw the frown on his face and knew that he was telling the truth.

"I was so ordinary." Even now, her childish fear that he'd begin to treat her as her family had lay like a malevolent shadow over her heart. "I sort of got lost among those three and their brilliance. I was just...me."

"Even in a crowd of a million people, Mina, you would stand out. I saw you with your family that first time and I saw only you." His voice was quiet but the words roared through her. "Your family did not appreciate your worth. It is good you came to me." With that, he folded her in his arms and dropped a kiss on her hair.

Seduced by his unexpected gentleness, she almost told him again that she loved him, but the part of her that needed so badly to be loved in return stopped her. She couldn't bear it if he ignored her, or worse, looked at her with puzzlement, because that was clearly not the nature of their relationship. As they stood there watching the sun set, a vague sense of impending wrongness worried her. She couldn't shake the feeling that she was going to lose Tariq.

However, as busy days drifted into sultry nights, her fears seemed to grow groundless and without substance, as airy as the desert wind. She convinced herself that she'd been imagining things, and stopped looking over her shoulder.

DAYS LATER, DRESSED IN AN ankle-length dress of pale green, her arms covered by full sleeves cuffed at the wrist, Jasmine circulated among Zulheil's people in the palace gardens, bathed in the fading evening light.

"Jasmine al eha Sheik." A touch on her elbow halted her.

She turned to smile at the elderly woman who'd stopped her. Absently, she made a note to ask Mumtaz exactly what the address meant. More than one person had greeted her that way this day. "Hello." She attempted Zulheil's native language.

The old woman's wrinkled face lit up. "You speak the language of Zulheil?" she asked in the same tongue.

Haltingly, Jasmine answered. "I try but...I am slow."

The woman patted her on the arm with the warm familiarity that the people of Zulheil seemed to feel toward their rulers. It was as if they were considered part of every single family in the land. She found the easy acceptance wonderful.

"You are of Zulheil. Soon you will speak the language well. My name is Haleah and I come from the farthest corner of Zulheil."

"A long journey."

Haleah nodded and fixed her with a shrewd eye. "I was sent to look at the new sheik's wife by the chieftain of our tribe."

Jasmine knew from her visit to Zeina that Zulheil's system of government was made up of a number of chieftains who exercised local power. In turn, they'd sworn allegiance to their sheik and followed his dictates with unswerving loyalty and even fiercer dedication.

"And what will...you tell...them?" She continued to speak in the beautiful lilting language of her sheik's land, not discomfited by learning the reason for Haleah's presence. For the past month, she'd been on the receiving end of such scrutiny from a number of messengers.

Haleah gave her a slow smile. "I will say that you have hair like fire and eyes like the blue of the sea on our coast. I will say your heart is open and that you will love our people as you love our sheik."

Jasmine's composure fractured. "I...thank you."

Haleah squeezed her arm. "No. I bring you the gratitude of my tribe for making our sheik feel happiness again. The sadness in his heart was felt keenly by all."

Jasmine bent and accepted the kiss on her cheek. Haleah moved away with a wave, heading for the car that would take her back to her lodgings and then to her home.

A tug on her arm brought Jasmine around to face Mumtaz.

"As your advisor, I have some information." Mumtaz's eyes held an amused look.

"Spit it out," Jasmine said, easy in the presence of this woman who'd become her closest friend.

"Keep your eye on that one." Mumtaz nodded discreetly toward an exotically beautiful woman.

"Why?" Jasmine hadn't talked to the woman, but had

admired the way she managed to dress demurely yet still look sexy.

"Hira's family is the most powerful one in Abraz and they wished for her to become Tariq's wife. She was also happy with the idea. Then you came. It does not hurt to know those who might bear you grudges." Mumtaz raised her brows and blended back into the gathering.

Though her confidence had grown since her marriage, Jasmine found it a shock to come face-to-face with her competition.

He'll forget you the minute some glamourpuss princess comes along.

Like a bad dream, her sister's contemptuous laughter whispered out of nowhere, perfectly describing Hira's lush sensuality. That same voice taunted that with women as stunning as Hira around, it was a wonder Tariq had married her at all. Love was a fool's dream. Jasmine gritted her teeth and fought off the ghosts. Tariq had married *her* and he wasn't a man who felt lightly.

Tariq watched Jasmine move about the garden. Her smile was bright and her grace unique. She was at home among his people, a confident woman, sure of herself. No hint remained of the needy child-woman who'd hurt him so badly that he'd had to return to his homeland to heal.

After her emotional confession, he'd made sure that she understood that she was accepted without question or hesitation. It had taken time, but his reward for patience had been seeing her faltering smile grow in brilliance. He was fascinated by her gentle blooming. Four years ago, she'd been a barely open bud who'd been badly mishandled, even by him. It was a hard thing to acknowledge, but he did it with the same ruthless honesty that made him a good leader.

He'd been older and emotionally far stronger. His wife's family had not nurtured the fragile confidence of his Jasmine, and as a result, she'd been easily bruised. He'd put pressure on a vulnerable eighteen-year-old to choose him against her family—an unfair choice. He could understand that child-woman's fears when faced with his arrogant demands, and even forgive her for the choice she'd made. And yet he couldn't deny that he still needed her to choose to fight for him, needed her to love him so much that fighting for him was the only choice she'd ever make.

The last time the choice had had to be made, her family had used her powerful need for acceptance to emotionally beat her into submission. Seeing this new Mina, he couldn't help but wonder whether, if the choice had to be made again, she'd stand firm and refuse to give him up.

Could it be so simple? The difference between the weakness of a child and the gentle strength of a woman? Perhaps he could chance trusting this lovely woman. This woman who quite simply took his breath away.

He planned to go to Sydney in a week, and this time, he decided, he wouldn't leave Mina behind. The woman his Jasmine had grown into deserved to be free. And she deserved his trust.

Seeing that she was having a quiet moment by the small reflection pool in the corner, he strode toward her.

"WHY SO QUIET, MY JASMINE?" Tariq's question was whispered against her ear.

"I'm amazed each time I realize that your people have

accepted me." It was neither a lie nor the whole truth. Haleah's words had made her wonder just how obvious her love for Tariq was. If his people could see it, why couldn't her husband?

The pensive look in his green eyes gentled. "You are my wife. There was never any question." He touched her lower back. "Now, tell me what is truly on your mind."

His perception startled her. "Hira."

His brows rose. "One of my advisors needs to learn discretion."

"She's my advisor now, thank you very much," Jasmine retorted. "I appreciate being in the know."

Tariq's eyes glinted with male amusement. "Gossip, you mean."

"Essential information." She smiled in return. "So?"

"How can women say so much in one word?" He squeezed her when she opened her mouth. "Hira's family wished a political match. I didn't."

The practicality of his words calmed Jasmine. "She's very beautiful."

"Beautiful women cause men only trouble." His eyes lingered on her, but it was the tenderness of his tone that made her heart stop beating.

Touched by the subtle compliment, she did something she rarely indulged in, unsure how Tariq would react. Reaching up on tiptoe, she dropped a quick kiss on the corner of his lips. "Ditto for outrageously handsome men."

His surprised laugh drew all eyes their way, bringing smiles to the faces of their audience. However, the royal couple weren't disturbed.

"What does Jasmine al eha Sheik mean?" she asked,

since she had him to herself for a few minutes, and the hand curved over her hip told her he was quite happy to be there.

Tariq's smile held an unusual hint of mischief. "You will not like it, my independent little wife."

She tilted her head to the side, struck by his tone. Unless she prompted him, her husband was rarely so playful. "What?"

"The literal translation is 'Jasmine who belongs to the sheik.' The sheik's Jasmine. They know you're mine."

She smiled and shook her head. "They are as bad as you."

He shrugged, unrepentant. "It is an address of honor. If they had not liked you, they would have called you this." He rattled off an unfamiliar phrase.

"What does that mean?"

"It means, 'One who is married to the sheik.'"

She frowned. "What's wrong with that?"

"Strictly speaking, it is respectful, but if a sheik's wife is addressed as such, the people do not believe that she is the one who should stand by their ruler's side."

"How strange. Does that mean you're Sheik al eha Jasmine?"

Tariq grinned but didn't get a chance to answer, because at that moment, a couple interrupted them to say their farewells. Kanayal and Mezhael were ambassadors from another corner of Zulheil.

"I wish you good journey." Tariq's demeanor underwent a subtle change. He remained warm and approachable, but the mantle of authority settled around him like an invisible cloak. It made Jasmine aware of just how different he was with her when they were alone.

Kanayal bowed at the waist, approval on his face. Mezhael clasped her hands together and bent her head in respect.

"We will go back to Razarah with joyful news for our tribe." Kanayal's eyes rested briefly on Jasmine. "I will tell them of sunsets and blue skies."

"All is well in Razarah?"

Jasmine knew that Tariq's question was more an issue of protocol than real inquiry. This afternoon, when the ambassadors had arrived, they'd both been invited to a private meal with Tariq. Her husband had insisted that Jasmine attend, telling her that he valued her intuitive insights.

Kanayal's hazel eyes were warm. "All is well in Razarah."

"As always, you will be in our prayers." Mezhael's eyes met hers. "Jasmine al eha Sheik, I will sing for you."

Not understanding the undercurrent in Mezhael's statement, Jasmine nevertheless knew that it was offered as a compliment. She inclined her head, imitating Tariq's regal action without conscious thought. "Thank you. I wish you good journey."

When they left, Jasmine saw that they'd been the last guests. The others had drifted out, happy to communicate their goodbyes through Hiraz, Mumtaz or the other advisors scattered around.

"Come, I will answer your question in our suite."

"How did you know I was going to ask you a question?" She let Tariq lead her inside the palace.

"You always get a certain determined look in your eye. It is most disfiguring. You should stop asking questions."

"You're a horrible tease, you know that, don't you?" She was laughing, safe in the knowledge that he liked her curiosity and her desire to learn.

"I have you to tell me." Tariq tugged her inside their bedroom and closed the door. He pressed her against the door before running his hands over the smooth material of her dress. "Where are the buttons?"

TARIQ'S PASSION WAS SO HOT, Jasmine felt scorched. As a result of the inferno, they didn't get around to dinner until very late. Jasmine only remembered to ask her question when they were in bed. She turned in Tariq's embrace and propped herself up on his chest.

"Why would Mezhael sing for me?"

Tariq's eyes were hooded, his expression that of a sated panther. He ran his finger across the fullness of her lower lip. "The Song of Gifting is unique to Zulheil." His tone was indulgent as he explained. "As you know, our country follows the old ways. It is what sets us apart from our neighbors."

"The Song of Gifting." She mulled that information over, enjoying Tariq's lazy but affectionate exploration of her face. "So she's singing it as a gift?"

"No. She will sing it to ask for a gift for you."

Jasmine kissed his fingers when he stopped at her lips again. He smiled and carried on, trailing his fingertips across her cheek to trace the rim of one ear.

"What gift?"

The glint in his eye was the only warning she had. "A child. There will be many such songs sung across Zulheil in the coming weeks." Tariq chuckled at her gasp. "My people have decided that you are the woman to bear the next sheik."

"They don't waste time, do they?" She wriggled up his body until her lips were over his.

"You are young, Jasmine, and not yet with child. If you wish, we will wait."

They'd already lost so much time, Jasmine thought with a pang of old pain. "I may be young but I've always known that I would bear your child."

His expression was suddenly bleak. "Come, Mina. Love me and convince me of that truth."

She gave him everything she had, but somehow knew that it wasn't enough. Tariq needed something else from her, something that he'd never ask for and that she couldn't divine. She fell asleep with a lump in her heart. The fear that had been eating away at her returned in full force, haunting her dreams with premonitions of loss and suffering.

CHAPTER TWELVE

"YOU ARE NOT EXCITED ABOUT this journey, my Jasmine?"

Jasmine turned her face from the airplane window. "Of course I am. Attending Australian Fashion Week will be a wonderful learning experience for me."

Tariq frowned. "Yet you seem preoccupied."

She bit her lip, thrown by his perceptiveness. "I guess I am a little. It's the first time you've let me leave Zulheil."

The hand he'd placed on her own tightened a fraction. "And you will return to Zulheil." His voice was hard, eliminating her misty dreams of trust.

"Yes." She would go wherever Tariq resided. "Will you be very busy with the energy conference?"

His face underwent a subtle change at her calm acceptance of his decree. However, the fact that he'd entertained even for a second the belief that she might defect, told her that deeper issues of trust and forgiveness lay buried within his heart. Even her agreeing to have his child had not rebuilt their broken bond.

"I'm sorry you cannot participate." His mouth twisted in a wry smile. "Zulheil may allow its women full participation, but most of the Arab states at this conference hold different views. Those who agree with Zulheil's approach are helping me to try and change the others' thinking, but progress is slow."

"And to challenge them openly with my presence at this juncture could well destroy everything that you've achieved?"

He threw her a quick grin. "Correct. Even though this conference involves the leaders of the Western world as well, including their women, our neighbors are the ones we must be careful of. I cannot afford to take a too-radical stance and alienate the massive powers that surround our borders."

She nodded, understanding the delicate balance he sought to maintain. "One step at a time. Perhaps by the time I'm fifty, I'll be able to chair such a conference," she joked.

Tariq didn't answer. When she turned her head, she found him staring at her. "What?"

"We will have been married for twenty-eight years by then."

"Goodness. I didn't even think of that."

"Then perhaps you should."

His enigmatic statement kept her company throughout the journey. They landed at Sydney Airport around 2:00 a.m. Going through customs, Jasmine confused her two passports.

"Sorry. This is the one you need." She handed over her newly issued Zulheil passport and put the other one away.

Tariq didn't say anything until they were in the limo on the way to the hotel. "Why did you bring both passports?"

Looking out at Sydney's lights, Jasmine replied absentmindedly, "The New Zealand one was in the pocket of my carry-on bag from when I entered Zulheil. I forgot all about it."

He didn't say anything further on the topic and came to sit beside her, teasing her for her open delight in the night scenery. She teased right back, but once in their hotel room, exhausted by the long flight, she fell into immediate slumber.

TARIQ WOKE JUST BEFORE DAWN. Mina was asleep, her head resting on his chest. He tangled his fingers in her glorious hair, feeling an urgent need to touch her, to appease the slowly healing creature inside him. He'd made the decision to trust Jasmine's loyalty on this trip, aware that she was no longer a teenage girl. What he hadn't counted on was his possessiveness and the frailty of this new accord between them. He'd needed his Mina to himself for a while longer.

He hadn't meant to snap at her on the plane, and had been immediately sorry that he had done it, seeing the hurt in her expressive eyes. But his generous wife had forgiven him. He would, he vowed, try to control his edgy possessiveness. It was not her fault that they were in this country, which had to remind her of her homeland. And it was not her fault that he was…afraid. Afraid that once again she'd make a choice that would shatter his soul. He hated that feeling.

Yet he couldn't have left her in Zulheil. It would have broken her tender heart if he'd forced her to remain behind—one more rejection on top of so many others. He touched her cheek and felt something deep inside him sigh in defeat.

Unbeknownst to her, his wife once more held his heart in her hands.

"I HAVE TICKETS TO MOST OF the shows." Jasmine waved the pieces of paper in Tariq's direction. He stopped in the process of buttoning up his white shirt and stalked over.

"You will be accompanied by Jamar."

She stood up to finish buttoning his shirt. "He'll be bored stiff."

Tariq gripped her wrists, forcing her to meet his vivid green eyes. "I do not do this to clip your wings, Mina. You are the wife of the Sheik of Zulheil. There are those who would hurt you to reach me." His words were gentle.

She gasped in surprise. "I hadn't considered that. I guess I'm still not used to being your wife." She knew she'd said the wrong words the moment they left her mouth.

Tariq's jaw firmed into a determined line that she knew well, and his grip on her wrists suddenly felt like steel handcuffs. "That will never change, so get used to it." He dipped his head and took her lips in a profoundly possessive kiss, his body rigid against hers. "You belong to me."

She thought he was going to leave her with that image of distrust, wounding her. Instead, he turned at the door and walked back to her, his shoulders taut. "Mina." His eyes were dark and turbulent. The gentle touch of his finger on her cheek was an apology.

Carefully, she reached up and kissed him softly on the lips. "I know I am your wife, Tariq. I *know*."

He nodded, an expression in his eyes that she couldn't read. "Take care, wife. I would not lose you." Then he was gone, leaving her shaken by the power of that statement.

WHETHER IT TOOK PLACE IN Sydney or Melbourne, Australian Fashion Week was one of the biggest shows on the planet, full of every type of style, color and decadence. Jasmine was entranced, though she never forgot Tariq's words. Did love drive her husband's possessiveness, or something less beautiful? Her mind continuously went over the words.

However, she didn't have to worry about Jamar. Her muscled bodyguard enjoyed watching the women on the catwalks, if not the fashions. He was commenting on a curvy brunette when a hand on her shoulder made Jasmine cry out in surprise. Jamar moved so fast she didn't see him shift. Suddenly, his big bulk blocked her field of vision.

A throaty feminine laugh breached the barrier.

"Jamar, it's okay." Shocked, Jasmine pushed around his side when he refused to budge from his protective stance. "She's my sister."

"Hello, Jasmine," Sarah drawled.

"Sarah." Her sister's beauty seemed even brighter.

Sarah's mouth curved into a smile that was without warmth. "So, what's it like being part of a harem?"

After all these years, Tariq's revelation had given Jasmine an insight into her sister's cruelty. "I'm Tariq's wife."

Sarah didn't hide her surprise fast enough. A bitter look tinted her beautiful eyes for a second. "Well, well. Caught the big fish, after all." She looked over her shoulder. "It's been lovely but I must rush. Harry's probably looking for me."

Sarah turned and disappeared into the dimness beyond the lights of the catwalk before Jasmine could reply. The minute-long meeting left her feeling a confusing mix of emotions.

"She is not like you." Jamar moved to her side once more, his blunt features set in disapproving lines.

"No. She's beautiful."

"And icy. That one is cold."

Jamar's words reminded Jasmine of Tariq's statements. Suddenly, her heart felt lighter, more carefree. Her husband had chosen her. He thought she was good enough just as she was, and that was what mattered.

"How did the initial negotiations go?" Jasmine asked Tariq over dinner. She'd decided to eat in their suite, aware that he'd be craving some peace and quiet.

He ran his hand through his damp hair, having just showered. Under the terry-cloth robe that he'd thrown on to placate her sense of modesty, his tanned skin glowed with health. "It is as I expected. Those with oil wish to keep their position of power and are unwilling to look at alternatives."

"Isn't that short-sighted? Oil will eventually run out."

His eyes gleamed with intelligence. "Exactly And it is not only money but our world that we must consider."

Jasmine reached across the table and touched his hand. "As an ex-New Zealander, I'd have to agree with you. Kiwis are very big on clean and green."

"Are you?" He trapped her hand beneath his.

"Am I what?"

"Are you an ex-New Zealander?"

She paused. "Aren't I? I thought after marrying you, I gained Zulheil citizenship?"

He nodded once. "Zulheil allows dual citizenship."

"I didn't know that." She smiled. "My heart belongs to you and your land, Tariq. It's home."

He began to rub his thumb in tiny circles across her wrist. "You have no wish to return to your family?"

She knew her smile was a little sad. Even though they'd hurt her so much, they were her family. A lifetime couldn't be easily dismissed. "I saw Sarah today."

"Your sister is well?" His question was innocuous, but his eyes were alert.

She shrugged. "You know Sarah."

He didn't say anything, simply watched her face with eyes that seemed to see through to her soul. When he stood and came around the table, she was ready for him. That night, his lovemaking was tender and careful, as if he was trying to soothe her hurt. She forgot Sarah's barbs with his first touch, her heart overflowing with love for her desert warrior.

Her grip on her husband's strong body was fierce, her loving equally tender, his comments at dinner having given her an insight into his mind. Her husband had been afraid that she'd be tempted by the proximity of her country of birth. He didn't know that Zulheil was the only place that she truly thought of as home, and only because it was his land.

JASMINE SPENT MOST OF THE next day shopping for gifts. Jamar tagged along like a good-natured, if extremely large, puppy, even offering suggestions on prospective purchases.

"Your sister is approaching us," he stated suddenly.

Jasmine looked up in surprise. Sure enough, Sarah was making her way through the small boutique in Darling Harbour.

"How about lunch, little sister?" For once, there was

no sarcasm or bitterness in her words, and Jasmine couldn't resist the invitation. Old habits were hard to break and this hint of an olive branch from an always-unapproachable sister was too good to pass up.

Before they reached the car, Sarah asked her if they could stop in at a travel agency. "Have to pick up some tickets." She smiled and wiggled her fingers at Jamar.

The bodyguard, who'd been hanging back, moved closer.

Jasmine smiled at him. "We're just going to stop by a travel agent's office. Can you tell the driver?"

Jamar frowned but did as she asked, taking the front passenger seat, while Jasmine sat in the back with Sarah. As the vehicle was a courtesy provided by the Australian government, there was no glass partition between the two compartments. Mindful of that, Jasmine kept her voice down as she chatted with Sarah, catching up. When she admitted to missing her family, Sarah said, rather loudly, "So, when do you want to leave for New Zealand? I'll book your ticket right now."

Jasmine responded in a quieter tone. "I'll see if Tariq has some free time after the conference." She wondered if she could convince her husband to return to the place where they'd hurt each other so much.

To her surprise, lunch was pleasant. Starved for news about her family, she drank in every one of Sarah's words. "Thank you," she said, after paying the bill for both their meals. "I needed to know about everyone."

Sarah smiled slowly. "Perhaps we'll see each other again. We're both adults now."

Jasmine nodded. She was no longer the naive girl she'd once been, and it seemed her sister respected that.

And maybe after marrying Boston blue-blood Harrison Bentley, Sarah had matured and forgotten her spiteful anger toward Tariq.

Jasmine had no premonition of the sheer wrongness of her belief until late that night.

SHE WAS IN THE SHOWER when Tariq returned sometime after eight. When she walked out into the bedroom, wrapped in a towel, she found him waiting for her, eyes glittering with what she immediately recognized as un-adulterated rage.

"Tariq? What is it?" She froze, suddenly afraid.

He remained on the other side of the room, his big body held tightly in check. "Did you have fun laughing at me, Jasmine?" His quiet voice vibrated with anger.

"W-what are you talking about?"

"Such innocence! And to think I'd believed you'd changed."

He raked her body with eyes that were so angry, she didn't want him anywhere near her. At the same time, it hurt that he stayed as far as physically possible from her.

"Unfortunately, your sister gave away your plans."

Her head jerked up. "What plans?"

"Your sister commiserated with me over your deser-tion. She said I had to understand that you could not bring yourself to marry a man like me."

Shocked, Jasmine just stared. When he ripped some-thing out of his pocket and threw it against her chest, she didn't move to get it.

"You did not tell her I was your husband! What were you planning to do after you left? File for divorce, or just ignore your Zulheil marriage?" The sharp pain in his voice cut her.

Sarah had done this, Jasmine thought dully. But she wouldn't win. Her lie was too enormous, too unbelievable. Surely Tariq would see the truth. He *knew* Sarah. "I'm not planning on leaving you. She lied."

He looked even more furious. "Do not make this worse with further lies. The plane ticket in your name that Sarah wished me to give you does not lie."

With shaking hands, Jasmine picked up the ticket, barely able to keep the towel around her. The ticket was in her name, and even worse, her passport details were listed. That was odd, but only seemed to damn her further in her husband's eyes.

"No," she cried. "I would never do this. My family had all these details on file."

His mouth twisted in disbelief. "Enough! I was foolish to believe in you despite it all, but Jamar heard you discussing your defection!"

Jamar had obviously not heard her response to Sarah's words. She reached for Tariq, forgetting the towel. "Listen—"

"The truth is clear. I have always known your choices. Your body is not enough to make me a fool again. Though if you wish, I can avail myself of the invitation." His dismissive glance broke her heart. He was so cold, so uninterested.

Unbearably ashamed of her nakedness, she pulled the towel around her with fingers that trembled, and tried to reason with him. "Please, Tariq, listen to me. I love you…" She gave him her heart in a frantic attempt to make him listen.

He laughed. "You must think me a great fool, Jasmine. Your love is worthless."

Brokenhearted at the bald-faced rejection, and no longer able to figure out a way to make him understand that her love and loyalty belonged to him without reservation, Jasmine threw the balled-up ticket in his face. "Yes, that's the truth!" she lied. "I'm going to New Zealand and I'm going to divorce you!"

Tariq didn't speak. His face resembled a mask carved out of stone. The rage driving him had been tempered to cold fury.

"I'll go back and marry someone more suitable. I don't know what I was thinking of, marrying you!" She wanted to break down and cry, but some final piece of pride held her in check. If she gave in to the urge, she might never stop.

"You will not leave Zulheil."

"I'm already out of Zulheil! I won't go back!"

The anger on his face should have scared her, but she was past fear, mercifully numb. "You will return," he declared.

"No!" Her anger crested. "You have no right to make me!"

"Get dressed. We are leaving today." His voice was without emotion, as if he'd suddenly tripped a switch. "If you try to make it difficult, I will personally make sure that you get to Zulheil."

"You wouldn't make a scene." The room separated them, but it was the distance in his eyes that broke her heart.

His eyes narrowed. "I will do what it takes."

Confronted with the Sheik of Zulheil, she knew that

she'd lost this battle. He had the political power to do whatever he wished. "I have nowhere else to go." The wistful words fell from her lips like long-held tears. "I gave up everything for you. Everything. *Everything*."

His only response was the slamming of the door behind him as he left the room.

SLUMPED OUTSIDE THE HOTEL door, his control shattered, Tariq could barely think. He knew what Sarah was like, and so, when she'd told him, he hadn't believed her. Even with the evidence of the ticket, he hadn't believed her. Making sure that she knew of his disgust with her for her troublemaking, he'd gone to find Jasmine. He'd wanted to protect her from her sister's maliciousness. Then Jamar had seen him heading to their suite, and had asked if Jasmine had talked to him about leaving for New Zealand. His expression had been dark.

"On their way to the travel agent's, her sister asked Jasmine al eha Sheik when she would like her ticket booked." The bodyguard had started to say something else, but was interrupted when the head of security beeped him. He'd excused himself.

Tariq had felt his heart break with Jamar's words. It was fortunate that the guard had left, because otherwise he would have seen his sheik's composure crack, like fine porcelain under a heavy boot.

Jamar was a loyal guard, one with no reason to lie, especially since he clearly adored Jasmine. Tariq called himself a fool for accepting Jasmine's explanation for carrying her New Zealand passport. He'd broken his longest-held vow and had trusted her when she'd said it was an oversight. Even after what she'd done to him the first time, he'd *trusted* her. He'd wanted to protect and keep her safe in his arms.

An image thrust into his mind, turning a knife inside him. Of a tiny woman with hair of flame pleading with him to believe her, her shoulders and legs bare. A woman with shame in her eyes when he'd mocked the inherent sensuality that was her nature. Sensuality that he had always treasured, that he'd taken time and care to nurture.

Another knife joined the first.

He forced himself to remember the reason for his anger. There was no reason for him to feel as if he'd broken something beyond value. Except he couldn't think for the anger and pain blinding him. The wounded thing inside him was in agony, but he refused to acknowledge that, refused to examine exactly why this betrayal hurt with the pain of a thousand suns on his naked skin. He'd survived Jasmine once before and he'd do it again.

Even if what he felt for her was a hundred times stronger than before...and the pain threatened to drive him to madness.

CHAPTER THIRTEEN

THEY LANDED IN ZULHEIL midmorning. Jasmine couldn't help but remember her first trip through the gleaming white corridors. Then, she'd believed that if she loved him enough, the man beside her would grow to love her, too.

Now, she knew that if he could convict her on such flimsy evidence, he had to have no trust in her loyalty. And no love in his heart. She'd failed to make him see that she was worth loving, and if Tariq couldn't see that, then the flaws in her had to be fatal. Battered by emotional storms, her defenses crushed, Jasmine couldn't fight those old demons any longer.

Once they reached the palace, she let Tariq haul her through the corridors, humiliating as it was, knowing that if she fought, he was angry enough to do something truly unforgivable. But when, after pulling her into his bedroom, he turned to leave, she stopped him. She wasn't someone he could lock away and forget.

"Where are you going?"

Tariq didn't even look at her. "Abraz."

Speak to me, she wanted to cry. *Give me something to hold on to.* Even after his accusations and distrust, her heart refused to give up. She loved him. Needed him. And this time, she would fight for him until there was no hope. "Why?"

He did look at her then, his eyes dark green with pure fury. "I am going to marry my second wife. You no longer amuse me. Perhaps she will have more loyalty than you have shown."

Jasmine's heart turned to ice. "You're taking another wife?"

"I will marry her in Abraz. You would do well to get used to a submissive role."

"How can you do this to me?" She prayed that he was only striking back at her because he was angry at her supposed betrayal. Then she remembered gorgeous Hira. Hira, who'd wanted to marry Tariq…and who lived in Abraz. Hira, the glamourpuss princess that Sarah had taunted her with so long ago. Jasmine's worst nightmare had just come to life.

Tariq's beautiful face was cruel with distaste as his merciless eyes raked her trembling body. "The same way you plotted to betray me."

"No! I didn't. Why don't you believe me?" She reached out to grab the edge of his jacket, but he shrugged her off.

"I do not wish to be late." Throwing her another dismissive glance over her shoulder, he walked out the door.

Jasmine didn't go out to the balcony this time. At that moment, something priceless deep inside her broke with an almost audible snap. But she couldn't allow herself to feel the pain, because if she did, she'd die from the wound. Instead, as a self-defense mechanism, she started to plan her escape. She'd been prepared to put up with Tariq's anger, his distrust, even his rejection of her, but this…

"I will never share him. Never."

Sarah's derisive voice seemed to haunt her, telling her she hadn't been woman enough to hold her husband.

"No!" Sarah had probably only meant to cause a fight, but Tariq's deep-rooted distrust of his wife had given her the greatest of victories. Jasmine refused to give her vindictive sister any more power.

Spinning on her heel, she walked to her room and locked the door. She needed to think. There was no way she was going to get a flight out of Zulheil. Tariq would have alerted his men to watch for any attempt on her part. He wanted her to suffer. He wanted to punish her. Previously, she'd let him, certain that her love would win through.

"Not anymore." He'd gone too far this time.

She couldn't take to the roads. The border guards were well-trained and scrupulous. Aside from that, her red hair was a beacon of recognition among the desert people.

"Water." She stopped, her heart pounding. Zulheil had a narrow seacoast and a thriving port. It would be relatively easy to slip on board one of the foreign ships when it stopped to refuel. Sailors were an independent lot, and the harbor authorities couldn't monitor each and every individual movement. Aside from that, they were more worried with keeping people out of Zulheil than policing those wanting to depart.

She knew she had to leave everything behind, so that no one would guess her plan. That seemed to sum up her fate. She was leaving everything. Her heart. Her dreams. Her hope.

Taking a calming breath, she went to the small safe in the bedroom. After their marriage, Tariq had shown her the safe and told her that it would always hold cash for her use. At the time, she'd been touched by his thought-fulness, but today, she just felt humiliated. Though she didn't want to take his money, accessing her New Zealand savings accounts would immediately give away her plans. Shouldering aside her pride, she keyed in the combination. There was enough cash to buy her passage and support her for a few weeks.

As she turned away from the safe, a flash of silver on a corner chair caught her eye. She had finished the beautifully beaded blouse with such hope, just before their departure to Australia. Now she could barely bear the sight of it. She folded it up and left it on the bed, with a note for Mumtaz. Her friend might hate her for fleeing, but she was the one for whom Jasmine had chosen the material.

Once she was ready, she walked to her writing desk and picked up a pen. Her fingers threatened to shake under the force of her emotions, but she disciplined them with strength that came from somewhere so deep inside, she'd never known it existed before that instant.

Tariq,
Ever since I came to Zulheil, you've been waiting for me to betray you and leave. Today, I'll live up to your lack of belief in me, but I won't leave in silence like a thief.

I love you so much that every time I breathe, I think of you. From the moment we reunited, I had no thought of ever leaving you. You were my first love, my only love. I thought I'd do anything for you, even bear your punishment over my choice four years ago, but today I've discovered my limits.

You're mine and mine alone. How can you ask me to share you?

Your pride will urge you to search for me, but I beg you, if you ever had any feelings for me, please don't. I could never live with a man who I loved but who hated me. It would kill me. I don't know what I'll do, I only know that my heart is broken and I must leave this place. Even if I never see you again, know that you'll always be my beloved.
Jasmine al eha Sheik

Dry-eyed, her pain too great even for tears, she folded the letter and sealed it in an envelope. When she'd begun, she'd thought to pen something hateful, hurting him as much as he'd hurt her, but she couldn't. Picking up her purse and the letter, she walked out to his study, the one place no one would venture until his return. She placed the letter in the center of his desk, where he would immediately see it. Her hands stroked the smooth mahogany in a final aching goodbye. In this room, they had come to learn about each other and she'd begun to help him shoulder his burdens.

"But it wasn't enough." Teeth gritted, she almost ran from the room, unable to bear the deluge of memories. Outside, she slipped on her sunglasses while the driver brought the car around. Within two minutes, she was on her way.

The beautiful minarets and colorful marketplace outside the windows of the car brought tears to her eyes. Her sense of loss was overwhelming. This place had become home. The exotic scents, the heavy heat, the bright-eyed and laughing people—they were all a part of her and would be forever.

Just like Tariq.

The docks were bustling. The driver parked in front of the popular waterside café she'd indicated. "I'm meeting a friend for lunch, so you can go elsewhere if you wish."

"I will wait here." His dark eyes didn't reflect his automatic smile.

She hadn't expected anything else. Tariq had been in a rage, but he'd given orders designed to keep her prisoner.

The minute she stepped outside, people waved and called out. They had accepted her without question, these generous desert people. Yet not even for them could she bear to share Tariq. After greeting her people with forced smiles, she made her way into the restaurant and sought out the hostess.

"Jasmine al eha Sheik, you will take a table?" The woman was beaming.

"Thank you, but I was wondering if you could help me?" Her voice was soft, but didn't waver as she'd half expected.

"Of course." The hostess's smile became impossibly wider.

"Somehow, a foreign news crew has managed to enter Zulheil and they've been tracking me. If you could show me your back entrance, my driver has instructed another driver to pick me up. It's annoying to be hounded like this."

The hostess's eyes lit up. Jasmine knew she should feel guilty about lying to her, but she was too numb to care. The back door opened onto a narrow alley. Though the lane was clean, there was a deserted, quiet air about it. The hostess looked around, a frown wrinkling her face.

"There is no driver here."

"Oh, he's waiting down there. Thank you." Before the woman could protest, Jasmine stepped out and began to stride confidently down the narrow cobbled path. Once out of sight, she changed direction and headed toward the water.

Lady Luck decided to give her a chance. A cruise ship was tethered at the docks, there only for a three-hour stop to refuel. In the crowd of European tourists allowed out to wander the docks, Jasmine no longer stood out. The authorities were vigilant about anyone attempting to get out, but nobody noticed a small female merging *into* the colorful mass of humanity.

Jasmine found that the cruise liner was happy to pick up an extra paying passenger, having lost some due to illness at the last stop. As an almost instinctive precaution, she used the New Zealand passport that had planted suspicions in Tariq's mind. Globe-trotting Kiwis were more likely to be present on the ships in port than the reclusive people of Zulheil. Or perhaps she used it because she couldn't bear to see her married name written there.

An hour later, she watched Zulheil's sparkling sand retreat to the horizon. She stood on the deck, her cheeks whipped by the wind, unable to look away. A part of her believed that if she didn't lose sight of the land, the final threads tying her to Tariq wouldn't be cut. Then night fell, spelling an end to even that impossible dream.

THE MOON SHIMMERED OVER the minarets of Zulheina, but Tariq could find no surcease from the gnawing sense of loss that seemed to reach inside his soul and steadily eat away at any hope of happiness.

He'd been halfway to Abraz by the time his sense of betrayal and anger had dissipated, gentled by his home-land. Pulsing hurt had taken its place. He'd given Mina his heart and she'd cut it to pieces for a second time. He hadn't quite known what he would do to survive. No one but Mina would ever be wife to him, but how could he remain with a woman who could betray him so easily?

His mind had kept replaying the most painful image— the naked agony in Mina's eyes when he'd told her that he was taking another wife. That he was rejecting her, just as her family had. He'd felt as if he'd struck her, as if *he* was the one who needed forgiveness.

Something desperate and primitive in him had kept saying that he'd made a mistake and had to return home. Searching for any hint of hope, he'd finally stopped re-acting and had started to listen.

When looked at logically, without the blindness caused by heartbreak, none of it made sense. If Jasmine had wished to leave him, she could have done so with-out Sarah's help. Dread had crept into Tariq's body when he'd realized that, but it was the memory of Jamar's rev-elation that had almost stopped his breath. Why would the bodyguard tell him about betrayal in such a casual way—in the hallway of a hotel, where anyone could have overheard?

Unwilling to believe that the mixture of distrust and anguish in him had caused him to make such a terrible mistake, but knowing deep inside that he had, Tariq had ordered the car to return to Zulheina in all haste. The wild part of him that had always belonged to Mina had *known.* He'd picked up the phone in the back of the car for something to do, a shield against his fear that he'd lost his wife for good.

The guard had answered after one ring. "Sir?"

"Jamar, I was thinking of a gift for my wife and recalled what you said in Australia. Was Jasmine enthusiastic when her sister asked about booking tickets to New Zealand?" His hand had been clenched tight around the phone.

"I heard Jasmine al eha Sheik say that she was going to speak to you about whether you might have some free time. I believe she would enjoy the gift of a trip." There had been a smile in his tone at being asked his opinion. "I was called away before I could ask if I could be her guard on any such trip. I know I ask much but...I did not like the feel of her sister." The guard's tone had been of someone expecting to be rebuked for the criticism, but he'd put his duty to protect above his own status. His judgment of Sarah also explained his scowling expression that day in Sydney.

"I agree, Jamar. And thank you." Tariq had been barely able to speak. His blood cold with the realization of his incalculable error, he'd returned to Zulheina.

Too late.

Far too late.

The crackle of paper made him glance down in surprise. He felt as if he was looking at a stranger's hand. A stranger who'd crushed the fragile material in his palm beyond recovery, with brutal efficiency. Uncurling those fingers that he was forced to acknowledge were his own, he pulled out the page and tried to flatten it against the dark wood of his desk. The whole time, he knew that no matter how hard he tried to smooth the wrinkles, it would never be enough.

As he would never again be able to enjoy the perfect joy of his Jasmine's love. He'd beaten and battered her heart so many times, in so many different ways, and yet she'd continued to love him, her feminine courage quiet and strong. But even her generous nature wouldn't forgive this most recent blow.

Tariq was prepared to accept that. He wasn't prepared to accept that he'd lost her for good. The woman his Mina had grown into had changed him forever. Her strength, her ability to lead beside him, her glorious sensuality…she was irreplaceable. He couldn't bear to live without the other half of his soul, even if she hated him.

"You belong to me, Mina." Only the desert heard his voice. Only the desert sent sighs of agreement on the wings of the cool, evening wind. Only the desert understood his desolation…and his determination.

JASMINE SPENT THE ENTIRE voyage secluded in her cabin, eschewing attempts by the social activities' staff to draw her out. She didn't cry. Her tears were frozen in her heart along with the rest of her emotions. She just wanted to forget.

Except Tariq wouldn't leave her alone. Each night, he came to her in her dreams, strong, virile, unwilling to accept her decision. She tossed and turned, her body covered with sweat, trying to fight him, but in the end he always won.

"You belong to me, Mina." His hands stroked her.

"No."

"Yes!" That male arrogance was apparent even in

her dreams. His shoulders gleamed in the moonlight, as they'd done those nights they'd spent in the desert. The desert, where she'd learned that a warrior's pride could be a harder thing to fight than any physical enemy.

"Tariq," she whispered, reaching out a hand to touch that warm, tempting skin. Nothing met her searching hands but cold emptiness. "Tariq, no!" Invariably, she woke up with his name on her lips, a cry for him to believe her...to love her.

The liner docked at a number of Middle Eastern destinations, but she didn't depart, not wanting to take the chance that someone might recognize her. Two weeks passed in self-imposed isolation. Then the ship made an unscheduled stop on a small Greek island, due to a passenger's need to disembark because of an emergency. Exhausted by her sense of loss and lack of sleep, Jasmine slipped off the ship and never returned. It was as good a place as any, she thought without enthusiasm. And because it wasn't a scheduled stop, even if Tariq searched for her, he'd be unlikely to locate her.

She managed to find a small garret apartment after she left the ship. On the night she arrived, she curled up on the bed and couldn't make herself move again. Thoughts of Tariq haunted her night and day, building shadows under her eyes and adding to the weight loss she'd suffered on board ship. Her mind replayed that final terrible fight over and over again, trying to find another way, another avenue. There were none.

"It's over. Accept it," she told herself each day, and each day she woke with her heart heavy with need and her body aching.

A week after her arrival, she dragged herself out the

door, fighting the depression. She was strong, she told herself. She'd survive. So what if half her soul was missing? She'd given that away by choice. And she couldn't bring herself to regret it. By chance, she saw a sign in a shop window seeking a seamstress. Taking a deep breath, she pushed open the door and walked inside.

That night, as she picked up a pair of scissors to begin an alteration, her numbness suddenly broke. It was as if her body realized that by doing something beyond bare survival, she'd decided to live again. With the sudden shift came thoughts and memories and heartache.

Her first emotion was fear—fear that she'd never forget Tariq. And then suddenly, she was terrified of forgetting. He lived inside her, part of her. Paradoxically, there was peace in knowing she would never stop loving him. Despite that knowledge, she avoided newspapers and magazines, aware that if she saw Tariq with his new bride, she would surely lose the tentative control she'd regained over her emotions.

TARIQ PICKED UP THE BRUSH and squeezed out paint the color of rich cream. Add a tinge of palest rose and he would have the living hue of his Jasmine's skin. A single stroke and one graceful arm came to life. She was almost complete, this creation of paint and emotion. Painstakingly, he began to fill in the details that made Mina unique. Pure sky-blue for those big, always innocent eyes. Even after he'd taught her the ways of pleasure, a part of Mina had remained forever the innocent.

A memory of those eyes bruised with hurt when he'd done something she couldn't forgive taunted him as he painted her portrait. It didn't matter if she never forgave him. He couldn't let her go. He needed her more than she would ever need him. She made his life a gift rather than a burden. She was a piece of his soul, and if he had to, he'd search forever for her.

He told himself that she was no weak woman who would suffer in silence when he dragged her back. His Mina had spirit. She would fight him, and as long as there were words, he would fight for her.

There was a movement near the doorway. "Yes?" His concentration was immediately and utterly focused on Hiraz.

"We tracked down some passengers who saw her on board after the ship left the Middle East. They do not recall seeing her after Greece." Hiraz paused and suddenly said, "I cannot believe she has done this to you again. Let her go."

"Hold your words!" Tariq snapped. "Because you are my friend, I will forgive you that indiscretion, but you will never again speak against Mina. I am the one to blame." It would have been easy to blame Sarah, but Tariq knew it was his own fierce protection of his heart against further pain that had caused this. Sarah had merely been the catalyst.

His advisor's skepticism was obvious. "You? You treated her like a princess."

"I told her I was going to take another wife."

Hiraz froze. Sadness settled over his features, so deep it turned his brown eyes black. "I do not think even my Mumtaz would forgive me such a hurt."

"It does not matter. Jasmine is mine and I will never let her go." Tariq touched his hand to the letter that he constantly kept with him. "Prepare the aircraft. We will fly to Greece. You have a list of the stops the cruise ship made?"

Hiraz nodded. "There were only two." A brief flicker of hope glittered in his brown eyes.

Tariq didn't feel hope. He felt certainty.

JASMINE IGNORED THE impatient knocking for as long as she could. When it didn't stop, she put down some mending and made her way across the small garret, prepared to face off with her landlord. She'd paid up. He had no cause to hound her.

"You!" Her knees buckled when she saw the man filling the doorway. His arms reached out to catch her as she fell. Behind him, the door slammed shut. The garret seemed suddenly minuscule, the light slanting in under the eaves not bright enough to soften the intense darkness of emotion. "Let me go."

"You'll fall."

"I'm fine now." She pushed at Tariq's shoulders. To her surprise, he released her without complaint, holding her only long enough to gauge that she could stand on her own.

Stumbling backward, she wrapped her hands around her waist and stared. "You've lost weight." His face was shadowed with the beginnings of a beard, and his eyes looked dark and haunted, but it was the way his clothes hung on him that worried her. "What's happened?"

"You left me."

Jasmine hadn't expected that response. She shook her head and backed up until she hit the wall. "How did you find me?"

He didn't release her from his bleak gaze. "I went to New Zealand first."

Her heart thudded at that.

"You didn't tell me that you'd completely turned your back on your family to come to me."

Jasmine didn't answer, torn up at the thought that he'd cared enough to search for her. Perhaps, a traitorous part of her wondered, half of him was better than nothing? Immediately, she discarded that dangerous idea. No. No. No!

"You chose *me*, Mina." His voice was rough with the understanding of what she'd done. "You chose me above all others, above everyone else in the world. Did you think I would let you walk away once you'd become mine?"

"I won't come back." Seeing him with another woman would rip her to shreds.

"Mina." He reached out his hand.

"No!"

He didn't heed her, moving to trap her against the wall. The white silk of his shirt was soft under her fingertips when she tried to push him away. At the same time, she hunched her body against the exposed beams of the wall, afraid that her craving for his touch would override her vows to resist him.

"I won't share you." It took an effort to sound strong.

"Because you love me and you chose me."

She nodded, and lost the battle to stop the flow of tears. This close, she just wanted to hold him and forget her anguish in his arms. And the force of his words almost made her think that he believed in her love.

"Mina, you must come back with me. I cannot live

without you, my Jasmine. I need you like the desert needs rain." Framing her face with his hands, Tariq used his thumbs to gently rub away her tears.

The pain in his green eyes echoed her own. She tried to shake her head but he held her in place. "I chose you, Jasmine. You are my wife. It is not a bond that can be broken." The fervor of his words made her body thrum in recognition. "I love you. I *adore* you."

"But you've taken…" She couldn't complete her sentence.

"I would never do such a thing," he murmured. "I was very angry with you that day, but I was also hurting. I believed that you had trampled on my heart again. It was the only weapon I possessed and I used it. Then, I did not believe that you cared enough to be heartbroken. I am so sorry, Mina."

"You weren't planning to take another wife?" She managed to get the question past the obstruction in her throat.

"Never. You are the only one. *Always* you'll be the only one. In my heart and in my soul, I have known from the moment we met that you would be the only one. That is why I felt so betrayed. I would never marry another."

"Never?" she whispered, beginning to understand, to believe. Her husband had turned on her like a wounded animal that day, shattered by her apparent betrayal after they'd seemed to be reaching peace. The broken pieces inside her began to heal under the heat of the truth in his eyes. Unconsciously, her hands drifted to rest at his waist.

"I waited four years for you to grow up. I stayed faithful to the love between us. Do you think I could ever take another woman to my bed, much less into my heart?" His eyes glittered with the power of what he was confessing.

Stunned, she didn't know what to say. She hadn't known of the depths of her panther's devotion. Her heart seemed to be crying and laughing at the same time, but all she could do was drown in the promise she saw in his eyes.

"Forgive your foolish husband, Mina. Around you, he does not always think with calm." His expression was penitent, but the way he had her trapped against the wall told her that he intended to persuade her, no matter how long it took.

Her husband might be apologizing, but he didn't know the meaning of being humble. Jasmine smiled slowly. She wouldn't have him any other way. "Only if he'll forgive me for making the wrong choice four years ago."

"I forgave you the instant you stepped foot on my land, Mina." He smiled his predator's smile. "I just needed time to salvage my pride."

"And is it salvaged? Will you doubt me again?"

"All I needed to know was that you'd choose to fight for me if you ever had to make the decision again."

So simple, and yet she hadn't been able to figure it out. She touched his hair with tentative fingers. "There is no question of choice. You come first."

"I know that now, Mina." He leaned into her gentle caress.

There was something more she had to know. "Do you think...loving me is a weakness?"

There was no pause. "Loving you is my greatest strength. The assassins sought to blind me to that truth. With heart, I can reach those who would otherwise be lost. I have never stopped loving you." His hands moved down her body to clasp her buttocks and press her close. "Will you return with me?"

Jasmine laughed at the way he was trying to act as if he was giving her a choice, when they both knew he wasn't leaving the room unless she was with him. "Do you promise to be a good, amenable husband from now on and follow my every command?"

He scowled. "You're taking advantage of me."

"It's not working, is it?"

"I don't know." He glanced speculatively at the tiny bed in the corner. "If that cot holds up under our weight, I'll permit you to take advantage of me." The sparkle in his eyes belied his solemn tone, but before Jasmine could accept the offer, she had to know.

"I love you. Do you believe that?"

Tariq's face was fierce with joy. "Mina!" He crushed her to him. "Your love for me is in your eyes, in your touch, in your every word. Even your farewell letter, which you wrote when you were feeling abandoned and so hurt, rings with the richness and truth of your love. I do not feel worthy of it, but I will not give you up. You are mine."

Jasmine swallowed and laid one fear to rest. There was no room for doubt in the passion of her husband's voice. "Do you believe I betrayed you?" She leaned back so she could look into his eyes.

He laid his forehead against hers as his big body curved over hers in a familiar protective stance. Vibrant male heat seeped into her bones, a deep caress that made her want to melt, but there were questions yet to be answered.

"Once I was no longer blinded by pain and anger, I realized the truth. I did not need Jamar's explanation. My heart knew you would never do such a thing to me." Tenderly, he cupped her cheek in one hand. "I am afraid I am possessive beyond reason where you are concerned, and the closeness of your homeland had me on edge. My fear of losing you turned me a little mad. I was returning to beg your forgiveness when I was told that you had disappeared."

"I didn't want to go," she confessed.

"You will promise to never leave me again. Promise," he growled, no longer gentle and compassionate, the panther tying his mate to him. "Fight, get angry, but do not leave!"

"I promise, but you must talk to me. Promise me that."

He smiled. "I promise you, my Jasmine, that I will talk to you. I cannot change who I am. I am possessive and you will have to become adept at dealing with such a husband."

"As long as you let me deal with you. Don't push me away. Don't go cold and silent on me. When you do that, it's like a part of me is missing."

He pulled her to him again, the hand on her nape holding her against his chest. "Forgive me, Mina, because I cannot forgive myself for the hurt I have caused you."

"I think I could forgive you anything." Her vulnerability to him no longer terrified her, not when he loved her with all of the passion in his warrior's heart. "My only regret through everything is that we wasted four years."

He chuckled. "Not wasted, Mina. I thought I would give you five years to grow up. I was being very patient, was I not?"

She smiled and touched his cheek in a familiar caress. He turned his face into her hand, his stubble rough but enticing against her skin. "You were. And after five years?"

"You would have decided to take a trip to the desert."

"I would have?"

"Umm." He leaned down and kissed her, as if he couldn't resist. She softened, she melted, she became his. When he drew away, the masculine scent of him swirled around her, enclosing her in an embrace more intimate than the physical one. "And once there, you would have married a man who has always known that you were meant to be his."

"So I could've waited another year and saved myself the trouble?" she dared to tease.

"Perhaps I would not have lasted five years. My patience was wearing thin." His next words were uncompromising. "You were born to be mine, Mina."

The strength of his vow made her want to weep. Tariq loved her, flaws and all. The hole inside her heart closed forever. She leaned up and kissed him, a soft, loving kiss that held everything she felt.

"Does this mean I am truly forgiven?" he asked.

"Just give me your promise to talk to me if you ever feel angry or hurt, and we'll wipe the slate clean."

"I do not intend to let you out of my sight, so that is a moot point." He laughed when she pushed at his chest and raised her scowling face to his.

"You still don't trust me?"

"I trust you with my heart and soul," he told her, his green eyes bright. "I also need you so fiercely that it would please me should you wish to spend your hours by my side." He touched his fingers to her throat in a light caress. "You asked me a question once. The answer is yes, as you are Jasmine al eha Sheik, I am Tariq al eha Jasmine. I belong to you."

The raw honesty of his words humbled her and yet made her heart burst. Tariq was proud and strong, as enduring in his vows as Zulheil Rose was in its beauty. For him to surrender to her in this way meant more than could ever be put into words. Her panther had placed his happiness into her keeping, and she intended to protect that trust with every breath in her body.

"Do your people hate me?" She bit her lip.

"*Our* people are used to the tempestuous women of sheiks." He grinned. "In the first years of my parents' marriage, my mother once camped in Paris for two months."

"Oh." Though the news about their people made her happy, Jasmine was even more pleased to hear the affection in Tariq's voice. It appeared that his frustrated anger toward his mother was passing with time.

"It is I who would be considered a poor sheik if I could not persuade you to return." He leaned close. "My honor is in your hands." There was a teasing light in his eyes.

"Come, husband who belongs to me." She tugged his hand. "Your wife wishes to take advantage of you."

"I would never deny my wife, Mina," he breathed into her mouth.

The cot did indeed hold their weight.

EPILOGUE

THERE WAS A ROAR FROM THE crowd below when Jasmine stepped out onto the balcony, her six-month-old baby son cradled in her arms. Behind her, Tariq put a protective arm around her waist and leaned down until his lips touched her temple. "You are loved, my Jasmine." His smile was tender.

Jasmine stretched up and touched her lips to his. "I know," she whispered. The roar of the crowd was drowned out by the passionate thunder racing through her veins. "As are you, Tariq al eha Jasmine. From the heart and soul."

This incredible man was hers, she thought, without limits or restrictions. Or worry. His birthday present to her had been the repeal of the old law that had made her believe his angry threat to take another wife.

"Our son will be a warrior." Tariq touched one waving fist. "He was conceived in passion."

"Tariq, hush." Her cheeks bloomed at the memory of their reunion on that tiny Greek island. Out of their love and hunger, they'd created a tiny, beautiful human being.

"Our people cannot hear us." He smiled.

That smile made her heart beat faster and her mouth go dry. Every day that they spent together, she fell more in love with her husband. In front of her eyes, he was growing into a powerful, compassionate leader, adored by his people and respected by both his allies and his foes. But what turned her heart over was the way he loved her. The way he saw greatness in her, too.

"I could not have chosen a better woman to lead by my side. You are magnificent." His hand stroked the fiery fall of her hair, unconsciously echoing her thoughts.

Jasmine thought back over the past year and a half. "I feel like I've grown more since I married you than I did in all the years before." Tariq's faith in her had made her dig deep to find the skills he needed in a wife. She'd become adept at behind-the-scenes negotiations, and even better at listening to what people didn't say.

He touched her cheek and the caress turned the crowd wild. "You have also taught me much. Your gentle ways are turning foes into allies. That's why I married you, of course."

His teasing of her hadn't changed. "I told you, by the time I'm fifty, women will be at those conferences."

"I have faith that you will accomplish the impossible." Tariq's confidence in his wife ran deep and true. Mina could do whatever she put her mind to. Look how well her designing was going. His lovely little wife was becoming famous, not only for her diplomacy but for her artistry.

"You are not working too much?" He looked down at her luminous beauty and could understand why their people openly thanked the stars for her. Just as her husband did.

"How could I?" She turned an exasperated face up at him. "If it's not you, it's Mumtaz or Hiraz telling me to rest. Honestly, I could shoot that man at times."

"My advisors know how important you are to their

sheik's happiness." Tariq's tone was light, but his need for her very real. Without her, he would not be the man he was today. She had taught him about love so strong it humbled him. He could never articulate all that she meant to him, but he could say, "Thank you." It was a rough whisper.

He looked down at that tiny being cradled in his wife's arms and thanked him, too—for teaching him about a parent's love. The minute Jasmine had laid Zaqir in his arms, he'd forgiven his mother for her choice.

"You're welcome." Jasmine's throat closed with withheld tears. She understood what her desert warrior couldn't say. Tariq no longer hid either his very real love or his need for her. He'd filled the emptiness in her with so much love that sometimes she hurt with the beauty of it.

Moving closer to him until he was supporting their son with an arm under hers, she raised her free hand to the gathered masses. These desert people were her family, her home. Zaqir was a beloved son, the embodiment of the love between her and Tariq. Her husband was her hope and joy.

"We are going in. You are cold." After one final wave, Tariq rubbed her arms and nudged her inside.

Once there, she raised her face to his. "I think we should dine alone tonight. In our private dining area."

He raised a brow, his eyes darkening at her husky tone. "Will the little sheik be asleep?"

"Your son is beginning to be very well behaved." She kissed their baby's soft cheek. "Unlike his father."

Tariq laughed. "If I began to behave, Mina, you'd be

most disappointed. Bored." He pulled her into the circle of his arms, warm and strong.

She let him cuddle her to him, their baby between them. "I don't think forever with you would bore me."

"Come then, Jasmine al eha Sheik, let us put this one to bed." He nuzzled her and then kissed Zaqir, his love for their child open and unashamed. "I wish to adore my wife, little one. You will have to be good tonight."

Jasmine smiled in sheer joy. Around them, the rare beauty of the Zulheil Rose glowed with an inner warmth, but between her and Tariq, there burned an even more precious incandescence. As she went to lay Zaqir in his crib, Tariq by her side, Jasmine knew that this glory would only grow stronger with time. Like the crystal, it would endure.

* * * * *

PARANORMAL

Dark and sensual paranormal romance stories
that stretch the boundaries of conflict and desire, life and death.

n o c t u r n e™

COMING NEXT MONTH
AVAILABLE DECEMBER 27, 2011

#127 CLAIM THE NIGHT
The Claiming
Rachel Lee

#128 WOLF WHISPERER
The Pack
Karen Whiddon